An ignoble death

"The King will summon you at [...] Marquis said quickly, all trace of the draw[...] has been making a fool of Debe[...] tains and stealing our horses an[...] mind: Either you surrender, sp[...] ble, or he's ging to make an example of you [...] morrow. Not a noble's death, but a criminal's."

"Criminal's?" I repeated stupidly, my voice nearly gone.

"It will last all day," he said with a grimace of distaste. It was the first real expression I'd ever seen from him, but by then I was in no mood to appreciate it.

The door shut, the footsteps withdrew, and I was left in silence. It was then that I hit the low point of my life.

FIREBIRD—WHERE FANTASY TAKES FLIGHT™

Crown Duel
Sherwood Smith

(originally published as the novels
Crown Duel and *Court Duel*)

FIREBIRD
AN IMPRINT OF PENGUIN PUTNAM INC.

This story is dedicated to my agent,
Valerie Smith.

With special thanks to my writing group,
the Foam Riders, and to Kathleen
Dalton-Woodbury, for reading this in draft

FIREBIRD

Published by the Penguin Group
Penguin Putnam Inc.,
345 Hudson Street,
New York, New York 10014, U.S.A.
Penguin Books Ltd, 80 Strand, London WC2R ORL, England
Penguin Books Australia Ltd, Ringwood, Victoria, Australia
Penguin Books Canada Ltd, 10 Alcorn Avenue,
Toronto, Ontario, Canada M4V 3B2
Penguin Books (N.Z.) Ltd, 182–190 Wairau Road,
Auckland 10, New Zealand

Penguin Books Ltd, Registered Offices: Harmondsworth, Middlesex, England

Originally published in the United States of America
by Harcourt Brace & Company, 1997 and 1998
Published by Firebird, an imprint of Penguin Putnam Inc., 2002

9 10 8

Crown Duel, Book I copyright © Sherwood Smith, 1997
Court Duel, Book II copyright © Sherwood Smith, 1998
Crown Duel (Books I and II) and "Vidanric's Birthday Surprise"
copyright © Sherwood Smith, 2002
All rights reserved
ISBN 0-14-230151-5
Printed in the United States of America

Part One

PROLOGUE

HOPE ANY OF MY DESCENDANTS READING THIS KNOW exactly what the Covenant and the Code of War are, but there is always the chance that my story has been copied by the scribes and taken to another land that will consider Remalna distant and its customs strange.

The Covenant has to do with wood—and with Fire Sticks.

We share the land with the Hill Folk. They were here before our people came. One legend has it they were once trees, given human form by some powerful sorcerer. They certainly look more like trees than they do like people. Other stories insist they came through one of the fabled World Gates and settled here because of our trees.

For the trees in our country are unique. We have the common kinds, of course. But high in our mountains we also have the remarkable colortrees: huge, long-lived goldwoods and bluewoods and greenwoods and redwoods, so named because the grains of these trees run rich with gleaming colors.

For centuries Remalna made itself wealthy by cutting them down and selling them to other lands. But our greed nearly caused disaster. The Hill Folk, who were being driven from their homes among the trees, readied themselves to fight. Not in war, because they don't use weapons. Remalna faced a magical fight that we ha̶ no hope of winning. Peace was made only when our people prom̶ ised that trees would never again be cut down. Wood would b̶ gathered only if it fell. In return, each autumn the Hill Folk woul̶ give us Fire Sticks, which would burn by magic until well into th̶ next summer.

Rich or poor, every family within the borders of Remalna— from the King to the poorest street sweeper—gets Fire Sticks. I̶ proportion not to their riches but to their number. And anyon̶ who tries to take Fire Sticks, or to sell them, somehow receive̶ fewer the next year.

The Fire Sticks are given out by magicians from a distant coun̶ cil, who then disappear. There is a simple spell we say to start th̶ fire, and to stop it—*Words of Power*, we call it, though the spell can̶ actually do anything else.

Since the days the Covenant was made, no more colortrees hav̶ been chopped down. What wood we use is gathered from windfal̶ and it is used carefully. Our old wooden furniture is treasured.

And so we've existed peacefully beside the Hill Folk for man̶ hundred years.

Unfortunately, neighboring countries have not let us exist i̶ peace.

For centuries we fought battles hand-to-hand. Several genera̶ tions ago someone brought to our continent bows and arrow̶ which can kill from a distance. These changed the character ̶ battle so much that a Code of War was agreed on by most of th̶ countries on our continent. The only weapons permitted would b̶ those held or thrown by hand.

When my story began, these rules had kept us relatively pros̶ perous and in relative peace. I say "relative" because real peace an̶ real prosperity are not possible when you are ruled by a bad kin̶ who thinks he is above all the laws.

ONE

HE BROKEN SHUTTER IN THE WINDOW CREAKED A
warning. I flung myself across the table, covering as best I could
my neat piles of papers, as a draft of cold wind scoured into the
room. Dead leaves whispered on the stone floor, and the corners
of my moat of papers rustled. Something crashed to the floor behind me. I turned my head. It was the soup bowl I'd set that morning on an old, warped three-legged stool and promptly forgotten.

The rotted blue hanging in the doorway billowed, then rippled
to quiescence. The whispers and rattles in the room stilled, and I
sat up with care and looked at the bowl. Could it be mended? I
knew Julen would be angry with me. Julen was the blacksmith's
sister, and the mother of my friend Oria. After my mother died she
looked after me, and she had of late taken over cooking for us.
Crockery was hard to come by these days.

I reached for the pieces, my blanket ripped—and cold leaked
up my arm.

I sat back on my cushion, staring down in dismay at the huge
tear at my elbow. I did not look forward to the darning task
ahead—but I knew that Julen would give me one of those looks she
was so good at and calmly say that practicing my darning would
teach me patience.

"Mel?"

The voice was Bran's. He tapped outside the door, then lifted the hanging. "Meliara, it's time to go see Papa."

Ordinarily Branaric never called me Meliara, but I was too distracted to notice right then.

"Bran!" I leaped to my feet. "I did it—just finished! Look!" I pulled him into the room, which had once been a kind of parlor for the servants, back when the castle had had plenty of servants. Pointing proudly at the table, I said, "I know how to cheer Papa, Bran. I've found us a way to pay this year's taxes! It's taken me two days, but I really believe I have it. It'll buy us another year—you know we need another year. Look," I babbled, stooping down to tap each pile of papers. "Every village, every town in Tlanth, and what it has, what it owes, and what it needs. Not counting the gold we set aside for our Denlieff mercenaries—"

"Mel."

I looked up, my mouth still moving; but when I saw the stricken look in Bran's dark blue eyes, all the plans fled from my mind as if that cold wind had swept them into the shadowy corners with the dead leaves.

Branaric looked back at me, his face suddenly unfamiliar. My brother always smiled—with his mouth, his eyes, even the little quirk in his straight brows. Julen once said that he'd been born smiling, and he'd probably die the same. But there was no smile on his wide mouth now.

"Papa?" I asked, my throat suddenly hurting.

He nodded just once. "Wants us both. We'd better be quick."

I batted aside the door hanging and ran out. My bare feet slapped the cold stone flooring, and I shivered and yanked my blanket closer. I felt the old wool give and the hole at my elbow widened as I dashed past the warmth of the kitchen and up the tower stairs.

Bran was just behind me. Neither of us spoke as we toiled round and round, up to the little room at the top of the tallest tower of our castle. The cold was bitter, promising a fierce winter. As I ran

4

pulled my blanket tighter, tucking the ends through the rope I used as a sash.

The fourth round brought us to Papa's room. To my surprise he was completely alone—the villagers who had taken turns sitting with him had been sent away—and the windows were wide open. Despite two of our three precious Fire Sticks burning brightly in the fireplace and on a makeshift brazier near the bed, the room was shockingly cold.

"Papa—" I cried, flinging myself down by the high, narrow bed. "It's not good for you to be so cold when you're sick—"

"Leave it, child." His voice was just a whisper. "I want to die hearing the windharps. Already the Hill Folk mourn me..."

I heard it then, a faint, steady humming on the wintry breeze, carried down from the distant mountain peaks. The sound was eerie but strangely calming, and I turned away from the window, the cold air forgotten.

"Papa—" That was Bran.

Our father's gray beard stirred as he turned his head. He gave Bran a weak, tired smile, no more than a twitching of the lips, and wrenched at my heart. "Be not sad, my boy. Be pleased," Papa said slowly. "The Hill Folk honor me. All my life I have kept the Covenant, and I shall die keeping it. They know it, and they send their music to guide my spirit from the mortal realm."

I took his hand, which felt cold and dry. Pressing it against my cheek, I said, "But Papa, you are not to worry about Greedy Galdran's tax demand. I've found a way to pay it—I just finished!"

The gnarled fingers briefly gripped my hand. "It's no longer time for taxes, child. It's time to go to war. Galdran's demand was not meant to be fulfilled. It was an excuse. His cousin wants our lands."

"But we're not ready," I protested numbly. "Just one more year—" I heard the scrape of a shoe behind me, and Bran touched my shoulder.

Papa smiled wearily. "Meliara. Branaric and Khesot know the

5

time is come, but that is what they are trained for. Indeed, daughter, they are ready because of the help you have given them this past year."

I fell silent, and he looked from me to my brother and then back, and then spoke slowly and with increasing difficulty.

"Remember, my children...although your mother chose to adopt into my family, she was a Calahanras...the last of the very finest royal house ever to rule Remalna. If she had wanted, she could have raised her banner, and half the kingdom would have risen, gladly, in her name. You two are half Calahanras. You have her wit, and her brains. You can take Remalna, and you will be better rulers than any Merindar ever was."

I stared at my father, not knowing what to say. To think. It was the first time he had mentioned our mother since that horrible day, nearly ten years ago, when the news had come that she had died so suddenly and mysteriously while on a journey to the capital, Remalna-city.

"Promise me," he said, struggling up on one elbow. His breath wheezed in and out, and his skin was blotchy with the effort, but his voice was strong. "Promise me!...You will...fight Galdran... protect Tlanth...and the Covenant..." He fell back, fought for breath.

"Papa," I quavered.

Beside me, Bran reached for the frail old hand. "Papa, please. Rest. Be easy—"

"Promise!" He gripped both our hands, pulling us toward him. "You must...promise me..."

"I promise," I said quickly.

"And I," Branaric said. "Now, Papa, you must try to rest."

"It's too late for..." His eyes closed, and his fingers loosened from mine, and wandered without purpose over the bedclothes. "Khesot...You and Khesot, Branaric...as soon as our hirelings get here from Denlieff, then you attack. Surprise...will carry you a long way."

6

Bran nodded. "Just as you say, Papa."

"And trust Azmus," Papa said, trembling with the effort it took ›peak clearly. "He was your mother's liegeman... If—if he had n with her on that cursed trip, she would be with us now... :en to him. I didn't, once, and..." Grief wracked his face, grief pain.

"We understand, Papa," Bran said quickly. I couldn't talk—my ›at hurt too much.

Our father gave a long sigh of relief and fell back on his pillows. u're a good boy, Branaric. No, a man now... a man these four rs. And Meliara, almost grown..." He turned his head to look ne. Horror seized my wits when I saw the sheen of tears in his s. "Meliara, so like your mother. I wronged you, my daughter. ase forgive me for neglecting you..."

Neglect? I thought of the years that Bran had reluctantly gone to the tower to wrestle with musty old learning-books while I free with Oria and the other village children and, in summers, med the high mountains to dance with the Hill Folk under the moon. My father had always seemed a distant, preoccupied , and after Mother's death he had become even more distant. ›as her I'd missed, and still missed.

Now I sucked in my breath, trying hard not to cry. "But I was py, Papa," I said. "It wasn't neglect, it was freedom."

My father smiled. The tears shone in the furrows beside his s. "Free..." I don't know if he was repeating what I said or inning a new thought; whichever, it was destined to remain un-shed, at least in this world.

He fell silent, his hands reaching again. This time when we h gripped his fingers, there was no response, and after a moment breath slowed, then stopped.

Branaric stood helplessly, looking down at the still figure in the . Feeling numb—unreal—I took Papa's thin hands, which were warm, and laid them gently across his breast. Then I turned my brother. "There's nothing we can do now, except gather

7

the villagers…" *And prepare the funeral fires.* I couldn't say th
words.

Bran's chest heaved in a sob, and he pressed the heels of hi
palms to his eyes. His grief dissolved my numbness, and I began t
weep.

Bran opened his arms and I cast myself into them, and we stoo
there for a long time, crying together while the cold wind swirle
round us and the distant windharps of the Hill Folk hummed.

It was Bran who pulled away suddenly. He gripped my shoul
ders. "Mel, we have to keep that promise. Both of us. But you don'
know—" He shook his head and knuckled his eyes. "Together.
know I'm the oldest, and Papa named me the heir, but I promis
right now, we'll share the title. Half and half, you and me, even i
we disagree—which I hope won't happen. All we have now is thi
old castle, and the county's people to protect—and each other."

"I don't want to be a countess," I said, sniffling. "Look at me
Wearing a horse blanket and running about with bare feet! I don'
know the first thing about being a countess."

"You're not going to Court," Bran said. "You're going to wai
And about that"—he winced—"about that, I think you know jus
about as much as I do."

"What do you mean?"

Bran looked quickly at Papa's body and then said, "I know it'
stupid, but I don't feel right about telling you these things up here
Let's stop the fires and go downstairs."

Each of us moved to one of the blazes and said the Words o
Power over a Fire Stick. The fires flickered out with a snap. I picke
up my Stick, which was still warm; I wrapped my chilled finger
around it and waited as Bran slowly, with a last glance at the stil
figure on the bed, picked his up.

"Have you been keeping secrets from Papa?" I asked, full o
foreboding, as we started down the long spiral.

"Had to." Bran took a deep, unsteady breath. "He aged ter
years when Mama was killed, and every year since, he's seemed t

8

add another ten. Until this year. Of late each *day* seems to have added ten."

"Better tell me, then," I said.

"There's no way to make this easy," Bran warned as we reached the ground floor again. "First you should know why Papa wanted us to go on the attack right away: Azmus has proof that the King, and his cousin, plan to break the Covenant. It's a letter that Debegri wrote. It's full of fancy language, but what it means is he's offering our colorwoods for sale outside our kingdom. For gold."

I sucked in a deep breath. "What about the Hill Folk? The woods are theirs! It's been that way for centuries!"

Branaric shook his head slowly. "Not if Debegri gets his way —and Azmus knows the King is behind this scheme, because it was his messengers who were sent to carry the letter."

"But we haven't heard from those warrior captains we hired—"

"Now it's time for you to hear the secret I kept from Papa." Bran looked grim. "Those mercenaries from Denlieff took our money and vanished."

I stopped and faced him. "What? Do we know that for certain? Could they have been delayed—or ambushed—by Galdran?"

Bran shrugged. "I don't know. The only reliable informant we could send to find out would be Azmus."

"But isn't he still in the capital with Papa's letter to the King?"

Branaric nodded. "Awaiting the signal to deliver it and disperse copies through all the Court, just as Papa ordered. But as to the mercenaries from Denlieff, both our messengers have come back and said the commander isn't to be found. No one's even heard of him or his troop." Bran added sourly, "I thought all along this was as risky as trusting skunks not to smell."

I nodded as we stopped by the empty kitchen and laid the Fire Sticks on the great table. "But Papa was so certain they'd believe in our cause."

"Mercenaries don't have causes—or they wouldn't be swords

9

for hire," Bran said. "We really need someone trained to captain our people and teach us the latest fighting techniques."

"We can't hire anyone else; we haven't the gold," I said. "I just spent two days trying to work around the sums we had to send for the taxes."

Bran raised his hands. "Then we are on our own, sister."

I groaned as we walked the last few steps to the old stewards' parlor, and I swatted aside the hanging. Then I stopped again and groaned louder. I'd forgotten the broken window. All my careful piles of paper were strewn around the room like so much snow.

Bran looked around and scratched his head. "I sure hope you wrote down your figures," he said with a rueful smile.

"Of course I didn't," I muttered.

He slewed around and stared at me. "You didn't?"

"No. I hate writing. It's slow, and my letters are still ill formed, and the ink blobs up, and my fingers get stiff in the cold. I simply separated all the villages' lists of resources and figured out who could give a bit more. Those papers went in one pile. The villages that are overreached went in another pile. I made mental trades in my mind until I managed to match the totals demanded by Galdran. Then I was going to find Oria and tell it all to her so she could write it down." I shrugged.

Though I'd only learned to read and write the year before, it was I who kept track of our careful hoard of supplies, and the taxes, and the plans—and now all my work was scattered over the stone floor of the room.

We both stared until the *plop-plop* of raindrops coming through the broken window and landing on the papers forced us into action.

Working together, we soon got all the papers picked up. Bran silently gave me his stack, and I pressed them all tightly against me. "I still have the totals in my head," I assured him. "I'll find Oria and get her to write it out, and we can see where we are. We'll be all right, Bran. We will." I wanted desperately to see that stricken look leave his eyes—or I would begin crying all over again.

Bran lifted his gaze from the mess of rain-spattered papers in my arms and smiled crookedly. "A horse blanket, Mel?"

I remembered what I was wearing. "It tore in half when Hrani tried washing it. She was going to mend it. This piece was too small for a horse, but it was just right for me."

Bran laughed a little unsteadily. "Mel. A *horse blanket*."

"Well, it's clean," I said defensively. "Was—at least, it doesn't smell of horse."

Bran sank down onto the three-legged stool, still laughing; but was a strange, wheezy sort of laugh. "A countess wearing a horse blanket and a count who hates fighting, leading a war against a wicked king who has the largest army the kingdom has ever known. What's to become of us, Mel?"

I knelt down—carefully, because of the broken crockery—set my papers aside, and took his hands. "One thing I've learned about doing the figures: You don't look at the problem all at once, or it's like being caught in a spring flood under a downpour. You tackle the problem in pieces...We'll send our letter to the King. Maybe Galdran will actually listen, and abide by the Covenant, and ease taxes, so we don't have to go to war. But if he doesn't, some of those courtiers ought to agree with us—they can't all be Galdran's toadies—which means we'll surely get allies. Then we'll gather the rest of our supplies. And then..."

"And then?" Bran repeated, his hands on his knees, his dark blue eyes even darker with the intensity of his emotions.

"And then..." I faltered, feeling overwhelmed with my own emotions. I took a deep breath, reminding myself of my own advice. *Pieces. Break it all into small pieces.* "And then, if Galdran attacks us, we'll fight back. Like I said, maybe we'll have help. The courtiers will see it in Papa's letter to the King: We are not doing this for ourselves. We're doing it to protect the Hill Folk, for if Papa is right, and Galdran's cousin wants to break the Covenant and start chopping down the great trees again, then the Hill Folk will have nowhere to live. *And* we're doing it for our people—though not

11

just them. For all the people in the kingdom who've had to pay those harsh taxes in order to build Galdran that big army."

Branaric got to his feet. "You're right. In pieces. I'll remember that...Let's get through today first. We have to tell everyone in the village about Papa, and send messengers throughout Tlanth, and get ready for the funeral fire."

My first impulse was to run and hide, for I did not look forward to facing all that pity. But it had to be done—and we had to do it together.

And afterward, when the village was quiet and lights went out, I could slip out of the castle and run up the mountainside to where I could hear the reed flutes mourning.

The Hill Folk would emerge, looking a little like walking trees in the moonlight, and wordlessly, accompanied by their strange music—which was a kind of magic in itself—we would dance slowly, sharing memory, and grief, and promise.

TWO

T WAS EXACTLY A MONTH LATER THAT JULEN, ORIA, rani the weaver, and I gathered in the kitchen—the only warm om in the castle—and studied Bran from all angles.

He flushed with embarrassment but turned around willingly lough while we judged the fit of the tunic Hrani had remade for m. The old green velvet, left from Papa's wardrobe, nicely set off ran's tall, rangy build. His face was long and sharp boned, like ather's had been.

The only features Bran and I shared were wide-spaced dark lue eyes and wavy red-brown hair—both inherited from our other. The green of the tunic was just right for his coloring.

"This tunic might not be the fashion—" Julen began.

"Of course it's not the fashion," Oria cut in, her dark eyes full scorn for the vagaries of courtiers. "When from all accounts their shions change from week to week—maybe day to day."

"This tunic might not be the fashion," her mother repeated as Oria had not spoken, "but it looks good. And wear your hair tied ck, not loose or braided. Better stay with the simple styles than ok foolish in what might be old styles."

Bran shrugged. He had as little interest in clothing as I did. s long as they don't take one look and laugh me back into the snow, I'm content." He turned to me and sighed. "But I can't help wishing you were going. You've a much quicker mind than I have."

Quick to laugh, quick to act—and much too quick to judge. How many times had I heard that warning? I stole a look at Julen, who pursed her lips but said nothing.

I shook my head. "No, no, you got all the charm in this family—along with the imposing height. All I got was the temper. This is a mission to win allies, not enemies, and if they laughed *me* back into the snow, you *know* I'd go right back at them, sword in hand, and try to make them listen!"

Bran and Oria laughed, and even Julen smiled. I crossed my arms. "You know it's true."

"Of course," Bran agreed. "That's why it's funny. I can just see you taking on a palace full of sniffy courtiers twice your size, as if they were a pack of unruly pups—"

"Here, my lord, try the blue one now," Julen said. Despite the title—which she had insisted on using since Father's death—her tone was very much like the one she reserved for little Calaub and his urchin friends. "And that's enough nonsense. You'll do well if you go down to those barons and talk like you mean it. And you, my lady," she rounded on me, "if you wish to be helpful, you can see if Selfan has finished resoling the blackweave boots."

I got up, knowing a dismissal when I heard one.

Oria started after me but paused at the door, looking back, a considering expression on her pretty face. I looked as well, but I saw only Bran unlacing his tunic as he talked to Julen about those boots.

Oria gave a tiny shrug and pushed me out the door.

"Something wrong?" I asked.

Her dark eyes gleamed with humor now. "Mama is very cross, isn't she? I don't think she wants your brother going to the lowlands."

It was not quite an answer, but during the last couple of years I'd gotten used to Oria's occasional mysterious evasions. "Can't be

14

lped. Azmus wrote out copies of our letter to the King and gave
em to prominent courtiers, but not one response have we re-
ived. It's time to get some allies with face-to-face meetings, or
e're finished before we even start."

She pursed her lips, the humor gone. "I made him up some
od things to eat," she said. "Let me fetch the pack."

ot too much later we all stood in the castle courtyard as Branaric
ished tying his travel gear onto the saddle of his horse. Then he
ounted, gave us a quick salute, and soon was gone from sight.

He didn't like saying farewells any more than I did. I retreated
to the castle, and for a time wandered from room to empty room
cold drafts of wintry wind chilled my face. Inevitably my path
ought me to the library, empty these ten years. Black scorch
arks still stained the walls and ceiling, potent reminders of the
rrible night we found out about my mother's death. Crying in
ge, my father had stamped into this room, where generations of
tiars had stored their gathered knowledge, and deliberately—one
ok at a time—set it all ablaze. The only books that had escaped
re a half dozen dull tomes in the schoolroom.

After, Father had retreated to his tower, and never again re-
rred to that night. But his determination to see Galdran toppled
m the throne had altered from desire to obsession.

I paced the perimeter of the room, looking at the grimy ash-
ackened stones, my mood dark.

Oria's voice broke my reverie: "Amazing, isn't it, how one can
e in a mess and never really notice it? Perhaps we ought to scour
ese rooms out come spring."

I turned around. Oria stood in the open doorway—the hanging
d rotted entirely away a few years back. "Why? The weather will
st blow more leaves in, and we can't afford windows."

"The wind won't blow ten years' worth in at once," Oria said
actically.

15

I looked around, wondering why I resisted the idea. Was this room a kind of monument? Except I knew my mother would not have liked a burnt, blackened room as a memorial. In her day, the furnishings might have been old and worn, for taxes even then had been fierce, but each table and cushion and candlestick had been mended and polished, and the castle had been cozy and clean and full of flowers. And this room…

"She loved books," I said slowly. "It was Papa who declared war on them, just as he did on Galdran. I really don't know why Papa burned this room. Nor do I know how to find out." I reached a decision. "Maybe we should clean it. Except—what a chore!"

Oria grinned. "A challenge. I've wanted to set this castle to rights for—" She stopped suddenly and shook her head. "Mama said to bring you down to the smithy. You can sleep in the loft. That way we can add this Fire Stick to the two we've already put in our supply pack."

I nodded, glad to be relieved of having to sleep alone in the castle. It wasn't the sadness of the past lingering in shadowy corners that bothered me so much as my own fears about the future.

During the long, snowbound month that followed, I kept busy. The few times I had nothing to do, Julen assigned me chores. She called herself my maid, and her directions were framed in the form of a question ("Would you care to deliver these mended halters to the garrison, my lady?"), but otherwise she treated me much as she treated Oria. I found this comforting. I didn't feel so much like an orphan.

We spent a lot of time at the old garrison—a leftover from the days when every noble had some kind of private army—training in swordfighting with all those who had volunteered to help in the war. Our army was comprised mostly of young people from villages across Tlanth.

In charge now was Khesot, a man whose seventy years had been

evoted to the service of the Counts and Countesses of Tlanth—
ur father, and his grandmother before him—except for a five-year
int fighting for the old King during the long siege when the in-
mous pirate fleet called the Brotherhood of Blood had tried to
ain access to the coastal cities. It was these five years' service as a
oldier that had gotten him placed in the position he was in now.
e'd never risen higher than leader of a riding, but he knew enough
f war to realize his own shortcomings. And he was the best we
ad.

The huge, drafty building echoed with the clanks and thuds
nd shouts of mock battle. Khesot walked slowly up and back, his
ild brown eyes narrowed, considering, as he watched us work.

"Get that shield arm up," he said to a tough old stonemason.
Remember you will likely be fighting mounted warriors, and I very
uch fear that most of us will be afoot. The mounted fighter has
e advantage; therefore you must unhorse your opponent before
ou can hope to win…"

We had spent days affixing shiny metal bits to our shields to
flect sunlight at the horses and cause them to rear. We had also
acticed slicing saddle belts, hooking spears or swords around legs
nd heaving warriors out of the saddle. And we learned other meth-
ds of unhorsing warriors, such as tying fine-woven twine between
o trees at just the right height so that the riders would be knocked
f their horses.

Khesot turned around, then frowned at two young men who
ad assumed the old dueling stance and were slashing away at one
other with merry abandon, their swords ringing.

"Charic! Justav! What do you think you are doing?"

The men stopped, Charic looking shamefaced. "Thought we'd
fine a little, in case we take on one o' them aristos—"

"Many of whom are trained in swordplay from the time they
gin to walk," Khesot cut in, his manner still mild; but now both
ung men had red faces. "By the very best sword masters their
ealthy parents can hire. It would take them precisely as long as it

amused them to cut you to ribbons. Do not engage their officers in a duel, no matter how stupid you might think them. Two of you moving as I told you, can knock them off balance…"

He went on to lecture the two, who listened soberly. Several others gathered around to listen as well.

Oria and I had been working with one another until I stopped to watch. Now Oria lowered her sword arm and eyed me. "What's wrong?"

I dropped my point, absently massaging my shoulder. "Did I frown? I was—well, thinking of something."

She shrugged, and we went back to practice. But I kept part of my attention on Khesot, and when he drew near to us, I disengaged and said, "I have a question for you."

Khesot nodded politely, and as we walked to the side of the room, he said, "May I compliment you, my lady, on your improvement?"

"You may," I said grimly, "but I know I'm still not good enough to face anyone but a half-trained ten-year-old."

He smiled. "You cannot help your stature."

"You mean I'm short and scrawny, and I'll always be short and scrawny, and short and scrawny makes for a terrible warrior."

His smile widened; for a moment he was on the verge of laughter. As he positioned himself so he could continue to watch the practice, he said, "You have a question for me?"

"Something I've been worrying about; what you told Chari and Justav put me in mind of it. Even if we have the best-trained warriors in the world, how can we really hope to defeat that army of Galdran's? I can see how long it takes to beat just one person and you know that even Faeruk, who is our best, won't be able to take on whole ridings."

"I am hoping that the most the King will send against us will be a couple of wings," Khesot said. "Twice-nine ridings, with their foot soldiers, we can probably handle, if we plan well and use our familiarity with the territory to our advantage."

"Well," I said, "I was thinking: Instead of having to do all this .cking and slashing, could it be possible to try other means to feat them—through discouragement or even dismay?"

"What have you in mind?"

"It is the King's cousin, Baron Debegri, who wants our lands," aid. "Rumor has it he is a pompous fool. If we were to make him ok foolish, might he give it up as a bad business and go home?" 1esot was silent, so I continued, outlining my plans. "Supposing : could, oh, turn aside a stream uphill from their camp and swamp em in their bedrolls. Or sneak in and add pepper to their food. sit in trees and drop powdered itchwort on them as they ride neath."

Khesot paused, his eyes distant. Finally he turned to me, his pression curious, and said, "Who is to execute these admirable ms?"

"I will," I said immediately. "I know I'm never going to be 1ch good in these hand-to-hand battles, but climbing trees is mething I can do better than most. I'll ask for volunteers. I know ria will join me, and Young Varil. Old Varil says he's too small to ndle a sword, and he wants so badly to help. And—"

Khesot lifted a hand. "I had not considered that you would tually go into battle with us, my lady. I thought your practice re was mostly for diversion."

I felt my face go hot. "I guess that's a polite way of telling me at I really *am* bad with the sword, then?"

He smiled a little. "No, it's just that members of the nobility n't usually lead battles unless they've been trained their whole es."

"But I will never ask anyone from our village—from any village Tlanth—to risk his or her life unless I'm willing to myself."

"You must realize, my lady, if Galdran's people catch you, they ll treat you like any other prisoner..."

"We're all equally at risk," I said. "But my plan is to be sneaky, they are surprised."

He bowed. "Then I leave it to you, my lady."

I bowed back. "I'll get started right away!"

Though I still missed my brother and worried because he sent no message, having a plan to work on made the wintry days move faster. I was very busy, often from the first ring of the gold-candle bell at dawn to the single toll of midnight, when those who kept night watches lit the first white candle.

I had a group of five, all younger than Oria and I. We left the good fighters to the ridings, which Khesot was pulling together slowly, as he evaluated the best leaders.

It being midwinter, herbs were hard to come by, but assiduous poking into ancient grottoes seldom touched by the weather, and patient communication through friends and relatives, uncovered some surprising stores. Thus by Midwinter's Day, which was also Oria's Name Day, I had laid by a good supply of itchwort and sneezeweed and three kinds of pepper, plus a collection of other oddments.

Thus I was in a happy mood when I put on a gown that Oria had outgrown and walked out with her to the village square to begin the celebration. For it wasn't just her Name Day, but also her Flower Day; though she'd been doing the women's dances for several years, after today she would no longer dance the children's dances. Young men and women who passed their Flower Days were considered of an age to marry.

A heavy snow over the previous two days had trapped those who might otherwise have gone home to celebrate Midwinter with their families, so we had a larger group than usual. The stars overhead were stunningly clear, as only winter skies can make them. Our breath puffed white as we formed up circles, and some shivered; but we knew we'd soon be warm enough as the musicians began thrumming and tapping a merry tune.

Everyone looked our way. Oria stepped back, smiling, and I

fted the deep blue cheli blossoms I'd found in one of those old
rotected grottoes, and tossed them high in the air. They fluttered
own around her. She twirled about, her curly black hair brushing
gainst her crimson sash. Then, slowly, stepping to the music, she
alked between the two great blazes in the square made by every-
ne bringing their Fire Sticks. And all her friends flung flowers.

Sometimes she bent to pick them up. Not any special ones, that
, from any special person. She hadn't been twoing with anyone,
ven though she could have been anytime these past three years.
s I watched her deft fingers twist the stems of the blossoms into
garland, I felt a kind of swooping sensation inside when I realized
at we *both* had been of the age to be twoing with the young men
r three years.

My Flower Day was coming up in just weeks. My Flower
)ay—and I was still happiest dancing with the children.

But there was no time to consider this. The circle walk ended,
nd Oria carefully placed her garland on her head, then held out
er hands to me. "Come, Mel, let's dance!"

We moved into the cleared space, which was now dappled with
lossoms in a kind of mirror to the brightly colored jewels in the
ky. Warmth radiated from the fires, and soon we were flushed from
1e dance.

Before the young men could move out for their own first dance,
1e sound of horses' hooves approaching made the musicians falter.
1emory of imminent war, forgotten for a short time, now rushed
ack on us. I could see it in the quick looks, the hands that strayed
) knife hilts or stooped for rocks.

A horse and rider emerged from the shadows into our silence.
watched in surprise as my brother rode directly up to us, and just
ehind him a small, round-faced man on another horse—Azmus.

Bran's mount halted in the center of our dance square, its limbs
embling, and my brother slid off, almost pitching forward. Several
eople sprang forward to help, some to hold him up, others to take
1e horse away to be cared for. Behind, Azmus dismounted, and

21

though he didn't lose his balance, his face was haggard. His horse was also led away.

I ran to Branaric and stared with dismay into his drawn face. His hair had come loose and hung in wet strings across his brow and down over his soggy cloak. He opened his mouth, but no words came out.

Her garland askew, Oria handed Branaric a steaming cloth. He buried his face and hands gratefully in it for a long moment. The only sound in the square was the crackling of the flames.

Finally he looked up, his skin blotchy but his eyes clearing. "War," he said, and cleared his throat. "Azmus found out, and came to get me. The King has sent his cousin to take Tlanth for non-payment of taxes. And for conspiring to break the Covenant."

THREE

ALDRAN HAD TWO FORTRESSES ON THE BORDER OF
anth, one to the south, called Vesingrui, and a smaller one on
r northwest border, called Munth. This castle was much closer
the wealthy and powerful and somewhat mysterious principality
Renselaeus—about whose leaders we knew little, other than that
y were allied with Galdran.

It was the castle of Munth that would see the start of the war.
unth was closest to our castle and the heart of Tlanth. If Munth
re kept well supplied, Galdran's forces would find it the easier
settle in all winter and throw warriors against us.

Some of the younger people wanted to attack Vesingrui first,
that would be more daring, it being closest to the lowlands. But
esot wisely pointed out that we couldn't actually hold it; we'd
divided in half, and a small army divided into two tiny forces
uldn't be much good for anything.

So two days after Oria's Flower Day, just ahead of a terrible
owstorm, Azmus rode south to return to Remalna-city for spying
rposes while the rest of us marched down the mountains to
unth. We found it nearly empty, though the soldiers there were
viously preparing for more inhabitants. We surprised them in the
dst of a huge cleanup.

The fight was short, and soon Galdran's people were locked in their own dungeon. The storm struck while we were snug in the castle.

While our army celebrated its first victory, Khesot called Bran and me and our riding leaders together. The echoes of happy songs rang off the mossy ancient stones as we met in the high round room set aside for the commander. Outside the wind howled, and the thick windows showed pure white. But we lit one of our own castle's Fire Sticks and huddled around it, drinking hot cider, until the room had lost some of its chill.

On a huge wood table was spread the map I'd carefully made the summer before. It showed all of Tlanth, every village, every mountain, and all the rivers and valleys I knew so well.

"Debegri is on his way here," Khesot said finally, gesturing with his pipe at the map. "None of our prisoners would tell us when they received their orders, but I suspect, from the evidence around us, he and his warriors are expected imminently."

"Good!" Bran said, laughing as he brandished his cider cup. "So what's next? A welcome party?"

"A welcome party of ghosts, I think," Khesot said. "We don't know how many Debegri is leading, and we don't have enough supplies to outlast a siege. I wish our timing had been better—before the army but after their supplies got here. Then we could have held out indefinitely."

"Except they could have penned us here and attacked the rest of Tlanth, couldn't they?" I asked doubtfully.

"Exactly, my lady," Khesot said, giving me a thin smile of approval. "Whatever forces they have are probably hunkered down somewhere, waiting out this storm. No one's going anywhere until it ends. Therefore what I suggest is that we use the time the storm lasts to completely destroy this castle. Render it unusable for them, forcing them to carry their supplies with them—at least for the time being."

"And we can pick away at them, getting some of those supplies," Old Varil said grimly.

"And keep them away from our villages, so they can't set up bases there," Hrani added, tucking her shawl around her more tightly as an especially fierce gust of wind sent a trickle of icy air stirring through the room.

"But that's defensive work," I protested. "Aren't we going to go on the attack?"

Khesot puffed at his pipe and nodded at me. "The time has come to ignore all the rhetoric. We call this war a revolt. They call us traitors. The truth is, Galdran has attacked us here in our homeland, and we have to defend it."

"At least until we get some allies," Branaric said, still smiling. "They're all afraid of Galdran, every single person I spoke with. Take Gharivar of Mnend—he's right below us, and if Debegri wants more land, Mnend will be next. I may not be as quick at understanding hints as Mel, but I could see he agreed with me, even though he didn't dare promise anything. Orbanith listened as well. And a couple of the coastal barons."

Khesot frowned slightly but just puffed away at his pipe without speaking. It was then that I began to believe that we were going to have to fight this one all alone.

We worked for the four days of that blizzard, loosening the mortar in the lower stones of Castle Munth. The wind and storm did the rest; after the walls fell, we melted snow from uphill with our combined Fire Sticks. The resulting flood was impressive.

By the next morning, when the scouts we left behind saw the first of Debegri's soldiers march up the road, the whole mess had frozen into ice, with our ex-prisoners wandering around poking dismally at the ruins. It would take a great deal of effort to make any use of Munth, and the scouts were still laughing when they came to report.

———

25

For five whole weeks, this was how it went.

We froze the roads ahead of Debegri's marching warriors. We changed road signs, removed landmarks, used snow to alter the landscape. Three times we sat on the cliffs above and cracked jokes while the army milled around in confusion far below us.

We attacked their camps at night, flinging snow and stones at those on the perimeter and then disappearing into the woods before the angry Baron could assemble a retaliation party.

The only one we couldn't get at was Debegri, for he had a splendid—even palatial—tent that was closely guarded in the very center of their camp. He also had lancers riding in double columns on either side of him whenever his army moved.

But we actually did get to use the itchwort.

As soon as I saw Galdran's army I realized it would be impossible to drop itchwort on them, for they were much better bundled up than we were. Steel helms, thick cloaks, chain mail, thick gauntlets, long battle tunics—brown and green, dark versions of the gold and green of Remalna—and high blackweave boots kept everything covered. In disappointment I'd told my little band to put the packets of itchwort at the bottoms of our carryalls.

But one night, after we'd flooded their camp by blocking up a stream just above them, the chance came. The weather was ugly, slashing sleet and stinging rain rendering the world soggy. Debegri, always recognizable in his embroidered gold cloak and the white-plumed helm of a commander, stalked out through a line of torch bearers and waved his arms, yelling.

Half of his army marched off into the darkness, presumably in search of us. The rest labored to strike the camp. Varil, Oria, and I perched high in trees, watching. At one point something happened at the other end of the camp, and for a short time Debegri's mighty tent lay collapsed and half rolled on its ground cover.

I looked over at Oria. "Itchwort," I murmured.

Varil snorted into the crook of his elbow so the sound wouldn't carry.

"I don't know," Oria whispered doubtfully. "Those sentries may come marching back just as quickly…"

"You stay and watch," I whispered back. "Give the crow call if you see danger. Varil, we'll have to crawl through mud—"

Varil was already digging through his pack.

We scrambled down from our tree and elbow-crawled our way through the mud to the partially folded tent. There both of us emptied our packs into it and scattered the dust as best we could, then we retreated—and just in time. The tent was soon packed up, loaded onto its dray.

When Debegri camped again, we were lined up in the rocks of cliff to the east, watching eagerly. To our vast disappointment, he didn't emerge at all—for three days.

For the week after that he had almost the entire army guarding him, which made it easy to harass their sentries. And one night we managed to steal half their horse picket.

That was the last and most triumphant of our exploits; we celebrated long past midnight, sure that if the war was going to be like this, we'd win before the spring thaws came to the mountains.

We celebrated too soon.

The next time Debegri sent a wing after us, they broke the Code of War and used arrows. Debegri had archers with him, probably hired from another land. Three of our people were hit, and from then on we were forced to stay under the cover of forestland.

And so for a time we were at an impasse; they did not advance, but we were more cautious about attacking. They had broken the Code of War, but we had no one to complain to. Against my wishes, Branaric sent some of our people to find bows and arrows, and to learn how to shoot them.

Then the day came when a new column was spotted riding up behind Debegri's force. We almost missed them, for we had also begun staying in a tight group. As well, Khesot, cautious since his days in the terrible Pirate Wars, still sent pairs of scouts on rounds all four directions twice a day.

It was Seliar, of my group, who spotted them first. She reported to me, and the rest of us crept down the hillside to watch the camp below. We saw at the head of the column a man wearing a long black cloak.

Debegri emerged, bowed. The newcomer bowed in return and handed the Baron a rolled paper. They went inside Debegri's tent, and when they emerged, the stranger had the white plume of leadership on his helm. Debegri's glower was plain even at the distance we watched from.

Backing up from our vantage, we retreated to our camp.

Bran and Khesot and the other riding leaders were all gathered under our old, patched rain cover when we reached them. Seliar blurted out what we'd seen.

Branaric grinned all through the story. At the end I said, "This is obviously no surprise. What news had you?"

Bran nodded to where a mud-covered young woman sat in front of one of the tents, attacking a bowl of stew as if she hadn't eaten in a week. "Messenger just arrived from Azmus, or it would have been a surprise. Galdran has taken his cousin off the command. He'd apparently expected us to last two weeks at most."

"Well, who is this new commander? Ought we to be afraid?"

Bran's grin widened until he laughed. "Here's the jest: He's none other than the Marquis of Shevraeth, heir to the Renselaeus principality. According to Azmus, all he ever thinks about are clothes, horse racing, and gambling. And did I mention clothes?"

Everyone roared with laughter.

"We'll give *him* two weeks," I crowed. "And then we'll send him scurrying back to his tailor."

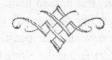

FOUR

T TOOK ONE LONG, DESPERATE WEEK TO PROVE JUST
w wrong was my prophecy.

"The revolution is not over," Branaric said seriously some ten
ys later.

But even this—after a long, horrible day of real fighting, a
sperate run back into the familiar hills of Tlanth, and the advent
rain beating on the tent over our heads—failed to keep Branaric
rious for long. His mouth curved wryly as he added, "And today's
tion was not a rout, it was a retreat."

"So we will say outside this tent." Khesot paused to tap his
peweed more deeply into the worn brown bowl of his pipe, then
looked up, his white eyebrows quirked. "But it *was* a rout."

I said indignantly, "Our people fought well!"

Khesot gave a stately, measured nod in my direction, without
oving from his cushion. "Valiantly, Lady Meliara, valiantly. But
urage is not enough when we are so grossly outnumbered. More
now that they have an equally able commander."

Bran sighed. "Why haven't we heard anything from Gharivar
Mnend, or Chamadis from Turlee, on the border? I *know* they
th hate Galdran as much as we do, and they as much as promised
help."

"Perhaps they have been cut off from joining us, Lord Branaric," Khesot said, nodding politely this time to Bran.

"Cut off by cowardice," I muttered. My clothes were clammy, my skin cold; I longed to change into my one other outfit, but we had to finish our own war council before facing the riding leaders. So I perched on the hard camp cushion, arms clasped tightly around my legs.

Bran turned to me, frowning. "You think they lied to me, then?"

"I just think you're better off not counting on those Court fools. Remember, Papa always said they are experts at lying with a smile, and their treaties don't last as long as the wine haze after the signing."

Bran's eyes went serious again under his straight brows. "I know, Mel," he said, plainly unhappy as he picked absently at a threadbare patch on his cushion. "But if we don't get help...Well, we're just not enough."

Leaving us staring at the grinning skull of defeat. I shook my head, shivering when my wet clothes shifted on my back and sent a chill down my flesh. Now Bran looked worn, tired—and defeated—and I was angry with myself for having spoken. "Khesot has the right of it," I said. "Perhaps they really were cut off."

I looked up, caught a glance of approval in Khesot's mild brown eyes. Heartened, I said, "Look. We aren't lying to our people when we say this is a retreat. Because even if we *have* been routed, we're still in our own territory, hills we know better than anyone. Meanwhile we've evaded Greedy Galdran's mighty army nearly all winter. A long time! Didn't Azmus say Galdran promised the Court our heads on poles after two days?"

"So Debegri swore," Bran said, smiling a little.

"That means we've held out all these weeks despite the enormous odds against us, and word of this has to be reaching the rest of the kingdom. Maybe those western Counts will decide to join us—and some of the other grass-backed vacillators as well," I finished stoutly.

Bran grinned. "Maybe so," he said. "And you're right. The gher Shevraeth drives us, the more familiar the territory. If we an aright, we can lead them on a fine shadow chase and pick them f as they run. Maybe more traps..."

Khesot's lips compressed, and I shivered again. "More traps? ou've already put out a dozen. Bran, I really hate those things."

Branaric winced, then he shook his head, his jaw tightening. This is war. Baron Debegri was the first to start using arrows, espite the Code of War, and now Shevraeth has got us cut off om our own castle—and our supplies. We have to use every eapon to hand, and if that means planting traps for their unwary et, so be it."

I sighed. "It is so...dishonorable. We have outlawed the use f traps against animals for over a century. And what if the Hill olk stumble onto one?"

"I told you last week," Bran said, "my first command to those lacing the traps is to lay sprigs of stingflower somewhere nearby. he Hill Folk won't miss those. Their noses will warn them to ead lightly long before their eyes will."

"We are also using arrows," I reminded him. "So that's two ains on our honor."

"But we are vastly outnumbered. Some say thirty to one."

I looked up at Khesot. "What think you?"

The old man puffed his pipe alight. The red glow in the bowl oked warm and welcome as pungent smoke drifted through the ent. Then he lowered the pipe and said, "I don't like them, either. ut I like less the thought that this Marquis is playing with us, and nytime he wishes he could send his force against us and smash us one run. He has to know pretty well where we are."

"At least you can make certain you keep mapping those traps, o our folk don't stumble into them," I said, giving in.

"That I promise. They'll be marked within a day of being set," ranaric said.

Neither Branaric nor Khesot displayed any triumph as Branaric eached for and carefully picked up the woven tube holding our precious map. Branaric's face was always easy to read—as easy as my own—and though Khesot was better at hiding his emotions, he wasn't perfect. They did not like using the traps, either, but had hardened themselves to the necessity.

I sighed. Another effect of the war. *I've been raised to this almost my entire life. Why does my spirit fight so against it?*

I thrust away the nagging worries, and the dissatisfactions, and my own physical discomfort, as Bran's patient fingers spread out my map on the rug between us. I focused on its neatly drawn hills and forests, dimly lit by the glowglobe, and tried hard to clear my mind of any thoughts save planning our next action.

But it was difficult. I was worried about our single glowglobe, whose power was diminishing. With our supplies nearly gone and our funds even lower, we no longer had access to the magic wares of the south, so there was no way to obtain new glowglobes.

Khesot was looking not at the map but at us, his old eyes sad.

I winced, knowing what he'd say if asked: that he had not been trained for his position any more than nature had suited Bran and me for war.

But there was no other choice.

"So if Hrani takes her riding up here on Mount Elios, mayhap they can spy out Galdran's numbers better," Branaric said slowly. "Then we send out someone to lure 'em to the Ghost Fall Ravine."

I forced my attention back to the map. "Even if the Marquis fails to see so obvious a trap," I said, finally, smoothing a wrinkle with my fingers, "they're necessarily all strung out going through that bottleneck. I don't see how we can account for many of them before they figure out what we're at, and retreat. I say we strike fast, in total surprise. We could set fire to their tents and steal all their mounts. That'd set 'em back a little."

Bran frowned. "None of our attempts to scare 'em off have worked, though—even with Debegri. He just sent for more reinforcements, and now there's this new commander. Attacking their camp sounds more risky to us than to them."

Khesot still said nothing, leaning over only to tap out and re-load his pipe. I followed the direction of his gaze to my brother's face. Had Branaric been born without title or parental plans, he probably would have found his way into a band of traveling players and there enjoyed a life's contentment. Did one not know him by sight, there was no sign in his worn dress or in his manner that he was a count—and this was even more true for me. I looked at Khesot and wondered if he felt sad that though today was my Flower Day there would be no dancing—no music, or laughter, or family to celebrate the leaving of childhood behind. Among the aristocrats in the lowlands, Flower Day was celebrated with fine dresses and satin slippers and expensive gifts. Did he pity us?

He couldn't understand that I had no regrets for something I'd never known—and believed I never would know. But I controlled my impatience, and my tongue, because I knew from long experi-ence that he was again seeing our mother in us—in our wide, dark-lashed eyes and auburn hair—and she had dearly loved pretty clothing, music, her rose garden.

And Galdran had had her killed.

"What do you think?" Bran addressed Khesot, who smiled ruefully.

"You'll pardon an old man, my lord, my lady. I'm more tired than I thought. My mind wandered and I did not hear what you asked."

"Can you second-guess this Shevraeth?" Branaric asked. "He seems to be driving us back into our hills—to what purpose? Why hasn't he taken over any of our villages? He knows where they lie —and he has the forces. If he does that, traps or no traps, arrows or no arrows, we're lost. We won't be able to retake them."

Khesot puffed again, watching smoke curl lazily toward the tent roof.

In my mind I saw, clearly, that straight-backed figure on the apple-gray horse, his long black cloak slung back over the animal's haunches, his plumed helm of command on his head. With either phenomenal courage or outright arrogance he had ignored the possibility of our arrows, the crowned sun stitched on his tunic gleaming in the noonday light as he directed the day's battle.

"I do not know," Khesot said slowly. "But judging from our constant retreats of the last week, I confess freely, I do not believe him to be stupid."

I said, "I find it impossible to believe that a Court fop—really, Azmus reported gossip in Remalna claiming him to be the most brainless dandy of them all—could suddenly become so great a leader."

Khesot tapped his pipe again. "Hard to say. Certainly Galdran's famed army did poorly enough against us until he came. But maybe he has good captains, and unlike Debegri, he may listen to them. *They* cannot all be stupid," Khesot said. "They've been guarding the coast and keeping peace in the cities all these years. It could also be they learned from those first weeks' losses to us. They certainly respect us a deal more than they did at the outset." He closed his eyes.

"Which is why I say we ought to attack them at their camp." I jabbed a finger at the map. "There are too many of them to carry their own water. They'll have to camp by a stream, right? Oh, I suppose it isn't realistic, but how I love the image of us setting fire to their tents, and them swarming about like angry ants while we laugh our way back into the hills."

Branaric's ready grin lightened his somber expression. He started to say something, then was taken by a sudden, fierce yawn. Almost immediately my own mouth opened in a jaw-cracking yawn that made my eyes sting.

"We can discuss our alternatives with the riding leaders after we eat, if I may suggest, my lord, my lady," Khesot said, looking anxiously from one of us to the other. "Let me send Saluen to the cook tent for something hot."

Khesot rose and moved to the flap of the tent to look out. He made a sign to the young man standing guard under the rain canopy

short distance away. Saluen came, Khesot gave his order, and we
watched Saluen lope down the trail to the cook tent.

Khesot stayed on his feet, beckoning to my brother. With careful fingers I rolled up our map. I was peripherally aware of the
other two talking in low voices, until Branaric confronted me with
surprise and consternation plain on his face.

Branaric waited until I had stowed the map away, then he
grabbed me in a sudden, fierce hug. "Next year," he said in a husky
voice. "Can't make much of your Flower Day, but next year I
promise you'll have a Name Day celebration to be remembered
forever—and it'll be in the capital!"

"With us as winners, right?" I said, laughing. "It's all right,
Bran. I don't think I'm ready for Flower Day yet, anyway. Maybe
being so short has made me age slower, or something. I'll be just
as happy dancing with the children another year."

Bran smiled back, then turned away and resumed his quiet conversation with Khesot. I listened for a moment to the murmur of
their voices and looked at but didn't really notice the steady rain,
or the faintly glowing tents.

Instead my inner eye kept returning to the memory of our people running before a mass of orderly brown-and-green-clad soldiers, overseen by a straight figure in a black cloak riding back and
forth along a high ridge.

FIVE

AFTER A HASTY SUPPER I SAT IN THE BIG TENT WE'D
fashioned from three smaller ones and looked at each tired, worried face in the circle of riding leaders, and made a private res-
olution.

The truth was, the riding leaders were afraid to attack the
Galdran camp. I didn't blame them. Each had a turn to speak.
Some were hesitant, some apologetic. They didn't sound like warriors, but simply like exhausted men and women. Calaub: a blacksmith by trade, brother to Julen. Hrani: a weaver. Moraun: a miller.
Faeruk: wounded thirty years before, when fighting pirates for the
old King. Only Jusar favored the idea, but he was a rarity: a young
man trained in arms, though for defense of the castle, not for the
field.

And even Jusar seemed tense, voicing his worry that trying to
locate the enemy's main camp might bring trouble down on us.
"They'll surely have more sentries watching than we can find," he
said.

"More sentries than we have warriors," Faeruk joked, and the
others laughed uneasily.

"Who knows? Galdran might even have managed to hire some
magician. For that matter, how did they get so many Fire Sticks?"

Irani said. Her voice held a little of her old spirit, but there was stricken expression in her eyes that I could not account for.

"One person in each riding took his or her family's Sticks," usar said. "Heard rumors about what is required of new recruits: bey or die."

Calaub's heavy brows met over his big nose. "Makes sense. Galdran's not going to care about Fire Stick custom—not if he's reaking the Covenant."

"Or trying to," Khesot said with a faint smile, bringing the ubject back. "So let's use our alternate plan. Tomorrow, if this eather clears, we can sort out the details."

I stayed quiet as the war council wound up. Then I followed s they filed down the trail to the cook tent to get their evening ose of the thick soup that was tasting each day more of ground orn and stale vegetables and less of stock and herbs.

What we need is information, I thought. *And no one wants to send ayone on what might be a suicide mission, to spy out their camp.* The roblem was, we had only one good spy—Azmus. And he was in he capital trying to garner fresh news.

During Debegri's command we'd used some of the older chilren as horse tenders and arms bearers, but only in isolated places. ome of these youths had willingly climbed very tall trees to survey ad report on distant movements. Now, with Shevraeth in comand, no one wanted to send a child into direct danger.

Staring upward through a tangle of branches at the glowering inks of rain clouds, I saw a break, just for a moment. If the latest orm lifted that night, I decided to do the job myself.

As the last of the light disappeared, the showers diminished, id early stars glimmered between the silent clouds moving southard. Wind whipped through the camp, drumming the tent walls. moved toward my tent, thinking that if I really were to go spying at night, I'd better get to sleep early.

Just before I reached the tent I heard a giggle, sharply broken f. I lifted the flap—and gasped.

37

Oria stood there grinning, her dark eyes crinkled. All around my little tent were flowers, early spring blooms of every color, some of them from peaks a long ride away. The air was sweet with their combined scents.

"Everybody brought one," she said. "I know it doesn't make up for no music and no dancing, but... Well, it was my idea. Do you like it?"

"It's wonderful." I sniffed happily at a silvery spray of starliss.

"Sit down, Mel," Oria said. "Forget the war, just for a bit. I'll brush out your hair for you."

With a sigh of relief I untucked the end of my braid and let it roll down my back behind me. Perching on a camp stool, I shut my eyes and sat in silence as Oria patiently fingered the long braid apart and then brushed it out until it lay in a shining cloak down nearly to my knees. The steady brushing was soothing, and I felt all the tensions of the long day drain out of me.

When she was done, I said, "Thanks, Ria. That's as good as an afternoon nap in the summer."

"A shame you have to put it up again," she said, smiling. "It's so pretty—the color of autumn leaves. Promise you'll never cut it."

"I won't. It's the only thing I have left to share with my mother, the color of our hair. And she always wanted me to grow it out." My fingers worked quickly from old habit as I braided it up again, wrapped it twice around my head, and tucked the end in. "But I can't parade around in long hair during a war. Or, I suppose I could, except then I'd end up carrying half the mountain in it."

"You can wear it down after we win, then, and start a new fashion."

"You'll be the one starting the fashions," I said, laughing up at her.

"Duchess Oria," she said, swishing around my tiny tent. "New silk shoes every day—twice a day! I can hardly wait."

"That'll do," Julen said to Oria. She was vigorously brushing mud off my alternate pair of woolen trousers. "You stop your non-

38

ase and go and get your rest. We'll have to make a supply run
again tomorrow." Oria stuck her tongue out at her mother, grinned
at me, and ran out. Julen laid my other tunic down. "This is the
best I can make of these trousers; the mud will not come out. Your
other's old tunic looks even worse," she said, frowning heavily.
"I wish I could wash these properly! Even so, they wouldn't look
much better. 'Tis shameful, you not dressing to befit your station.
Especially on this day."

I dropped onto my bedroll, grinning. "For whom?" I asked.
"Everyone has seen me like this since I was small. And truth to tell,
Oria would look a lot prettier in fancy clothes than I would."

Julen's square, worn face looked formidable as she considered
this. She said slowly, " 'Tisn't proper. When I grew up, we dressed
to fit our places in life. Then you knew who was what at a glance
and how to deal with 'em."

"But that means an orderly life, and when has Tlanth been
orderly?" I asked, sobering. "Not in my memory."

Julen gave a short nod. "It's just not right, your runnin' barefoot and ignorant with the village brats. I count my two among
them," she added with a wry smile.

"But they're my friends," I said, leaning on one elbow. "We
know each other. We'll defend each other to the death. You think
Beruk and the rest would have left their patches of farm or their
work to follow us if I'd stayed in the castle, spending tax money on
gowns and putting on airs?"

Julen pursed her lips. "Friends in war—and I hope you'll remember us when things are put right. But you know we all will
eventually have to take up our work again, and you won't be knowing how to have friends among your own kind."

"I don't miss what I never had."

"I've said my piece. Except," Julen added strongly, "I'll continue to curse the day Galdran Merindar's mother didn't strangle
him at birth."

"Now, *that*," I said with a laugh, "is a fine idea, and one I'll

39

join with enthusiasm! Now, tell me this: What's amiss with Hrani? Both her older children are fine. I saw them in camp tonight, joking around with the others. Yet she looked unhappy."

Julen's lips compressed. "It's the youngest. Tuel came down with messages from the hideaway today, bringing some of you blooms." Julen lowered her voice. "Hrani's baby is fine, it's just that she's no longer a baby, and Hrani wasn't there to see her leave off diapers and use the Waste Spell." She gave a quick look over her shoulder to see if any men happened to have sneaked into the tent and were listening.

I nodded. "So they had the ceremony, and Hrani was here with us instead of welcoming her daughter to childhood. Now I see. Poor Hrani!"

"Don't say aught of it to her. Might make her feel worse." Julen sighed and pointed at my other tunic. "Change now, before you catch your death."

"All right," I said, feigning a yawn. It wouldn't do for her to figure out what I was up to. "And then I think I'll get some sleep."

She bustled about the tent a little while longer while I hastily changed. I wrapped myself up in my blankets and lay down on the cot. By the time she was done I was almost warm. She blew out the candle and left.

Moonlight flooded my tent when I rose, jammed my feet into my winter mocs, pulled on my ancient hat, and slipped out. The ground was still muddy, but I had long ago learned how to move across soggy ground. The air was now still and almost balmy. As I slipped between the tents, tugging my battered hat close about my ears, I looked up, awed by the spectacular blaze of stars scattered gleaming across the sky. The moon was up, big enough that its silvery glow gave me just enough light to make out my pathway.

A few paces beyond the last tent, I heard a sudden noise and a voice: "Who's there?"

40

Pleased at this evidence of an alert sentry, I said, "It's Meliara, Devan. I'm going scouting."

"Countess!" Devan dropped down from a tree branch into my path and squinted into my face. "Alone?"

"I think I'll be the faster this way," I said. "And it's so beautiful tonight, I think I'll enjoy the going."

He paused, a big man used to millstones and bushels of wheat, not to clutching a sword. "Ain't there someone else to go?"

"This is *my* mission," I said.

"Well, be safe," he said, hoisting himself back up into the mighty tree. "And quick. I'll be on the watch for your return."

I thanked him and sped down the pathway, stopping only to check my bearings. Well as I knew the terrain, everything is different at night—unless night is what one is accustomed to. Picturing my map, I located myself in reference to our camp, and to where theirs was likeliest to be.

What I had to watch out for was their sentries, who, since the camp couldn't possibly be hidden, probably would be. Debegri had kept them close, probably to guard his precious person the better, but the Marquis sent his out at much wider range—something we'd discovered too late, which had precipitated our first, and worst, battle.

Deciding to approach from above and on the other side of the river, I made my way swiftly along an old animal path to where I knew there was a big tree bridging the ravine. Careful scanning revealed no humans about, so I crossed the massive trunk without looking down. Not far away was a jut of rock from which a good portion of the valley below could be seen. I lay behind some shrubs and watched the rock's silhouette for a time. There was nothing obviously amiss, but as the approach was bare, affording a clear field of vision, I didn't want to risk walking until I knew it was safe.

Three times I'd almost decided to move, then changed my mind and watched a bit longer before I saw what I'd feared: One of the unevennesses on the jut stirred. Just slightly—but it was enough to make it plain that one soldier, and probably more, crouched there in the rubble.

So I had to find another way down, but at least—I told myself as I carefully withdrew back into the shrubbery—I'd been right about the location of their camp.

With painstaking care I made my way to another slope and climbed one of the great sky-sweeping pines. Peering down through a gap in the branches, I saw the camp at last. And what I saw made my heart thud with dismay. The entire hillside below gleamed with little reddish campfires, not just dozens of them, but nearer a dozen dozen. Where indeed had they gotten so many Fire Sticks? I knew they couldn't be burning wood, for then there would have been smoke, and smell, and possibly the drums of the Hill Folk. How could Galdran justify forcing his soldiers to take Sticks from so many families?

Anyway, I sat and tried to estimate how many Fire Sticks they had, and therefore how many unknown households must be going cold. Then I tried to estimate the rows of tents that I could just make out between the fires.

Had Galdran sent his *entire* army up against us?

I clutched the swaying branch, pine scent sharp in my nostrils, and stared down, realizing slowly what this meant. There was no way we could win. Even with the old commander against us, the sheer weight of numbers would have ground us down to nothing. But under this new commander, how long would it take before Galdran had Bran and me paraded down the Street of the Sun on our way to a public execution?

And what about our people?

And after they were disposed of, what about the Covenant?

I closed my fists and pounded lightly on the tree branch. We had to do something—fast! But what?

All I could think as I climbed down was that desperate situations required desperate measures. And then I had to laugh at myself as I ran up the path. That sounded properly heroic, but how to make it *work*?

I looked up at the black interlacing of leaves, through which the rainbow-hued stars made a pattern of heedless beauty. The stars, the mountains, the rustling trees formed a silent testimony to the shortsighted futility of the humans who struggled below. I thought of Hrani missing her child's passing from the innocent abandon of babyhood into childhood. And suddenly I wished I were rid of the war, shed of hunger, of tiredness, and dirt, and could wander at will through the forest, enjoying its peace.

Only, one cannot put aside a war, even for a moment.

Ah, Branaric.

My head was back, my eyes still on the stars as I walked. All the warning I had was a metallic *klingg!* and then red-hot pain blazed from my ankle up to my skull and closed my consciousness for an immeasurable time behind a fiery red wall.

The first thought to penetrate was a desperate one: *Don't scream, don't scream.* My breath rasped in my throat as I struggled up. My nose stung, and I sneezed—I had landed facedown on a sprig of stingflower.

I ran my fingers lightly over the fanged steel closed around my ankle, whimpering, "Got to get it off, got to get it off..."

Why had I refused to touch them, to learn how to disable them? And how came this one here? As another white-hot spear of agony shot through me, I fell back, realized that this one had not been on the map. My hand fumbled for the sprig of stingflower and I sniffed it, sneezing again. The pain was terrific, but this was better than fainting. *The herb is fresh,* I thought, glad I could still think. *Keep busy...think...They must have laid this one just a while ago, and there's been no time yet to write it down...*

I rolled to my knees, wondering if I could somehow manage to walk despite the thing, but just the slightest movement flattened me again. Then I heard crashing in the shrubbery down the trail, and when I turned my head, the weird fractured shadows cast by bobbing torches hurt my eyes.

Our people wouldn't be carrying torches so close to their camp—

The thought wormed its way through my fading consciousness.

43

I had just enough presence of mind to fling myself back into the sheltering branches of a spreading fern before the roaring in my ears overwhelmed me and cast me into darkness.

A strong taste tingled in my mouth and burned its way into my throat. I gasped when the banked fire of pain sent flame licking up my body.

"Another sip."

Something pressed insistently against my lips, which parted. Another wash of pungent fluid cleared some of the haze from my brain. I swallowed, gasped again. My eyes teared, opened, and I drew a long, shaky breath.

"That's it," the same voice said with satisfaction. "Here y'are, m'lord. She's awake."

"Bran?" I croaked.

"What was that?" a new voice murmured, on my other side.

"Your trap," I said, my voice hardly strong enough to be called a whisper. I tried to blink my eyes into focus, but my vision stayed hazy. "I knew...this would happen...to one of us."

"Fair enough," the new voice said, amusement shading the slow, drawling words. "It's happened to nine of us."

A harsh laugh from a different direction smote my ears. "Take this fool out and hang her," this new voice grated. "And the trap with her. Let the slinking rebels find *that*."

"Softly, Baron, softly," said the quiet voice.

The voices—all unfamiliar—the words penetrated then, and I realized I was in the hands of the enemy.

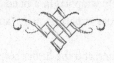

SIX

THE HAZE PROMPTLY SWALLOWED ME, AND IT WAS A
ng time before I woke up again. This time I was aware of a head-
he first, and of correspondingly intense pain radiating up my left
g. Even though I couldn't lift my head I could move it; within
e space of two breaths I realized I was lying in a tent, and there
as a young woman wearing a brown cloak with the sigil of a healer
tched on one side.

My gaze traveled up to her face. She was young, with ordinary
atures and patient brown eyes. Her dark hair was drawn back into
single braid clipped short at shoulder length.

"Here's water," she said. "Drink."

With practiced care she lifted my head, and I slurped eagerly
the water. My lips were dry; my mouth felt worse. When she
fered a second dipperful, I accepted gratefully.

"Think you some soup would go down well?" she asked, her
ice neutral.

"Try." My voice sounded like an old frog's.

She nodded and left the tent. I heard the murmur of voices,
d then I remembered, with a pang of anger-laced fear, that I was
prisoner. As if to corroborate it, my fingers moved to my waist,
und that my knife belt was indeed gone.

Wincing against the headache, I rose on my elbows, looked down at my legs. The one was securely wrapped in a bandage. My moc was gone. I wiggled my bare toes experimentally, and then wished I hadn't.

The tent flap opened a moment later, and the healer reappeared with a steaming mug in either hand. The familiar smell of camp soup met my nose, and the light, summer-fields aroma of lister-blossom tea.

She offered the tea first. Knowing it would help ease the pain a little, I drank it down, wincing as it scalded my tongue and throat. Even so, it was wonderful. The soup was next, and way in the back of my mind a bubble of humor arose at how much it tasted just like the stuff we'd been eating in our camp these long weeks. Only, this had a few more spices to render the boiled vegetables a little more palatable.

When I was done I lay back, exhausted by even that much effort. "Thanks," I said. Again the healer nodded, then she went out.

I closed my eyes, feeling sleep steal over me; but the pleasant lassitude fled when the tent flap opened again, this time pulled by a rough hand. Cold air swirled in. I blinked up at a burly helmeted soldier. He held the tent flap aside for a much lighter-boned man, who walked in wearing an anonymous black cloak. The guard let the flap fall, and I heard the gravel crunch under his boots as he took up position outside the tent.

The new arrival sank down onto the camp stool the healer had used, but he didn't say anything, so for a short time we studied one another's faces in the dim light. Large gray eyes surveyed me from my filthy scalp to my bandaged leg. I could read nothing in the man's face beyond that leisurely assessment, so I just stared back, trying to gather my wits as I catalogued his features: a straight nose, the chiseled bones of someone at least Bran's age, a long mouth with the deep corners of someone on the verge of a laugh. All this framed by long pale blond hair tied simply back, under a broad-rimmed but undecorated black hat. His rank was impossible to guess, but his job wasn't—he had to be an interrogator.

So I braced myself for interrogation.

And watched his eyes register this fact, and those mouth corners deepen for just a moment. Then his face blanked again, his gaze resting on mine with mild interest as he said, "What is your name?"

It took a moment for the words to register—for me to realize he did not know who I was! His eyes narrowed; he had seen my reaction, then—and I stirred, which effectively turned my surprise into a wince of pain.

"Name?" he said again. His voice was vaguely familiar, but the vagueness remained when I tried to identify it.

"I am very much afraid," he said presently, "that your probable future is not the kind to excite general envy, but I promise I can make it much easier if you cooperate."

"Eat mud," I croaked.

He smiled slightly, both mouth and eyes. The reaction of anerless humor was unexpected, but before I could try to assess it, he said, "You'll have to permit me to be more explicit. If you do not willingly discourse with me, I expect the King will send some of his experts, who will exert themselves to get the information we require, with your cooperation or without it." He leaned one hand across his knee, watching still with that air of mild interest—as if he had all the time in the world. His hand was long fingered, slim of form; he might have been taken for some minor Court scribe except for the callused palm of one who has trained all his life with the sword.

The import of his words hit me then, and with them came more fear—and more anger. "What is it you want to know?" I asked.

His eyes narrowed slightly. "Where the Astiars' camp lies, and their immediate plans, will do for a start."

"Their camp lies in their land...on which you are the trespasser...and their plans are to...rid the kingdom of...a

47

rotten tyrant." It took effort to get that out. But I was reasonably proud of my nasty tone.

His brows lifted. They were long and winged, which contributed to that air of faint question. "Well," he said, laying his hands flat on his knees for a moment, then he swung to his feet with leisurely grace. "We have a fire-eater on our hands, I see. But then one doesn't expect to find abject cowardice in spies." He stepped toward the flap, then paused and said over his shoulder, "You should probably rest while you can. I fear you have an unpleasant set of interviews ahead of you."

With that he lifted the flap and went out.

Leaving me to some very bleak thoughts.

He did that on purpose, I told myself after a long interval during which I tried not to imagine what those "experts" would try first in order to get me to blab—and how long I'd last. I'd faced the prospect of dying in battle and was ready enough, but I'd never considered the idea of torture.

And the worst of it is, I thought dismally, *there's nothing to be gained, really. We don't have any kind of master plan, and the camp will probably be changed by tomorrow. But if I say any of that willingly, then I am a coward, and they'll be sure to let everyone know it soon's they find out who I am.*

As soon as—

Think! My head ached anew, but I forced myself to follow the thought to its logical conclusion. The enemy did not know who I was. *That means they cannot use me against Bran.*

That was the secret I had to keep my teeth closed on as long as I could, I realized. My person was worth more than what was in my head—*if* Galdran found out.

So he can't find out, I resolved, and I lay back flat, closed my eyes, and tried my best to suspend my thoughts so I could sleep.

When I woke again, I was in darkness.

Fighting my way to awareness, I realized I'd heard sharp voices.

ells echoed back and forth, calling commands to different ridings; om the distance there came the clang and clash of steel.

It's Bran, I thought, elated and fearful. *He's attacking the camp!*

As if in answer, I heard his voice. "Mel! *Mel!*"

I rolled to my knees, fighting against invisible knives of pain.)ne more cry of "Mel!" at slightly more of a distance enabled me) gather my courage and stand up.

Diving through the tent flap, I screamed with all my failing rength, *"BRAN!"* And I clutched at the tent to keep myself from lling full-length on the muddy ground. A light mist bathed my ice, making me shiver—a distant part of me acknowledged that in ddition to everything else I had a pretty hot fever going.

"Meliara! Mel! *Mel!*" A number of voices took up the cry, and realized that all our people must have attacked.

Again I gathered all my strength and started forward. Which as a mistake. My left foot simply refused to carry my weight.

I started to fall, felt hard hands catching one of my arms. My g jolted—and thank goodness, that finished me.

Vhen I woke again there were voices, only this time close, and ey hurt my ears. A particularly harsh one prevailed. As I struggled gainst waves of fog to identify that voice, some of its words came .ear: "…your responsibility, unless you want to formally relin- uish her to me. I know what to do with rebels…"

The fog closed in again, clearing to a steady roaring noise that owly resolved into the sound of rain on the tent roof. Again there ere voices in the distance, but the lassitude of heavy fever made impossible for me to make sense of what I heard.

The next thing I was aware of was the fitful red beating of fire arough my eyelids. Someone lifted my head and pressed a cup to y lips. I smelled listerblossom tea, with another, sharper scent eneath it. I opened my eyes and drank. The taste was bitter, but was thirsty.

The bitterness had to be some kind of sleep herb; my head

49

seemed to separate from my body as I was jostled and moved about
But the pain stayed at a distance, for which I was grateful, and I
gave up trying to fight for consciousness.

When I did come to again, it was to the slow recognition of patterned movement. Next I realized that I was more or less upright
kept in place by the uncompromising grip of an arm. And at last I
saw that I was on horseback and someone was with me.

"Bran?" I murmured hopefully.

The arm did not slacken its grip as its owner hesitated, ther
said, "It desolates me to disappoint you, but your brother is no
here. Despite two really praiseworthy attempts at rescue." I recognized that drawling voice: the interrogator's.

The hint of amusement irritated me, and sick and hurt as I was
I simply had to retort *something*. "Glad...at least...you're desolated."

As a crack it was pretty weak, but the amusement deepened ir
the light voice above my ear as he added, "I must add, when you
hill rebels get truly riled, they do fight well. We didn't catch any
of 'em. Several dead, but they're of no use to anyone. And they
accounted for rather more of us than they ought to have."

"*Haha*," I gloated.

The voice continued, polite but utterly devoid of any emotion
save that hint of amusement: "Your hat disappeared somewhere the
other night, and it did not seem appropriate under the circumstances to request someone in our army to surrender a replacement."

"It's of no consequence—" I began loftily, then I grunted with
pain as the horse made a misstep and veered around some obstruc-
tion in the road.

And a new fact registered: *He knows who I am.*

That means we must be on the way to Remalna-city—and Galdran

A sick feeling of terror seized my insides, and I was glad the

an holding me could not see my face. My head was tucked against
s shoulder, with my left leg as straight as possible across the
orse's withers, my right dangling. I thought immediately of strug-
ing, trying to fight free, except I remembered what had happened
hen I had tried to take a step.

Well, then, somehow I have to escape—and take the horse, I told
yself. *There's almost a three-day journey ahead. Anything can happen
I am on the watch.*

I turned my attention to my surroundings. We were riding at
slow, steady pace downhill toward the west. The long bands of
ouds above were cold blue on top, their undersides yellow and
nk, and the reflected peachy gold glow touched the valleys and
elds with warm light. Behind me, I knew, were the high mountains
d ancient, tangled forest where I'd grown up. Below me the
ountains opened slowly into farmland, with dark marches of forest
aching toward the distant sea. Such profligate beauty lifted my
irits, and despite the situation, I couldn't believe I would come
ill.

Unfortunately, this elevated mood disappeared with the sun.
or the light steadily grew more diffuse and lost its warmth, the
adows closed in, and a steady, drizzling rain began to fall. Faintly,
the distance, I heard bells tolling for blue-change, and even they
unded mournful. My various aches seemed to increase with the
rkness, and once or twice when the tired horse stumbled, wrench-
g my left leg, I couldn't help making noise, but I turned each into
muttered curse.

My captor left the road before it was completely dark, and rode
th a sense of sureness that indicated he knew the terrain. After a
ne we stopped in a secluded glade against a rocky palisade, under
e sheltering branches of a great-grandfather oak. A short distance
vay a little stream plashed off the rocks and wound its way among
e trees. The east wind did not penetrate there, nor did much of
e rain.

In silence the man reined in his horse, dismounted, lifted me down to a high grassy spot that was scarcely damp. In the gathering gloom he tended to his horse, which presently cropped at the grass. My eyes had become accustomed to the darkness; the flare of light from a Fire Stick, and the reddish flicker of a fire, startled me.

At first I turned away, for the unsteady flame hurt my eyes, but after a time the prospect of warmth brought me around, and I started inching toward the fire.

The man looked up, dropped what he was doing, and took a step toward me. "I can carry you," he said.

I waved him off. "I'll do it myself," I said shortly, thinking, *Why be polite now? So I'll be in a good mood when you dump me in Galdran's dungeon?*

He hesitated. I ignored him and turned my attention to easing forward. After a moment he returned to whatever he had been doing. After a little experimenting, I found that it was easiest to sit backward and inchworm along, dragging my left leg.

Soon enough I was near to his fire, which was properly built in a ring of rocks. Using the tip of his rapier, he held out chunks of bread with cheese, toasting them just enough. The smell made my mouth water.

In silence he divided the food into two portions, laying mine on a flat rock near my hand.

Then he held up a camp kettle. "Want tea? Or just water?"

"Tea," I said.

He walked off toward the waterfall. I peered after him into the gloom, saw the horse standing near the pool where the water fell. One chance of escape gone. I'd never get to the horse before he could stop me.

With a small sense of relief, I turned my attention to the bread. I was suddenly ravenous, and even though the cheese was still hot, I wolfed my share down and licked my fingers to catch the last crumbs.

By then the man had returned and set the kettle among the

mbers. Then he looked up, paused, then picked up his share of
he bread and reached over to put it in front of me.

"That's yours," I said.

"You appear to need it more than I do," he said, looking
mused. "Go ahead. I won't starve."

I picked up the bread, feeling a weird sense of unreality: Did
e expect me to be grateful? The situation was so strange I simply
ad to turn it into absurdity—it was either that or sink into fear
nd apprehension. "Well, does it matter if I starve?" I said. "Or do
Galdran's torturers require only plump victims for their arts?"

The man had started to unload something from the saddlebag
t his side, but he stopped and looked up with that contemplative
aze again, his broad-brimmed black hat just shadowing his eyes.
The situation has altered," he said slowly. "You must perceive how
our value has changed."

His words, his tone—as if he expected an outbreak of hys-
erics—fired my indignation. Maybe my situation was desperate,
nd sooner than later I was going to be having nightmares about
—but not for the entertainment of some drawling Court-bred
unky.

"He'll try to use me against my brother," I said in my flattest
oice.

"I rather suspect he will be successful. In the space of one day
our brother and his adherents attacked our camp twice. It would
ppear they are not indifferent to your fate."

I remembered then that he had said something about an attack
arlier, but I'd scarcely comprehended what he meant. "Do you
now who was killed?" I asked quickly.

The firelight played over his face. He watched me with a kind
f narrow-eyed assessment impossible to interpret. "You know
iem all, don't you," he commented.

"Of course I do," I said. "You don't know who—or you just
on't tell me, for some rock-headed reason?"

He smiled. "Your determined bravado is a refreshment to the

53

spirit. But if you know them all by name, then the loss of each is immeasurably greater. Why did you do it? Did you really think you could take a few hundred ill-trained village people into war and expect anything but defeat?"

I opened my mouth to retort, then realized I'd be spoiling what little strategy we did have.

But then he said wryly, "Or did you expect the rest of the kingdom to follow your heroic example and rise up against the King?"

Which is, of course, exactly what we *had* expected.

"So they sit like overfed fowl and watch Galdran Merindar break the Covenant by making secret pacts to sell our woods overseas?" I retorted.

He paused in the act of reaching for the camp jug. "Break the Covenant? How do you know about that? I don't recall you've ever been to Court."

Tell him about Azmus, and the intercepted letter, and have him send minions to make certain both disappeared? No chance. "I just know. That's all *you* need to know. But even if it weren't true, Debegri would still go up to take the County of Tlanth by force. Can't any of you Court people see that if it happens to us, it can happen to you? Or are you too stupid?"

"Possibly," he said, still with that dispassionate amusement. "It's also possible your...somewhat misguided actions are inspired by misguided sources, shall we say?"

"Say what you want," I retorted. "It's not like I can duff off in a huff if you're impolite."

He laughed softly, then shook his head. "I ought not to bait you. I apologize."

The implication seemed pretty clear: Soon enough I'd have a hard time of it. The prospect silenced me.

He didn't seem to notice as he brought out the jug and then poured two mugs of steaming water. A moment later he opened a little bag and brought out dried leaves, which he cast into one mug.

other bag provided leaves for the other mug. The wonderful ent of tea wafted through the air. I did not recognize the blend or blends. Instinct made me sigh; then I realized I'd done it and shed I hadn't.

The man came around, set a cup down by my hand. "Are you ry uncomfortable?"

"Does it matter?" I said, and wrapped my chilled hands around e cup—which was not of the battered metal I'd expected, but ry fine ceramic. Exquisite gilding ran round the lip, a stylized aid of argan leaves.

"Whether it does or not, you shall have a better conveyance the morrow," he said. "Drink your tea and sleep. We shall con- ue our discourse when you have had some rest."

I couldn't resist one more crack. "Is that a promise or a threat?"

He just smiled.

SEVEN

MY FIRST DUTY WAS TO ESCAPE. AS I LAY UNDER THE
blanket the man had given me, I tried to figure out how I might
get myself to where the horse stood without rousing its owner from
his slumbers. Once I was on the animal's back, it wouldn't matter
if the man woke up—in fact, it might be nice to see that Court-
bred composure shattered.

I drifted off while estimating steps from tree to shrub, and
didn't waken until the thud of horses' hooves under my ear brought
me to drowsy wakefulness.

Waves of exhaustion ebbed and flowed over me as I watched in
dreamy bemusement. The interrogator still sat in the same place,
staring down into some kind of stone that cast a weird bluish light
over his face and glowed in two bright pinpoints in his eyes. It was
magic. A summons-stone. A rarity that made me wonder just who
he was—or whether we had vastly underestimated Galdran's access
to wizard wares. Beyond him the soft, steady *plop-plop* of raindrops
on leaves tapped out a pleasant rhythm.

I think I drifted again, without meaning to, because when I
opened my eyes again it was to see a young equerry dismount from
a hard-breathing charger and bow low. "My lord," she said, holding
out another blue-glowing stone.

The man sat where he was, merely taking the stone as he said, "Your report."

"Baron Debegri has dispatched your orders about the carriage. It should be waiting at the Lumm-at-Akaeriki bridge by green-change tomorrow."

"And our friends the Tlanthi?"

"Are silent, my lord. Your message was sent under white flag, and Lord Jastra reported it was given into their hands. Nothing from that time until I left."

"Promising," was the answer. "It seems likely we'll be back in civilization well in advance of the Spring Festival, after all," he finished, the Court drawl very pronounced. "Return. Tell the Baron to be so good as to carry on as ordered."

The equerry bowed again. I saw her stifle a yawn as she threw herself into the saddle; she was soon out of the circle of firelight, but I listened to the sound of the horse's hooves diminish, questions looming in my mind. As I struggled with them, I sank once more under the tide of slumber and didn't waken until the lovely scent of tea worked its way into my dreams and banished them.

I sat up, fought against dizziness. Somewhere in the distance a single bell rang out the pattern for gold-candles and the beginning of another day.

"Drink."

The cup was near to hand. I rose on one elbow and reached for it. Some sips later I felt immeasurably better. My eyesight cleared, and so did my thoughts.

I remembered the interlude during the night, and frowned across the fire at my companion. He looked exactly the same as ever—as if he'd sat up for a single time measure and not for an entire night. The plain hat, simply tied hair, ordinary clothing unmarked by any device; I squinted, trying to equate this slight figure with that arrogant plume-helmed commander riding on the ridge above the last battle. *But if he is who I think he is, they're used to being up all night at their stupid Court parties*, I thought grimly.

"You seem to know who I am," I said. "Who are you?"

"Does it matter?"

His use of my own words the night before surprised me a little. Did he expect flattery? Supposedly those so-refined Court aristocrats lived on it as anyone else lives on bread and drink. I considered my answer, wanting to make certain it was not even remotely complimentary. "I'm exactly as unlikely to blab our secrets to an anonymous flunky as I am to a Court decoration with a reputation as a gambler and a fop," I said finally.

"'Court decoration'?" he repeated, with a faint smile. The strengthening light of dawn revealed telltale marks under his eyes. So he *was* tired. I was obscurely glad.

"Yes," I said, pleased to expand on my insult. "My father's term."

"You've never wished to meet a...Court decoration for yourself?"

"No." Then I added cheerily, "Well, maybe when I was a child."

The Marquis of Shevraeth, Galdran's commander-in-chief, grinned. It was the first real grin I'd seen on his face, as if he were struggling to hold in laughter. Setting his cup down, he made a graceful half-bow from his seat on the other side of the fire and said, "Delighted to make your acquaintance, Lady Meliara."

I sniffed.

"And now that I've been thoroughly put in my place," he said, "let us leave my way of life and proceed to yours. I take it your revolt is not engineered for the benefit of your fellow-nobles, or as an attempt to reestablish your mother's blood claim through the Calahanras family. Wherefore is it, then?"

I looked up in surprise. "There ought to be no mystery obscuring our reasons. Did you not trouble to read the letter we sent to Galdran Merindar before he sent Debegri against us? It was addressed to the entire Court, and our reasons were stated as plainly as we could write them—and all our names signed to it."

"Assume that the letter was somehow suppressed," he said ryly. "Can you summarize its message?"

"Easy," I said promptly. "We went to war on behalf of the Hill 'olk, whose Covenant Galdran wants to break. But not just for aem. We also want to better the lives of the people of Remalna: ae ordinary folk who've been taxed into poverty, or driven from aeir farms, or sent into hastily constructed mines, all for Galdran's ersonal glory. And I guess for the rest of yours as well, for whose aoney are you spending on those fabulous Court clothes you never 'ear twice? Your father still holds the Renselaeus principality—or as he ceded it to Galdran at last? Isn't it, too, taxed and farmed ɔ the bone so that you can outshine all the rest of those fools at Court?"

All the humor had gone out of his face, leaving it impossible ɔ read. He said, "Since the kind of rumor about Court life that ɔu seem to regard as truth also depicts us as inveterate liars, I will ɔt waste time attempting to defend or deny. Let us instead discuss ɔur eventual goal. Supposing," he said, reaching to pour more tea ɪto my cup—as if we were in a drawing room, and not sitting ɪutside in the chill dawn, in grimy clothes, on either side of a fire ɪst as we were on either side of a war—"Supposing you were to efeat the King. What then? Kill all the nobles in Athanarel and ɪt yourselves up as rustic King and Queen?"

I remembered father's whisper as he lay dying: *You can take emalna, and you will be better rulers than any Merindar ever was.*

It had sounded fine then, but the thought of giving any hint of aat to this blank-faced Court idler made me uncomfortable. I aook my head. "We didn't want to kill anyone. Not even Galdran, ntil he sent Debegri to break the Covenant and take our lands. As r ruling, yes we would, if no one else better came along. We were ɔing it not for ourselves but for the kingdom. Disbelieve it all you ant, but there's the truth of it."

"Finish your tea," he said. "Before we find our way to a more ɔmfortable conveyance, I am very much afraid we're both in for a

59

distasteful interlude." He reached into the saddlebag and pulled out a wad of bandage ticking and some green leaves.

I sat up suddenly, winced, then stretched my hands over the bandage on my ankle, which (I dared a quick look) was filthy. "Oh no, you don't."

"I promised Mistress Kylar. And if I don't keep that promise, chances are you might lose that foot. So brace up. I'll be as quick as I can."

"Give me the stuff and let me do it," I said. "I know how. I've helped patch up all our wounded."

"Here's a knife. Let's see how far you get in taking the old bandage off." And he tossed a dagger across the fire. It spun through the air and landed hilt-deep in the ground next to my hand.

"Chance throw," I said snidely, suspecting that it hadn't been. He said nothing, which confirmed my suspicions. So I turned my back in order to avoid seeing that bland gray gaze, and I yanked the knife free. At first I wanted to wipe it clean on my clothes, but a quick perusal of my person reminded me that I'd already been wearing grimy clothes before I'd walked into the trap, fallen full length in the mud, and spent two days lying in a tent. So I wiped the dagger on the grass, then slit the bindings on the bandage. Spots of brown that had leaked through and hardened on the outside of the bandage warned me that this was probably going to be the least favorite of all my life experiences so far.

I gulped, held my breath, pulled the bandage quickly away. The keem leaves were all wrinkled and old. I started to pull the first one free, gasped, and was nearly overwhelmed by a sudden loud rushing in my ears.

When it subsided, my companion was right next to me. The dagger was back in its sheath at his belt, and he handed me a length of wood that had fallen from a nearby tree. "Hang on," he said briskly. "I'll be as fast as I can."

I barely had time to take hold of the wood with both hands; then I felt warm water pour over my ankle. I didn't squeak, or cry, or make any sound—but as soon as the fresh keem leaves were on

60

y torn flesh and the new bandage was being wrapped quickly round and around, I clutched that wood tight and started cursing, ot pausing except to draw breath.

When it was done and he took the mess away to bury, I lay ack and breathed deeply, doing my best to settle my boiling omach.

"All right," he said, "that's that. Now it's time to go, if we're reach Lumm by green-change." He whistled, and the dapple-ray trotted obediently up, head tossing.

I realized I ought to have been more observant about chances r escape, and I wondered if there were any chance of taking him surprise now.

First to see if I could even stand. As he went about the chore f resaddling the horse, I eased myself to my feet. I took my time it, too, not just because my ankle was still protesting its recent bandaging; I wanted to seem as decrepit as possible. My head felt eirdly light when I made it to my feet, and I had to hang on to a ranch of the oak—my foot simply wouldn't take any weight. As on as I tried it, my middle turned to water and I groped for the ranch again.

Which meant if I did try anything, it was going to have to be ithin reach of the horse. I watched for a moment as he lashed own the saddlebags then rammed the rapier into the saddle sheath. here was already that knife at his belt. This did not look prom-ing, I thought, remembering all the lessons on close fighting that hesot had drilled into us. *If your opponent is better armed and has e longer reach, then surprise is your only ally. And then you'd better pe he's half-asleep.* Well, the fellow had to be tired if he'd sat up night, I thought, looking around for any kind of weapon.

The branch he'd handed me to hang on to was still lying at my et. I stooped—cautiously—and snatched it up. Dropping one end, discovered that it made a serviceable cane, and with its aid I hob-ed my way a few paces, watching carefully for any rocks or roots at might trip me.

Then a step in the grass made me look up. The Marquis was

61

right in front of me, and he was a lot taller than he looked seated across a campfire. In one hand were the horse's reins, and he held the other hand out in an offer to boost me up. I noticed again that his palm was crossed with calluses, indicating years of swordwork. I grimaced, reluctantly surrendering my image of the Court-bred fop who never lifted anything heavier than a fork.

"Ready?" His voice was the same as always—or almost the same.

I tipped my head back to look at his face, instantly suspicious. Despite his compressed lips he was clearly on the verge of laughter.

For a moment I longed, with all my heart, to swing my stick right at his head. My fingers gripped…and his palm turned, just slightly; but I knew a block readying when I saw one. The strong possibility that anything I attempted would lead directly to an ignominious defeat did not improve my mood at all, but I dropped the stick and wiped my hand down the side of my rumpled tunic.

Vowing I'd see that smile wiped off his cursed face, I said shortly, "Let's get it over with."

He put his hands on my waist and boosted me up onto the horse—and I couldn't help but notice it didn't take all that much effort.

All right, defeat so far, I thought as I winced and gritted my way through arranging my leg much as it had been on the previous ride. *All I have to do is catch him in a single unwary moment…* He mounted behind me and we started off, while I indulged myself with the image of grabbing that stick and conking him right across his smiling face.

The less said about that morning's ride, the better. I would have been uncomfortable even if I'd been riding with Branaric, for my leg ached steadily from the jarring of the horse's pace. To be riding along in the clasp of an enemy just made my spirits feel the worse.

We only had one conversation, right at the start, when he apol-

gized for the discomfort of the ride and reminded me that there
ould be a carriage—and reasonable comfort—before the day was
one.

I said, in as surly a tone as possible, "You might have thought
f that before we left. I mean, since no one asked my opinion on
.e matter."

"It was purely an impulse of disinterested benevolence that
recipitated our departure," he responded equably—as if I'd been as
olite as one of his simpering Court ladies.

"What do you mean by that?"

"I mean that it seemed very likely that your brother and his
dherents were going to mount another rescue attempt, and this
me there was no chance of our being taken by surprise."

He paused, letting me figure that out. He meant the King's
arriors would have killed everyone, or else taken them all prisoner,
d he had forestalled such a thing. Why he should want to prevent
is opportunity to defeat all our people at once didn't make sense
me; I kept quiet.

He went on after a moment, "Since the King requires a report
1 our progress, and as it seemed expedient to remove you, I de-
ded to combine the two. It appears to have worked, at least for a
me."

That meant he'd stalled Branaric—with what? Threats against
y life if our people tried anything? The thought made me wild
ith anger, with a determination to escape so strong that for a time
took all my self-control not to fling myself from that horse and
un, bad leg or no.

For at last I faced the real truth: that by my own carelessness,
might very well have graveled our entire cause. I knew my brother.
ranaric would not risk my life—and this man seemed to have
gured that much out.

The Marquis made a couple other attempts at conversation, but
ignored him. I have to confess that, for a short time, hot tears of
ge and self-loathing stung my eyes and dripped down my face. I

didn't trust my voice; the only consolation I had for my eroding self-respect was that my face couldn't be seen.

When the tears had dried at last, and I had taken a surreptitious swipe at my nose and eyes with my sleeve, I gritted my teeth and turned my thoughts back to escape.

EIGHT

THE SUN WAS DIRECTLY OVERHEAD AND MERCI-
essly hot when we reached the Akaeriki River. What ought to have
een a cool early-spring day—as it probably was, high in our
mountains—felt like the middle of summer, and my entire body
rotested by turning into one giant itch. Even my braid, gritty and
amp, felt repellent.

In addition to everything else, not long after the village bells
all over the valley merrily rang the changeover from gold to green,
ay stomach started rumbling with hunger.

It was a relief when we reached the village of Lumm. We did
ot go into it but rode on the outskirts. When the great mage-built
ridge came into view I felt Shevraeth's arm tighten as he looked
his way and that.

On a grassy sward directly opposite the approach to the bridge
plain carriage waited with no markings on its sides, the wheels
nd lower portions muddy. The only sign that this might not be
ome inn's rental equipment were the five high-bred horses waiting
earby, long lines attached to their bits. A boy wearing the garb of
stable hand sat on a large rock holding the horses' lines; nearby
footman and a driver, both in unmarked clothing but wearing
ervants' hats, stood conversing in between sips from hip flagons.

Steady traffic, mostly merchants, passed by, but no one gave them more than a cursory glance.

The gray threaded through a caravan of laden carts. As soon as the waiting servants saw us, the flagons were hastily stowed, the horse boy leaped to his feet, and all three bowed low.

"Hitch them up," said the Marquis.

The boy sprang to the horses' mouths and the driver to the waiting harnesses as the footman moved to the stirrup of the gray.

No one spoke. With a minimum of fuss the Marquis dismounted, pulled me down himself, and deposited me in the carriage on a seat strewn with pillows. Then he shut the door and walked away.

By then the driver was on her box, and the horse boy was finishing the last of the harnesses, helped by the footman. Levering myself up on the seat, I watched through the window as the footman hastily transferred all the gear on the gray to the last waiting horse, and then the Marquis swung into the saddle, leaning down to address a few words to the footman. Then the gray was led out of sight, and without any warning the carriage gave a great jolt and we started off.

Not one of the passersby showed the least interest in the proceedings. I wondered if I had missed yet another chance at escape, but if I did yell for help, who knew what the partisanship of the Lumm merchants was? I might very well have gotten my mouth gagged for my pains.

This did not help my spirits any, for now that the immediate discomforts had eased, I realized again that I was sick. How could I effect an escape when I had as much spunk as a pot of overboiled noodles?

I lay back down on the pillows, and before long the warmth and swaying of the carriage sent me off to sleep.

———

When I woke the air was hot and stuffy, and I was immediately aware of being shut up in a small painted-canvas box. But before I could react with more than that initial flash of distress, I realized that the carriage had stopped. I struggled up, wincing against a thumping great headache, just as the door opened.

There was the Marquis, holding his hand out. I took it, making a sour face. At least, I thought as I recognized an innyard, he looks as wind tousled and muddy as I must.

But there was no fanfare, no groups of gawking peasants and servants. He picked me up and carried me through a side door, and thence into a small parlor that overlooked the inn-yard. Seated on plain hemp-stuffed pillows, I looked out at the stable boy and driver busily changing the horses. The longshadows of late afternoon obscured everything; a cheap time-candle in a corner sconce marked the time as green-three.

Sounds at the door brought my attention around. An inn servant entered, carrying a tray laden with steaming dishes. As she set them out I looked at her face, wondering if I could get a chance to talk to her alone—if she might help a fellow-female being held prisoner?

"Coffee?" the Marquis said, splintering my thoughts.

I looked up, and I swear there was comprehension in those gray eyes.

"Coffee?" I repeated blankly.

"A drinkable blend, from the aroma." He tossed his hat and riding gloves onto the cushion beside him and leaned forward to pour a brown stream of liquid into two waiting mugs. "A miraculous drink. One of the decided benefits of our world-hopping mages," he said.

"Mages." I repeated that as well, trying to marshal my thoughts, which wanted to scamper, like frightened mice, in six different directions.

"Coffee. Horses." A careless wave toward the innyard.

67

"Chocolate. Kinthus. Laimun. Several of the luxuries that are not native to our world, brought here from others."

I could count the times we'd managed to get ahold of coffee, and I hadn't cared for its bitterness. But as I watched, honey and cream were spooned into the dark beverage, and when I did take a cautious sip, it was delicious. With the taste came warmth, a sense almost of well-being. For a short time I was content to sit, with my eyes closed, and savor the drink.

The welcome smell of braised potatoes and clear soup brought my attention back to the present. When I opened my eyes, there was the food, waiting before me.

"You had probably better not eat much more than that," said the Marquis. "We have a long ride ahead of us tonight, and you wouldn't want to regret your first good meal in days."

In weeks, I thought as I picked up a spoon, but I didn't say it out loud—it felt disloyal somehow.

Then the sense of what he'd said sank in, and I almost lost my appetite again. "How long to the capital?"

"We will arrive sometime tomorrow morning," he said.

I grimaced down at my soup, then braced myself up, thinking that I'd better eat, hungry or not, for I'd need my strength. "What is Galdran like?" I asked, adding sourly, "Besides being a tyrant, a coward, and a Covenant breaker?"

Shevraeth sat with his mug in his hands. He hadn't eaten much, but he was on his second cup of the coffee. "This is the third time you've brought that up," he said. "How do you know he intends to break the Covenant?"

"We have proof." I saw his eyes narrow, and I added in my hardest voice, "And don't waste your breath threatening me about getting it, because you won't. You really think I'd tell you what and where it is, just to have it destroyed? We may not be doing so well, but it seems my brother and I and our little untrained army are the only hope the Hill Folk have."

The Marquis was silent for a long pause, during which my

nger slowly evaporated, leaving me feeling more uncomfortable by the moment. I realized why just before he spoke: By refusing to tell im, I was implying that he, too, wanted to break the Covenant.

Well, doesn't he?—if he's allied with Galdran! I thought.

"To your question," the Marquis said, setting his cup down, 'What is Galdran like?' By that I take it you mean, What kind of reatment can you expect from the King? If you take the time to onsider the circumstances outside of your mountain life, you might e able to answer that for yourself." Despite the mild humor, the ght, drawling voice managed somehow to sting. "The King has een in the midst of trade negotiations with Denlieff for over a ear. You have cost him time and money that were better applied sewhere. And a civil war never enhances the credit of the govern-ent in the eyes of visiting diplomats from the Queen Yustnesveas f Sartor, who does not look for causes so much as signs of slack ontrol."

I dropped my spoon in the empty soup bowl. "So if he cracks own even harder on the people, it's all our fault, is that it?"

"You might contemplate, during your measures of leisure," he aid, "what the purpose of a permanent court serves, besides to quander the gold earned by the sweat of the peasants' brows. And onsider this: The only reason you and your brother have not been Athanarel all along is because the King considered you too harm-ss to bother keeping an eye on." And with a polite gesture: "Are ou finished?"

"Yes."

I was ensconced again in the carriage with my pillows and ach-g leg for company, and we resumed journeying.

The effect of the coffee was to banish sleep. Restless, angry ith myself, angrier with my companion and with the cruel hap-enstance that had brought me to this pass, I turned my thoughts nce again to escape.

Clouds gathered and darkness fell very swiftly. When I could o longer see clearly, I hauled myself up and felt my way to the door. The only plan I could think of was to open the door, tumble out, and hopefully lose myself in the darkness. This would work only if no one was riding beside the carriage, watching.

A quick peek—a longer look—no one in sight.

I eased myself down onto the floor and then opened the door a crack, peering back. I was about to fling the door wider when the carriage lurched around a curve and the door almost jerked out of my hand. I half fell against the doorway, caught myself, and a moment later heard a galloping horse come up from behind the carriage.

I didn't look to see who was on it, but slammed the door shut and climbed back onto the seat.

And composed myself for sleep.

I knew I'd need it.

Noises and the dancing flickers and shadows of torchlight woke me once. The coach was still. I sat up, heard voices, lay down again. The headache was back, the fever—my constant companion for several days—high again. I closed my eyes and dropped into a tangle of nasty dreams.

When I woke, sunlight was streaming in the window. I sat up, feeling soggy and hot, but forgot my discomfort when I saw two armed and helmed soldiers in the brown and green of Galdran's army. Turning my head, I saw two more through the other window, and realized that at some point during the night we had picked up an escort.

Was this Shevraeth's attempt to bolster his prestige in front of the King? I was glad he hadn't deemed me worth impressing; the trip had been awful enough, but to have had to be stuck riding cross-country in the center of a pompous military formation would have been just plain humiliating.

Another glimpse through the window revealed we were passing buildings, and occasional knots of people and traffic, all drawn aside m the road to let us pass. Curious faces watched the cavalcade.

We had to be in Remalna-city. The idea made my stomach
amp up. Very soon they'd haul me out to my fate, and I knew I
d to do my best not to disgrace our people.

For the first time—probably ever—I turned my thoughts to my
pearance. There was nothing to be done about it, I thought dis-
ally as I stared down at my clothes. Old, worn, bag-kneed woolen
ousers, their dun color scarcely discernible for the splotches of
ud and dried gore (on the left side). One scuffed, worn old moc
d one filthy bare foot. The old brown tunic, once Bran's, was a
ess, and my braid, which had come undone, looked like a thigh-
agth rattail. Hoping for the best, I spit on the underside of my
nic hem and scrubbed my face; the gritty feel did not bode well
r success.

So I gave up. There was nothing for it but to keep my chin
gh, my demeanor as proud as possible; for after all, I had nothing
be ashamed of—outside of being caught in the first place. Our
use was right, those nasty cracks about mountain rabble and
rmlessness notwithstanding.

I folded my arms across my front, ignoring the twinges and
hes in my leg, tried to steady my breathing, and looked again out
e window. It appeared we were drawing nearer to Athanarel, the
yal palace, for the buildings were fewer and what I did see was
signed to please the eye. Despite my disinclination, I was im-
essed. Ordered gardens, flower-banked canals, well-dressed peo-
e now decorated the view. A sweet carillon rang the change from
ld to green: It was noon.

The carriage swept through two wrought-iron gates. I leaned
ward and caught a glimpse of a high wall with sentries visible
it. Then we rolled down a tree-lined avenue to a huge flagged
urt before the biggest building I had ever seen.

The coach slowed. A moment later the door opened.

"Countess," someone unfamiliar said.

Feeling hot and cold at once, I slid from my pillow seat to the floor of the carriage and pushed my left leg carefully out, followed by my right. Then, sitting in the doorway, I looked up at two enormous soldiers, who reached down and took hold of my arms, one each. Positioned between them in a tight grip, I could make a pretense of walking.

They fell in the midst of two rows of guards, all of whom seemed to have been selected for their height and breadth. *To make me look ridiculous?* I thought, and forced my chin up proudly.

Remember, you are Meliara Astiar of Tlanth, your mother was descended from the greatest of Remalna's royal families, and you're about to face a tyrant and a thief, I told myself firmly. Whatever happened, whatever I said, might very well get carried back to Branaric. I owed it to the people at home not to rug-crawl to this villain.

So I exhorted myself as we progressed up a broad, sweeping marble stair. Two magnificent doors were flung open by flunkies in livery more fabulous than anything anyone in Tlanth—of high degree or low—had ever worn in my lifetime, and *klunk-klunk-klunk*, the rhythmic thud of boot heels impacted the marble floor of a great hall. High carved beams supported a distant ceiling. Windows filled with colored glass were set just under the roof, and beneath them hung flags—some new, some ancient. Under the flags, scattered along the perimeter of the marble floor, stood an uncountable number of people bedecked in silks and jewels. They stared at me in silence.

At some unseen signal the long line of guards around me stopped and their spears thudded to the floor with a noise that sounded like doom.

Then a tall figure with a long black cloak walked past us, plumed and coroneted helm carried in his gloved right hand. For a moment I didn't recognize the Marquis; somewhere along the way he'd gotten rid of his anonymous clothing and was now clad in a long black battle tunic, Remalna's crowned sun stitched on its breast. At his side hung his sword; his hair was braided back. He passed by without so much as a glance at me. His eyes were slack lidded, his expression bored.

He stopped before a dais, on which was a throne made of carved wood—a piece of goldwood so beautifully veined with golds and reds and umbers it looked like fire—and bowed low.

I was tempted to try hopping on my one good foot in order to get a glimpse of the enemy on the throne, but I didn't—and a moment later was glad I hadn't, for I saw the flash of a ring as Galdran waved carelessly at the guards. The four in front promptly stepped to each side, affording a clear field of vision between the King and me. I saw a tall, massively built man whose girth was running to portliness. Long red hair with gems braided into it, large nose, large ears, high forehead, pale blue eyes. He wore a long, carefully cultivated mustache. His mouth stretched in a cruel smile.

"So you won your wager, Shevraeth, eh?" he said. The tone was jovial, but there was an ugly edge to the voice that scared me.

"As well, Your Majesty," the Marquis drawled. "The dirt, the stretches of boredom...really, had it taken two days more, I could not have supported it, much as I'd regret the damage to my reputation for reneging on a bet."

Galdran fingered his mustache, then waved at me. "Are you certain someone hasn't been making a game of you? That looks like a scullery wench."

"I assure you, Your Majesty, this is Lady Meliara Astiar, Countess of Tlanth."

Galdran stepped down from his dais and came within about five paces of me, and looked me over from head to heels. The cruel smile widened. "I never expected much of that half-mad old man, but this is really rich!" He threw back his head and laughed.

And from all sides of the room laughter resounded up the walls, echoing from the rafters.

When it had died, Galdran said, "Cheer up, wench. You'll have your brother soon for company, and your heads will make a nice matched set over the palace gates." Once again he went off into laughter, and he gestured to the guards to take me away.

I opened my mouth to yell a parting insult but I was jerked to one side, which hurt my leg so much all I could do was gasp for breath. The echoes of the Court's laughter followed into the plain-walled corridor that the soldiers took me down, and then a heavy steel door slammed shut, and there was no sound beyond the marching of the guard and my own harsh breathing.

NINE

HE CELL I WAS LOCKED INTO SEEMED ESPECIALLY elected for its gloom and dampness.

I didn't hear any other victims in any of the surrounding cells, nd I wondered if they'd put me squarely in the center of an empty ring. I could hear every noise down the corridor, for the dungeon eemed to be made of stone, save only the door, which was age-ardened wood with a grilled window. The cell's furniture consisted f a narrow and rickety rusty iron cot with rotten straw-stuffed cking inadequately covering its few slats. In the corner was an qually rusty metal jug half filled with stale water.

Opposite the door was a smaller window set high up in the wall f the cell. Even without the grating, a cat would have had difficulty queezing through the opening. The grating didn't keep out the ccasional spurts of dust that clouded in, kicked up by passing orses or marching guards. I wondered if the window were set at round level, which would bring a spouting of water onto me at ae next rain. It certainly didn't keep out the cold.

The day wore on, marked only by subtle changes in the gloomy ght in the cell, and by the distant sound of time-change bells. By s end I almost wished I *had* been handed off to the torturers, for t least after the inevitable interval of unimaginable nastiness I ould have been more or less insensate.

Instead, what happened was a kind of refined torture that I hadn't expected: People came, in twos and threes and fours, to stare at me. The first time it happened I didn't know what to expect—except for those possible torturers—and I lay on the narrow, blanketless cot with my back to the door, my hands sweating.

But the door didn't open. Instead I heard the murmur of singsong, pleasingly modulated voices, and then the titter of young women.

I kept my back to the door, glad they could not see my crimson face.

At the end of the day, after countless repeats of the curiosity-in-the-cage treatment, I wondered why Galdran had bothered to have me locked up at all, if he was permitting half the Court to troop down to gawk at me.

The answer came the next day. I might have understood it sooner, but by then the dampness and my continual fever had made it hard to think of much beyond my immediate surroundings. When the door first opened, I didn't turn around, and other than a flash of fear, I didn't really react.

Someone prodded me in the shoulder, and when I turned a grim-faced guard said, "Drink it. Fast." She held out a battered metal-handled mug.

Surprised, I took the mug, smelled a soup whose main component seemed to be cabbage. By then cabbage smelled more delicious than any meal in memory, and I downed the lukewarm soup with scarcely a pause for breath. The soldier grabbed the mug from my hands and went out, locking the door hastily.

Not too long after, another one came in, this time with a mug of tea, which I also had to gulp down. I did—and happily, too. Then, just after dark, two soldiers came, both standing in the doorway holding torches while a healer—an elderly man this time—with practiced haste unwrapped the bandage on my leg. Much as it hurt, I knew I needed a change, so I gritted my way through. I couldn't look at my own flesh, but kept my gaze on his face. His

76

ps were pruned in heavy disapproval, and he shook his head now
nd then but didn't speak until he was done.

"The keem leaves have kept infection out," he murmured, "but
's not healing. Have you fever?"

"My closest companion," I said hoarsely—and realized it had
een two days since I'd spoken.

"You'll need an infusion of willow bark..." He stopped,
rabbed up the mess with a quick swipe of his hand, then left with-
ut another word.

The throbbing was just settling into a dull ache when the
oor opened again, and this time a completely new soldier came
, bearing a mug and a bundle under his arm. The bundle was a
anket, and the steam from the mug smelled familiar...At the
rst refreshingly bitter sip I realized that here was my infusion
willow bark, and it finally sank into my fevered brain that
aldran probably didn't know about any of this. What I had ex-
erienced for the past two days, from the gawks to the gifts, were
e effects of bribery. Those Court people paid to get a look at
e—and, it seemed, some had for whatever reason bought me what
mfort they could.

Bribery! If things could come in, couldn't something go out?
mething like me? Except I had nothing at all to bribe anyone
th. And I suspected that the going price for smuggling somebody
t would be a thumping great sum beyond whatever anyone had
id to slip me a cup of soup.

A half-hysterical bubble of laughter tried to fight its way up
m somewhere inside me, but I controlled it, afraid once I began
might start wailing like a wolf when it sees the moons.

After a short time the willow did its work upon me, and I fell
to the first good sleep I'd had in days.

eep ended abruptly the next morning when the cell door opened
d my blanket was unceremoniously snatched off me. Within a

short space I was shivering again, but I did feel immeasurably better than I had. Even my foot ached a bit less.

That day it rained, and the window leaked. Ignoring the twinges in my foot, I dragged my cot away, which was a mistake because its legs promptly collapsed. I sat on it anyway, more or less out of the wet.

More gifts that day: some hot stew, more tea, and a castoff tunic that smelled of mildew and was much too large, but I pulled it on gratefully. At night, another blanket, which disappeared the next morning—this time with an apologetic murmur from the guard who removed it.

The gifts helped, but not enough to counteract the cold or my own state of health. Somewhere in the third or fourth day infection must have set in, for the intermittent fever that had plagued me from the start mounted into a bone-aching, chill-making burner.

I was sicker than I'd ever been in a short but healthy life, so sick I couldn't sleep but lay watching imaginary bugs crawl up the walls. And of course it had to be while I was like this—just about the lowest I'd sunk yet—that the Marquis of Shevraeth chose to reappear in my life.

It was not long after the single bell toll that means midnight and first-white-candle. Very suddenly the door opened, and a tall, glittering figure walked in, handing something to the silent guard at the door, who then went out. I heard footsteps receding as I stared, without at first comprehending, at the torch-bearing aristocrat before me.

I blinked at the resplendent black and crimson velvet embroidered over with gold and set with rubies, and at the rubies glittering on fingers and in pale braided hair. My gaze rose to the rakish hat set low over the familiar gray eyes.

He must have been waiting for me to recognize him.

"The King will summon you at first-green tomorrow," the Marquis said quickly, all trace of the drawl gone. "It appears that your brother has been making a fool of Debegri, leading him all

ver your mountains and stealing our horses and supplies. The King
as changed his mind: Either you surrender, speaking for your
rother and your people, or he's going to make an example of
ou in a public execution tomorrow. Not a noble's death, but a
riminal's."

"Criminal's?" I repeated stupidly, my voice nearly gone.

"It will last all day," he said with a grimace of distaste. It was
he first real expression I'd ever seen from him, but by then I was
a no mood to appreciate it.

Sheer terror overwhelmed me then. All my courage, my firm
esolves, had worn away during the time-measures of illness, and I
ould not prevent my eyes from stinging with tears of fear—and
hame. "Why are you telling me this?" I said, hiding my face in
y hands.

"Will you consider it? It might...buy you time."

This made no sense to me. "What time can I buy with dis-
onor?" All I could imagine was the messengers flying eastward,
nd the looks on Bran's and Khesot's faces—and on Julen's and
alaub's and Devan's, people who had risked their lives twice trying
o rescue me—when they found out. "I know why you're here." I
nuffled into my palms. "Want to gloat? See me turn coward?
Vell, gloat away..." But I couldn't say anything more, and after
bout as excruciating a pause as I'd ever endured, I heard his heels
a the stone.

The door shut, the footsteps withdrew, and I was left in silence.

It was *then* that I hit the low point of my life.

don't know how long I had been sniffing and snorting there on
y broken bunk (and I didn't care who heard me) when I became
vare of furtive little sounds from the corridor. Nothing loud—no
ore than a slight scrape—then a soft grunt of surprise.

I looked up, saw nothing in the darkness.

A voice whispered, "Countess?"

A voice I recognized. "Azmus!"

"It is I," he whispered. "Quickly—before they figure out about the doors."

"What?"

"I've been shadowing this place for two days, trying to figure a way in," he said as he eased the door open. "There must be something going on. The outer door wasn't locked tonight, and neither is this one."

"Shevraeth," I croaked.

"What?"

"Marquis of Shevraeth. Was here gloating at me. The guard must have expected him to lock it, since the grand Marquis sent the fellow away," I muttered as I got shakily to my feet. "And he —being an aristocrat, and above mundane things—probably assumed the guard would lock it. *Uh!* Sorry, I just can't walk—"

At once Azmus sprang to my side. Together we moved out of the corridor, me hating myself for not even *thinking* of trying the door—except, how could I have gotten anywhere on my own?

At the end of the corridor a long shape lay still on the ground. Unconscious or dead, I didn't know, and I wasn't going to check. I just hoped it wasn't one of the nice guards.

Outside it was raining in earnest, which made visibility difficult for our enemies as well as for us. Azmus took a good grip on me, breathing into my ear: "Brace up—we'll have to move fast."

The trip across the courtyard was probably fifty paces or so, but it seemed fifty days' travel to me. Every step was a misery, but I managed, heartened by the reflection that each step took me farther from that dungeon and—I hoped fervently—from the fate in store if Galdran got his claws into me again.

We went through a discreet side door in a low, plain side building. Lamps glowed at intervals on the walls, seeming unnaturally bright to my dark-accustomed, feverish eyes. Breathing harshly, Azmus led the way down the hall and up some narrow stairs to a small room.

As soon as the door was shut he touched a glowglobe on a table, and in its faint bluish light, he sprang to a long cupboard and yanked it open. Shelves and shelves of folded cloth were revealed. "Here," he said. "Put this on, my lady. Quickly—make haste, make haste. We can get through the grounds as servants only if a search is not raised."

I held up what he had handed me and saw a gown. It was much too wide. As I looked at it rather helplessly, he bit his lip, his round face concerned; then he grabbed it back and pulled something else out. "There. That's for a stable hand, but it ought to fit better—they are mostly young."

I realized he was already wearing the livery of a palace servant. Not the fabulous livery of the foot servants who waited on the nobles in the palace, but the plain garb of the underservants. Short, stocky, with an unprepossessing face, Azmus was easily overlooked in any crowd. I didn't know his age, and it was impossible to guess from his snub-nosed face, all of which made him the perfect spy.

Wincing, I pulled off the mildewed tunic some unknown benefactor had gifted me with, and I yanked the livery over my filthy, rumpled clothes. I left my braid inside the tunic, pulled a cap on, and shoved my feet into a pair of shoes that were much too big. The tunic came down to just below my knees. We both looked at my trousers, which were not unlike the color of the stable hands', and he said with a pained smile: "In the dark, you'll pass. And our only hope of making it is now, while no one can see us." He bundled my mildewed tunic and my one moc under his own clothes.

"Where are we going?" I asked as he helped me down the stairs.

"Stable. One chance of getting out is there—if we're fast."

Neither of us wasted any more breath. He had to look around constantly while bearing my weight. I concentrated on walking.

At the stable, servants were running back and forth on errands, but we made our way slowly along the wall of a long, low building toward a row of elegant town carriages.

I murmured, "Don't tell me...I'm to steal one of these?"

Azmus gave a breathless laugh. "You'll steal a ride—if we can get you in. Your best chance is the one that belongs to the Princess of Renselaeus—if we can, by some miracle, get near it. The guards will never stop it, even if the hue and cry is raised. And she doesn't live within Athanarel, but at the family palace in the city."

"Renselaeus..." I repeated, then grinned. The Princess was the mother of the Marquis. The Prince, her husband, who was rumored to have been badly wounded in the Pirate Wars, never left their land. I loved the idea of making my escape under the nose of Shevraeth's mother. Next thing to snapping my fingers under *his* nose.

Suddenly there was an increase in noise from the direction of the palace. A young girl came running toward us, torch hissing and streaming in the rain. "Savona!" she yelled. "Savona!"

A carriage near the front of the line was maneuvered out, rolling out of the courtyard toward the distant great hall.

Keeping close to the walls, we moved along the line until we were near a handsome equipage that looked comfortable and well sprung, even in the dark and rain. All around it stood a cluster of servants dressed in sky blue, black, and white.

Two more names were called out by runners, and then came, "Renselaeus!"

But before the carriage could roll, the runner dashed up and said, "Wait! Wait! Get canopies! She won't come out without canopies—says her gown will be ruined."

One of the servants groaned; they all, except the driver, dashed inside the stable.

Next to me, Azmus drew in his breath in a sharp hiss. "Come," he said. "This is it."

And we crossed the few steps to the carriage. A quick look. Everyone else was seeing to their own horses, or wiping rain from windows, or trying to stay out of the worst of the wet. At the back of the coach was a long trunk; Azmus lifted the lid and helped me imb up and inside. "I do not know if I can get to the Renselaeus .lace to aid you," he warned as he lowered the lid.

"I'll make it," I promised. "Thanks. You'll be remembered for is."

"Down with Merindar," he murmured. "Farewell, my lady."

And the lid closed.

Lying flat was a relief, though the thick-woven hemp flooring raped at my cheek. Around me muffled voices arrived. The car-ige rocked as the foot servants grabbed hold. Then we moved, owly, smoothly. Then stopped.

Faintly, beckoning and lovely, I heard two melodic lines traded .ck and forth between sweet wind instruments, and the thrum-ing of metallic harp strings.

A high, imperious voice drowned the music: "Come, come! loser together! Step as one, now. I mustn't ruin this gown...The ing himself spoke in praise of it...I can only wear it again if it not ruined...Step lively there, and have a care for puddles. here!"

I could envision a crowd of foot servants holding rain canopies er her head, like a moving tent, as the old lady bustled across the ud. She arrived safely in the carriage, and when she was closed , once again we started to roll.

"Ware, gate!" the driver called presently. "Ware for Rense-eus!" The carriage scarcely slowed. I heard the creak of the great on gates—the ones that were supposed to be sporting my head thin a day. They swung shut with a *graunch*ing of protesting etal, and the carriage rolled out of Athanarel and into the city.

y next worry, of course, was how to get out of the trunk without ing discovered. I'd seen how busily all those servants cleaned their rriages as they waited in the rain, so I knew the first thing the nselaeus lackeys would want to do the moment they stopped uld be to rub the elegantly painted canvas with rainproofing wax polish. Would that mean opening the luggage trunk? My heart was pounding loud enough to be heard at the palace, it seemed to me, when we finally came to a halt.

And then came the imperious voice again; I'd discounted the vanity of an old lady. "No, no, leave that. Where are my canopies? Take me across the yard. Come, come, don't dawdle!"

Footsteps moved away, and I knew I had to move right then—or risk discovery.

Shouldering the lid up, I eased out, falling to the straw-covered ground when I tried to step on my left foot. A few paces away I saw a pitchfork leaning against a wall. Hauling myself to my feet, with my heart still thumping somewhere near my throat, I lunged my way across to the pitchfork, steadied myself on it, and used it as a brace for my left leg.

A quick look either way, then I was out the stable door, into a narrow alley. I hobbled into its welcome gloom, turned the first moment I could, and kept moving until I was thoroughly lost and soaked right to the skin. By then my hands were sore from the pitchfork's rusty metal, and my racing heart had slowed. It was time to find a place to hide, and rest, and plan my next move.

I was on a broad street, which was dangerous enough. As yet there was still some traffic, but soon that would be gone.

Light and noise drew my attention. Farther down, my street intersected another. On the corner was a great inn, its stableyard lit by glowglobes. As I watched, a loaded coach-and-six slowly lumbered in. Stable hands ran out and surrounded it. I hobbled my way along the wall, then stepped into the courtyard. At the side was a great mound of hay covered by a slanting roof. What a perfect bed that would be! My body was, by then, one great ache, and I longed to stretch out and sleep and sleep and sleep.

I kept my eyes on the hay. Every other step I moved my pitchfork around, as though tidying the yard. No one paid me the least heed as I stepped closer, closer—

"Boy! You there!"

I turned, my heart slamming.

The innkeeper stood on a broad step, his apron covering a scrawny chest. Nearby a soberly dressed man wearing the hat of a prosperous farmer dismounted from a fine mare. "Boy—girl? Here, take this gentleman's horse," the innkeeper said, snapping his fingers at me.

Trying not to be obvious about my pitchfork crutch, I stepped slowly nearer, toward the light. Warmth and food smells wafted out from a cheerfully noisy common room. Clearly this inn never knew quiet, night or day.

"Hey, is that palace livery? A palace hand, are you? What you doing here?"

"Errand," I said, trying desperately to make up a story.

But that appeared to be good enough. "Look, you, our hands are busy. You trim down this horse and put him with the hacks, and there'll be a hot toddy waiting inside for ye. How's that?"

I ducked my head in the nod that I'd seen the stable hands use at the palace. The man standing next to the innkeeper surrendered the reins to me and pulled off the saddlebags, yawning hugely as he did. "Wet season ahead, Master Kepruid," he said, following the innkeeper inside. "I know the signs..."

And I was left there, holding a horse by the reins.

My inner debate lasted about the space of one breath. I looked at the mare, which was as wet as I but otherwise seemed fine; she had not been galloped into exhaustion.

So I led the mare back toward the entry to the stable, my shoulder blades feeling as if a hundred unfriendly eyes watched. Then I leaned against her, standing on my bad foot, which almost gave out. I hopped up—ignoring the sharp pain—and grabbed the saddle horn, throwing my good leg over the saddle.... And I was mounted!

The pitchfork dropped; I gathered the reins and nudged the animal's sides. She sidled, tossed her head, nickered softly—and then began to move.

Several streets later, I kicked off the awful shoes, and when we had left the last of the houses of Remalna-city behind I decided I'd better get rid of the palace livery in case everyone around recognized it. I was so wet there was no chance of being warm—the tunic was merely extra weight on me. Gladly I pulled it off and balled it up, and when we crossed a bridge topped with glowglobes, I dropped my burden into a thicket near the water's edge.

So…where to go, besides east?

My body needed rest, warmth, sleep; but my spirit longed for home. Once I'd left the city and the last of what light there was, I could see nothing of the rain-swept countryside. The horse moved steadily toward the eastern mountains, which were discernible only as a blacker line against the faintly glowing sky. Gradually, without realizing it, I relinquished to the mare the choice of direction and struggled just to keep awake, to stay on her back.

After an interminable ride I tried lying along her neck. Beneath the rain-cold mane her muscles moved, and faint warmth radiated into me. I drifted in and out of dreams and wakefulness until the dream images overlay reality like dye-prints on silk. Looking back, I realize I'd slipped into delirium; but at the time I thought I was managing to hold on to consciousness, only that my perception of the world had gradually diminished to the fire in my leg and the rough horse hair beneath my cheek.

Dawn was just starting to lift the darkness when the mare walked into a farmyard and stopped, lifting her head.

I gripped weakly at her mane with both fists to keep myself from falling, and I sat up. The world swam sickeningly. Somewhere was the golden light of a window, and the sound of a door opening, and then voices exclaiming.

"Heyo, Mama, Drith is back—but there's someone else on her instead of Papa." And then a sharp voice: "Who are you?"

I opened my mouth, but no sound came out. The whirl of the universe had increased, and it drew me inexorably into the vortex of welcoming darkness.

TEN

WHEN I FIRST OPENED MY EYES—AND IT TOOK
...out as much effort as had the entire escape from Athanarel—
...meone made me drink something. I think I fell asleep again in
...e midst of swallowing.

Then I slept, and dreamed, and slept some more. I woke again
...en someone coaxed me into a bath. I remember the delicious
...se of warm water pouring over my skin, and afterward the clean
...ell of fresh sheets, and myself in a soft nightgown.

Another time I roused to the lilting strains of music. I thought
...was back at the palace, and though I wanted to go closer, to hear
...e sound more clearly, I knew I ought to get away.... I stirred
...tlessly...and the music stopped.

I slept again.

Waking to the sound of the bells for third-gold, I found myself
...ring up at a pair of interested brown eyes.

"She's awake!" my watcher called over her shoulder. Then she
...rned back to me and grinned. She had a pointed face, curly dark
...ir escaping from two short braids, and a merry voice as she said,
...plat!" She clapped her hands lightly. "We were fair guffered
...en you toppled right off Drith, facedown in the chickenyard
...d. Good it was so early, for no one was about but us."

I winced.

She grinned again. "You're either the worst horse thief in the entire kingdom, or else you're that missing countess. Which is it?"

"Ara." The voice of quiet reproach came from the doorway.

I lifted my eyes without moving my head, saw a matron of pleasant demeanor and comfortable build come into the room bearing a tray.

Ara jumped up. She seemed a couple years younger than I. "Let me!"

"Only if you promise not to pester her with questions," the mother replied. "She's still much too ill."

Ara shrugged, looking unrepentant. "But I'm dying to know."

The mother set the tray down on a side table and smiled down at me. She had the same brown eyes as her daughter, but hers were harder to read. "Can you sit up yet?"

"I can try," I said hoarsely.

"Just high enough so's we can put these pillows behind you." Ara spoke over her shoulder as she dashed across the room.

My head ached just to watch her, and I closed my eyes again.

"Ara."

"Mama! I didn't do *anything*!"

"Patience, child. You can visit with her next time, when she's stronger. If she likes," the woman amended, which gave me a pretty good idea they knew which of the two choices I was. *So much for a story*, I thought wearily.

In complete silence the mother helped me by lifting my cup for me to sip from, and by buttering bread then cutting it small so I wouldn't have to tear it. Soon, my stomach full, my body warm, I slid back into sleep.

The next time I woke it was morning. Clear yellow light slanted in an open window, making the embroidered curtains wave in and out in slow, graceful patterns. I lay without moving, watching with sleepy pleasure.

I might have drifted off again when there was a quick step, and Ara appeared, this time with pink blooms stuck in her braids. "You're awake," she said happily. "Do you feel better?"

"Lots," I said. My voice was stronger.

"I'll tell Mama, and you'll have breakfast in a wink." She whirled out in a flash of embroidered skirts, then bobbed back into view. Lowering her voice as she knelt by the bed-shelf, she said, "Feel like talking?"

She sounded so conspiratorial I felt the urge to smile, though I don't think the impulse made it all the way to my face.

"That thing on your ankle was pret-ty nasty. But we have keem leaves, and herbs from Grandma. Mama thought you were going to die." Ara grimaced. "At first Papa was mad about the horse, for he had to pay out all his profits to hire another, plus the bother of returning it, but he didn't want you to die, nor even want to report you—not after the first day. And not after we *Found Out.*" The last two words were uttered in a tone of vast importance, her eyes rounding. "Luz will tell you he heard it first, but it was I who went to the Three Rings and listened to the gossip."

I swallowed. "Luz?"

She rolled her eyes. "My brother. He's ten. Horrid age!"

I thought of Branaric, who had always been my hero. Had he ever thought I was at a horrid age? A complex of emotions eddied through me. When I looked up at Ara again, she had her lower lip between her teeth.

"I'm sorry," she said. "Have I spoken amiss?"

"No." I tried a smile. It felt false, but she seemed relieved.

The mother came in then, carrying another tray. "Good morning. Is there anything you wish for?"

"Just to thank you," I said. "The—horse. I, um, didn't think about theft. I just...needed to get out of Remalna-city."

"Well, she brought you right home." The mother's eyes crinkled with amusement. "I think the hardest thing was my spouse having to endure being chaffed at the inn for losing Drith. He—we—decided against mentioning the theft to anyone as yet."

I tried to consider what that meant, and failed. Something must have showed in my face, because she said quickly, "Fret not. No one has said anything, and no one will, without your leave. There's time enough to talk when you are feeling stronger."

I sighed. And after a good breakfast, I did feel a great deal stronger. Also, for the first time, I didn't just slip back into sleep. Ara, hovering about, said, "Would you like to sit on my balcony? It faces away from the farm, so no one can see you. I have a garden—it's my own. All the spring blooms are out. Of course," she hastened to add, "it's just a farm garden, not like any palace or anything."

"I haven't had a garden since my mother died. I'd like to see yours very much."

"Try walking," Ara said briskly, her cheeks pink with pleasure. "Mama thinks you should be able to now, for your ankle's all scabbed over and no bones broke, though they might be bruised. Here's my arm if you need it."

I swung my legs out and discovered that my hair, clean and sweet smelling, had been combed out and rebraided into two shining ropes.

Standing up, I felt oddly tall, but the familiar ache had dulled to a bearable extent, and I walked without much difficulty from the small room onto a wide balcony. A narrow wicker bench there was already lined with pillows. I sank down and looked out over a blooming garden. Through some sheltering trees, I glimpsed part of the house, and a bathhouse, and gently rolling hillocks planted closely in crop rows. And beyond, purple in the distance, the mountains. My mountains.

"This is the best view." Ara waved her arms proudly. "I tried it from several rooms. See, the roses are there, and the climbing vine makes a frame, and ferris ferns add green here…"

"Ara, don't chatter her ear off." The mother appeared behind us. "Here's another cup of listerblossom tea. I don't think you can drink too much of it," she added, putting it into my hands.

I thanked her and sipped. Ara stayed quiet for the space of two swallows, then said, "Do you like my garden?"

"I do," I said. "Moonflowers are my favorite—especially that shade of blue. They mostly grow white up in our mountains."

"We have only blue here. Though I'm getting slips of some that grow pale lavender at the center, and purple out." She sat back, her profile happy. "I love the thought that I will be able to sit my whole life on this balcony and look out at my garden."

"You're the heir?" I asked.

She nodded, not hiding her pride. Then, turning a round gaze on me she said, "And you really are the Countess of Tlanth?"

I nodded.

She closed her eyes and sighed. "Emis over on Nikaru Farm is going to be *soooo* jealous when she finds out. She thinks she's so very fine a lady, just because she has a cousin in service at Athanarel and her brother in the Guard. There *is* no news from Athanarel if we doesn't know it first, or more of it than anyone."

"What is the news?" I asked, feeling the old fear close round me.

She pursed her lips. "Maybe Mama is right about my tongue running like a fox in the wild. Are you certain you want all this now?"

"Very much," I said.

"It comes to this: The Duke of Savona and the Marquis of Shevraeth have another wager, on which one can find you first. The King thinks it great sport, and they have people on all the main roads leading east to the mountains."

"Did they say anything about my escape?"

She shook her head. "Luz overheard some merchants at the Harvest—that's the inn down the road at Garval—saying they thought it was wizard work or a big conspiracy. I went with Papa when he returned to the Three Rings in Remalna-city, and everyone was talking about it." She grinned. "Elun Kepruid—he's the innkeeper's son at Three Rings, and he likes me plenty—was telling me all the *real* gossip from the palace. The King was very angry, and at first wanted to execute all the guards who had duty the night you got out, except the ones he really wanted had disappeared, and everyone at Court thought there was a conspiracy, and they were afraid of attack. But then the lords started the wagers and turned it all into a game. Savona swore he'd fling you at the King's feet inside of two weeks. Baron Debegri, who was just returned from the mountains, said he'd bring your head—then take it and fling it at your brother's feet. He's a hard one, the Baron, Emis's brother said." She grimaced. "Is this too terrible to hear?"

"No…No. I just need…to think."

She put her chin on her hands. "Did you see the Duke?"

"Which duke?"

"Savona." She sighed. "Emis *has* seen him—twice. She gets to visit her cousin at Winter Festival. She says he's even *more* handsome than I can imagine. Four duels…Did you?"

I shook my head. "All I saw was the inside of my cell. And the King. And that Shevraeth," I added somewhat bitterly.

"He's supposed to have a head for nothing but clothes. And gambling." Ara shrugged dismissively. "Everybody thinks it's really Debegri who—well, got you."

"What got me was a trap. And it was my own fault."

She opened her mouth, then closed it. "Mama says I ought not to ask much about what happened. She says the less I know, the less danger there is to my family. You think that's true?"

Danger to her family. It was a warning. I nodded firmly. "Just forget it, and I'll make you a promise. If I live through this mess, and things settle down, I'll tell you everything. How's that?"

Ara clapped her hands and laughed. "That's nacky! *Especially* if you tell me all about your palace in Tlanth. *How* Emis's nose will turn purple from envy—when I can tell her, that is!"

I thought of our old castle, with its broken windows and walls, the worn, shabby furnishings and overgrown garden, and sighed.

———

fter a time Ara had to do her chores, leaving me on the porch
ith a fresh infusion of tea to drink, her garden to look at, and her
ords to consider.

Not that I got very far. There were too many questions. Like:
Where did those guards go? Azmus had overcome one, but I didn't
member having seen any more. Then there were the unlocked
pors. The one to my cell could be explained away, but not the
utside one. If there was a conspiracy, was Azmus behind it? Or
meone else—and if so, who; and more importantly, to what end?

It was just possible that those dashing aristos had contrived my
cape for a game, just as a cruel cat will play with a mouse before
e kill. Their well-publicized bet could certainly account for that.
he wager would also serve very nicely as a warning to ordinary
ople not to interfere with their prey, I thought narrowly.

Therefore, if I had left any clue to my trail, I had better move
. Soon.

While considering all this I fell asleep again with the half-filled
ug in my lap. When I woke the sun was setting and my hands
re empty. A clean quilt lay over me. Somewhere someone was
aying music: the steel strings of a tiranthe, and a pipe. I listened
a wild melody that made me wish I could get up and dance
nong Ara's flowers, followed by a ballad so sad I was thrown back
memory to the days after my mother died.

It was during the third song that two quiet figures came out
to the balcony. The man I recognized after a moment as the one
no had handed me his horse's reins that night an age ago. He set
wn a lamp and sat in a wicker chair nearby. His wife brought me
ore tea, then took her place in another chair.

The man said, "Are you well enough to discuss plans, mylady?"

"Of course." I sat up straight. "I'm in your debt. What can I do?"

He looked over at his wife, who said quietly, "Master Kepruid
members the stable hand from the palace who was supposed to
for Drith. He has said nothing about our story of the dropped
ins and the need to hire a horse to chase a mare who has made

93

the trip into the city every month for six years. And he won't, if you can promise you won't carry your war into the city."

"Carry my war," I repeated, feeling a cold wash of unpleasantness through me. "It—it isn't *my* war."

"Yours and the Count of Tlanth's," the man said. "We understand that much."

"Then...you are content under Galdran Merindar?" I asked.

"Am I?" the man said. "I am content enough. The merchants in the city buy goods from our village, and I receive my portion of their profits for arranging the selling, which covers our taxes. The farm does just well enough to keep us fed. If the taxes do not rise too steeply again, we will manage. I cannot answer for others."

The mother said, "Rumor has it your war is intended to protect the Covenant, but the King insists it was you who was going to break it. Rumor also has it you and your brother said you were going to war for the betterment of Remalna."

"It's true, I assure you," I said. "I mean, about our going to war for the Covenant. The King intends to break it—we have proof of that. And we *do* want to help the kingdom."

"Perhaps it is true." The mother gave me a serious look. "But you must consider our position. Too many of us remember what life was like on the coast during the Pirate Wars. No matter who holds a port, or a point, it is our lands, and houses, that get burned, our food taken for supplies, our youths killed. And sometimes not just the youths. We could have a better king, but not at the cost of our towns and farms being laid waste by contending armies."

These words, so quietly spoken, astounded me. I thought of my entire life, devoted to the future, in which I would fight for the freedom of just such people as these. Would it all be a waste?

"And if he does raise the taxes again? I know he has four times in the last ten years."

"Then we will manage somehow." The man shook his head. "And mayhap the day will come when war is necessary, but we want put that day off as long as we can; for when it does come, it will ot be so lightly recovered from. Can you see that?"

I thought of the fighting so far. Who had died while trying to scue me? Those people would never see the sun set again.

"Yes. I do see it." I looked up and saw them both watching me xiously.

The woman leaned forward and patted my hand. "As he says, e do not speak for everyone."

But the message was clear enough. And I could see the justice it. For had I not taken these people's mare without a thought to e consequences? Just so could I envision an army trampling Ara's arden, their minds filled with thoughts of victory, their hearts cerin they were in the right.

"Then how do we address the wrongs?" I asked, and was hamed at the quiver in my voice.

"That I do not know," the man said. "I concern myself with hat is mine, and I try to help my neighbors. The greater quesons—justice, law, and the rights and obligations of power—those em to be the domain of you nobles. You have the money, and the aining, and the centuries of authority."

Unbidden, Shevraeth's voice returned to mind, that last conrsation before the journey into Remalna, *You might contemplate ring your measures of leisure what the purpose of a permanent court ves...And consider this: The only reason you and your brother have t been in Athanarel all along is because the King considered you too rmless to bother keeping an eye on.*

I sighed. "And at least three of the said aristocrats are busy oking for me. Maybe it's time I was on my way."

There was no mistaking the relief in their faces.

"I did the best I could with your clothes, but they did not rvive washing," the woman said. "However, Ara has an old gown id by. It's a very nice one, but she no longer fits into it."

"Anything," I said. "And I don't mind wearing my old clothes. hole or two won't hurt me. Actually, I'm used to them."

She laughed. "I very much fear they disintegrated, or the tunic did, anyway. The trousers I bade Ara bury out in the turned field, for I knew there'd be no bringing those bloodstains out." She got to her feet. "Does Ara's music distress you anymore?"

"It never did." I looked at her in surprise. "I like it very much."

She gave me an odd, slightly troubled glance, then took my empty mug and led the way back to the little room I'd been sleeping in.

The next morning Ara seemed resigned about my leaving. She reminded me of my promise three times, then offered to brush out my hair for me. I agreed, sipping the last cup of their healing tea and wondering how far I'd get.

When she was done she flexed her fingers and stood back admiringly. "Knee-length hair! Not even Lady Tamara Chamadis—you know, daughter of the Countess of Turlee—has hair that long."

"I haven't cut it since my mother was killed. Swore I wouldn't until—well, she was avenged," I finished rather lamely, thinking of my conversation with her parents, who still had not told me their names, nor permitted their son or other dependents anywhere in my presence.

"Well, don't even then. It's the prettiest color in the world—not just brown, but brown and red and gold and wheat. Like the colorwoods!"

"My brother's is the same color." I figured that hair, at least, was a safe-enough topic. Pulling mine from long habit into separate strands, I braided it tightly as Ara chattered about the hair colors of her friends.

She opened a trunk and pulled out folded lengths of material. "Mother thought this one might fit. Put it on!"

I'd had my first real bath early that morning; I went to the bathhouse with Ara, wearing her mother's cloak, and no one had seen us. As I reached for the underdress, I realized how very relucant I was to leave. Ara's parents wanted me gone. I needed to get ome. But there was a strong part of me that would have been appy to sit in their garden and listen to music.

"It's a bit long, but you can kirtle it up." Ara looked me over ritically.

The underdress was white linen, embroidered at the volumi- ous sleeves, the neck, and the hem with tiny crimson birds and owers. The overdress was next, with a heavy skirt of robin's-egg lue, then the bodice, which laced up to a square neck that was ld-fashioned but pleasing.

"There. 'Tis beautiful! Hoo, I've never had that small a waist, ven when I was Luz's age." Using both hands, she brought out a ng, narrow mirror and set it on the trunk, tipping it back.

I looked down, hardly recognizing the person staring back at 1e. She looked much older than I was used to looking: a bony face, rge blue eyes that—I realized—matched the skirt of the gown. o myself I just looked thin, with a wary gaze, but Ara sighed with appy sentimentality. "You are so graceful, just like a bird. And eautiful!"

"Now, that I'm not," I said, half laughing and half exasperated.

"Well, not in the way of Lady Tamara, whose eyelashes are mous, and whose features get poems written on them, according Emis. But it's the way your face changes…" She flipped her ands up.

I laughed again, feeling foolish. I realized that no one had com- 1ented on my appearance since I was small; I simply *was*. I certainly ad not looked into a mirror for many seasons, and what clothing had was chosen for freedom of wear, and for warmth.

She looked at me in blatant surprise. "Don't say—have you no irts?"

"No." I shrugged. "Never have."

"Well." I could see her struggling not to think the less of me. 've had them since I turned fifteen. Master Kepruid's son is just 1e! Makes the dances ever so much more fun." She shrugged and grinned again. "Mama doesn't want me twoing before my Flower Day, at the least. And in truth, her rule is not so hard, for it's nacky having lots of flirts. Emis thinks she's more popular than I am, with those cousins and all, but—"

The door hanging flapped open, and Ara blinked in surprise. I found myself reaching for a weapon at my belt, and of course there was none.

But no enemy came in, only a gangling boy just about my height. His round cheeks were flushed with exertion. Staring at me with frank curiosity, he said, "They're searching cross-country from the river east…Daro says that his brother in the Guard told them they found palace livery in the river."

Ara bit her lip. "We're more south than east."

"But it's close enough that I'd better go. Thank you, Luz," I said.

The boy grinned. "I better lope, or Mama'll have my hide. But I won't tweet, oak-vow!" He slapped his forearm and touched his brow, then he dashed out again.

I sighed. "If I can have one more thing—a hat—I do swear I'll repay you somehow, someday."

Ara giggled as she dived into the trunk; I realized then that I had been using her room. "I don't have an extra hat, for I've just begun to wear them, but you can take this." She held out a long fringed scarf with dancing animals and birds embroidered on it. "You look young enough to wear a kerchief. But don't tie it under your chin. Behind, like we do." With quick fingers, she fixed the scarf.

Ara's mother came in then, and her relief to find me dressed and ready to go was plain. "I don't think we have any shoes to fit you," she said.

"That's all right. I'm used to being barefoot, and in much colder weather than this."

They seemed surprised, but neither of them spoke as we walked out. It was the first time I had seen any of the house besides the bedroom. I glanced with great curiosity over a landing into a big

ntral room with two stories of doors leading off it. In the center
as a round ceramic stove tiled in colorful patterns—a very old
buse, then. Built before stoves with vents to rooms were built, but
ter the Hill Folk gave Remalna the Fire Spell; for people used to
ut their Fire Sticks in such rounded stoves, thinking the heat
ould go out in a circle.

We went down a narrow flight of stairs. The mother glanced
uickly down two clean, shiny-floored hallways before gesturing me
to a tiny storeroom. "My cousin, who does all the kitchen work,
ustn't see you. He's a fine young man, but gabby. So all that tea
as been for my feigned illness." She smiled wryly. "Here is some
od—"

"Mama, that's an old basket," Ara protested. "Why don't you
ve her one of Sepik's nice ones?"

The mother hesitated, looking at me.

I said firmly, "Not if Sepik, whoever that is, makes baskets with
distinctive pattern. The old one will suit me much better."

I was handed a basket covered with a worn cloth. The weight
the basket was promising.

"Can I walk her to the hidey-path?" Ara asked.

"No. You are already late for your chores. I am going to take
walk for my health. Not a word more."

Ara pressed her lips together, winked at me, then fled.

I followed the mother through a side door. We walked down
rough the garden and beneath a pleasant copse of spreading trees.
he land sloped away toward a stream, which wound its way
rough a tangle of growth. Through this a narrow footpath par-
leled the stream.

She did not speak as we walked. I concentrated on keeping up
ith her brisk pace. My ankle, I was glad to find, only ached dully,
d the skirt kept twigs and brush from touching my still-sensitive
in. I didn't know how I'd feel later, but thus far I was doing well
ough to get off the farm with the haste they seemed to think
cessary.

"Here's our border," she said, stopping suddenly. We stepped off the path, and she parted the hanging leaves of a willow to point at rounded hills with an ancient stone wall crossing them. It was low and worn, just tall enough to keep sheep in. "If you cross that way, you'll catch up with the path leading to Ruka-at-Nimm, which is a good-sized village. It's also well south of the Akaeriki road, which is the main road east."

"I'll take it from here. The closer I get to the mountains, the faster I know how to cross the terrain. I'm grateful to your family."

She pressed her lips together, looking for a moment very much like her daughter. "There are some who talk revolution, and wistfully, too. Sepik, who makes the baskets, is one. But my man comes from a line of scribes, and most of them were killed in the Pirate Wars—none of them knew aught of fighting. He's more pacifist than some."

I nodded. "I understand."

She half reached out her hand, and I took it and clasped it With a brief curtsy she turned and disappeared back down the trail.

I wasted no time lingering but splashed down through the stream with my blue skirts held high; I toiled up the other side, crossed over the stone wall, and was on my way.

ELEVEN

KEPT WALKING UNTIL MY ANKLE ACHED, THEN I
stopped under a tree to eat. I hoped when I got to a more wooded
area I might find a fallen branch that would serve as a cane. Meantime, at each of the two trickling spring streams I'd crossed, I
paused long enough to drink and to soak my foot in the shocking
cold water. The numbness helped.

My picnic was a quiet one, there in the shade of an old oak. I
listened to birds chasing through the long grasses and distant
hedgerows, and looked up at the benign blue sky. It was hard to
believe right then that a great search was going on just for me.

I ate only one bread stuffed with cheese and herbs, and one
fruit tart, leaving all the rest for later. I wanted the food to last as
long as possible—as if the sense of peace that I'd gotten from Ara's
family might disappear along with their food.

Late in the afternoon I limped my way down the last leg of the
path, which joined up with a stone-paved road. My heart thumped
when I saw people on the road, going both ways. I walked slowly
down, relieved that none of them were warriors. Hoping this was
a good sign, I fell in behind an ox-drawn cart full of early vegetables. Occasionally horses trotted up from behind. I resisted the urge
to look behind me, and I made myself wait until they drew abreast.
Each time it was only ordinary folk who rode by.

The traffic increased when I reached the village, and when I walked into the market square I saw a large crowd gathered at one end. For a few moments I stood uncertainly, wondering whether I ought to leave or find out what the crowd was gathered for.

Suddenly they parted, and without warning two soldiers in brown and green rode side by side straight at me. Dropping my gaze to my dusty feet, I pressed back with the rest of the people on the road near me, and listened with intense relief as their horses cantered by without pausing.

The decision as to whether I should try to find out what was going on was settled for me when the crowd around me surged forward, and a man somewhere behind me called, "Hi, there! Molk! What's toward?"

"Search," a tall, bearded man said, turning. Around me people muttered questions and comments as he added, "That Countess causing all the problems up-mountain. Milord Commander Debegri has taken over the search, and he thinks she might end up this far east."

"Reward?" a woman's shrill voice called from somewhere to the left.

"Promised sixty in pure gold."

"Where from?" someone else yelled. "If it's Debegri, I wouldn't count no gold 'less I had it in hand, and then I'd test it."

This caused a brief, loud uproar of reaction, then the bearded man bellowed, "The King! Sixty for information that proves true. Double that for a body. Preferably alive, though they don't say by how much."

Some laughed, but there was an undertone of shock from others.

Then: "What's she look like, and is she with anyone?"

"Might be on a brown mare. Filthy clothes, looks like a human rat, apparently. No hat. Dressed like a dockside beggar."

"That's some help." Another woman laughed. "I take it we look for whiskers and a long tail?"

"Short, scrawny, brown hair, long—very long. Blue eyes. Ban-

ged left leg, got caught in a steel trap. Probably limping if not
ounted."

Limping. I looked down, wondering if any of the people
essed around me had been watching me walk.

Time to move on. Now, I thought, and I took a step sideways,
en backward, easing my way out of the crowd. I didn't hear all
the next shouted question, but the answer was clear enough:
Commander Debegri said that if anyone is caught harboring or
ding the fugitive, it means death."

One step, two: I turned and walked away, forcing myself to keep
even pace, as my heart thumped like a drum right under my ears.

f course I couldn't get away from that village fast enough.

On my way in I'd turned over various plans in my mind,
ostly false tales about stolen money and a desperately ill relative,
eant to get me a free bed (or a corner in a barn), for it was in-
easingly apparent that rain was on the way. Now I abandoned
ose, glad I had spoken to no one. When the rain started I clutched
y basket to me and tried to hurry my pace, to look like I had
mewhere to go, because it seemed to me that passersby glanced
me curiously.

As soon as I could find a side road I turned down it, and then
even smaller one than that, scarcely more than a cow path.
at brought me unexpected aid; just as the sun was setting, I
otted an outbuilding on what seemed to be a good-sized farm. A
utious scouting proved it to be empty of anyone but a number of
ickens. They put up a squawk and murmur when I first walked
, but when I'd settled myself on some piled straw, they ignored
e after a time.

The last of the light sufficed to enable me to get some food
d repack my basket, then I arranged the straw into as comfortable
ile as I could, curled up, and fell asleep to the steady beat of rain
the metal roof.

By sunup I was on my way again. Remembering that nasty

comment about the filthy dockside beggar, I dusted myself off and straightened my bodice and skirt, then I took the added precaution of wrapping my braid around my head in a coronet, tucking the end under, then retying the kerchief. This way, I hoped, I looked as anonymous as possible.

My ankle felt much the same as it had the previous morning, which boded well enough if I were careful. I ate as I walked, resolving to try to find something to use as a cane at least for a time. My plan was to make my way steadily east, then worry about the southern trip once I was safely into the mountains. Around me now were rolling hills, some forest-covered. This made for nice cover and some protection from the intermittent rain, but unfortunately the clouds were so thick and low they thoroughly obscured the sun—and the distant mountains. I had nothing to guide myself by.

I tried to choose larger hills to traverse, figuring that this would bring me steadily east and mountainward. It was good theory but bad practice—which I didn't realize until I topped a rocky cliff and looked down at a wide river meandering its way along. It had to be the Akaeriki—there was no river this large north of Remalna-city except the Akaeriki. And there were no rivers at all running north-south.

I looked back. Tired, footsore, I did not want to simply retrace my steps. So I turned east and walked along the ridge parallel to the river, deciding that I would choose a direction if I reached civilization. Otherwise—since I was there—I'd look for an easy way to cross the river, which had to be done sometime anyway.

On the far side was the main Akaeriki road. Twice I saw the continuous stream of traffic pull aside for galloping formations of spear-carrying soldiers. The second time I saw them riding headlong toward the west, my worry was replaced by a kind of gloating triumph.

This gave me the impetus to push on, threading my way steadily through increasingly wild country. The rain had largely abated, though out on the horizon a solid black line of clouds made me determined not to stop for the night until I'd found some kind of substantial shelter.

The impending rain was on my mind when I reached an intersecting path that led down an ancient ravine to an old, narrow bridge. No one was on it. As I watched, hesitating, a white-bearded shepherd approached from the other side, clucking to a flock of sheep.

No one appeared to disturb them as they crossed. A short time later the sheep appeared on the path just below me, and I ducked behind a rock as they trotted by, followed up by their shuffling human.

One more glance—and I slipped down the trail and stepped out onto the bridge, which vibrated with each step. Avoiding looking down at the rocky river below, I hurried across, then stepped onto the south bank with a sense of relief.

I crossed the road quickly, saw only a boy driving a cart loaded with hay. Scrambling up the low ridge on the other side, I soon achieved the relative safety of a scattering of trees.

And so for a time—I heard bells echo through the valley, tolling second-green and third-green—I walked above the road where days ago I had been taken in the other direction by Shevraeth on his dapple-gray. That journey was on my mind as I toiled through grass and over stones and the thick tree roots of ancient hemlock.

The forestland thickened at one point, and without warning it opened onto a road. Fading back behind a screen of ferns, I watched the traffic. It appeared I'd reached a major crossroads. A stone marker at the intersection indicated the Akaeriki road downhill, and to the south lay the small town of Thoresk.

A town. Surely one anonymous female could lose herself in a town? And while she was at it, find some shelter?

Big raindrops started plopping in the leaves around me. The coming storm wouldn't be warded by tree branches and leaves, that was for certain. Clutching my half-empty basket to my side, I started up the road, careful not to limp if anyone came into view from the opposite direction.

I saw a line of slow wagons up ahead, with a group of small children gamboling around them. I hurried my pace slightly so I would look like I belonged with them; I had nearly caught up when a deep thundering noise seemed to vibrate up from the ground.

"Cavalcade! Cavalcade!" a high childish voice shrieked.

The farmers clucked at their oxen and the wagons hulked and swung, metal frames creaking, over to one side. The children ran up the grassy bank beside the road, hopping and shrieking with excitement.

Feeling my knees go suddenly watery, I scrambled up the bank as well, then sat in the grass with my basket on my lap. I checked my kerchief surreptitiously and snatched my hand down as two banner-carrying outriders galloped into view around the bend I'd walked so shortly before.

Behind them a single rider cantered on a nervous white horse. The rider was short but strongly built. A gray beard, finicky mustache, and long hair marked him as a noble; his mouth and eyes were narrowed, whether in habit or in anger I didn't know—but my instinctive reaction to him was fear.

He wore the plumed helm of a commander, and his battle tunic was brown velvet. He had passed by before I realized that I had very nearly come face-to-face with Baron Nenthar Debegri, Galdran Merindar's former—and now present—commander.

Then behind him came row on row of soldiers, all formidably armed, riding three abreast. Dust and mud flew from the horses' hooves, and the noise was enough to set the oxen bellowing in distress and pulling at their traces. Seven, eight, nine ridings—a full wing.

A full wing of warriors, all to search for me? I didn't know whether to laugh or to faint in terror. So I just sat there numbly and watched them all ride by—a very strange kind of review.

As the end of the cavalcade at last drew nigh, the children were lready skidding down the bank. My eyes, caught by a change in olor, lifted. Instead of rows of brown-and-green battle gear, the ast portion were in blue with black and white, their device three tars above a coronet. As my astonished mind registered that this vas the Renselaeus device, my gaze was drawn to the single rider eading their formation.

A single rider on a dapple-gray. Tall in the saddle, long blond air flying in the wind, hat so low it shadowed the upper portion f his face, the Marquis of Shevraeth rode by.

And as he drew abreast, his head lifted slightly, turned, and he tared straight into my eyes.

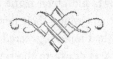

TWELVE

There was no time to react, of course.

My heart gave one great thump and scampered like the rat they'd called me as the gray rode on unchecked, followed by the remainder of the cavalcade.

Ahead of me, the oxen drivers and their children moved back slowly onto the road, the adults exclaiming and wondering what was going on, and the children whooping and waving imaginary swords.

The only thought in my mind was to put as much distance as possible between that town and myself.

Go west, I thought. *They won't expect that.*

And I turned my nose back into the forest from which I'd emerged, and started hurrying along as fast as I could.

In the meantime my mind was busy arguing with itself. I could see Shevraeth's face clearly—as if the moment had been painted against the insides of my eyelids. It was impossible to say that there had been recognition; maybe only a reminder. His expression certainly hadn't changed from what had to be a kind of resigned boredom.

And it's not like he's ever seen me with a clean face, I thought, grimacing as I remembered that bearded man's description. My hair

as hidden, I was wearing a gown usually worn by prosperous farm
irls, and of course I'd been sitting, so there was no limp or bandage
give me away.

Just a scare, I told myself. *He was watching the crowd to pass the
me.* But my heart persisted in hammering at my ribs, and my feet
ed along as though there were fire at my heels.

The rain was coming down in earnest when I dropped onto a
otpath. With relief I turned and followed this, and I soon
merged from the forest into a sheltered little dell.

The welcome gold of lit windows glowed through the gathering
arkness. I was in a tiny village.

They can't possibly find me here, I thought as I splashed down the
ath. *Probably no one but the inhabitants even knows where the vil-
ge is.*

So thinking, I scouted my way around the nearest buildings,
ad when I found a huge barn, I didn't even hesitate to slip in-
de.

It had to be a common barn; there were numerous animals
oused inside. But it was warm and dry, and someone had even left
lamp sitting on a hen coop just inside the door.

I looked around, saw a hayloft and a ladder. In the space of
ree breaths I was up it and lying down on a pile of fresh, sweet-
elling hay. Shivering from my wet clothes, I wished I dared to
ke them off as I rummaged in my basket for some food.

The bread had grown hard and the cheese dry, but the fruit
as still tasty. I decided I had to finish the last of the bread,
d save the fruit tart for the morrow. After that, I'd be on my
vn.

As if to taunt me, savory food smells wafted up to my rafter. I
ghed—then realized that the door below must have been opened.
nd a moment later I rolled over toward the ladder and stared into
pair of wary green eyes.

"Awk!" I squeaked.

The eyes crinkled. The owner took another step up the ladder, and a buxom young woman around my own age, with a cloud of curling red hair, faced me. Her face was moon-round, her eyes interested. "You left wet footprints across the dirt," she said.

I sighed. "It's just the storm. I was on my way home, and it rained so very hard, and I'll go if you like."

She shrugged, smiling a little. "Truth is, I don't care a bit, but if Grandfer comes out, he'll raise a ruckus. Inn does bad enough in these times, as he reminds us every time we want a new hair ribbon or a coin to go to the fair."

"Haven't any coins. Shall I sweep the prints away?"

"I will, soon's I feed the animals." She winked. "Go ahead and sleep. I won't tell—truth is, times aplenty I've thought of running away from Grandfer, except what would I do to earn my keep anywhere else except tend farm stock? May's well do that at home, for who's to say that anyone who might hire me might not be three times worse?"

She think's I'm a runaway apprentice. "Oh, thank you!"

She shrugged again, started down, then stopped when her eyes were once more level with the edge of the rafter. They crinkled as she said, "I just wish you'd been a boy instead, and as handsome, for then I'd have demanded a kiss as payment."

And with a gurgling laugh, she descended the rest of the way.

I chewed at my tough bread and listened to the rain on the roof and the pleasant sounds of the animals getting their food. Presently I heard the rhythmic *wisp*ing of a broom, and then the door closed.

And it seemed I'd just shut my eyes and drifted off to sleep when light flickered into my dreams and I opened my eyes on the red-haired girl, clutching a candle whose flame flickered wildly. Her face was white with excitement and fear.

"Are you a countess?" she whispered.

A pang smote my chest, and I sat up. "Who is out there?"

She pointed behind her. "Warriors. A whole riding, at least. And a lord. Rings, a sword—" She gestured, obviously impressed,

en the fear was back. "Going from house to house. I told Grand-
r I was checking on the cow about to calve," she added from down
n the barn floor. "If they find out you're here—"

"I'll go."

She was gone in a trice, leaving me to feel my way down in the
arkness. *Leastwise if I can't see, no one can see me—unless they have
torch, and then I'll see their light first*, I thought.

The barn had several doors. I eased one open a crack as some-
here nearby a horse shifted weight and nickered softly. Terrified
at the sound would carry, I slipped out the door and shut it.

Rain hit me in the face, hard and cold. I stumbled out into
, my feet splashing in deep puddles. Running as fast as I could,
crossed behind another building and then nearly hit a tree. Its
rny leaves warned me to stop. I reached, felt the bole of a
ighty hemlock, and after only a short hesitation, I tucked my
asket securely up under my arm and climbed the tree as high as I
uld.

Shivering, my fingers and toes numb, I stared down through
e branches until I saw lights flickering, and over the steady drum-
ing of the rain I heard horses' hooves. The streaming torches
ounced away up a trail and disappeared.

I clung to the tree until my arms were so numb I couldn't tell
I was holding on or not. This made me panicky again; and shakily,
oving with excruciating slowness, I climbed back down.

On the muddy ground I hesitated, wishing I dared to retreat to
e barn again. But I remembered that business about "harboring
e fugitive" and "death," and reluctantly I felt my way farther back
to the forest, until the growth around me was so tangled the rain
as a mere nuisance instead of a downpour.

Worming my way into the thickest part of a patch of ferns, I
rled up and passed the remainder of a miserable night. Sleep was
termittent, for sudden drips of cold on my skin, or the tickle of
me unseen insect, would keep jerking me awake. The night
emed endless, but at last a bleak, cheerless blue light lifted the

111

shadows just enough for me to make out the shapes of branches and foliage. By then I had wound myself into a tight ball, and what little warmth I could generate made me ill inclined to move.

But I knew I had to move eventually, if only to better shelter. My joints ached, my foot itched, and I was afraid that once again I might get sick, and this time there would be no Ara and her nice family to rescue me.

Still I stayed where I was until the light was stronger, and then shafts of yellow stabbed into my hidey-hole. I realized that the sun had come out. Hoping for warmth, I moved, this time with alacrity, and soon I was making my way westward into the forest, moving from sun patch to sun patch.

By noon I had dried out. I stopped once and beat as much of the dirt off as I could, which rendered my clothing a little less stiff. When I came to a stream I washed my face and hands. Whatever happened, I did not want to look like that filthy dockside beggar they were noising about over half the countryside.

On my walk I ate the last of my food, and when I found another stream, I drank enough to fill my middle.

Now I had an additional worry: finding food. And as the day wore on, it became increasingly obvious that this was going to be as hard as staying out of sight of searchers.

When I reached the end of the patch of forest I was ready to run out into the bright sunshine—but before I'd passed the last tree I saw a line of riders racing across a distant field.

Ducking instinctively behind the tree, I peered over a branch, shading my eyes against the glare of the sun, and saw that they rode in two-by-two formation, and that they were not following any road.

Now, it *might* have been the riders had nothing to do with me, but I was not about to take that chance. As I looked out across the rolling terrain, I realized that they probably had me boxed in. They new approximately where I was—that business the night before made it pretty clear—but not exactly. As for my part, I had to spot their perimeter...and cross it.

And get something to eat.

Without endangering any innocent people.

Standing there watching the diminishing formation, I was intensely aware of how alone I was—but it was not the same terrible, helpless feeling I'd had when I first discovered that I was a prisoner. Then I couldn't walk and couldn't get free. Now I was free, and I could walk, and as I remembered what Ara had said about that accursed Shevraeth and his abominable friend making sport of finding me, I got angry. There is nothing like good, honest, righteous anger to infuse a person with energy.

All right, I thought. *Either I keep blundering about in all four directions, or else I locate these searchers—they have to be a limited number—and then move when and where they are least expecting it.*

And so I turned my steps east and started stumping along in the direction the cross-country racers had gone.

I crossed two hills, cresting the last to look down into a pleasant little valley. Water ribboned between the hills from a small lake, probably going to join up with the Akaeriki north of me. Along the lakeside lay a small town. There was no sign of my search party anywhere around; they were probably in the town. So I found a good spot in the shelter of a thick shrub—for by then the sun was hot—made certain that no part of me formed a silhouette, and sat down to watch.

I was fighting drowsiness when they finally emerged and started riding southward, again across the hills. I stared after them until my eyes watered. They kept disappearing beyond the hills but then eventually reappeared, each time getting smaller and smaller. Then they disappeared for a long time: another village or town. I made myself wait and watch. Again I was trying not to nod off when I saw a second line appear on the crest of a hill directly west of me, on the other lip of the valley.

The urge to sleep fled. I watched the line—it was a long one this time, with tiny bright dots at the front that indicated banners —descend into the town.

The banners meant the commander. Was the Marquis still with him, or had he finally gotten bored and gone back to the silk-and-velvet life in Athanarel?

"You might contemplate the purpose of a court..." You brainless, twaddling idiot, I thought scornfully. I wished he were before me. I wished I could personally flout him and his busy searchers, and make him look like the fool he was. And watch the reaction, and walk away laughing.

While I was indulging my fulminating imaginings, the long line emerged again, much more quickly than the previous one had. Delight suffused me: They had obviously discovered that the previous group had been there, and had probably decided that the place was therefore safe.

Excellent. Then that was where I would go.

The sun was setting and a cold wind had started fretting at the tops of the grass, fingering my skirts and kerchief, when I topped the last rise on my approach to the lakeside town. Keeping well to the undergrowth, I skirted the place, looking for a likely hidey-hole, preferably one in which I might also find something to eat. Barns seemed the best choice. I had only to sneak in when the owners were safely abed. And maybe there'd be some early vegetables or even some preserves.

I waited until dark had fallen and then started slinking my way down along someone's garden wall. Dropping onto a brick pathway, I straightened up with my basket on my arm and tried to look unconcerned. People were walking about, and the ironwork lamps on poles lighting the streets indicated this was customary. Obviously this wasn't a market town that closed its doors at sundown. Perhaps it was one of those towns where wealthy merchants bought second house in pleasant surroundings for purely social purposes. Certainly a lakeside would be pleasant enough.

As I emerged onto a lovely brick-patterned street some of the noise I heard resolved into music. My steps turned automatically that way, and I saw an inn, its windows bright with golden light, its doors wide open. As always when I heard music, my heart felt light and the tiredness in my body diminished. This was good music, too, not just the awkward plunkings and tweetings that served merely to mark the right melody for enthusiastic but untrained singers, as I was used to in Tlanth. It had been a very long while since a minstrel, much less wandering players, had dared our mountain heights. Though we did love entertainment, the word had probably spread down-mountain that about all they'd get from us for their pains would be loud applause and a bit of plain food.

But this inn seemed to have no such problem. Stepping inside, I counted six different instruments, all of them played well. The noises of people having a good time made listening difficult, so I pressed between merrymakers, trying to get closer to the musicians.

Someone moved, someone else changed position, and I found myself wedged against a table against one wall—a high table with ironwork chairs, instead of the usual low tables and cushions. The metal frame of the table dug into my hip, but at least no one could push me away, and I had a reasonably good view of the musicians.

And so I stood for a time, swaying and nodding with the complicated rhythms. People got up and danced, something I longed to do. I told myself it was just as well that I did not know any of the latest steps, for the last thing I needed was to risk drawing attention to myself—especially if my ankle suddenly twinged and gave out.

It did ache, I realized as I stood there, and my stomach growled and rumbled. But it was so good to be warm, and to feel safe, and to listen to—

A player faltered; the musicians stopped. Around me the voices altered a little, from loud and jovial to questioning. I felt tension

115

dart through the room, like a frightened bird. Faces turned toward the door. Terror leaped in me as I shifted my shoulder just a little, then peeked swiftly under the gesturing arm of the man standing next to me.

Baron Debegri stood at the entrance. He negligently waved a gloved hand toward the table he wanted—a central table, with the best view of the musicians. Two stone-faced warriors motioned to the people already seated there.

No word had been spoken. The people at the table picked up their dishes and glasses and disappeared silently into the crowd. Debegri sat down, hands on thighs, looking well pleased with himself.

I stared at him, astounded by my rotten timing. But of course he wouldn't search at night. And of course he'd quarter himself in the best place available, and if this were indeed a resort town, the inns would be the best.

I couldn't stop sneaking peeks at him as he was served a substantial meal and a bottle of what had to be the very best bluewine. No one sat with him, but one of his personal guards stood at the doorway, another behind his chair, silent, watchful, awaiting his command. He didn't offer them anything to eat, just sat there and gorged himself.

As I watched, my fear slowly turned into anger, and then to rage. Heady with hunger, I struggled within myself. I felt if I didn't do something, make some kind of gesture, I would be a coward forever.

The rich smell of wine-braised onions met my nose, making me swallow. I turned, saw a harassed waiter laying down a bowl of some kind of stew for the people whose table I was wedged against. A flagon of mead and plate of fresh-sliced kresp were next. I met the eyes of the man seated adjacent. He met my gaze incuriously, then looked away with an air of slight annoyance. The other man paid me not the slightest heed as he piled kresp onto his plate and then ladled savory-smelling fish stew over it.

116

"Ungh," I groaned. But the sound was lost in the voices, which had risen again.

The music started up, this time a merry rhythm that made some people start clapping in counterpoint. Dancers appeared, at first staying well away from Debegri's table. However, after four or five songs, the crowd was thicker than ever, and slowly, surely, the dancers moved closer, until the flash of embroidered sleeves and the whirl of skirts flickered between me and the King's commander. For a time my attention was divided between sneaking glimpses at the two men beside me, who never once looked up from their meal before it was all gone, and the Baron, whose table was loaded with goodies, some of which he didn't even touch.

And as I watched the dancers moving unheeded around him, an idea formed in my mind, a reckless, useless, stupid idea, but one that promised such fun I could almost hear Bran's laughter.

It's been too long since I heard him laugh, I realized grimly. I was gloriously angry at the whole world—at the commander sitting there at his ease, at his numerous soldiery all looking for my dockside-rat self, at the Marquis for scorning us and our ideals, at the ordinary people for not caring that Bran had worn himself tired and grim on their behalf when he should have been laughing and moving right along with all these dancers.

The dancers had been a brightly colored mass, but now I watched individuals. One in particular drew my eye: a big bull of a man, obviously half-drunk. His partner could hardly stop laughing when he lurched and staggered as the others twirled and stamped. I watched the figures of the dance, learning the pattern. The observers seemed to know it well, for when the stomping and clapping occurred, those who wished to cross the room threaded their way among the dancers; then when the couples did hands-high, the floor cleared for the resulting whirls and partner trades.

The drunk man was starting to look tired. He'd want to stop soon, I knew. I'd have to move now, or not at all.

My heart clumped in counterpoint to the music as I slipped

117

through the crowd around the perimeter of the room and then, just as the clap-stamp-clap-stamp commenced, eased my way out among the dancers, ducking a tray here and a swinging arm there. My basket handle was over my elbow, so both hands were free.

When the horns signaled the next hands-high, I remembered my lessons from Khesot on Using Your Opponent's Weight Against Him. Steadying my hand against the drunken man's shoulder, I hooked my good foot around his ankle and yanked, pushing his shoulder at the same time.

He spun, bellowing, his fingers clutching at air, and fell—right across the commander's table. His partner shrieked, waving her arms. I dodged between her and Debegri, who had leaped up, cursing, as he mopped at the wine splashed down his front. With one hand I nipped a chicken pie and with the other a cup of mulled dessert wine, just before the table crashed over on its side, flinging the food everywhere. People screamed and shouted, pushing and shoving to get away from the mess. I ducked between two dancers and backed, laughing breathlessly, toward the door.

The drunken man was yelling, "Where is she? Where is she? Where's the little snipe that tripped me?"

"Calm yourself, sir," Debegri grated, his voice harsh and somehow familiar. "Guards! Right this table…"

Trying to smother my laughter, I turned around on the doorstep and saw another chance. A single warrior stood holding the reins of the beautiful white horse. As I watched, the soldier stifled a yawn and looked over at the door, to where the two guards were busy with Debegri's table.

Flinging the mulled wine squarely into her face, I jumped up across the horse's back, and as it bucked and sidled, I jammed my heels in its ribs and it leaped forward.

The reins went flying. I grabbed at them with my free hand and thrust the meat pie into my mouth with the other.

The warrior sprang to stop me but the horse was too fast. I dashed my basket against the warrior's head and slapped the reins on the horse's white neck.

A spear whizzed right past my shoulder, and a few moments
er something sharp pricked my neck. Ducking as low as I could,
lung desperately to the reins. The horse stretched its legs into a
lop, and then a canter. Behind I heard the blare of a summons
rn.

The chase was on!

THIRTEEN

I KNEW IT HAD BEEN A STUPID THING TO DO—AND
worse, dangerous. But I simply could not stop laughing. Half of my
meat pie fell away in my struggle to get and keep my balance. What
little I did manage to hang on to tasted wonderful—and woke up
my appetite like some kind of ravening beast.

I stayed low, for the white horse was astonishingly fast and I
was afraid to fall. I was also afraid of spears, or worse; remembering
the sharp prick at my neck, I touched my skin cautiously and found
the slime of blood and a long rent in my kerchief. That warrior
had recovered pretty fast from the mulled wine in the face. If her
aim had been just a fraction better, Debegri would have had a head
all ready for the King's gatepost.

But for now the worry lessened slightly; my horse was faster
than the pursuers'. The problem was I had no idea where I was
going. Every curve frightened me, even though my mount pulled
steadily ahead. I kept scanning the hilltops fearfully, expecting a
contingent to top the rise and cut me off.

Despite my lengthening lead—and maybe because of it—the
pursuers stayed hot to task.

Finally I thought of the forest and looked around again, this
time to get my bearings. As soon as we rounded a likely curve in

the stone road I yanked the reins to the side. The horse leaped to obey, and with a heave and a snort started plunging crosswise up the hill to the east.

I didn't really think this would fool the pursuers, and sure enough, after a short time I saw their outlines against the uneasy dark of the sky. And moments after that, a cold sweep of wind brought the first spattering of another rainstorm.

It would slow me, but so would it slow the others. The forest line neared...neared...much faster to reach now than it had been to leave by foot. I realized as my mount flashed past the first trees that I'd make it—but what then? Try to lose them? That tactic wouldn't last long, not with a great white horse crashing and smashing through the undergrowth.

And...for the first time I thought of the handsome saddle equipage on the animal's back. What if Debegri had one of those summons-stones? All they'd have to do was follow along and pounce when it was convenient.

Yet if I somehow managed to ditch the horse in the forest and it emerged without me, they'd have a most conveniently narrow perimeter in which to search.

But if they thought I was still on its back...

The trees were closer together. Unseen branches whipped at my face and head. I let the animal slow just a little as I fumbled the basket off my arm and hooked the handle over the pommel. How to keep it there? I thought of the kerchief. With a pang of regret I pulled it off. I wouldn't be able to wear it anymore anyway, not with that great rent in it, and no doubt splashes of gore from where the warrior's knife had nicked my skin.

Tying one end around the basket handle and the pommel, I let the other end flap in the breeze. Would that fool them into thinking I was still on the horse? I'd have to try.

The rain was now coming down in earnest, roaring through the trees. I could not see or hear the pursuit, but that meant nothing. Slowing the white horse as much as I dared, I pulled my legs up, readying. Ahead I saw open space, and I realized I'd have to make my move immediately.

So I guided the horse to a tree with a nice low branch, stood on the saddle...reached...gripped rough bark...and with my right foot gave the horse's flank a good smack. "Run!" I yelled, scrambling up onto the branch.

My braid came loose, its coils catching round my neck and nearly strangling me, but I ignored it as I fought my way up into the tree and then held on tightly. The wet, slick branches swayed with the wind, and rain stung my face.

I scarcely had time to get a good grip. A frighteningly short interval passed before I heard crashing noises above the roar of rain, and through the tossing branches saw a weird reddish glow bobbing crazily below. The pursuit passed right below me, following the trail of smashed grass and small bushes that the white horse had made.

If I'd been just a little slower, they would have seen me.

Instinct was strong. I wanted to hug that tree tight and stay there for the duration, but I knew this would be a mistake. I had to get out of that forest, and fast, for I couldn't count on my basket decoy lasting too long.

So, slipping and grunting, I climbed down and then stumbled back along the trail the plunging horses had made.

It wound around a bit, certainly more than I had been aware of when on horseback. Trying to decide whether this was bad or good, I toiled on, gasping for breath and looking frequently behind me.

When I emerged from the forest, I wondered, *What now?*

The town. Why not? They will never expect me there again.

And so, as exhaustion slowed my steps, I made my way for the second time back to the town, stopping only once, to drink from a cold, fresh-running stream.

I kept well away from the inn. The streets were mostly clear. Occasional pairs of warriors clopped by on horseback, bearing orches and spears. By then I was too tired to react much beyond ducking into the shadows.

I found a garden with little open-air gazebos placed at intervals along a path, and a very pretty bathhouse on a stream. These were a temptation, but I avoided them. They'd be the first thing *I* would check if I were searching.

So, once again, I found a thick ferny plant to crawl under, and there I passed the night.

Despite my discomfort I slept heavily, but I woke feeling like I needed a goodly week more of sleep. My face, hands, and legs below my knees hurt as though they'd been stung by a thousand nettles, and when I looked, I saw my skin crisscrossed by red welts from the branches and twigs the night before.

My ankle throbbed warningly. Two of the healing scabs had been ripped off and the whole thing was fairly messy again—though of course not as bad as it had been at first. Just once I looked at the bathhouse, from which I could hear congenial voices echoing, and I yearned for a bath. How long had it been, aside from the one day at Ara's? *Never again will I complain about our old bathhouse*, I thought grimly as I flexed my foot. I knew I wasn't going to be walking any great distances that day. So what I had to do was to find a way to get a ride.

Of course the first thing I thought of was all those wagons I'd seen on my peregrinations. But I was certain there were warriors topping every cart that came along any of the main roads. And the little side paths were too narrow for wagons.

Just then the bells for first-gold rang. Dawn. The fewer people who saw me the better, I thought, looking down at the once-pretty blue skirt. Now it was splotched with mud and striped with grass and leaf stains.

I thrust my braid down the back of my underdress to hide its length, smoothed my bodice and skirt as best as I could, and made

123

certain no one was around before I crawled out from beneath my fern.

It seemed strange not to have the basket on my arm. I missed its comforting weight, even though it would have served no further use.

I miss Ara's clean bed, and her pretty garden, and that hot food...

I shook my head, ignoring the pangs through my temples. No use in regrets—I had to keep my spirits up.

I crossed the garden, staying near the hedgerow borders until the pathway debouched onto one of the lovely brick streets. A quick glance down the street revealed scarcely any traffic—but way up at the other end were two tall, armed individuals wearing blue and black-and-white livery.

Oh, joy. The Marquis was somewhere around.

For a moment I indulged in a brief but satisfying daydream of scoring off him as I had off the Baron the night before. But amusing as the daydream was, I was *not* about to go searching him out.

First of all, while I didn't look like I had before, the dress wasn't much of a disguise; and second...I frowned. Despite his reputation as a fop and a gamester, I wasn't all that certain he would react as slowly as Debegri had.

I retreated back to the garden to think out my next step. Mist was falling, boding ill weather for the remainder of the day. And my stomach felt as if it had been permanently pressed against the back of my spine.

I pulled the laces of the bodice tighter, hoping that would help, then sat on a rock and propped my elbows on my knees.

"Are you lost?"

The voice, a quiet one, made me start violently. My shoulders came up defensively as I turned to face an elderly man. He was elegantly dressed, wearing a fine hat in the latest fashion, and carried no weapons.

"Oh no. I was supposed to meet someone here, and..." I shrugged, thinking wildly. "A—a flirt," I added, I don't know why. "I guess he changed his mind." I got to my feet again.

The man smiled a little. "It happens more frequently than not when one is young, if you'll forgive my saying so."

"Oh, I know." I waved my hands as I backed up one step, then another. "They smile, and dance, and then go off with someone else. But I'll just find someone better. So I'll be on my way," I babbled.

He nodded politely, almost a bow, and I whirled around and scurried down the path.

Even more intensely than before, I felt that crawling sensation down my back, so I dropped off the path and circled back. I was slightly reassured when I saw the old man making his way slowly along the path as though nothing out of the ordinary had happened; but my relief was very short lived.

As I watched, two equerries in Renselaeus livery strode along the path, overtook the man, and addressed him. I watched with my heart thumping like a drum as the man spoke at some length, brushed his fingers against his face—*the scratches from the trees!*—and then gestured in the direction I had gone.

Expecting the two equerries to immediately take off after me, I braced for a run. *Why had I babbled so much?* I thought, annoyed with myself. *Why didn't I just say "No" and leave?*

But the equerries both turned and walked swiftly back in the direction they'd come, and the old man continued on his way.

What does that mean?

And the answer was not long in coming: They were going back to report.

That meant a whole lot of them searching. And soon.

Yes, I'd really widened my perimeter, I thought furiously, cursing the Baron, music, inns, resorts, food, and the Baron again, throwing in Galdran Merindar *and* the Marquis of Shevraeth for good measure. I slipped back through the garden to the street. Spotting an alley behind a row of houses, I ducked into that.

And when I heard the thunder of approaching horses' hooves, I dove toward the first door, which was miraculously open. Slipping inside, a sickly smile on my face, I concocted a wild story about deliveries and the wrong address as I looked about for inhabitants angered at my intrusion.

But my future had brightened. The hallway was empty. Behind me was a stairway leading upward, and next to it one leading to a basement. For a moment I wanted to fling myself down that, to hide in the dark, but I restrained myself: There was generally only one way out of a basement.

At my right a plain door-tapestry opened onto a storeroom of some sort. I peeked inside. There were two windows with clouded glass, and a jumble of dishes, small pieces of furniture, trays, and a row of hooks with aprons and caps on them. That outer door was the servants' entrance, I realized, and this room was their storeroom.

Colors flickering in the clouded glass brought my attention around. Moving right up next to the window, I listened, and heard the slow clopping of hooves. The rhythm broke, then stopped; from another direction came more hooves, which swiftly got closer.

The house I was in was a corner house, the first in a row. Two search parties met right outside my window, where the alley conjoined with the street.

"Nothing this way, my lord," someone said.

A horse sidled; another whickered.

Then a familiar voice said, not ten paces from me: "Search the houses."

FOURTEEN

O THERE I WAS, LIGHT-HEADED WITH HUNGER, FOOT-
ore, with the perimeter of safety having closed to about ten paces
ound me, and the Marquis of Shevraeth standing just on the
her side of the wall.

At least he didn't—yet—know it.

As if in answer, I heard the *klunk* of footsteps on the tiled floor
rectly above me. Someone else had been listening at a window
d was now moving about. To come downstairs? Would the
archers go to the front or come to the back?

I thought about, then dismissed, the idea of begging safety from
e inhabitants. If they were not mercifully inclined, all they'd need
do was shout for help and I'd be collared in a wink. And if they
ere merciful, they faced a death sentence if caught hiding me.

No, what I had to do was get out without *anyone* knowing I'd
een inside the house. And nippily, too.

Hearing the clatter of hooves and the jingle of harnesses and
eapons, I edged close to the window and peered out again. All I
uld see was the movement of smeary colors, but it sounded like
e riding had moved on. To divide up and start on the houses?

What about the other group?

Dark-hued stalks stood directly outside the window. Did one
them have a pale yellow top?

I could just *see* him standing there narrow eyed, looking around. Then maybe he'd glance at the window and see something flesh-colored and blue just inside the edge...

I closed my eyes, feeling a weird vertigo. Of course he couldn't see me—it was dark inside and light out. That meant the window would be a blank, dark square to him. If he even gave it a look. I was letting fancy override my good sense, and if I didn't stop it, his searchers would find me standing there daydreaming.

I took a deep breath—and the stalks outside the window began to move. Soon they were gone from sight, and nothing changed in the window at all. I heard no more feet or hooves or swords clanking in scabbards.

It was time for me to go.

My heart thumped in time to the pang in my temples as I opened the storeroom door, peeked out, then eased the outside door open. Nothing...nothing...I slipped out into the alley.

And saw two posted guards at the other end. They were at that moment looking the other way. I whisked myself behind a flowering shrub that bordered the street, wincing as I waited for the yells of "Stop! You!"

Nothing.

Breathing hard, I ran full speed back across the street and into the garden where I'd spent the night before. And with no better plan in mind, I sped along the paths to the shady section, found my fern, and crawled back in. The soil was still muddy and cold, but I didn't mind; I curled up, closed my eyes, and tried to calm my panicking heart and aching head.

And slept.

And woke to the marching of feet and jingling of weaponry. Before I could move, there was a crackling of foliage and a spear-head thrust its way into my bush, scarcely an arm's length above my head. It was withdrawn, the steps moved on, and I heard the smashing sound of another poke into the shrubbery there.

"This is my third time through here," a low voice muttered.

"I tell you, if we don't get a week's leave when this is over, I'm going back to masonry. Just as much work, but at least you get enough time to sleep," another voice returned.

There was a snorting laugh, then the footsteps moved on.

I lay in frightened relief, wondering what to do next. My tongue was sticky in my mouth, for I'd had nothing to drink since the night before, and of course nothing to eat but those few bites of the meat pie.

How much longer can I do this?

Until I get home, I told myself firmly.

I'd wait until dark, sneak out of that town, and never return. *I'll travel by night and go straight east,* I decided. How I was to get food I didn't know, but I was already so light-headed from hunger, all I could think of was getting away.

Just before sunset it started to rain again. I told myself that this was good, that it limited visibility for the searchers. Therefore it would help me, because I needed to go west, and I'd been trapped on the east side of the town for two days.

Thus I rationalized sneaking through the town rather than going around it, which might be a small problem to those on horseback—but to someone who was tired, footsore, and unenthusiastic about slogging knee-deep in mud when she could traverse more quickly the beautifully paved streets, it was a lure that could not be overcome.

So, keeping to dark alleys and tree-shaded parkways, I started to make my way through the town, always edging north, since I remembered that the lake lay along the southeast border. I was going all right until my growing thirst got so bad I could think of little else.

Where to get a drink? In the countryside this was less of a problem, but now I began to regret having stayed in the town just to make it easier on my feet. The streams had been turned into canals, with windowed bathhouses everywhere along them, and house windows overlooking everything else. It was impossible to sneak to a canal for a drink and not be seen. Holding my mouth open to catch raindrops on my tongue only made my thirst more intense.

So when I stumbled onto a little circular park with a fountain in its center, I simply couldn't resist. A quick glance showed the square to be completely deserted. In fact, so far I hadn't seen any people at all, but I didn't consider that, beyond my brief gratitude that the rain had kept them all inside.

I hopped over a little flower border. The blooms—ghostly white in the soft glow from the lamps around the park's circumference—ran up the brick walkway and gripped the stone lip of the fountain. I opened my mouth, leaned in, and took a deep gulp.

And heard hooves. Boots.

"You, there, girl! Halt!"

Who in the *universe* ever halts when the enemy tells them to?

Of course I took off in the opposite direction, as fast as I could: running across grass, leaping neatly tended flowers. But the park was a circle, which made it easy for the riders to gallop around both ways and cut me off. I stopped, looked back. No retreat.

Meanwhile another group came running across the lawns, swords drawn. I backed up a step, two; looked this way and that; tried to break for it in the largest space, which of course was instantly closed.

There must have been a dozen of them ringing me, all with rapiers and heavier weapons gleaming gold tipped in the light from the iron-posted glowglobes and the windows of the houses.

"Report," someone barked; and then to me, "Who are you? Don't you know there is a sunset curfew?"

"Ah, I didn't know." I smoothed my skirts nervously. "Been sick. No one mentioned it…"

"Who are you?" came the question again.

"I just wanted a drink. I was sick, I think I mentioned, and idn't get any water…"

"Who are you." This time it wasn't even a question.

The game was up, of course, but who said I had to surrender eekly? "Just call me Ranisia." I named my mother, using my hardst voice. "I'm a ghost, one of Galdran Merindar's many victims."

Noises from behind caused the ring to tighten, the weapons all ointing a finger's breadth from my throat. My empty hands were : my sides, but these folks were taking no chances. Maybe they ought I *was* a ghost.

No one spoke, or moved, until the sound of heels striking the rick path made the soldiers withdraw silently.

Baron Debegri strode up, his rain cape billowing. Under his ppish mustache his teeth gleamed in a very cruel grin. He stopped ithin a pace of me, and with no warning whatever, backhanded e right across the face. I went flying backward, landing flat in a ower bed. The Baron stepped onto my left knee and motioned a rch bearer over. He stared down at the half-healed marks on my nkle and laughed, then jerked his thumb in a gesture of command. wo soldiers sprang to either side of me, each grabbing an arm and ulling me to my feet.

"What have you to say now, my little hero?" the Baron gloated.

"That you are a fool, the son of a fool, and the servant of the iggest—"

He swung at me again, and I tried to duck, but he grabbed me y the hair and then hit me. The world seemed to explode in ars—for a long time all I could do was gasp for breath and fight gainst dizziness.

When I came out of it, someone was binding my hands; then vo more someones grabbed my arms again, and I was half carried ack to the street. My vision was blurry. I realized hazily that a em on his embroidered gloves must have cut my forehead, for a arm trickle ran nastily down the side of my face, which throbbed ven worse than my ankle.

I got thrown over the back of a horse, my hands and feet bound to stirrups. From somewhere I heard Debegri's harsh voice: "Lift the curfew, but tell those smug-faced Elders that if anyone harbored this criminal, the death penalty still holds. You. Tell his lordship the Marquis that his aid is no longer necessary, and he can return to Remalna-city, or wherever he wants."

Quick footsteps ran off, and then the Baron said, "Now, to Chovilun. And don't dawdle."

Chovilun…

One of the four Merindar fortresses.

I closed my eyes.

I do not like to remember that trip.

Not that I was awake for much of it—for which I am grateful. I kept sliding in and out of consciousness, and believe me, the *out*s were more welcome than the *in*s.

I knew that Chovilun Fortress lay at the base of the mountains on the Akaeriki River, which bisects the kingdom, but I didn't know how long it took to reach it.

All I can report is that I felt pretty sick, nearly as sick as I'd been when I fell into Ara's chickenyard. Sick at heart as well, for I knew there was no escape for Meliara Astiar after all; therefore I resolved that my last job was to summon enough presence of mind to die well.

Not, of course, that the truth would ever get to Branaric. The Merindars had captured and held a kingdom by a winning combination of treachery, bullying, and lying. I had made the Baron look silly during that episode at the inn, and I knew he was going to take his revenge on me in the privacy of his fortress, making it last as long as possible. And every weakness he could get me to display was going to get noised as excruciatingly as possible over the entire kingdom—especially aimed at Tlanth.

So my only hope, therefore, was to make him so angry he'd kill me outright and save us both a lot of effort.

These were my cheery thoughts—not that my head was any too clear—as we clattered into a stone courtyard at last. The ever-present rain had nearly drowned me. My hands and feet were numb. When the guards cut me loose I fell like an old bundle of laundry onto the stone courtyard, and once again hands gripped my upper arms and yanked me upright.

This time I made no pretense of walking as I was borne into a dank tunnel, then down steep steps into an even danker, nasty-smelling chamber.

And what I saw around me was a real, true-to-nightmare dungeon. Shackles, iron baskets, various prods and knives and whips and other instruments whose purpose I didn't know—and didn't want to know—were displayed on the walls around two great stained and scored tables.

A huge, ugly man in a bespattered blackweave apron motioned for the soldiers to put me into a chair with irons at arms and feet. As they did, he said, "What am I supposed to be finding out?"

Behind, the Baron said harshly, "I want to shed these wet clothes. Don't touch her until I return. This is going to last a long, long time." His gloating laugh echoed down a stone passageway.

The huge man pursed his lips, shrugged, then turned to his fire, selecting various pincers and brands to lay on a grate in the flames.

Then he came back, lifted one bushy brow at the soldiers still flanking me, and said in a low voice, "Kinda little and scrawny, this one, ain't she? What she done?"

"Countess of Tlanth," one said in a flat voice.

The man whistled, then grinned. He had several teeth missing. Then he bent closer, peered at me, and shook his head. "Looks to me like she's half done for already. Grudge or no grudge, she won't last past midnight." He grinned again, motioning to the nearest warrior. "Go ahead and put the irons on. Shall we just have a little fun while we're waiting?"

He pulled one of his brands out of the fire and stepped toward me, raising it. The sharp smell of red-hot metal made me sneeze—and when I looked up, the man's mouth was open with surprise.

My gaze dropped to the knife embedded squarely in his chest, which seemed to have sprouted there. *But knives don't sprout, even in dungeons,* I thought hazily, as the torturer fell heavily at my feet. I turned my head, half rising from the chair—

And saw the Marquis of Shevraeth standing framed in the doorway. At his back were four of his liveried equerries, with swords drawn and ready.

The Marquis strolled forward, indicated the knife with a neatly gloved hand, and gave me a faint smile. "I trust the timing was more or less advantageous?"

"More or less," I managed to say before the rushing in my ears washed over me, and I passed out cold right on top of the late torturer.

FIFTEEN

ΛWARENESS CAME BACK SLOWLY, AND NOT VERY asantly. First were all the aches and twinges, then the dizziness, d last the sensation of movement. Before I even opened my eyes ealized that once again I was on a horse, clasped upright by an n.

The Marquis again? Memories came flooding back—the dun-on, the Baron's horrible promise, then the knife and Shevraeth's mment about timing. The Marquis had saved me, with about the sest timing in history, from a thoroughly nasty fate. Relief was foremost emotion, then gratitude, and then a residual embar-sment that I didn't understand and instantly dismissed. He had ed my life, and I owed him my thanks.

I opened my eyes, squinting against bright sunlight, and turned head, words forming only to vanish when I looked up into an familiar face. I closed my eyes again, completely confused. Had reamed it all, then? Except—where was I, and with whom?

The horse stopped, and the stranger murmured, "Drink."

Something wet touched my lips. I swallowed, then gasped as uid fire ignited its way down my gullet, the harsh taste of distilled stic with other herbs. I swallowed again, and my entire body ewed—even the aches diminished.

"Not too much," someone else warned.

The liquid went away. I opened my eyes again and this time saw three or four unfamiliar faces looking at me with expressions ranging from interest to concern.

I twisted my head to look into the face of the young woman holding me. She was tall and strong, with black hair worn in a coronet around her head under a plain helm. She held out a flask to someone else, who took it, capped it, dropped it into a saddlebag

The peachy light of early morning touched the faces around me. All of them were unfamiliar. There was no sign of the Marquis of Shevraeth—or of Baron Debegri, either. I blinked, sat up straighter, then grimaced against a renewal of all my aches.

"Am I holding too tight, Lady Meliara?" the woman asked.

"I'm all right," I said a little hoarsely.

"I don't think you can ride alone quite yet."

"Sure, I can," I replied instantly.

To my surprise they all laughed—but it wasn't unkind laughter, like Baron Debegri's, or heartless laughter, like that of Galdran's Court in the throne room at Athanarel.

"We'll see, my lady," was all she said. And lifting her head "Let's move."

Suddenly businesslike, the others ranged themselves around us in a protective formation, and the horses started forth at a steady canter.

The glow from the bristic faded, leaving me with the lassitude of someone who feels truly awful.

After a time the riders slowed, then stopped, and the woman holding me said, "Here's a good spot. Flerac, you and Jamni see to the mounts. Loris, and you three, set us up a perimeter. Amol, the Fire Stick and the stores. My lady, you and I are going down to that pool over there."

So saying, she dismounted, then lifted me down. She paused, rummaged in her saddlebag, pulled out a bundle, then said, "I am Yora Nessaren, captain of this riding. Please come this way, my ady." And she even bowed, then held out her arm for my support. I took it gratefully.

This was certainly a new twist on the various treatments I'd received. I was even more surprised when we topped a little rise shaded by trees, and looked down at a clear pool. One end was shaded, the other golden and glittering in the sun.

"First order of the day," she said with a grin, "you are to have a bath and new gear." She opened a small, carved box. A scent of summer herbs rose from it. She dug two fingers in, then slapped something gritty onto my palm. "There's some of my sandsoap." Then, putting the box away, she reached again into her bag and pulled out a new teeth cleaner. "I always carry an extra in the field."

"Thanks," I said gratefully, thinking, as I stepped down to the pool, of all those days I'd had to use the edge of my increasingly dirty underdress.

I found a flat rock on which to put my waiting soap and teeth cleaner. Moments later I flung off the last of my dirt-stiff clothes and dived into the pool. The water was clear and cold, instantly soothing the stings got from hiding in scratchy shrubs, and the rope burns on my wrists and ankles from my journey as a saddle pack to Debegri's fortress. After a good scrub from head to toe, I reached for my clothes in order to wash them out. Yora Nessaren, who'd sat on the rise staring up at the trees, turned, then shook her head. "We'll burn those old clothes, my lady—they're ruined." And she pointed to where she'd laid out a long, heavy cotton shirt, and one of the blue and black-and-white tunics, and a pair of leggings. Renselaeus's colors.

"I don't mind putting that dress back on, dirty or not," I said. "I'm used to dirt."

She gave me a friendly shrug but shook her head. "Orders."

I considered that as I rinsed the last of the sandsoap from my hair and twisted it to get the water out. Orders from whom? Once again my mind filled with recent memories. More awake now, I knew that the rescue at Chovilun had been no dream. Was it possible that the Marquis had seen the justice of our cause and had switched sides? The escort, the humane treatment—surely that meant I was being sent home. Once again I felt relief and gratitude. As soon as I got to the castle I'd write a fine letter of thanks. No, I'd get Oria to write down my words, I decided, picturing the elegant Marquis. At least as embarrassing as had been the idea of waking up in his arms again was the idea of his trying to read my terrible handwriting and worse spelling.

"Don't stay in too long, my lady."

The voice recalled me to the present—and I realized my skin was getting chilled. Reluctantly I climbed out of the pool. At once my various aches and pains clamored for attention, and all I wanted to do was lie there in the sun and sleep forever.

But then delicious smells wafted from the other side of the rise, which woke up my appetite. Wringing out my hair, I hastily put on the clothes Yora Nessaren had laid out. They were hopelessly large on me—and when she saw it, she bit her lip, hard, in a praiseworthy attempt not to laugh. I looked down, saw the three stars that should have been in the middle of my chest resting over my stomach. I shook my head. "This is better than the dress?" I asked as she packed up the extra gear.

"Well, it's clean," she said, "and we'll belt it up. But when we ride, it's nine equerries for House Renselaeus that people will be seeing, my lady."

I was too tired to wonder what this meant—except I knew it was no immediate threat to me. So without asking any further questions, I followed her back over the rise to where a young man with two red braids tied back had laid out a little camp. In the distance I saw the horses being tended as they drank from the stream that fed my pool, but the others were nowhere in sight.

"Here, Lady Meliara." Yora Nessaren tossed me a carved shell comb.

As I attacked my hair she cut my old dress up and burned it bit by bit. I thought of Ara and was sorry to see it used thus.

The young man finished his preparations, then said, "All ready, Ness."

Just then the equerries who had been tending the horses came through the trees and sat down.

The riding captain looked at them, said, "We'll eat, then rotate positions so the others can have their meal. Then we're on the road."

And that's what happened. The red-haired young man, Amol, handed me a toasted length of bread that turned out to have meat, cheese, and greens stuffed into it. He also gave me a generous tin of tea, all without looking directly at me.

I sat on a rock with my hair hanging down to the grass all around me, drying in the warm breeze. The equerries ate quickly, with a minimum of conversation, and they studiously ignored me. When Nessaren and her group finished, they went by twos to replace the ones doing guard duty. Then everyone helped clean up. I was still working on my braid when they began to remount, and then I saw that there was a ninth horse. But Nessaren looked from me to it, frowning, then said, "We'll proceed as we started, I think, if you don't object, my lady." And bowed without a trace of ironic intent.

I knew I was too weak to ride on my own, and I realized I was not uncomfortable with the idea of riding with her on the same horse. So I just shrugged, finished my braid at last, wrapped it hastily around my head, and tucked the end under. One of them silently handed me a helm.

Nessaren was smiling faintly as she boosted me up onto her mount, but she said nothing beyond, "Ride out."

The others fell into formation, and away we went.

And that was the pattern for several days. The second day Nessaren offered me that last horse, which, of course, I accepted. We rode at a steady pace, occasionally cantering when the horses were fresh.

The first few times I rode alone I felt inordinately weary toward the end of each ride. But just when it seemed I was going to fall off, we'd make a stop for food and water, or to camp.

They had an extra bedroll for me, and we slept under the stars, or in a tent when it rained. We always stopped near a stream so that we could start our ride with a proper morning bath. We also stopped once at midday, when a hard rainstorm overtook us, and camped through the duration.

A time or two a pair of the riders would peel off and disappear, to reappear later with fresh supplies, or once with a sealed letter, which was given into Yora Nessaren's hands. She got that the day we stopped for the rainstorm, and since I had nothing else to do, I watched her read it.

As usual she said nothing, but she looked over at me with a faintly puzzled expression that I found disturbing because I couldn't interpret it.

Yora and the others were all scrupulously polite, and until that day, carefully distant. We had a big tent in which six or seven could sleep more or less comfortably. Four of them were in the tent with me, the rest busy with either the horses or guarding.

Nessaren sat cross-legged on her bedroll, tapping her letter against her knee. Finally she looked up. "Red, you and Snap go into Bularc. Falshalith is in charge of the garrison there—report in, say you've been on the search up in the hills and you want an update."

The red-haired fellow fingered the gold ring in his ear, then frowned. He glanced at me, then his gaze slid away. He said, "Think they'll talk?"

The woman they called Snap twiddled her fingers. "Why not? The more ignorant we are, the more Falshalith will condescend." Her brown eyes widened with false innocence. "After all, we're just servants, right?"

Snap and the redhead both looked at me; then she looked away and Amol said, "More tea, my lady?"

"No, thanks." I considered my next words.

For those first days it had taken all my energy just to keep up and not embarrass myself. But the regular food, and the rest, had restored a lot of my energy, and with it came curiosity.

I said tentatively, "You know, I have one or two questions..."

Amol's eyelids lifted like he was thinking, *Just one or two?* and Snap took her underlip firmly between her teeth. She seemed to have the quickest temper, but she was also the first to laugh. Both of them turned expectantly to their captain, who said calmly, "Please feel free to ask, Lady Meliara. I'll answer what I can."

"Well, first, there's that dungeon. Now, don't think I'm complaining, but the last thing I remember is Shevraeth's knife coming between me and a hot poker, you might say. I wake up with you, and we're on the road, going south. Remalna-city is north. I take it I'm not on my way back to being a guest of Greedy Galdran?"

Snap's head dropped quickly at the nickname for the King, as to hide her laughter, but Amol snickered openly.

"No, my lady," Nessaren said.

"Well, then, it seems to me we're just about to the border. If we're going to Tlanth, we ought to be turning east."

"We are not going to Tlanth, my lady."

I said with a deep feeling of foreboding, "Can you tell me where we *are* going?"

"Yes, my lady. Home. To Renselaeus."

Not home to me, I thought, but because they had been so decent, I bit the comment back and just shook my head. "Why?"

"I do not know that. My orders were to bring you as quickly as was comfortable for you to travel."

"I'd like to go home," I said, polite as it was possible for me to be.

Nessaren's expression blanked, and I knew she was about to tell me I couldn't.

I said quickly, "It's not far. I just want to see my brother, and let him know what has happened to me. He must be worried—he might even think me dead."

At the words *my brother* her eyes flickered, but otherwise there

141

was no change in her expression. When I was done speaking she said quietly, with a hint of regret, "I am sorry, my lady. I have my orders."

I tried once again. "A message to Branaric, then? Please. You can read it—you can *write* it—"

She shook her head once, her gaze not on me, but somewhere beyond the trees. We'd ceased to be companions, even in pretense—which left only enemies. "We're to have no communication with anyone outside of our own people," she said.

My first reaction was disbelief. Then I thought of that letter of thanks I'd planned on writing, and even though I had not told anyone, humiliation burned through me, followed by anger all the more bright for the sense of betrayal that underlay it all. Why betrayal? Shevraeth had never pretended to be on my side. Therefore he had saved my life purely for his own ends. Worse, my brother was somehow involved with his plans; I remembered Nessaren's subtle reaction to his mention, and I wondered if there had been some sort of reference to Bran in that letter Nessaren had just received. What else could this mean but that I was again to be used to force my brother to surrender?

Fury had withered all my good feelings, but I was determined not to show any of it, and I sat with my gaze on my hands, which were gripped in my lap, until I felt that I had my emotions under control again.

When I realized that the silence had grown protracted, I looked up and forced a polite smile. "I don't suppose you know where your Marquis is?" I asked, striving for a tone of nonchalance.

A quick exchange of looks, then Nessaren said, "I cannot tell you exactly, for I do not know, but he said that if you were to ask, I was to tender his compliments and regrets, but say events required him to move quickly."

And we're not? I thought about us waiting out the rain, and those nice picnics, and realized that Nessaren had been watching me pretty carefully. It was no accident that we'd stopped for rests, then;

essaren had very accurately gauged my strength. A fast run would
have meant riding through rain and through nights, stopping only
to change horses. We hadn't even had to do that.

Once again my emotions took a spin. I had had a taste of the
way prisoners could be conveyed when the Baron had me thrown
over a saddle for the trip to Chovilun. Nessaren and her riding had
made certain that my journey so far was as pleasant as they could
make it.

Is this, I wondered acidly, *possibly an attempt to win me to
Shevraeth's side in whatever game he's playing with the King and the
Baron?* Just the thought made me wild to face their Marquis again
and give him the benefit of my opinions.

But none of this could be shown now, I told myself. My quarrel
was not with Nessaren and the equerries, who were just following
orders. It was with their leader.

I glanced up, saw that they seemed to be waiting. For a
reaction?

"Anyone know a good song?" I asked.

SIXTEEN

TURNED OUT THIS WAS JUST THE RIGHT QUESTION. Of the eight of them four played musical instruments, and Amol had a wonderful singing voice. They carried their instruments in their saddlebags, but in deference to me had not brought them out. After I made it clear I liked music, we had singing every night, and sometimes during long stretches of lonely country where no one else was about.

A lot of the songs were in Rensare, the very old dialect that apparently most of the people in the principality spoke. I knew little about Renselaeus, other than that it *was* a principality, a wealthy one, and for centuries had owed its allegiance directly to the ancient kingdom of Sartor, and only the most nominal allegiance to Remalna. Apparently one of our kings in the more recent past had won some kind of concessions from the Renselaeus ruler, and in turn the Renselaeans had been granted the county of Shevraeth, which lay on the coast in Remalna proper, hard against their southern border. This title went to the Renselaeus heir. The only things I knew about the Prince and Princess were that they were old, and that they had had a single heir late in life, the present Marquis.

My companions couldn't hide their surprise at my ignorance, but after I asked a few questions about the background of the songs, hey started telling me about the homes, and life, and history there. nd though they assiduously stayed away from the vexing topic of urrent events, I garnered a few interesting facts—not just about heir loyalty to the Renselaeus family instead of to the Merindar rown, but the fact that the principality seemed to have its own rmy. A very well trained one, too.

This became really clear when Amol and Jamni returned from heir mission. Both were excited, Amol laughing. "Report went to he King that the mysterious attack on Chovilun was by mountain aiders," he said.

"So my lord must have been right about those greens." Flerac ulled thoughtfully at his thin mustache. *Greens*, I'd gathered, was heir nickname for Galdran's warriors.

"I'm just glad we didn't have to kill them," Snap put in, rolling er eyes. "Those two in the dungeon were sick as old oatmeal about eing ordered to stand duty during torture. I can tell when some- ne's haystacking, and they weren't."

"What happened?" I asked, trying to hide my surprise. "I take there was fighting when you people pulled me out of that Ierindar fortress?"

They all turned to me, then to Nessaren, who said, "Some. Ve let some of them go, on oath they'd desert. There are plenty f greens who didn't want to join, or wish they hadn't."

"What about that lumping snarlface of a Baron?" I kept y voice as casual as possible, wondering what all this meant. Vas Shevraeth, or was he not, Debegri's ally? "I hope he got ounced."

"He ran." Flerac's lip curled. "Came out, found his two body- uards down, got out through some secret passage while we were ying to get in through another door. Don't think he saw any of s. Don't know, though."

Then they were no longer allies. What did *that* mean? Was hevraeth trying to take Debegri's place in Galdran's favor?

"Report could be false," Amol said soberly.

Nessaren nodded once. "Let's pick up our feet, shall we?"

By which they meant it was time to ride faster.

As we made our way steadily southward, their spirits lifted at the prospect of home, and leave-time to enjoy it. From remarks they let fall it seemed that the Marquis had had them on duty day and night, with no breaks, during all the days of my run for freedom. I really liked Nessaren and her riding. With good-natured generosity they treated me as a companion rather than as a prisoner. The last four mornings they even let me run through their morning sword drills with them. Some of it I knew from our own exercises with Khesot, but they had far better ones. I did my best to memorize the new material for taking back to our people in Tlanth.

The problem was, I realized as we raced across the southern hills, I was still furious with their leader.

My duty was clear: I had to escape.

Our last night before crossing the border we spent in a well-stocked cave, tucked up high on a rocky hill near a waterfall. The roar of the water was soothing, and the moist, cool air felt great after a long, hot ride. Until we were settled in I didn't notice that we were seven instead of nine, but as no one seemed concerned, I realized that two of them—tired as they must have been—had ridden on ahead.

As I rolled up in my sleeping bag, I felt an intense wave of homesickness. How many times had I camped out in just such places, high up in Tlanth? The sounds and smells of home permeated my dreams, making me wake up in a restless mood.

I was still restless when we rode over the bridge that spanned the river border. Restless and angry and apprehensive by turns. Not long after we crossed the border we stopped at an outpost, and there changed horses. Nessaren and the others all wanted to ride flat out for the capital. I wasn't asked my opinion.

Don't think I wasn't on the watch for a chance to peel off, but anything their formation was now even tighter around me. I don't think it was even conscious—but there it was, I had about as much chance of getting away from them as a lone chicken had from a family of foxes.

Our road skirted a city built against a mountain. I caught glimpses of the terraced capital between cultivated hills. At the highest level was a castle, built on either side of a spectacular waterfall. A bridge lined with old trees crossed from one side to the other.

The castle slid out of sight as we rounded a hill and started up a road whose stones were worn smooth with age. Sentries in blue and black-and-white saluted us. I realized they thought I was one of them, and though no one even glanced twice at me, I felt more uncomfortable than ever.

After an uphill ride we emerged into a courtyard, horses' hooves clattering. The two members of the riding who'd left the night before came running out, along with several other people, all of them in the Renselaeus livery; some were in battle tunics, like Nessaren, and some in the shorter tunics and loose trousers of civilian wear.

Two of these latter came forward and for a moment they looked confused. With a smile—and accompanied by laughs from the others—Yora Nessaren indicated me. The two servants bowed. "Will you honor us by following this way, my lady?"

Behind me the others were chattering happily, exchanging news as they unloaded the horses. Soon they were out of earshot, and once again I walked with silent servants up a hallway. They were on either side of me, just out of reach, which diminished my chances of tripping them and scooting away. *All right, then*, I decided, *I will just have to make my break after whatever unpleasant interview is awaiting me.*

The hallway led to a circular stairway with two or three doors on each landing. Round four or five times upward, then we entered a very different type of hallway. Instead of the usual stone, or the tile of the wealthy, the floors were of exceptionally fine mosaic in a complicated pattern; but that only drew my eye briefly. Along one wall were high, arched windows whose diamond-shaped panes of clear glass looked out onto the terraced city below. It was an impressive sight.

At the end of the hall we trod up more stairs, wide, shallow, and tiled, passing beneath a domed glass ceiling. Around me small, carefully tended trees grew in pots.

Beyond those to another hall, with four doors—not woven doors, but real colorwood ones—redwood, bluewood, goldwood, greenwood—beautifully carved and obviously ancient.

The servants opened one and bowed me into a round-walled room that meant we were in a tower; windows on three sides looked out over the valley. The room was flooded with light, so much that I was dazzled for a moment and had to blink. Shading my eyes, I had a swift impression of a finely carved and gilded redwood table surrounded by blue satin cushions. Then I saw that the room was occupied.

Standing between two of the windows, almost hidden by slanting rays of sun, was a tall figure with pale blond hair.

The Marquis was looking down at the valley, hands clasped behind him. At the sound of the door closing behind me he looked up and came forward, and for a moment was a silhouette in the strong sunlight.

I stood with my back to the door. We were alone.

"Welcome to Renselaeus, Lady Meliara." And when I did not answer, he pointed to a side table. "Would you like anything to drink? To eat?"

"Why am I here?" I asked in a surly voice, suddenly and acutely aware of how ridiculous I must look dressed in his livery. "You may as well get the threats out at once. All this politeness seems about as false as…" *As a courtier's word,* I thought, but speech wouldn't come and I just shook my head.

He returned no immediate answer; instead seemed absorbed in

pouring wine from a fine silver decanter into two jewel-chased goblets. One he held out silently to me.

I wanted to refuse, but I needed somewhere to look and something to do with my hands, and I thought hazily that maybe the wine would clear my head. All of the emotions of the past days seemed to be fighting for prominence in me, making rational thought impossible.

He raised his cup in salute and took a drink. "Would you like to sit down?" He indicated the table. The light fell on the side of his face, and, like on that first morning after we came down from the mountain, I saw the marks of fatigue under his eyes.

"No," I said, and gulped some wine to fortify myself. "Why aren't you getting on with the sinister speeches?" I had started off with plenty of bravado, but then a terrible thought occurred, and I squawked, "Bran—"

"No harm has come to your brother," he said, looking up quickly. "I am endeavoring to find the best way to express—"

Having finished the wine, I slammed the goblet down onto a side table, and to hide my sudden fear—for I didn't believe him— I said as truculently as possible, "If you're capable of simple truth, just spit it out."

"Your brother has agreed to a truce," the Marquis started.

"Truce? What do you mean, a 'truce'?" I snarled. "He wouldn't surrender, he *wouldn't*, unless you forced him by threats to me—"

"I have issued no threats. It was only necessary to inform him that you were on your way here. He agreed to join us, for purposes of negotiation—"

A sun seemed to explode behind my eyes. "You've got Bran? You used me to get my brother?"

"He's here," the Marquis said, but he didn't get any further.

Giving a wail of sheer rage, I plucked a heavy silver candleholder and flung it straight at his head.

SEVENTEEN

HE CAUGHT IT ONE-HANDED, SET IT GENTLY BACK
in its place.

I clenched my teeth together to keep from screaming.

The Marquis stepped to the door, opened it. "Please bring
Lord Branaric here."

Then he sat down in one of the window seats and looked out
as though nothing had happened. I turned my back and glared out
the other window, and a long, terrible silence drained my wits entirely until the door was suddenly thrust open by an impatient hand;
and there was my brother, tall, thinner than I remembered, and
clean. "Mel!" he exclaimed.

"Bran," I squawked, and hurled myself into his arms.

After a moment of incoherent questions on my part, he patted
my back then held me out at arm's length. "Here, Mel, what's this?
You look like death's cousin! Where'd you get that black eye? And
your hands—" He turned over my wrists, squinting down at the
healing rope burns. "Curse it, what's toward?"

"Debegri," I managed, laughing and crying at once. "Oh, Bran,
that's not the worst of it. Look at this!" I stuck out my bare foot
to show the purple scars. "That horrid trap—"

"We pulled 'em all out," he said, and grimaced. "It was the

ill Folk sent someone to tell us about you—that's a first, and did
scare me!—but by the time we got down the mountain, you were
ne. I'm sorry, Mel. You were right."

"I was s-s-s-*stupid*. I got caught, and now we're both in
ouble," I wailed into his shoulder.

The carved door snicked shut, and I realized we were alone. I
ve a great sob that seemed to come up from my dusty bare toes,
d all those pent-up emotions stormed out. Bran sighed and just
ld me for a long time, until at last I got control again and pulled
ay, hiccoughing. "T-Tell me how everyone is, and what hap-
ned?"

"Khesot, Julen, both are fine. Hrani cut up bad, but coming
rough. We lost young Omic and two of those Faluir villagers.
aat was when we tried a couple of runs on the greenie camp.
terward, though, we got up Debegri's nose but good," he said
th a grin. "Ho! I don't like to remember those early days. Our
ople were absolutely wild, mostly mad at me about those accursed
ps. After our second run, Shevraeth sent a warning under truce.
id you were on your way to Remalna-city, and we should hole
against further communication. Then we found out that the
ng had gone off on one of his tantrums—apparently wasn't best
eased to find that this fop of a marquis had done better in two
eks than his cousin had in two months, and gave the command
ck to Debegri. We enjoyed that." He grinned again, then winced.
Until Azmus appeared. Nearly killed himself getting to our camp.
ld us about the King's threat, and your escape, and that you'd
sappeared and he couldn't find you. Debegri left, with half his
my, and we knew it was to search for you. We waited for word.
d time, there."

"*You* think it was bad..." I started.

"Mmm." He hugged me again. "Tell me."

Vivid images chased through my mind: Shevraeth over the
mpfire; Galdran's throne room and that horrible laughter; the
cape; what Ara's mother said; that fortress. I didn't know how to

151

begin, so I shook my head and said, "Never mind it now. Tell me more."

He shrugged, rubbing his jaw. "Shevraeth sent us a message about six days ago, white flag, said he had you and wanted to discuss the situation with me—on our ground. He knew where we were! And next morning, there *they* were. We met at the Whitestream bridge. His people on one side, ours on the other. I was as itchy as a cat in dogland, afraid one or the other side would let loose on either me *or* him and either way there'd be blood for certain. He strolled out like it was a ballroom floor, cool as you please, said you were safe in his care—what's that?"

"I said, 'Hah!' "

He grinned. "Well, anyhow, he told me that Debegri was promised not just our lands but a dukedom if he could flush us out once and for all. Baron plans to fire us out, soon's the rains end. Shevraeth promised safe passage to and from Renselaeus—on his word—if I came along with him for a talk. He told me you were on your way, and said if I came, whatever we decided, you could return to Tlanth with me. Didn't see any way around it, so—" He lifted his hands. "Here I am. Rode all day two days, and all night last night, got here this morning. Must say, he's been decent enough—"

"I *hate* him and those Court smirkers!" I cried. "Hate, hate, hate—"

The door opened behind us, and we both whirled around rather guiltily.

A servant appeared, bowed, said, "My lord, my lady, His Highness Prince Alaerec requests the honor of your company at dinner. Should you wish to prepare, we are instructed to provide everything necessary."

Bran chuckled. "Wait until you see the bath they have here. One of these ice-faced Renselaeus toffs has to have been thick a thieves with a first-rate mage. No lowly bathhouses for this gang."

My face felt like a flame by then, but Bran didn't notice. "I'l have a little of that wine while you go on," he added, rubbing his hands.

This left me with nothing to do but follow the servant back down the hall and down one level of stairs to another hall. He opened a door, bowed, waited until I passed him, then closed the door again.

This left me in a room I had never seen anything even remotely like.

It reminded me of a stream in a forest. Trees grew alongside a wide running bath, all tiled and blue and clean. High windows let in clear light. *Magic, indeed*, I thought as I moved to the edge of the eddying water, I dipped a hand in, found that it was warm. *Lots of magic.*

A quiet rustle brought my head around; three maidservants gowned in blue and white came forward, bowed; and one said, "My lady, His Highness sends his compliments and begs you to make use of Her Highness's wardrobe."

I thought of that imperious voice at the palace and tried not to laugh. The change from oversized livery to an elderly lady's court frills and furbelows would probably manage to make me look more ridiculous than ever. But what alternative was there? My own clothes—such as they were—had been burned by Ara's mother a long time ago.

As soon as I was in that bath, though, these thoughts, and most of my other worries, were soothed away from my mind as the various aches were soothed from my body. It felt as if I were sitting in a rushing stream; only, the water was warm, and soft as finespun silk, and the soaps were subtly scented and made my skin glow. Everything was laid out for me, from comb to teeth cleaner.

There was even a salve to work through one's hair, one of the maids pointed out. She did it for me (which almost put me right to sleep, tired as I was) and afterward, the comb seemed to slide right through my hair.

Then, wrapped in a cape-sized towel that had been kept warm

153

on heatstones, I followed the maids into an adjacent room as large as the bath. There were trunks and trunks of fabrics of every type and hue.

Feeling like a trespasser, I fingered through the nearest, stopping when I saw a gown of green velvet. Tiny golden birds had been embroidered at the neck and down either side of the bodice laces. The sleeves, unlike the present fashions, were narrow, and embroidered at the cuffs. Tiny slits had been made at shoulders and elbows to pull through tufts of the silken underdress of pale gold. The fabrics whispered richly as the maids helped me to pull them on without tangling my hair, which hung, wet and free, to my knees. When the overdress settled around me, I discovered that the Princess was not much larger than I, which made me want to laugh.

Someone brought slippers, and I thought of Julen as I put them on and laced them. They were tight—the Princess obviously had tiny feet—but they were so soft it didn't much matter. Certainly they fit better than the outgrown mocs I'd gotten from the blacksmith's son.

When the gown was laced and the sleeves adjusted, one of the maids brought out a mirror. I looked in surprise at myself; the gown made me look taller, but nothing could make me seem larger. My face looked *old* to my eyes, and kind of grim, the black eye ridiculous.

I turned away quickly. "I'm ready. Where is my brother?"

In answer one of the maids bowed and scurried out the door, her steps soundless on the tiles. One of the others bore away Nessaren's clothes, and the third opened a door for me and bowed; and I walked through, feeling like a real fool. I was afraid I'd forget about the train dragging behind me, trip, and go rolling down the stairs, so I grabbed fistfuls of skirt at either side and walked carefully after her.

"Ho, Mel! You look like you're treading on knives." Branaric's voice came from behind me.

"Well, I don't want to ruin this gown. Isn't mine," I said.

He just grinned, and we were led down another level to an elegant room with a fire at one end and windows looking out over the valley. The sun was setting, and the scene below was bathed in the rosy-golden light.

We went forward. There were cushioned benches on either side of the fire, and directly before it a great carved chair. Shevraeth rose from one of the benches, making a gesture of welcome. Indicating the chair, in which sat a straight-backed old man dressed in black velvet, he said, "Father, I have the honor of introducing Lady Meliara Astiar." And to me, in the suavest voice, as if I hadn't flung a candleholder at his head just a little while before, "Lady Meliara, my father, Prince Alaerec."

The old man nodded slowly and with great dignity. He had keen dark eyes, and white hair which he wore loose on his shoulders in the old-fashioned way. "My dear, please forgive me if I do not rise. I am afraid I do not get about with ease or grace anymore."

I felt an impulse to bow, and squashed it. I remembered that Court women sweep curtsys—something my mother had tried once to teach me, when I was six. I also remembered that I was there against my will—a prisoner, despite all the fine surroundings and polite talk—so I just crossed my arms and said, "Don't think you have to walk about on my behalf."

Bran gave me a slightly bemused look and bobbed an awkward bow to the old man.

A servant came forward, silent and skillful, and passed out goblets of wine. The Prince saluted me in silence, followed by Bran and Shevraeth. I looked down at my goblet, then took a big gulp that made my nose sting.

In a slow, pleasant voice, Prince Alaerec asked mild questions—weather, travel, Bran's day and how he'd filled it. I stayed silent as the three of them worked away at this limping conversation. The Renselaeus father and son were skilled enough at nothing-talk, but poor Bran stumbled over half his words, sending frequent glances at me. In the past I'd often spoken for both of us, for truth was he

155

felt awkward with his tongue and was somewhat shy with new people, but I did not feel like speaking until I'd sorted my emotions out—and there was no time for that.

To bridge his own feelings, my brother gulped at the very fine wine they offered. Soon a servant came in and announced that dinner was ready, and the old Prince rose slowly, leaning heavily on a cane. His back was straight, though, as he led the way to a dining room. Bran and I fell in behind, I treading cautiously, with my skirts bunched in either hand.

Bran snickered. I looked up, saw him watching me, his face flushed. "Life, Mel, are you supposed to walk like that?" He snickered again, swallowed the rest of his third glass of wine, then added, "Looks like you got eggs in those shoes."

"I don't *know* how I'm supposed to walk," I mumbled, acutely aware of that bland-faced, elegantly dressed Marquis right behind us, and elbowed Bran in the side. "Stop laughing! If I drop these skirts, I'll trip over them."

"Why didn't you just ask for riding gear?"

"And a coach-and-six while I was at it? This is what they *gave* me."

"Well, it looks right enough," he admitted, squinting down at me. "It's just—seeing you in one of those fancy gowns reminds me of—"

I didn't want to hear what it reminded him of. "You're drunk as four skunks, you idiot," I muttered, and not especially softly, either. "You'd best lay it aside until you get some food into you."

He sighed. "Right enough. I confess, I didn't think you'd really get here—thought that there'd be another bad hit."

"Well, I don't see we're all that safe yet," I said under my breath.

The dining room was formidably elegant—I couldn't take it in all at once. A swift glance gave the impression of the family colors, augmented by gold, blended with artistry and grace. The table was igh, probably to accommodate the elderly Prince. The chairs, one or each diner, were especially fine—no angles, everything curves nd ovals and pleasing lines.

The meal, of course, was just as good. Again I left the others to vork at a polite conversation. I bent my attention solely to my ood, eating a portion of every single thing offered, until at last— nd I never thought it would happen again, so long it had been— was truly stuffed.

This restored to me a vestige of my customary good spirits, nough so that when the Prince asked me politely if the dinner had een sufficient, and if he could have anything else brought out, I miled and said, "It was splendid. Something to remember all my ife. But—" I realized I was babbling, and shut up.

The Prince's dark eyes narrowed with amusement, though his nouth stayed solemn—I knew I'd seen that expression before. Please. You have only to ask."

"I don't want a thing. It was more a question, and that is: If ou can eat like this every day, why aren't you fatter than five xen?"

Bran set his goblet down, his eyes wide. "Burn it, Mel, I was ust thinking the very same!"

That was the moment I realized that, though our rank was as igh as theirs, or nearly, and our name as old, Branaric and I must ave sounded as rustic and ignorant as a pair of backwoods twig atherers. It ruined my mood. I put my fork down and scrutinized ne Prince for signs of the sort of condescending laughter that vould—no doubt—make this a rich story to pass around Court as oon as we were gone.

Prince Alaerec said, "During my peregrinations about the vorld, I discovered some surprising contradictions in human nature.)ne of them is that, frequently anyway, the more one has, the less ne desires."

His voice was mild and pleasant, and impossible to divine any irect meaning from. I turned for the first time to his son, to meet that same assessing gaze I remembered from our first encounter. How long had *that* been trained on me?

Now thoroughly annoyed, I said, "Well, if you're done listening to us sit here and make fools of ourselves, why don't we get on to whatever it is you're going to hold over our heads next?"

Neither Renselaeus reacted. It was Bran who blinked at me in surprise and said, "Curse it, Mel, where are your wits at? Didn't Shevraeth tell you? We're part of their plan to kick Galdran off his throne!"

EIGHTEEN

WHAT?" I YELLED. AND I OPENED MY MOUTH TO
complain *Nobody told me anything*, but I recalled a certain interview,
not long ago, that had ended rather abruptly when a candleholder
had—ah—changed hands. Grimacing, I said in a more normal
voice, "When did this happen?"

"That's the joke on us." Bran laughed. "They've been at it as
long as we have. Longer, even."

I looked from father to son and read nothing in those bland,
polite faces. "Then...why...didn't you respond to our letter?"

As I spoke the words, a lot of things started making sense.

I thought back to what Ara's father had said, and then I remembered Shevraeth's words about the purpose of a court. When
I glanced at Prince Alaerec, he saluted me with his wineglass; just
a little gesture, but I read in it that he had comprehended a good
deal of my thoughts.

Which meant that *my* face, as usual, gave me away—and of
course this thought made my cheeks burn.

He said, "We admire—tremendously—your courageous efforts
to right the egregious wrongs obtaining in Remalna."

Thinking again of Ara's father and Master Kepruid the innkeeper, I said, "But the people don't welcome armies trampling

through their houses and land, even armies on their side. I take it you've figured out some miraculous way around this?"

Bran slapped his palm down on the table. "That's it, Mel— where we've been blind. We were trying to push our way in from without, but Shevraeth, here, has been working from within." He nodded in the Prince's direction. "Both—all three of 'em, in fact."

I blinked, trying to equate with a deadly plot an old, imperious voice whose single purpose seemed to be the safety of her clothing. "The Princess is part of this, too?"

"She is the one who arranged your escape from Athanarel," Shevraeth said to me. "The hardest part was finding your spy."

"You knew about Azmus?"

"I knew you had to have had some kind of contact in Remalnacity, from some of the things you said during our earlier journey. We had no idea who, or what, but we assumed that this person would display the same level of loyalty your compatriots had when you first fell into our hands, and I had people wait to see who might be lurking around the palace, watching."

Questions crowded my thoughts. But I pushed them all aside, focusing on the main one. "If you're rebelling, then you must have someone in mind for the throne. Who?"

Bran pointed across the table at Shevraeth. "He seems to want to do it, and I have to say, he'd be better at it than I."

"No, he wouldn't," I said without thinking.

Bran winced and rubbed his chin. "Mel…"

"Please, my dear Lord Branaric," the Prince murmured. "Permit the lady to speak. I am interested to hear her thoughts on the matter."

Rude as I'd been before, my response had shocked even me, and I hadn't intended to say anything more. Now I sneaked a peek at the Marquis, who just sat with his goblet in his fingers, his expression one of mild questioning.

I sighed, short and sharp. "You'd be the best because you *aren't* Court trained," I said to Bran. It was easier than facing those other wo. "Court ruined, I'd say. You don't lie—you don't even know how to lie in social situations like this. I think it's time the kingdom's leader is known for honesty and integrity, not for how well he gambles or how many new fashions he's started. Otherwise we'll just be swapping one type of bad king for another."

Bran drummed his fingers on the table, frowning. "But I don't want to do it. Not alone, anyway. If you are with me—"

"I'm not going to Remalna-city," I said quickly.

All three of them looked at me—I could feel it, though I kept my own gaze on my brother's face. His eyes widened. I said, "You're the one who always wanted to go there. I've been. Once. It's not an experience I'd care to repeat. You'd be fine on your own," I finished weakly, knowing that he wouldn't—that I'd just managed, through my own anger, to ruin his chances.

"Mel, I don't know what to say. Where t'start, burn it!" Bran ran his fingers through his hair, snarling it up—a sure sign he was upset. "Usually it's you with the quick mind, but this time I think you're dead wrong."

"On the contrary," the Prince said, with a glance at his son. "She makes cogent points. And there will be others aside from the royalists in Tlanth who will, no doubt, share a similar lack of partisanship."

"Your point is taken, Father," Shevraeth said. "It is an issue that I will have to address."

Sensing that there was more meaning to their words than was immediately obvious, I looked from one to the other for clues, but of course there were none that I could descry.

Branaric filled his glass again. "So, what exactly is it you want from us?"

"Alliance," Shevraeth said. "How that will translate into practical terms is this: You withdraw to your home, to all appearances willing to negotiate a truce. I shall do my best to prevail upon Galdran to accept this truce, and we can protract it on technicalities for as long as may be, which serves a double purpose—"

"End the fighting, but honorably," Bran said, nodding. "I understand you so far. What if Debegri comes after us anyway?"

"In apprehension of that, my people are taking and holding the Vesingrui fortress on your border. For now they are wearing the green uniform, as servants of the Crown. If Debegri goes on the attack, I will send this force against him. If not—"

"They'll leave us be?"

"Yes."

"And if Debegri doesn't come?"

"You wait. I hope to achieve the objective peacefully, or with as little unpleasantness as possible. If it transpires that I do require aid in the southeast, I would like to be able to rely on you and your people as a resource."

"And after?"

"As we discussed. Honor the Covenant. No more forced levies; tax reform; trade reestablished with the outside, minus the tariffs that went into the Merindar personal fortune. That's to start."

Bran shrugged, rubbed his hands from his jaw to through his hair, then he turned to me. "Mel?"

"I would prefer to discuss it later," I said.

"What's to discuss?" Bran said, spreading his hands.

"The little matter of the crown," Shevraeth said dryly. "If we are finished, I propose we withdraw for the evening. We are all tired and would do the better for a night's sleep."

I turned to him. "You said to Bran we can leave, whatever we decide."

He bowed.

"Good. We'll leave in the morning. First light."

Bran's jaw dropped.

"I want to go home," I said fiercely.

The Prince must have given some signal undiscernible to me, for suddenly a servant stood behind my chair, to whom Prince Alaerec said, "Please conduct the Countess to the chamber prepared for her."

I got up, said to Bran, "I'll need something to wear on the ride ome."

He slewed around in his chair. "But—"

I said even more fiercely than before, "Do you really think I ught to wear *this* home—even if it were mine, which it isn't?"

"All right." Branaric rubbed his eyes. "Curse it, I can't think r this headache on me. Maybe I'd better turn in myself."

He fell in step beside me and we were led out. I walked with s much dignity as I could muster, holding that dratted skirt out way from my feet. My shoulder blades itched; I imagined the two enselaeuses staring, and I listened for the sound of their laughter ng after we'd traversed the hall and gone up a flight of stairs.

slept badly.

It wasn't the fault of the room, which was charmingly furnished, r the bed, which was softer than anything I'd ever slept on. And wasn't as if I weren't tired, for I was. After restless tossing half ie night, I decided I just needed—desperately—to be home, and rose and sat in the window seat to look up at the stars.

I fell asleep there at last, and didn't waken until a maid came .. She looked slightly surprised at seeing me sitting in the window my borrowed nightgown, my head on my knees, but said no- ing beyond, "Good morning, my lady." Then she bowed and id a bundle on the bed. "His Highness requests the honor of ur company at breakfast, whenever you are ready. Do you need ything?"

"No. Thanks."

She bowed again and withdrew.

After another bath in that wondrous room I put on the clothes ie maid had brought, which turned out to be an old shirt, that een tunic Hrani had remade for Branaric, now considerably the orse for a winter's wear, and some trousers. I had to use the laces om the shirt to belt up the trousers, and the sleeves were much

163

too long, making awkward rolls at my wrists, but the outsized tunic covered it all.

I was just brushing my hair out when there was a quick knock at the door. Branaric came in. "Ready?"

"Nearly," I said, my fingers quickly starting the braid. "I suppose you don't have extra gloves, or another hat?" I eyed the battered object he held in his hand. "No, obviously not. Well, I can ride bareheaded. Who's to see me that I care about?"

He smiled briefly, then gave me a serious look. "Are you certain you don't want to join the alliance?"

"Yes."

He sank down heavily onto the bed and pulled from his tunic a flat-woven wallet. "I don't know, Mel. What's toward? You wouldn't even listen yesterday, or hardly. Isn't like you, burn it!"

"I don't trust these cream-voiced courtiers as far as I can spit into a wind," I said as I watched him pull from the wallet a folded paper. "And I don't see why we should risk any of our people, or our scarce supplies, to put one of them on the throne. If he wants to be king, let him get it on his own."

Bran sighed, his fingers working at the shapeless brim of his hat. "I think you're wrong."

"You're the one who was willed the title," I reminded him. "I'm not legally a countess—I haven't sworn anything at Court. Which means it's just a courtesy title until *you* marry. You can do whatever you want, and you have a legal right to it."

"I know all that. Why are you telling me again? I remember we both promised when Papa died that we'd be equals in war and in peace. You think I'll renege, just because we disagree for the first time? If so, you must think me as dishonest as you paint them." He jerked his thumb back at the rest of the Renselaeus palace. I could see that he was upset.

"I don't question you, Bran. Not at all. What's that paper?"

Instead of answering, he tossed it to me. I unfolded it carefully, for it was so creased and battered it was obvious it had seen a great deal of travel. Slowly and painstakingly I puzzled out the words—then looked up in surprise. "This is Debegri's letter about the colorwoods!"

"Shevraeth asked about proof that the Merindars were going to break the Covenant. I brought this along, thinking that—if we were to join them—they could use it to convince the rest of Court of Galdran's treachery."

"You'd *give* it to them?" I demanded.

Bran sighed. "I thought it a good notion, but obviously you don't. Here. You do whatever you think best. I'll bide by it." He dropped the wallet onto my lap. "But I wish you'd give them a fair listen."

I folded the letter up, slid it inside the waterproof wallet, and then put it inside my tunic. "I guess I'll have to listen to the other, at any rate, over breakfast." As I wrapped my braid around my head and tucked the end under, I added, "Which we'd better get to as soon as possible, so we have a full day of light on the road."

"You go ahead—it was you the Prince invited. I'll chow with Shevraeth. And be ready whenever you are."

It was with a great sense of relief that I went to the meal, knowing that I'd only have to face one of them. *And for the last time ever*, I vowed as the ubiquitous servants bowed me into a small dining room.

The Prince was already seated in a great chair. With a graceful gesture he indicated the place opposite him, and when I was seated, he said, "My wife will regret not having had a chance to meet you, Lady Meliara."

Wondering what this was supposed to mean, I opened my hands. I hoped it looked polite—I was not going to lie and say I wished I might have met her, for I didn't, even if it was true that she had aided my palace escape.

The door opened, and food was brought in and set before us. The last thing the server did was to pour a light brown liquid into a porcelain cup. The smell was interesting, though I didn't recognize it.

"What is this?" I asked.

The servant had withdrawn. "Chocolate," said Prince Alaerec. "From the southeast. I thought you might enjoy it."

I took a cautious taste, then a more enthusiastic one. "It's good!"

He smiled and indicated I was to help myself from the various chafing dishes set before us. Which I did, with a very liberal hand, for I didn't know when or where Bran and I would eat next.

When we were finished, the Prince said, "Have you any further questions concerning the matter we discussed last night?"

"One." While I felt no qualms about being rude to his son, I was reluctant to treat the elderly man the same. "You really have been planning this for a long time?"

"For most of my life."

"Then why didn't you respond? Offer to help us—at least offer a place in your alliance—when Bran and I sent our letter to the King at the start of winter?"

The Prince paused to take a sip of his coffee. I noted idly that he had long, slim hands like his son's. Had the Prince ever wielded a sword? *Oh yes—wasn't he wounded in the Pirate Wars?*

"There was much to admire in your letter," he said with a faint smile. "Your forthright attitude, the scrupulous care with which you documented each grievance, all bespoke an earnestness, shall we say, of intent. What your letter lacked, however, was an equally lucid plan for what to do after Galdran's government was torn down."

"But we did include one," I protested.

He inclined his head. "In a sense. Your description of what the government ought to be was truly enlightened. Yet…as the military would say, you set out a fine strategy, but failed to supplement it with any kind of tactical carry-through." His eyes narrowed ghtly, and he added, "It is always easiest to judge where one is norant—a mistake we made about you, and that we have striven correct—but it seemed that you and your adherents were ide- stic and courageous, yet essentially foolhardy, folk. We were very uch afraid you would not last long against the sheer weight of aldran's army, its poor leadership notwithstanding."

I thought this over, looking for hidden barbs—and for hidden eanings.

He said, "If you should change your mind, or if you simply ed to communicate with us, please be assured you shall be lcome."

It seemed that, after all, I was about to go free. "I confess I'll l a lot more grateful for your kindness after I get home."

He set his cup down and steepled his fingers. "I understand," murmured. "Had I lived through your recent experiences, I ex- ct I might have a similar reaction. Suffice it to say that we wish u well, my child, whatever transpires."

"Thank you for that," I said awkwardly, getting to my feet.

He also rose. "I wish you a safe, swift journey." He bowed over y hand with graceful deliberation.

I left then, but for the first time in days I didn't feel quite so d about recent events.

ound Bran in the courtyard below. Two fresh, mettlesome horses aited us, and Bran had a bag at his belt. Shevraeth himself was ere to bid us farewell—a courtesy I could have done without. npatient to be gone, I stayed silent as he and my brother ex- anged some last words.

Then, at last, Shevraeth stepped back. "Do you remember the ute?"

Bran nodded. "Well enough. My thanks again—" He looked er at me, then sighed. "Another time, I trust." I realized then at he actually *liked* the Marquis—that in some wise (as much as

167

a Court decoration and an honest man ill trained in the niceties of high society could) they had become friends.

Shevraeth turned to me, bowed. There was no irony visible in face or manner as he wished me a safe journey. I felt my face go hot as I gritted out a stilted "Thank you." Then I turned in my saddle and my horse spun about. Branaric was with me in a moment, and side by side we rode out.

And in silence we began our journey. The horses seemed to want speed, which gladdened my heart. I turned my back on the terraced city with its thundering fall; faced east and home.

We stopped at noon to rest the horses, and to eat the packet of food someone had given Bran while I was at breakfast. Sitting under a tree, dabbling my feet in a stream, I felt my restlessness wash away and my spirits soar. Branaric seemed unusually quiet. His face, customarily so good-humored, was somber.

"Cheer up," I said. "We'll soon be home."

He looked up, his bread half forgotten in his hand. "And forsworn."

A cold feeling went through me. "No." I shook my head. "Galdran will fall—*if* they're telling the truth—which is what Papa wanted."

"He wanted us to help, and to lend our strength to rebuilding afterward. Now we're to sit and watch it all from a distance." He looked down at his bread and pitched it across the stream, where a flock of noisy blue-plumaged tzillis squabbled over it. "Why do you persist in thinking they are liars? They haven't lied to me. What lies did they tell you?"

"Half-truths," I muttered. "Court-bred..."

"You keep plinking out that same tune, Mel, but the truth is—" He stopped, shook his head.

"Go ahead." The coldness in my middle turned to a sick feeling. "Get it out."

"No use." He shrugged. "If I were going to pitch into you, I ought to have done it last night, but it didn't seem fair to do it on their turf. Come on, let's go home." He climbed back onto his horse. I followed, and in silence once more we took to the road.

That night we stayed at an inn. We had good rooms, and an excellent meal, all paid for by Renselaeus beneficence. Bran's mood stayed somber even through the fine music of some wandering minstrels who played for the common room, and he went early to bed.

Enough of his mood lingered that, for the first time, I did not slip into the magical spell of music but listened with only part of my mind. The other part kept reviewing memories I would rather forget, and portions of conversations, until at last I gave up and went to my room. There I took out and puzzled my way through Debegri's entire letter, which made me angry all over again. I spent a very restless night.

Branaric woke me the next morning with an impatient knock. As soon as we'd bathed, dressed, and breakfasted, we were on the road, with new horses. Bad weather followed us; the wind chased coldly through the trees, and the air was heavy with the smell of impending rain. The edge of a storm caught us in the last afternoon, but we kept riding until sundown. It became apparent that Bran was looking for somewhere specific. We finally reached a small town and slowed until we rode into the courtyard of an inn on its market square.

This was just as the rain hit in earnest.

That night I lay in another clean bed, listening to the wind howl and a tree scratch at the window with twiggy fingers. It was a mournful, uncanny sound that disturbed my dreams.

The storm passed west and south just before dawn, leaving a cold, dripping world. Now we had reached the heavy forestland at the base of the mountains; by midday we would reach the lowest border of Tlanth.

Even Bran seemed slightly more cheery at the prospect of

getting home, and we both rose early and ate quickly, eager to get going.

Until that morning most of the journey had been made in silence, our stops to eat and change horses—again, Renselaeus beneficence: all we had to do was mention their name, and the horses were instantly available—too brief for much converse. When we did stop, we were both too tired to talk. But that day the roads were too muddy for fast travel, and Branaric suddenly turned to me and asked for my story, so I gave him a detailed description of my adventures.

I had just reached the episode at the fountain with Debegri, and was grinning at the fluency and point of Bran's curses, when we became aware of horses behind us.

Traffic had been nonexistent all day, which we had expected. No traders had been permitted to go up into Tlanth for months. We were on the southernmost road into Tlanth, well away from Vesingrui, the fortress that the Renselaeus forces supposedly held, so we didn't expect any military traffic, either.

"Sounds like at least one riding," I said, remembering that pattern well. Danger prickled along my nerves, and I wished I had a weapon.

"Something must have happened." Bran sounded unconcerned. "They must need to tell us—"

"Who? What?"

Bran shrugged. "Escort. Shevraeth sent it along to keep us safe. Knew you would refuse, so they've been behind us the whole way."

I was peering through the trees, anger and apprehension warring inside me. Annoyed as I was to be thus circumvented—and to have my reactions so accurately predicted—I realized I'd be well satisfied to find out that the approaching riders were indeed Renselaeus equerries.

The Renselaeus colors would have stood out, but the green-and-brown of Galdran's people blended into the forest; they were almost on us before we saw them, and Bran yelled, "It's a trap!"

"Halt!" The shout rang through the trees.

Of course we bolted.

"Halt, or we shoot," came a second yell.

"Bend down, bend—ah!"

Bran's body jerked, then he fell forward, an arrow in his back.

NINETEEN

OUR HORSES PLUNGED UP THE TRAIL.

"Go on...Go!" Bran jerked one hand toward the mountains, then swayed in his saddle.

Another arrow sang overhead.

"I won't leave you," I snapped.

"Go. Our people...Carry on the fight."

"Bran—"

In answer he yanked the reins on his terrified horse, which lunged toward mine. Gritting his teeth, he leaned out and whipped the ends of his reins across the mare's shoulder. *"Go!"*

My mount panicked, leaped forward. My neck snapped back. I clutched to the horse's mane with all my strength. The last glimpse I had of Bran was of his white face and his anxious eyes watching me as he and his mount fell back.

And then I was on my own.

For a time the mare raced straight up the trail while the only thought I could hold in my mind was, *A trap? A trap?* And then the image, seen endlessly, of Bran being shot.

Then a scrap of memory floated up before my inner eye. Again I saw the elegant Renselaeus dining room, heard the Marquis's refined drawling voice: *My people are taking and holding the Vesingrui ortress on your border. For now they are wearing the green uniform...*

A trap. Cold fury washed through me. *They have betrayed us.*

It was then that I recovered enough presence of mind to realize that I was in my home territory at last, and I could leave the trail anytime. The horse had recovered from the panic and was trotting. So I recaptured the reins, leading the horse across the side of the mountain toward the thickest, oldest part of the local forest. It didn't take me long to lose the pursuit, and then I turned my tired mare north, permitting her to slow as I thought everything through.

It made perfect sense, after all. Bran and I were certainly an inconvenience, especially since we'd refused to ally. For a moment guilt tweaked at my thoughts—if it hadn't been for me, we'd both be alive and well in their capital. And in their hands, I told myself. If they could cold-bloodedly plan this kind of treachery, wasn't this sort of end waiting for us anyway?

And now Bran is dead. Branaric, my fun-loving, trusting brother, the one who pleaded with me to give them a fair chance. Who wanted to be their friend.

All my emotions narrowed to one arrow of intent: revenge.

It was nightfall, under a heavy storm, when I reached Erkan-Astiar, home to my family for over five hundred years. I didn't even go to the castle, which looked dark and cold. I went straight to the smithy, and there found Julen and Calaub sitting down to tea and porridge.

Within a short time all our leaders were crowded together in their tiny kitchen. Celebration at my appearance was short-lived, for as soon as I had them together I told them what had happened, withholding no detail.

Anger—grief—fear—questions—disbelief: These were the reactions from our people. Some expressed a variety of these reactions, as questions and amplifications went back and forth.

Finally, there in the old smithy under a howling wind, I

173

formally set everyone free of the oath they'd sworn to Bran and me. "We can't win, not now," I said, with tears burning my eyes. "But those who want to take a few of them with us when we go down, come with me."

Devan gripped his club, glowering up at the ceiling. "We goin' against Vesingrui?"

I nodded, wiping my eyes on the sleeve of my tunic, wet as it was. "Supposedly they took it to watch for Debegri's soldiers, but I expect they're there to keep us divided from the rest of the kingdom. An all-out attack on that fortress will achieve something."

It was mostly the young—all Branaric's particular friends, and mine—who stepped forward. I said to them, "We'll leave as soon as you can get every weapon you can lay hold of. Choose only the experienced, surefooted mounts, for we'll travel all night and attack at dawn."

Khesot sat across from me at the table, silent, smoking his pipe. When everyone had left, some to get their weapons and others to go home, he squinted at me over the drifting silver smoke and said, "You ought to be certain you are right."

"I am."

He shook his head slowly.

"You don't believe me?" I demanded.

"I believe every word you have said, my lady," he murmured, his quiet tone a gentle reproof. "But there remain enough questions to make me feel that there might yet be another explanation."

"What else could there be? They were the only ones who knew where we were—and who."

He pursed his lips. "I swore I would stay with you until the end, whether victory or defeat, and so I will. But this seems a foolhardy death you lead our folk to. Let me propose this. I will come with you—and I expect others will follow, if I go—if you grant me one thing, an initial scouting party."

Instinct fought against common sense. My wish was to ride with steel in either hand to death and destruction, as quickly as possible.

Nothing, ever, could extinguish the terrible pain in my heart, except annihilation. But I had been raised to think of others, and so I forced myself to agree, though with no real grace.

He rose, bowed, and went out. I knelt there on Julen's soggy cushion, staring at my own hands wrapped around the squat mug I'd known since I was small. My hands looked like a stranger's, taut and white knuckled.

There was a quiet step, and I looked up.

"I saved this for you," said Oria, her pretty face unwontedly somber as she held out my short sword.

I took it, turned it over in my hands. "Are you coming with me?"

She looked over her shoulder. "Mama said I can do what I want. There are a lot of us whose families are arguing it out right now."

"I'm sorry," I said tightly, though I wasn't. *Go...our people... carry on the fight...* When I closed my eyes, I saw Bran's white, pain-grim face. I shook my head, resolving not to close my eyes again.

Oria dropped down on the cushion beside me. "I'd rather die tonight than live with—your brother gone, and us under Debegri's rule." She smiled sadly, her brown eyes shiny with unshed tears. "Why is it the songs all end with the good people winning, but in life they don't?"

"They don't make songs when the good lose," I muttered. "They make more war chants against the bad. So there won't be any songs for us." *Just laughter—*

Your brother has agreed to a truce. Shevraeth's smooth voice, and Galdran's harsh laughter, echoed with cruel antiphony through my aching skull. I got to my feet. "It's time to go."

Soon we were riding through the chill, wet night air, me in a bor-rowed hat probably older than I was. Despite the hiss of rain in the

175

trees, we could hear the weird high singing of the Hill Folk's harps, a different sound than any I'd heard yet. The sound seemed to thrum in my bones, and the horses were all skittish.

But we rode steadily, knowing the way despite the minimal light that the moon provided through the rain clouds. Taking little-known paths straight down the mountain, we reached the ridge directly above the fortress well before dawn. There we dismounted, hidden in the ancient trees. The mounts were led away, and the rest of us gathered behind the stones at the edge of the rough cliffs.

Khesot came forward. "We'll go now."

He and his chosen four scouts slipped down through the soggy brush toward the fortress, which was merely a dark bulk below us. The only clear light was on the bridge over the Whitestream, sputtering red torches that cast light on the four sentries walking back and forth.

My eyes stayed on those four half-discernible figures as I wormed my way slowly downhill and took up a position between some rocks, my sword gripped in my hand. A distant portion of my mind was aware of my shivering body; the rain trickling down my scalp into my tunic, which was already heavy with moisture; the tiny noises of the others moving into position around our end of the bridge; and the sound of the tumbling, rushing water below, which drowned the high keening of the Hill Folk harps on the peaks.

A faint movement distracted me as Oria elbow-crawled up to my side. Her profile was outlined by the light from those faraway torches as she looked down on the castle below.

"I'm sorry, Oria," I breathed.

She did not turn her head. "For what?"

"All our plans when we were growing up. All the fine things we'd have had after we won. Making you a duchess—"

She grunted softly. "That was no more than dream-weaving. I don't want to be a duchess. Never did. Well, after my fourteenth year, I didn't. That was you, wanting it for me."

For the first time a flicker of emotion broke briefly through the aching numbness around my heart. "But when we talked..."

She rested her chin on her tightly folded fists, staring down at the castle. I could see tiny reflections of the ruddy torches in her eyes, so steady and unblinking was her gaze. "The only way for me to be a noble is to become a scribe or a herald and work my way up through the government service ranks, and I don't want to write others' things, or to take records, and I don't want to get mixed up with governments—with the kind of people who want to rule over others. Seems like the wrong people get killed, the nice ones. I want..." She sighed and stopped.

"Tell me," I said. "We can dream-weave once more."

"I want to run a house. You can *control* that—make life comfortable, and pleasant, and beautiful. My dream was always that, or partly that..."

Once again she stopped, and this time the gleam of the torches in her eyes was liquid. A quick motion with her finger, a lowering of her long lashes, and the gleam was gone.

"Go on," I said.

She dropped her head down. "You never saw it, Mel. You're just what Mama calls you, a summer flower, a late bloomer."

"I don't understand."

She breathed a laugh. "I know. That's just it! Well, it's all nothing now, so why not admit what a henwit I've been? There's another way to be an aristo, and that's marriage. I never cared about status so much as I did about the idea of marriage. With a specific person."

"Marriage," I repeated, and then a blindingly new idea struck me. "You mean—Branaric?"

She shrugged. "I gave it up three summers ago, when I realized that our living like sisters all our lives meant he saw me as one."

"Oh, Ria." Pain squeezed my heart. "How I wish our lives had gone differently! If Bran were alive—"

"It still wouldn't have happened," she murmured. "And I've

177

already made my peace with it. That's an old dream. I'm here now because Debegri will do his best to kill our new dreams." She nudged me with her elbow. "Truth is, I rather liked being heart-free last summer, except you didn't notice that, either—you've never tried flirting, much less twoing. You just dance the dances to be dancing, you don't watch the boys watch you when we dance. You don't watch them dance." She chuckled softly. "You don't even peek at the boys' side at the bathhouse."

I reached back in memory, realized how much I had neglected to notice. Not that it had mattered.

My cold lips stretched into a smile. "The boys never looked at me, anyway. Not when they had you to look at."

"Some of that is who you are," she responded. "They never forgot that. But the rest is that you never cared when they did look at you."

And now it's too late. But I didn't say that. Instead, I turned my eyes to those four figures in their steady pacing and let my mind drift back to old memories, summer memories. How much of life had I missed while dedicating myself to Papa's war?

After an uncountable interval a voice murmured on my other side, "It's taking a long time." It was Jusar, our trained soldier. "Worries me."

With a jolt, I remembered Khesot and his party. Back to the war, and my losses. I steeled myself: no more dream drifting. "We'll watch the sentries, see if anyone comes out from the castle with a message for them," I whispered back. "That would mean trouble. Otherwise, as soon as we have light enough, we attack. Khesot or no."

He nodded. In the faint light from those torches below, I saw him swallow, then compress his lips, as though forming a resolve.

I returned to my vigil. The darkness seemed to endure forever, outside of me, inside. Now I wanted only to move, to run, to strike against a pair of watchful gray eyes and extinguish the light of aughter I saw there. And then be swallowed whole by the darkness, orever...

"Dawn."

I had dropped into another, darker reverie without knowing; Oria's soft voice broke it. I lifted my head, saw the faint bluish light ast barely distinguishing one tree from another. It touched the ortress, giving the flat bulk the dimension of depth, of height; and s I watched, the massive stones of the walls took on texture. From ae peaks there was silence.

Now that action was nigh, I felt a strange calm settle over me, lanketing me from emotion, from thought, even. Instinct would uide me. It remained only to give the signal, and emerge from our over, and attack.

I gripped my sword tighter and rose to my knees, bracing my-elf. Once I raised my arm, there would be no turning back.

A deep *graunch*ing noise, the protest of old metal, came from ae fortress, and I froze, waiting. My heart racketed in my chest as peered down through the early-morning gloom.

Slowly the big gates opened. Red-gold fire glow from inside lhouetted a number of figures who moved out toward the bridge, here the strengthening light picked out the drawn swords, the pears, the dark cloaks, and the helmed heads of the Renselaeus arriors. They were wearing their own colors, and battle gear. No veries, no pretense of being mere servants. In the center of their ormation were Khesot and the four others—unarmed.

There were no shouts, no trumpets, nothing but the ringing of on-shod boots on the stones of the bridge, and the clank of ready eaponry.

Could we rescue them? I could not see Khesot's face, but in ae utter stillness with which they stood, I read hopelessness.

I readied myself once again—

Then from the center of their forces stepped a single equerry, ith a white scarf tied to a pole. He started up the path that e meant to descend. As he walked the light strengthened, now illuminating details. Still with that weird detachment I looked at his curly hair, the freckles on his face, his small nose. *We could cut him down in moments*, I thought, and then winced the thought away. We were not Galdran. I waited.

He stopped not twenty-five paces from me and said loudly, "Countess, we request a parley."

Which made it obvious they knew we were there.

Questions skittered through my mind. Had Khesot talked? How otherwise could the enemy have seen us? The only noise now was the rain, pattering softly with the magnificent indifference of nature for the tangled passions of humans.

I stood up. "Here. State your message."

"A choice. You surrender, and your people can then disperse to their homes. Otherwise, we start with them." He pointed to the bridge. "Then everyone else." He lifted his hand, indicating the ridge up behind us.

I turned, and shock burned through me when I saw an un-countable host lined along the rocks we'd descended from half a night ago.

They had us boxed.

Surrounded. We had walked right into a waiting trap.

I looked down at the bridge again. Through the curtain of rain the figures were clearer now. Khesot, in the center, stood next to a tall slim man with pale yellow hair.

I closed my eyes, fought for control, then opened my eyes again. "Everyone goes to their homes? Including Khesot and the four down there?"

"Everyone," the boy said flatly, "except you, Countess."

Which meant I was staking my life against everyone else's. And of course there was no answer but one to be made to that.

With black murder in my heart, I flung my sword down rather than hand it over. Stepping across it, I walked past the equerry, whose footfalls I then heard crunching behind me.

Wild vows of death and destruction flowed through my mind

as I walked down the trail. No one moved. Only the incessant rain came down, a silver veil, as I slipped down the pathway, then reached the bridge, then crossed it, stalking angrily between the lines of waiting warriors.

When I neared the other end of the bridge, the Marquis turned his back and walked inside the fortress, and the others followed, Khesot and the four scouts still some distance from me. I could not see their faces, could not speak to them.

I walked through the big gates, which closed. Across the courtyard the south gates stood open, and before them mounted warriors waited.

With them were two saddled, riderless horses, one a familiar gray.

In silence the entourage moved toward them, and the Marquis mounted the gray, who sidled nervously, newly shod hooves ringing on the stones.

Khesot and the others were now behind me, invisible behind the crowd of warriors in Renselaeus colors, all of whom watched and waited in silence.

It was weird, dreamlike, the only reality the burning rage in my heart.

Someone motioned me toward the single riderless horse, and I climbed up. For a moment the ground seemed to heave under the animal's feet, but I shook my head and the world righted itself, and I glared through the softly falling rain to the cold gray gaze of the Marquis of Shevraeth, heir to Renselaeus.

His horse danced a few steps. He looked over his shoulder at me, the low brim of his hat now hiding his eyes.

"Ride," he said.

TWENTY

NO ONE ELSE SPOKE.

Surrounded by warriors but utterly isolated, I rode at a gallop through the quiet rain as daylight strengthened all around me. Birds squawked warnings, and once a deer crashed through a shrub and bounded with breathtaking grace across the road in front of us. Humans and horses stayed on their path, racing headlong.

I don't know how long we rode. At the time, the trip seemed endless; looking back, it was curiously short. Memory warps time, as it does the sights and sounds and smells of reality; for what shapes it is emotion, which can twist what seems clear, just as the surface of a pond seems to bend the stick thrust into the water.

I know only that we were still deep in the Old Forest, which meant a ride to the north, when at some point we left the road, and then the trails, and at last came to a clearing sheltered by ancient trees, in which stood a very old, mossy-stoned wood gatherer's cottage.

The riders fanned out, but my immediate escort rode straight to the overhanging rusty roof that formed a rudimentary barn. The Marquis dismounted and stretched out his hand to grip the bridle of my horse.

"Inside," he said to me.

I dismounted. Again the ground seemed to heave beneath my et, but I leaned against the shoulders of my mount until the world adied, and then I straightened up.

The Marquis walked toward the open doorway.

In a kind of blank daze, I followed the sweeping black cloak side and down a tiny hall, to a door made of old, rickety twigs und together. The Marquis opened this and waved me into a tle room. I took two steps inside it, looked—

And there, lying on a narrow bed, with books and papers strewn out him, was my brother, Branaric.

"Mel!" he exclaimed. "Burn it, you were right," he said past e. "Ran her to ground at Vesingrui, eh?"

A voice spoke behind me: "They were just about to drop on ."

I turned, saw the Marquis leaning in the doorway, a growing addle of rainwater at his feet.

For a long moment I could do nothing except stand as if rooted. he world seemed about to dissolve for a sickening moment, but I cked in a ragged breath and it righted again, and I threw myself wn on my knees next to the bed, knocking my soggy, shapeless t off, and hugged Branaric fiercely.

"Mel, Mel," Bran said, laughing, then he groaned and fell ack on his pillows. "Softly, girl. Curse it! I'm weak as a newborn tten."

"And will be for a time," came the voice from the doorway.)nce your explanations have been made, I exhort you to remem- er Mistress Kylar's warning."

"Aye, I've it well in mind," Bran said. And as the door closed, e looked up at me from fever-bright eyes. "He was right! Said ou'd go straight after 'em, sword and knife. What's with you?"

"You said, 'A trap.' I thought it was *them*," I muttered through ddenly numb lips. "Wasn't it?"

"Didn't you see the riding of greeners?" Bran retorted. "It was ebegri, right enough. He had paid informants in those inns, for he was on the watch for your return. Why d'you think Vidanric sent the escort?"

"Vidanric?"

"His name," Branaric said, still staring at me with that odd gaze. "You could try to use it—only polite. After all, Shevraeth is just a title, and he doesn't go about calling either of us Tlanth."

I'd rather cut out my tongue, I thought, but I said nothing.

"Anyway—life, sister—if he'd wanted me dead, why not in the comfort of his own home, where he could do a better job?"

I shook my head. "It made sense to me."

"It makes sense when you have a castle-sized grudge." He sighed. "It was the Renselaeus escort, hard on their heels, that attacked Debegri's gang and saved my life. Our friend the Marquis wasn't far behind—he'd just found out about the spies, he said. Between us we pieced together what happened, and what I said, and what you'd likely do. I thought you'd stay home. He said you'd ride back down the mountain breathing fire and hunting his blood. He was right." He started to laugh, but it came out a groan, and he closed his eyes for a long breath. Then, "Arrow clipped me on the right, or I'd be finished. But I can't talk long—I'm already feeling sick. Galdran is just behind Debegri. He's coming up to make an example of Tlanth himself. Talk all over the country-side..." He stopped, taking several slow breaths, then he squinted at me. "Ask Vidanric. He's the one explained it to me."

"First tell me, are we prisoners, or not?"

"No," Bran said. "But mark my words: The end is nigh. And we're either for Renselaeus or for Galdran."

"You mean Shevraeth is coming into the open?"

"Yes."

"Then—he's going to face the whole army?"

Bran breathed deeply again. "Galdran has very few friends," he murmured, then closed his eyes. "Go change. Eat."

I nodded, the numbness spreading from my lips to my brain, and to my heart. "Get your rest. We'll talk when you feel better."

I walked out, and closed the door, and leaned against it, my forehead grinding against the rough wood.

Finally I forced myself to look up, to move. A sudden, terrible weariness had settled over me. I saw an open door at the other end of the little hall, and yellow light pouring from it.

The light drew me more than anything. Straightening up, I crossed the hall. Inside the room Shevraeth sat at a rough stone table near a fireplace, in which a crackling fire roared. At one end of the table was spread a map, at the other a tray of food, as yet untouched. Against an adjacent wall was a narrow bed, with more papers and another map spread over its neatly smoothed blanket. Three or four warriors in the familiar livery sat on mats around the table, all talking in quiet voices, but when the Marquis saw me, they fell silent and rose to their feet.

In silence, they filed past me, and I was left alone with the person who, the day before, I'd wanted to kill even more than Galdran Merindar.

"Take a swig." Shevraeth held out a flagon. "You're going to need it, I'm afraid."

I crossed the room, sank cross-legged onto the nearest mat. With one numb hand I took the flagon, squeezed a share of its contents into my mouth; and gasped as the fire of distilled bristic burned its way inside me. I took a second sip and with stinging eyes handed the flagon back.

"Blue lips," he said, with that faint smile. "You're going to have a whopping cold."

I looked up at the color burning along his cheekbones, and the faint lines of strain in his forehead, and made a discovery. "So are you," I said. "Hah!" I added, obscurely pleased.

His mouth quirked. "Do you have any questions?"

"Yes." My voice came out hoarse, and I cleared my throat. "Bran said Galdran is coming after us. Why? I thought it had been made abundantly clear that—thanks to you—we were defeated, and that was after he'd already decided we were of no account."

"Here. Eat something." He pulled the tray over and pointed to the bread and cheese on it, and at the half of some kind of fruit tart.

I picked up the bread and bit into it as he said, "But his cousin did not encompass your defeat, despite the fact that you were outnumbered and outmaneuvered. This is the more galling for Galdran, you must understand, when you consider the enormous loss of prestige he has suffered of late."

"Loss of prestige? In what way?" I asked.

He sat back, his eyes glinting with amusement. "First there was the matter of a—very—public announcement of a pending execution, following which the intended victim escapes. Then…didn't you stop to consider that the countryside folk who endured many long days of constant martial interference in the form of searches, curfews, and threats might have a few questions about the justice of said threats—or the efficacy of all these armed and mounted soldiery tramping through their fields and farms unsuccessfully trying to flush a single unarmed, rather unprepossessing individual? Especially when said individual took great care not to endanger anyone beyond the first—anonymous—family to give her succor, to whom she promised there would be no civil war?"

I gasped. "I never promised that. How could I? I promised that Bran and I wouldn't carry our fight into their territory."

Shevraeth's smile was wry. "But you must know how gossip gets distorted when it burns across the countryside, faster than a summer hayfire. And you had given the word of a countess. You have to remember that a good part of our…influence…is vouch-safed in our status, after the manner of centuries of habit. It is a strength and a weakness, a good and an evil."

I winced, thinking of Ara, who knew more about history than I did.

"Though you seem to be completely unaware of it, you have become a heroine to the entire kingdom. What is probably more important to you is that your cause is now on everyone's lips, even if—so far—it's only being whispered about. With the best will in

186

the world, Galdran's spies could only find out what was being said, but not by whom. Imagine, if you can, the effect."

I tried. Too tired to actually think of much beyond when I might lay my head down, and where, I looked across the room at that bed—then away quickly—and said as stoutly as I could, "I hope it skewered him good."

"He's angry enough to be on his way to face us, but we shall discuss it later. Permit me to suggest that you avail yourself of the room next to your brother's, which was hastily excavated last night. We'll be using this place as our command post for the next day or so."

I wavered to my feet, swayed, leaned against the wall. "Yes. Well." I tried to think of something appropriate to say, but nothing came to mind.

So I walked out and found my way to the room, unlatched the door. A tiny corner hearth radiated a friendly heat from a fire. A fire—they used a Fire Stick just for me. Was there a family somewhere doing without? Or did the Hill Folk know—somehow—of the Marquis's cause, and had they tendered their approval by giving his people extras? I shook my head, beyond comprehending anything. Near the fireplace was a campbed, nicely set up, with a bedroll all stretched out and waiting, and a folded cloak for a pillow. Somehow I got my muddy, soggy clothes off and slid the wallet with Debegri's letter under the folded-cloak pillow. Then I climbed into that bed, and I don't remember putting my head down.

It was dark when I woke; I realized I'd heard the door click shut.

Turning my head, I looked into the leaping fire, saw lying on a stool in front of it—getting warm—some clothes. Next to the stool was an ewer with steaming water, a cloth, and a comb.

I could have lain there much longer, but I took this as a hint that I ought to get up, and when I remembered Bran lying in the next room, it was easier to motivate myself.

It did take effort, though. My skin hurt and my head ached,

sure signs that I was indeed coming down with some illness. I cleaned up as best as I could, combed out my rain-washed hair, and put on the familiar oversized Renselaeus livery donated by some anonymous person not even remotely my size. Again I stashed the letter inside the tunic, then I left the room.

I found the other two in Bran's room, and one look at their faces made it abundantly clear that they felt no better than I did. Not that the Marquis had a red nose or a thick voice—he even looked aristocratic when sick, I thought with disgust. But Bran sneezed frequently, and from the pungent smell of bristic in the air, he had had recourse to the flagon.

"Mel!" he exclaimed when I opened the door. And he laughed. "Look at you! You're drowning in that kit." He turned his head to address Shevraeth. "Ain't anyone undersized among your people?"

"Obviously not," I said tartly, and helped myself to the flagon that I saw on the bed. A swig of bristic did help somewhat. "Unless the sight of me is intended to provide some cheap amusement for the warriors."

"Well, I won't come off much better," Bran said cheerily.

"That I resent," the Marquis said with his customary drawl. "Seeing as it is my wardrobe that is gracing your frame."

Branaric only laughed, then he said, "Now that we're all together, and I'm still sober, what's the word?"

"The latest report is that the King is a day or two's march from here, well ensconced in the midst of his army. Debegri is with him, and it seems there have been some disagreements on the manner in which you two are to be dealt with. Galdran wants to lay Tlanth to waste, but Debegri, of course, has his eye to a title and land at last."

Bran rubbed his chin. "Only one of that family not landed, right?"

"To the Baron's festering annoyance. Despite their pose of eternal brotherhood, they have never really liked—or trusted—one another. It has suited Galdran well to have Nenthar Debegri serve as his watch-beast, for Debegri has been scrupulous about enforcing

Galdran's laws. Enthusiastic, I should say. If he cannot have land, Debegri's preference is to ride the countryside acting the bully. It has made him unpopular, which does Galdran no harm."

"So what's the plan?"

"I believe that our best plan is to flush them out. If we can capture them both, there will be little reason for the others to fight."

"But if they're in the midst of the army—" Bran started.

"Bait," I said, seeing the plan at once. "There has to be bait to bring them to the front." Thinking rapidly, I added, "And I know who's to be the bait. Us, right? Only, how to get them to meet us?"

"The letter," Branaric said. "They know now that we have it."

Both looked at me, but I said nothing.

"Even if we don't have it," the Marquis said easily, "it's enough to say we do to get them to meet us. If they break the truce or try anything untoward, a chosen group will grab them, and my warriors will disperse in all directions and reassemble at a certain place on my border a week later, at which time we will reassess. I can give you all the details of the plan if you wish them."

Bran snorted a laugh. "I'm in. As if we had a choice!"

"*Do* we have a choice?" I asked, instantly hostile.

"I am endeavoring to give you the semblance of one," Shevraeth replied in his most polite voice.

"And if we don't agree?" I demanded.

"Then you will remain here in safety until events are resolved."

"So we *are* prisoners, then."

Bran was chuckling and wiping his eyes. "Life, sister, how you remind me of that old spaniel of Khesot's, Skater, when he thought someone was going to pinch his favorite chew-stick. Remember him?"

"Bran—" I began, now thoroughly exasperated.

"Well, it isn't the goals, Mel, for we've the same ones, in essentials. It's you being stubborn, just like old Skater. Admit it!"

"I admit only that I don't trust *him* as far as I can throw a

189

horse," I fumed. "We're still prisoners, and you just sit there and laugh! Well, go ahead. I think I'll go back to sleep. The company is better." And I stalked to the door, went out, and slammed it.

Of course I could still hear Bran wheezing with laughter. The ancient doors were not of tapestry but of wood, extremely flimsy and ill-fitted wood, serving no real purpose beyond blocking the room from sight. Tapestry manners required I move away at once, but I hesitated until I heard Bran say, "She won't rat out on us. Let me talk to her, and she'll see reason."

"I'd give her some time before you attempt it," came the wry answer.

"She usually doesn't stay mad long," Bran said carelessly.

Again habit urged me to move. I knew to stay made me a spy-ears, which no one over the age of four is excused in being, yet I didn't move. I *couldn't* move. So I stood there and listened—and thus proved the old proverb about eavesdroppers getting what they deserve.

Shevraeth said, "I'm very much afraid it's my fault. We met under the worst of circumstances, and we seem to have misunderstood one another to a lethal degree."

Bran said, "No, if it's anyone's fault, it's ours—my parents' and mine. You have to realize our mother saw Tlanth as a haven from her Court life. All she had to do was potter around her garden and play her harp. I don't think Mel even knows Mother spent a few years at Alsais, learning courtly behavior at the Court in Colend. Mel scarcely talked before she started hearing stories on the immoral, rotten, lying Court decorations. Mama liked seeing her running wild with Oria and the village brats. Then Mama was killed, and Papa mostly lived shut in his tower, brooding over the past. He didn't seem to know what to do with Mel. She couldn't read or write, wouldn't even sit still indoors—all summer she would disappear for a week at a time, roaming in the hills. I think she knows more about the ways of the Hill Folk than she does about what actually happens at Court. Anyhow, I taught her her letters ust a year or so ago, mostly as an excuse to get away from my books. She liked it well enough, except there isn't much to read up here anymore, beyond what Papa thought I ought to know for preparing a war."

"I see. Yet you've told me she shared in the command of your rebels."

Bran laughed again. "That's because after she learned to read, Mel learned figuring, on her own, and took it over."

"You mean, she took charge of your business affairs?"

"Such as they were, yes. Taxes, all that. It's why I told her she had half the title. *Life!* She could've had the title, and the leadership, for all of me, except we promised Papa when he died that we'd go together. And working toward the war—it was easier when we did it together. She turned it into a game, though I think she saw it as real before I did." He sighed. "Well, I know she did. Curst maps prove it."

"Your family was reputed to have a good library."

"Until Papa burned it, after Mama died. Everything gone, and neither of us knowing what we'd lost. Or, I knew and didn't care, but Mel didn't even know. Curse it, her maid is sister to the blacksmith. Julen's never been paid, but sees to Mel because she's sorry for her."

"There has been, I take it, little contact with family, then?"

"Papa had no family left in this part of the world. As for Mama's royal cousins, when they moved south to Sartor, my parents lost touch, and I never did see any reason to try…"

I slipped away then, raging against my brother and the Marquis, against Julen for pitying me when I'd thought she was my friend, against nosy listeners such as myself… against Papa, and Galdran, and war, and Galdran again, against the Sartorans and every courtier ever born.

I sat in the room they'd given me and glared into the roaring fire, angry with the entire universe.

TWENTY-ONE

BUT AFTER A TIME EVEN MY TEMPER TANTRUMS HAVE to give way to rational thought, and I faced at last what ought to have been obvious from the very beginning: We'd lost because we were ignorant. And of the two of us, I was the worse off, because I hadn't even known I was ignorant.

An equerry tapped at the door and announced that supper was being served.

I sat where I was and waged a short fierce inner battle. Either I could sit and sulk—in which case they would want to know why—or I could go out there, pretend nothing was amiss, and do what needed doing.

The table in the Marquis's room was set for the three of us. I sniffed the air, which was pleasant with the summer-grass smell of brewing listerblossom. Somehow this eased my sore spirits just a little. I knelt down next to my brother, whose bed pillows cushioned him, and poured myself some of the tea. It felt good on my raw throat.

For a time I just sat there with my eyes closed, sipping occasionally, while the other two continued a conversation about the difficulties of supply procurement that they had obviously begun before I returned. At first I listened to the voices: Bran's husky, low, with laughter in it as a constant and pleasant undercurrent, and Shevraeth's soft, emotionless, with words drawn out in a court drawl to give them emphasis, rather than using changes in tone or timbre. The complexity of Shevraeth's reaction was thus masked, which—I realized—was more irritating to me than his voice, which didn't precisely grate on the ears. It was an advantage that I had no access to; I seemed to be incapable of hiding my reactions.

The tea restored to me enough presence of mind to bring the sense of their words, instead of mere sound. They were still discoursing on supply sources and how to protect supply lines, and Bran kept looking to me for corroboration, for in truth, I knew more about this than he did. Then I realized that it was an unexceptionable subject introduced so that I might take part; but I saw in that a gesture of pity, and my black mood threatened to descend again.

Then came the food—roasted fowl, with vegetables mixed into sauce made from the meat drippings, and a hot tart made with apples and spices and wine, by the smell. My appetite woke up suddenly, and for a time all I had attention for was my plate.

The others conversed little, and at the end of the meal I looked up, saw the unmistakable marks of fever in their faces. Branaric grinned. "What a trio we make! Look at us."

Annoyance flared anew. Glaring at him, I said hoarsely, "Look at yourself. I'd rather spare myself the nightmare, which would affright even a half-sighted gargoyle."

Bran gaped at me in surprise, then laughed. "Just keep that temper sharp. You'll need it, for we may be on the march tomorrow."

"Oh, good," I croaked with as much enthusiasm as I could muster.

It sounded about as false as it felt, and Bran laughed again; but before he could say anything, the Marquis suggested that we all retire, for the morrow promised to be a long day.

———

"Curse it," Bran said the next morning, standing before the fire in shirt and trousers with his shoulder stiffly bandaged. "You think this necessary?"

He pointed at the mail coats lying on the table, their linked steel rings gleaming coldly in the light of two glowglobes. It was well before dawn. The Marquis had woken us himself, with the news that Galdran's forces were nigh. And his messengers had brought from Renselaeus the mail coats, newly made and expensive.

"Treachery—" Shevraeth paused to cough and to catch his breath. He, too, stood there in only shirt and trousers and boots, and I looked away quickly, embarrassed. "We should be prepared for treachery. It was his idea to send archers against you in the mountains. He will have them with him now." He coughed again, the rattling cough of a heavy cold.

I sighed. My own fever and aches had all settled into my throat, and my voice was gone.

Bran was the worst off. Besides the wound in his shoulder, he coughed, sneezed, and sounded hoarse. His eyes and nose watered constantly. As well, the Renselaeus munificence extended to a besorceled handkerchief that stayed dry and clean despite its heavy use.

Groaning and wincing, Bran lifted his arm just high enough for a couple of equerries to slip the chain mail over his head. As it settled onto him, *ching*ing softly, he winced and said, "Feels like I've got a horse lying athwart my shoulders."

I picked up the one set aside for me and retreated to my room to put it on, and then the tunic they'd given me. Branaric's wallet containing Debegri's letter lay safe and snug in my waistband.

When I came back, Branaric started laughing. "A mouse in mail!" he said, pointing. He and Shevraeth both had battle tunics on, and swords belted at their sides; they looked formidable, whereas I felt I looked ridiculous. My mail shirt was the smallest

f the three, but it was still much too large, and it bunched and
olded beneath my already outsized tunic, making me feel like an
verstuffed cushion.

But the Marquis said nothing at all as he indicated a table where
choice of weapons lay, with belts and baldrics of various sizes and
yles. In silence I belted on a short sword similar to the one I'd
arown down in surrender above the Vesingrui fortress. I found a
elm that fit pretty well over my braid coronet, and then I was
eady.

Within a short time we were mounted on fresh chargers that
ere also armored. Despite the chill outside I started warm, for
e'd each drunk an infusion of listerblossoms against illness.

Our way was lit by torches as we raced over the ancient road,
nder trees that had been old before my family first came to Tlanth.
xcept for the rhythm of hooves there was no sound, but I sensed
aat forest life was watching us.

According to the plan two equerries were sent on ahead. The
est of us rode steadily as dawn started to lift the heavy shroud of
arkness. A fine rain still fell, and the trees dripped on us, spattering
ur faces with cold water. Strong was the green smell of wet loam
ad forest. I breathed deeply of it, finding it comforting in an odd
ay. No one talked much, but I kept thinking about the fact that
e were riding deliberately into danger—that Galdran would see
eachery as expedience. Our plan depended on the Renselaeus war-
ors being fast and accurate and brave, for they were as outnum-
ered as Bran and I had been up in the mountains.

I was also, therefore, intensely aware that my life was now in
ae hands of people I had considered enemies not two dawns ago.
id they still consider me one?

I tried to calm my nerves by laughing at myself; for someone
ho so recently had tried her best to ride to her death, my innards
ere a pit of snakes, and my palms were sweaty despite the rain.
ran was alive, I was alive, and suddenly I wanted to stay that way.
wanted to go home and clean out the castle and replant Mama's

garden. I wanted to see Oria and Julen and Khesot again, and I wanted to walk on the high peaks and dance with the Hill Folk on long summer nights, miming age-old stories to the windborne music...

I blinked. Had I just heard a reed pipe?

I lifted my head and listened, heard nothing but the thud of hooves and clatter of our accoutrements, and the soft rain in the leaves overhead.

At last the equerries returned—safe, I guessed, only because of Galdran's curiosity and his desire to get his bejeweled fingers around our throats.

"They're on the plain below the last hill, Your Grace," said one, pointing backward. "The King says he will meet you at the bridge over the Thereas River."

"Cover?" Shevraeth said, and coughed.

As if in sympathy Bran sneezed, and despite the danger, I felt a weird impulse to laugh. *If we win, will our colds be in the songs?*

"Thick, Your Grace. Trees, shrubbery. Both sides."

"Right. Then we can expect archers behind every bush, and swords waiting in the trees. Be ready for anything," he said, waving them on.

They raced off to spread the word.

"Well," Bran said, wincing as our horses moved forward again, "you wanted them in the forest."

"Equal things out a little," was the reply, still in the cool drawl. "Ready, Lady Meliara?"

"Let's get it over with," I croaked.

The Marquis gave me that assessing look, then turned to Bran. "Ready for a ride?"

"Certainly," my brother said, though without any of his usual humor.

Shevraeth reached into his saddlebag and pulled out the flagon. Wordlessly he passed it to Bran, who took a couple swigs, then, gasping, passed it to me. I helped myself, and with tearing eyes eturned it. The Marquis tipped back his head, took a good slug, hen stored it again, and we were off.

There's no use in talking about the plan, because of course nothing vent the way it was supposed to. Even the passage of time was horribly distorted. At first the ride to the hill seemed endless, with me sneaking looks at my brother, who was increasingly unsteady in his saddle.

The Marquis insisted on riding in front of us the last little distance, where we saw a row of four horse riders waiting—the outer two bearing banners, dripping from the rain, but the flags' green and gold still brilliant, and the inner two riders brawny and cruel faced and very much at ease, wearing the plumed helms of command.

"I just wanted to see if you traitors would dare to face me," Galdran said, his caustic voice making me feel sick inside. Sick—and angry.

The Marquis bowed low over his horse's withers, every line of his body indicative of irony.

Galdran's face flushed dark purple.

"I confess," Shevraeth drawled, "we had a small wager on whether you would have the courage to face us."

"Kill them!" Galdran roared.

And that's the moment when time changed and everything happened at once. At the edge of my vision I saw arrows fly, but none reached us. A weird humming vibrated through my skull; at first I thought it was just me, then I realized all the war horses, despite their training, were in a panic. For a few short, desperate breaths, all my attention was spent calming my own mount.

Galdran's reared, and he shouted orders at his equerries as he fought to keep his seat. The two banner-bearing warriors flipped up the ends of their poles, flicked away some kind of binding, and aimed sharp steel points at the Marquis as they charged. All around

197

me was chaos—the hiss and clang of steel weapons being drawn, the nickering of horses, grunts and shouts and yells.

"To me! To me!" That was Bran's cry.

Four Renselaeus warriors came to his aid. I kneed my mount forward and brandished my weapon, trying to edge up on Bran's weak side. Horseback fighting was something we'd drilled in rarely, for this was not mountain-type warfare. I met the blade of one of Bran's attackers, and shock rang up my arm. Thoughts chased through my brain; except for those few days with Nessaren's riding, I hadn't practiced for weeks, and now I was going to feel it.

Wondering how I would make it through a hand-to-hand duel, I glanced around—and just then I saw one of Galdran's equerries fall from his saddle, his banner-spear spinning through the air toward me. Instinctively my free hand reached up and I caught the spear by the shaft. Ignoring the sting in my hand, I jammed my sword into its sheath and started whirling the spear round and round, making the banner snap and stream as my prancing, sidling horse circled round my brother. Horses turned their heads and backed away; no one was able to edge up and get in a good blow at Bran, who swayed in his saddle, his bad arm hanging limp. The warriors fell back, and no one swung at me.

Dimly I became aware of an ugly, harsh voice shouting over the crash and thuds of battle. Keeping the banner whirling, I guided my horse with my knees and risked a glance back over my shoulder—and looked straight into Galdran's rage-darkened face. He said something, spittle flying from his mouth, as he pointed straight at me.

A moment later a flicker of movement on my immediate left caused me to glance round. Shevraeth was there, next to me. "Fall back," he ordered, his voice sharp.

"No. Got to protect Bran—"

There was no time for more. The Marquis was beset by furious attackers as the King shouted orders from a short distance away. Then more riders appeared from somewhere, and for a moment everything was too chaotic to follow. I found myself suddenly on

e edge of the battle; there were too many fighters on both sides
etween my brother and me. Too many fighters in the liveries of
e Baron and the King. Despair burned through me, cold as winter
e.

We were losing.

Then my horse plunged aside, I shifted in the saddle, and I
und myself face-to-face with Galdran. He glared at me with ha-
ed; I had this sudden, strange feeling that if we had both been
aall children facing each other in a village squabble he would have
reamed at me, *It's all your fault!*

His lips drew back from his teeth. "You, I will kill myself," he
arled, and he raised his great, flat-bladed sword.

I cast away the flimsy spear and drew my sword just a scarce
oment before Galdran struck. The first blow nearly knocked me
t off the horse. I parried it—just barely—pain shooting up my
m into my back. My arm was numb, so I used both hands to raise
y blade against the expected next blow.

But as Galdran's sword came down toward my head, it was met
a ringing strike that sent sparks arcing through the air. I
oked—saw the Marquis, hair flying, horse dancing, circling round
aldran and forcing his attention away. Then the two were fighting
sperately, the King falling back. I watched in fascination until
o of the King's guards rode to Galdran's aid, and Shevraeth was
ddenly fighting against three.

It seemed that the Marquis was going to lose, and I realized I
uldn't watch. Remembering my brother, I forced my mount
und so I could ride to his aid. But when I spotted him in the
aos of lunging horses and crashing weapons, he was staring past
y shoulder, his eyes distended.

"Meliara!" he yelled, trying to ride toward me.

I turned my head, saw the Marquis now fighting against three
ards; and once again the King was coming directly at me, sword
inging in a blur. I flung my sword at him and ducked. A blow
ught me painfully across the back of my helm, and darkness
shed up to swallow me.

TWENTY-TWO

I WOKE RELUCTANTLY, FOR MY HEAD ACHED LIKE A stone mountain had fallen on it. I sat up, ignoring the crashing in my skull, and swung my legs over the edge of my cot. I was back in the wood gatherer's cottage.

The fire was leaping, the room warm. I glanced at the window, saw light outside. As I stood I realized the chain mail was gone, as was the tunic. All I had on were the shirt and trousers I'd been wearing, wrinkled but dry. The wallet with Debegri's letter was still tucked safely in my waistband.

I looked around for the tunic so I could leave the room; not for worlds would I go out dressed thus into the midst of a lot of staring Renselaeus warriors.

Unless Galdran has won! The terrible thought froze me for a moment, but then I looked down at that fire and realized that if Galdran had beaten us, I'd hardly be in such comfortable surroundings again. More likely I'd have woken in some dungeon somewhere, with clanking chains attached to every limb.

I held my head in my hands, trying to get the strength to stand; then my door opened, thrust by an impatient hand. Branaric stood there, grinning in surprise.

"You're awake! Healer said you'd likely sleep out the day."

I nodded slowly, eyeing his flushed cheeks and overbright eyes. His right arm rested in a sling. "You are also sick," I observed.

"Merrily so," he agreed, "but I cannot for the life of me keep still. Burn it! Truth to tell, I never thought I'd live to see this day."

"What day?" I asked, and then, narrowly, "We're not prisoners, are we? Where is Galdran?"

"Dead," Bran said with a laugh.

I gaped. "Dead?"

"Dead and gone, though no one shed a tear at his funeral rite. And you should have seen his minions scatter beforehand! The rest couldn't surrender fast enough!" He laughed again, then, "Ulp! Forgot. Want tea?"

"Oh yes," I said with enthusiasm. "I was just looking for my tunic. Or rather, the one I was wearing."

"Mud," he said succinctly. "Galdran smacked you off your horse and you landed flat in a mud puddle. Hold there!"

I sat down on the bunk again, questions swarming through my mind like angry bees.

Branaric was back in a moment, carefully carrying a brimming mug in his one good hand, and some folded cloth and a plain brown citizen's hat tucked under his arm. "Here ye are, sister," he said cheerily. "Let's celebrate."

I took the mug, and as he toasted me with a pretend one, I lifted mine to him and drank deeply. The listerblossom infusion flooded me from head to heels with soothing warmth. I sighed with relief, then said, "Now, tell me everything."

He chuckled and leaned against the door. "That's a comprehensive command! Where to begin?"

"With Galdran. How did he die?"

"Vidanric. Sword," Bran said, waving his index finger in a parry-and-thrust. "Just after Galdran tried to brain you from the back. Neatest work I've ever seen. He promised to introduce me to his old sword master when we get to Athanarel."

" 'We'? You and the Marquis?"

201

"We can discuss it when we meet for supper, soon's he gets back. Life! I don't think he's sat down since we returned yestereve. I'm tied here by the heels, healer's orders, but there'll be enough for us all to do soon."

I opened my mouth to say that I did not want to go to Athanarel, but I could almost hear his rallying tone—and the fact, bitterly faced but true, that part of my image as the ignorant little sister guaranteed that Bran seldom took me seriously. So I shook my head instead. "Tell me more."

"Well, that's the main of it, in truth. They were all pretty disgusted—both sides, I think—when Galdran went after you. He didn't even have the courage to face me, and I was weavin' on my horse like a one-legged rooster. One o' his bully boys knocked me clean out of the saddle just after Galdran hit you. Anyway, Vidanric went after the King, quick and cool as ice, and the others went after Debegri—but he nearly got away. I say 'nearly' because it was one of his own people got him squarely in the back with an arrow— what's more, that one didn't sprout. Now, if that ain't justice, I don't know what is!" He touched his shoulder.

"What? Arrow? Sprout? Was that somehow related to that strange humming just as everything started—or did I imagine that?"

"Not unless we all did." Bran looked sober for a moment. "Magic. The Hill Folk were right there, watching and spell casting! First time I ever heard of them interfering in one of our human brangles, but they did. Those arrows from Galdran's archers all sprouted leaves soon's they left the bow, and they fell to the ground, and curse me if they didn't start takin' root. Soon's the archers saw that, they threw away their bows and panicked. Weirdest thing I ever saw. That hilltop will be all forest by winter, or I'm a lapdog."

"Whoosh," I said, sitting down.

He then remembered the cloth under his arm and tossed it into my lap.

I held up yet another tunic that was shapeless and outsized, but I was glad to see it was plain, thick, and well made.

"Found that in someone's kit. Knew you hated wearing these." Bran indicated his own tunic, another of the Renselaeus ones.

Thinking of appearing yet again as a ridiculous figure in ill-fitting, borrowed clothing, I tried to summon a smile. "Thanks."

He touched his shoulder with tentative fingers, then winced. "I'll lie down until Vidanric gets back. Then, mind, we're all to plan together, and soon's we're done here, we ride for Athanarel—all three of us."

"Why all three of us?"

"There's work that needs doing," Branaric said, serious again.

"What can I possibly do besides serve as a figure of fun for the Court to laugh at again? I don't *know* anything—besides how to lose a war; and I don't think anyone is requiring that particular bit of knowledge." I tried to sound reasonable, but even I could hear the bitterness in my own voice.

My brother sighed. "I don't know what I'll do, either, except I'll put my hand to anything I'm asked. That's what our planning session is to be about, soon's they return. So save your questions for then, and I don't want any more of this talk of prisoners and grudges and suchlike. Vidanric saved your life—he's been a true ally, can't you see it now?"

"He saved it twice," I corrected without thinking.

"He what?" My brother straightened up.

"In Chovilun dungeon. Didn't I tell you?" Then I remembered I hadn't gotten that far before Debegri's trap had closed about us.

Bran pursed his lips, staring at me with an uncharacteristic expression. "Interesting. I didn't know that."

"Well, you got in the way of an arrow before I got a chance to finish the story," I explained.

"Except, Vidanric didn't tell me, either." Branaric opened his mouth, hesitated, then shook his head. "Well, it seems we all have some talking to do. I'm going to lie down first. You drink your tea." He went out, and I heard the door to his room shut and his cot creak.

I looked away, staring at the merry fire, my thoughts ranging

203

back over the headlong pace of the recent days. Suddenly I knew that Shevraeth had recognized me outside that town, and I knew why he hadn't done anything about it: because Debegri was with him then. The Marquis and his people had searched day and night in order to find me before Debegri did—searched not to kill me, but in order to save me from certain death at Debegri's hands.

Why hadn't he told me? Because I'd called him a liar and untrustworthy, and had made it plain I wasn't going to change my opinion, no matter what. Then why hadn't he told my brother, who did trust him?

That I couldn't answer. And in a sense it didn't matter. What did matter was that I had been wrong about Shevraeth. I had been so wrong I had nearly gotten a lot of people killed for no reason.

Just thinking it made me grit my teeth, and in a way it felt almost as bad as cleaning the fester from my wounded foot. Which was right, because I had to clean out from my mind the fester caused by anger and hatred. I remembered suddenly that horrible day in Galdran's dungeon when the Marquis had come to me himself and offered me a choice between death and surrender. "It might buy you time," he'd said.

At that moment I'd seen surrender as dishonor, and it *had* taken courage to refuse. He'd seen that and had acknowledged it in many different ways, including his words two days before about my being a heroine. Generous words, meant to brace me up. What I saw now was the grim courage it had taken to act his part in Galdran's Court, all the time planning to change things with the least amount of damage to innocent people. And when Branaric and I had come crashing into his plans, he'd included us as much as he could in his net of safety. My subsequent brushes with death were, I saw miserably now, my own fault.

I had to respect what he'd done. He'd come to respect us for our ideals, that much was clear. What he might think of me personally…

Suddenly I felt an overwhelming desire to be home. I wanted

adly to clean out our castle, and replant Mama's garden, and walk
n the sunny glades, and think, and read, and *learn*. I no longer
vanted to face the world in ignorance, wearing castoff clothing and
ld horse blankets.

But first there was something I had to do.

I slipped out the door; paused, listening. From Branaric's room
ame the sound of slow, deep breathing. I stepped inside the room
hevraeth had been using, saw a half-folded map on the table,
 neat pile of papers, a pen and inkwell, and a folded pair of
loves.

Pulling out the wallet from my clothes, I opened it and ex-
racted Debegri's letter. This I laid on the table beside the papers.
Then I knelt down and picked up the pen. Finding a blank sheet
f paper, I wrote in slow, careful letters: *You'll probably need this to
onvince Galdran's old allies.*

Then I retreated to my room, pulled the borrowed tunic over
1y head, bound up my ratty braid, settled the overlarge hat onto
1y head, and slipped out the door.

At the end of the little hall was another door, which opened
nto a clearing. Under a dilapidated roof waited a string of fine
orses, and a few Renselaeus stable hands sat about.

When they saw me, they sprang to their feet.

"My lady?" One bowed.

"I should like a ride," I said, my heart thumping.

But they didn't argue, or refuse, or send someone to warn
omeone else. Working together, in a trice they had a fine, fresh
1are saddled and ready.

And in another trice I was on her back and riding out, on my
vay home.

Heee-*oh!*" The call echoed up from the courtyard. "Messenger!"

I straightened up slowly, wincing as my back protested. Skirting
1y neat piles, I went to the open window and looked down into

205

the sunlit courtyard far below, and saw Oria's younger brother, Calaub, capering excitedly about.

"Just stable the horse and send the messenger in for food, and the message can be left on the table," I called. And, over my shoulder to Oria, "I hope it's my book, but that would be miraculous, for I just sent the letter off—what, three? five? a few days ago."

"It's someone *new!*" Calaub's high voice was a bat squeak of excitement.

I laughed. The children his age had concocted an elaborate spy system to identify anyone coming up the main road to the castle—for no one quite believed, any more than I did, that we were truly safe, despite nearly two months of utter quiet. A quiet that had reigned since the day I rode into Erkan-Astiar on the borrowed mare with my head bandaged and, on my lips, the news that Galdran was truly gone.

Oria looked round the room, which had been Papa's refuge at the end of his life. It had not been touched since his death, and weather and mildew had added to the mess. Not long after my return we had commenced cleaning the castle from the basement up. Papa's room being at the very top of the tallest tower, I had left it for the last.

" 'Tis done," Oria said in satisfaction. She wiped her brow and added, "And not too soon, for the hot weather is nearly on us."

"Which is not the time for fires," I said, looking at the piles of things on the new-swept floor. Most of them were rubbish and would keep us warm at night, for our Fire Sticks had run out of magic. There was some furniture that could be mended, and a very small pile of keepsakes. These last I gathered myself as we went down the steps.

"The twins can bring everything down this afternoon," Oria said. "Mama is eager to get someone up there to scrub. You know she won't declare it's done until every stone is clean."

I set my pile carefully on a small table at the main landing, which was closest to the library. "And then the window work," I said, and bit my lip. We'd have to have shutters to all the windows that had stood open for years, or the place would be full of drafts and dirt by winter. I knew I ought to have glass put in, but also—desperately—wanted books. So to ease my conscience, I'd decided, as we got the wherewithal, to alternate windows and books, leaving my room for last.

We exited the tower and crossed the courtyard as a quicker route.

No one used the main hall—we all went in and out the side yard, which opened onto the warm kitchens. The spring rains had been tapering off, and though it was full summer in the lowlands, at our heights only of late had we begun feeling a breeze from over the mountains, carrying a warm herbal tang from the south. But the nights were still very chill, and often wet.

Oria and I walked into the kitchen to find Julen staring at a handsome young man with curly black hair and fine new livery in stiar colors.

His chin was up, and he swept a cool glance over us all as he said, "My errand is with my lady, the Countess of Tlanth."

"I am she." I stepped forward.

He gave me one incredulous look, then hastily smoothed his face as he bowed low. In the background, Julen clucked rather audibly. Next to me Oria had her arms crossed, her face stony. The young man looked about with the air of one who knows himself in unfriendly territory, and I reflected that for all his airs my brother had hired him or he wouldn't be here, and he deserved a chance to present himself fair.

"Surely you'll have been warned that we are very informal here," I said, and gave him a big smile.

And for some reason he flushed right up to his fine hairline. Bowing again, he said courteously, "My lady, I was to give this directly to you."

I held out one hand, noticed the dirt smudges, and hastily wiped on my clothes before putting it out again. When I glanced up at the equerry, I saw in his eyes just a hint of answering amusement at the absurdity of the situation, though his face was strictly schooled when he handed me the letter.

"Welcome among us. What is your name?" I said.

"Jerrol, as it pleases you, my lady." And again the bow.

"Well, it's your name if it pleases me or not," I said, sitting on the edge of the great slate prep table.

Julen clucked again, but softly, and I looked to the side, saw the preparations for tarts lying at the ready, and hastily jumped down again.

"Tell me, Jerrol," I said, "if a great Court lady mislikes the name of a new equerry, will she rename him or her?"

"Like…Frogface or Stenchbelly?" Calaub asked from the open window, and beyond him three or four urchins snickered.

Jerrol glanced about him, his face quite blank, but only for a moment. He then swept me a truly magnificent bow—so flourishing that no one could miss the irony—and he said, "An my lady pleases to address me as Stenchbelly, I shall count myself honored." He pronounced it all with awful elegance.

And everyone laughed! I said, "I think you'll do, Jerrol, for all your clothes are better than any of us have seen for years. But you will have heard something of our affairs, I daresay, and I wonder how my brother managed to hire you, and fit you out this splendidly, in our colors?"

"Wager on it yon letter will explain," Julen said grimly, turning to plunge her hands into her flour.

"Oh!" I had forgotten Jerrol's original purpose for arriving, and looked down at the letter with my name scrawled above the seal in Branaric's careless hand.

Looking down at the stiff, cream-colored rice paper—the good kind that came in the books that we had never been able to afford—I was both excited and apprehensive. Remembering my rather precipitous departure from that wood gatherer's house, I decided that much as I valued my friends, I wanted to read Bran's letter alone.

No one followed me as I walked out. Behind, I heard Oria saying, in a voice very different from what I was used to hearing from her, "Come, Master Jerrol, there's some good ale here, and I'll make you some bread and cheese..."

As I walked up to my room, I reflected on the fact that I *did* want to read it alone, and not have whatever it said read from my face. Then there was the fact that they all let me go off alone without a word said, though I knew they wanted to know what was in it.

It's that invisible barrier again, I thought, feeling peculiar. *We can work all day at the same tasks, bathe together at the village bathhouse, and sit down together at meals, but then something comes up and suddenly I'm the Astiar and they are the vassals...just as at the village dances all the best posies and the finest plates are brought to me, but the young men all talk and laugh with the other girls.*

Was this, then, to be my life? To always feel suspended midway between the aristocrat and the vassal traditions, and to belong truly to neither?

I sat down in my quiet room and worked my finger under the seal.

Dear Mel:

I trust this finds you recovered. Why did you have to run off like that? But I figured you were safe arrived at home, and well, or Khesot would've sent to me here—since you wouldn't write.

And how was I to pay for sending a letter to Remalna-city? I thought indignantly, then sighed. Of course, I *had* managed to find enough coin to write to Ara's family, and to obtain through the father the name of a good bookseller. But the first was an obligation, I told myself. And as for the latter, it was merely the start of the education that Branaric had blabbed to the world that I lacked.

I'm here at Athanarel, finding it to my taste. It helps that Galdran's personal fortune has been turned over to us, as repayment for what happened to our family—you'll find the Letter of Intent in with this letter, to be kept somewhere safe. Henceforth, you send your creditors for drafts on Arclor House...

I looked up at the ceiling as the words slowly sank in. "Personal fortune"? How much was that? Whatever it was, it had to be a vast improvement over our present circumstances. I grinned, thinking how I had agonized over which book to choose from the bookseller's list. Now I could order them all. I could even hire my own scribe...

Shaking my head, I banished the dreams of avarice, and returned to the letter—not that much remained.

...so, outfit yourself in whatever you want, appoint someone responsible as steward, and join me here at Athanarel as soon as you can. Everyone here wants to meet you.

"Now, that's a frightening thought," I said grimly.

And I think it's time for you to make your peace with Vidanric.

He ended with a scrawled signature.

I lowered the letter slowly to the desk, not wanting to consider why I found that last suggestion even more frightening than the first.

Behind Bran's letter, bearing three official-looking seals, was the Letter of Intent. In very beautiful handwriting, it named in precise terms a sum even higher than I'd dared to let myself think of, the remainder after the taxes for the army had been subtracted. Wondering who was getting *that* sum, which was even greater, I scanned the rest, which outlined in flowery language pretty much what Branaric had said. It seemed we now had a business house handling our money; previously I'd gathered the scanty sums and redispersed them myself, in coin.

I put that letter down, too. Suddenly the possibilities now available started multiplying in my mind. Not visiting Athanarel. I didn't even consider that; I'd tried to win a crown, and lost. But suppos-

dly all the wrongs I had fought for were being addressed, and
o—I vowed—I was done with royal affairs.

No, I told myself, my work now was Tlanth, and with this
money, all my plans could be put into action. Rebuilding, new
oads, booksellers...I looked around at the castle, no longer seeing
ne weather damage and neglect, but how it would look repaired
nd redecorated.

"Oria!" I yelled, running downstairs. "Oria! Julen! Calaub!
Ve're *rich*!"

Part Two

Part Two

ONE

STOOD AT MY WINDOW, AN OLD BUT COMFORTABLE
nket wrapped about me. The warmth of the low midwinter sun
rough the new paned glass was pleasant as I read again the letter
at had arrived that day.

Esteemed Countess Meliara:

*I have had the pleasure of meeting, and entertaining, your es-
timable brother, Count Branaric. At every meeting he speaks often
and fondly of his sister, who, he claims, was the driving spirit behind
the extraordinary events of last year.*

*He also promised that you will come join us at Court, but half a
year has passed, and we still await you. Perhaps the prospect of life
at the Palace Athanarel does not appeal to you?*

*There are those who agree with this sentiment. I am one myself.
I leave soon for my home in Merindar, where I desire only to lead a
quiet life. It is with this prospect in mind that I have taken up my
pen; I would like, very much, to meet you. At Merindar there would
be time, and seclusion, to permit leisurely discourse on subjects which
have concerned us both—especially now, when the country has the
greatest need of guidance.*

*Come to Merindar. We can promise you the most pleasant
diversions.*

I await, with anticipation, your response—or your most welcome presence.

And it was signed in a graceful, flourishing hand, *Arthal Merindar.*

A letter from a Merindar. I had brought about her brother's defeat. Did she really want friendship? I scanned it for perhaps the tenth time. There had to be a hidden message.

When I came to the end, I looked up and gazed out my window. The world below the castle lay white and smooth and glistening. We'd had six months of peace. Though the letter seemed friendly enough, I felt a sense of foreboding, as if my peace was as fragile as the snowflakes outside.

"Looking down the west road again, Meliara?"

The voice startled me. I turned and saw my oldest friend, Oria, peering in around the door tapestry. Though I was the countess and she the servant, we had grown up together, scampering barefoot every summer through the mountains, sleeping out under the stars, and dancing to the music of the mysterious Hill Folk. Until last winter, I'd only had Oria's cast-off clothing to wear; now I had a couple of remade gowns, but I still wore the old clothes to work in.

She smiled a little as she lifted the tapestry the rest of the way and stepped in. "I tapped. Three times."

"I was *not* looking at the road. Why should I look at the road? I was just thinking—and enjoying the sunshine."

"Won't last." Oria joined me at the window. "A whole week of mild weather? That usually means three weeks of blizzard on the way."

"Let it come," I said, waving a hand. I was just as glad to get off the subject of roads as I was to talk about all the new comforts the castle afforded. "We have windows, and heat vents, and cushions. We could last out a year of blizzards."

Oria nodded, but—typically—reverted right back to her subject. "If you weren't looking down the road, then it's the first time in weeks."

216

"Weeks? Huh!" I scoffed.

She just shrugged a little. "Missing your brother?"

"Yes," I admitted. "I'll be glad when the roads clear—Branaric did promise to come home." Then I looked at her. "Do you miss him?"

Oria laughed, tossing her curly black hair over her shoulder. "I know I risk sounding like an old woman rather than someone who is one year past her Flower Day, but my fancy for him was nothing more than a girl's dream. I much prefer my own flirts now." She pointed at me. "That's what you need, Mel, some flirts."

I too had passed my Flower Day, which meant I was of marriageable age, but I felt sometimes as if I were ten years younger than Oria. She had lots of flirts and seemed to enjoy them all. I'd never had one—and I didn't want one. "Who has the time? I'm much too busy with Tlanth. Speaking of busy, what make you of this?" I held out the letter.

Oria took it and frowned slightly as she read. When she reached the end, she said, "It seems straightforward enough, except... Merindar. Isn't she some relation to the old king?"

"Sister," I said. "The Marquise of Merindar."

"Isn't she a princess?"

"While they ruled, the Merindars only gave the title 'prince' or 'princess' to their chosen heir. She carries the family title, which predates their years on the throne."

Oria nodded, pursing her lips. "So what does this mean?"

"That's what I'm trying to figure out. I did help bring about the downfall of her brother. I think a nasty letter threatening vengeance, awful as it would be to get, would be more understandable than this letter."

Oria smiled. "Seems honest enough. She wants to meet you."

"But why? And why now? And what's this about 'guidance'?" Oria looked back at the letter, her dark brows slightly furrowed, then whistled softly. "I missed that, first time through. What do you think she's hinting at, that she thinks the new king ought not to be king?"

217

"That is the second thing I've been wondering about," I said. "If she'd make a good ruler, then she ought to be supported..."

"Well, would she?"

"I don't know anything about her."

Oria handed the letter back, and she gave me a crooked grin. "Do you want to support her bid for the crown, or do you just want to see the Marquis of Shevraeth defeated?"

"That's the third thing on my mind," I said. "I have to admit that part of me—the part that still rankles at my defeat last year—wants him to be a bad king. But that's not being fair to the country. If he's good, then he should be king. This concerns all the people of Remalna, their safety and well-being, and not just the feelings of one sour countess."

"Who can you ask, then?"

"I don't know. The people who would know her best are all at Court, and I wouldn't trust any of *them* as far as I could throw this castle."

Oria grinned again, then looked out the window at the sunlit snowy expanse.

Materially, our lives had changed drastically since the desperate days of our revolt against Galdran Merindar. We were wealthy now, and my brother seemed to have been adopted by the very courtiers whom we had grown up regarding as our enemies. While he had lingered in the capital for half a year, I had spent much of my time initiating vast repairs to our castle and the village surrounding it. The rest of my time was spent in banishing the ignorance I had grown up with.

"How about writing to your brother?" Oria asked at last.

"Bran is good, and kind, and as honest as the stars are old," I said, "but the more I read, the more I realize that he has no political sense at all. He takes people as he finds them. I don't think he'd have the first notion about what makes a good or bad ruler."

Oria nodded slowly. "In fact, I suspect he would not even like being asked." She gave me a straight look. "There is one person you could ask, and that is the Marquis of Shevraeth."

"Ask the putative next king to evaluate his rival? Not even I would do that," I said with a grimace. "No."

"Then you could go to Court and evaluate them yourself," she stated. "Why not? Everything is finished here, or nearly. We have peace in the county, and as for the house, you made me steward. Will you trust me to carry your plans forward?"

"Of course I will," I said impatiently. "But that's not the issue. I won't go to Court. I don't want to..."

"Don't want to what?" Oria persisted.

I sighed. "Don't want to relive the old humiliations."

"What humiliations?" she asked, her eyes narrowed as she studied me. "Mel, the whole country thinks you a heroine for facing down Galdran."

"Not everyone," I muttered.

Oria crossed her arms. "Which brings us right back," she said, "to that Marquis."

I sighed again. "If I never see him again, I will be content—"

"You'll not," Oria said firmly.

I shook my head and looked out sightlessly at the snow, my mind instead reliving memories of the year before. I could just picture how he must have described our encounters—always in that drawling voice, with his courtier's wit—for the edification of the sophisticates at Court. How much laughter had every noble in the kingdom enjoyed at the expense of the barefoot, ignorant Countess Meliara Astiar of Tlanth?

"Lady Meliara?" There was a tap outside the door, and Oria's mother, Julen, lifted the tapestry. Oria and I both stared in surprise at the three long sticks she carried so carefully.

"More Fire Sticks?" I asked. "In midwinter?"

"Just found them outside the gate." Julen laid them down, looked from one of us to the other, and went out.

Oria grinned at me. "Maybe they're a present. You did save the Covenant last year, and the Hill Folk know it."

219

"*I* didn't do it," I muttered. "All I did was make mistakes."

Oria crossed her arms. "Not mistakes. Misunderstandings. Those, at least, can be fixed. All the more reason to go to Court—"

"And what?" I asked sharply. "Get myself into trouble again?"

Oria stood silently, and suddenly I was aware of the social gulf between us, and I knew she was as well. It happened like that sometimes. We'd be working side by side, cleaning or scraping or carrying, and then a liveried equerry would dash up the road with a letter, and suddenly I was the countess and she the servant who waited respectfully for me to read my letter and discuss it or not as I saw fit.

"I'm sorry," I said immediately, stuffing the Marquise's letter into the pocket of my faded, worn old gown. "You know how I feel about Court, even if Bran has changed his mind."

"I promise not to jaw on about it again, but let me say it this once. You need to make your peace," Oria said quietly. "You left your brother and the Marquis without so much as a by-your-leave, and I think it's gnawing at you. Because you keep watching that road."

I felt my temper flare, but I didn't say anything because I knew she was right. Or half right. And I wasn't angry with *her*.

I tried my best to dismiss my anger and force myself to smile. "Perhaps you may be right, and I'll write to Bran by and by. But here, listen to this!" And I picked up the book I'd been reading before the letter came. "This is one of the ones I got just before the snows closed the roads: 'And in several places throughout the world there are caves with ancient paintings and Morvende glyphs.' " I looked up from the book. "Doesn't that make you want to jump on the back of the nearest horse and ride and ride until you find these places?"

Oria shuddered. "Not me. I like it fine right here at home."

"Use your imagination!" I read on. " 'Some of the caves depict constellations never seen in our skies—' " I stopped when we heard he pealing of bells. Not the melodic pattern of the time changes, but the clang of warning bells at the guardhouse just down the road.

"Someone's coming!" I exclaimed.

Oria nodded, brows arched above her fine, dark eyes. "And the Hill Folk saw them." She pointed at the Fire Sticks.

" 'Them?' " I repeated, then glanced at the Fire Sticks and nodded. "Means a crowd, true enough."

Julen reappeared then, and tapped at the door. "Countess, I believe we have company on the road."

She looked in, and I said, "I hadn't expected anyone." Then my heart thumped, and I added, "It could be the fine weather as melted the snows down-mountain—d'you think it might be Branaric at last? I don't see how it could be anyone else!"

"Branaric needs three Fire Sticks?" Oria asked.

"Maybe he's brought lots of servants?" I suggested doubtfully. "Perhaps his half year at Court has given him elaborate tastes, ones that only a lot of servants can see to. Or he's hired artisans from the capital to help forward our work on the castle. I hope it's artisans," I added.

"Either way, we'll be wanted to find space for these newcomers," Julen said to her daughter. She picked up the Fire Sticks again and looked over her shoulder at me. "You ought to put on one of those gowns of your mother's that we remade, my lady."

"For my brother?" I laughed, pulling my blanket closer about me as we slipped out of my room. "I don't need to impress him, even if he has gotten used to Court ways!"

Julen whisked herself out.

Oria paused in the doorway. "What about your letter?"

"I guess I will have to ask Bran," I said, feeling that neck-tightening sense of foreboding again. "But later. When I find the right time."

She ducked her head in a nod, then disappeared.

I pulled the letter from my pocket, crammed it into a carved box near my bed, and ran out of the room.

The flags were chilly on my feet, but I decided against going back in for shoes. If it really was Bran, I wanted to be in the court-yard to see his face when he discovered the improvements to the castle.

The prospect of Bran's arrival, which we had all anticipated so long, made me slow my steps just a little, to look at the familiar work as if it were new: windows, modernized fireplaces, and best of all, the furnishings. My prizes were the antique plainwood tables from overseas, some with inlaid patterns, some with scrollwork and thin lines of gilding; all of it—to my eyes, anyway—beautiful. Half the rooms had new rugs from faraway Colend, where the weavers know how to fashion with clear colors the shapes of birds and flow-ers, and to make the rugs marvelously soft to the feet.

As I trod down the main stairway, I looked with pleasure at the smooth tiles that had replaced the worn, uneven stones. They made the area look lighter and larger, though I hadn't changed anything in the walls. The round window at the front of the hall had stained glass in it now, a wonderful pattern that scattered colored light across the big stairway when the sun was just right.

Oria reappeared as I crossed the hall to the front door.

"I wish the tapestries were done," I said, giving one last glance around. "Those bare walls."

Oria nodded. "True, but who will notice, with the new tiles, and these pretty trees?"

I thanked her, feeling a little guilty. I had stolen the idea of the potted trees from the Renselaeus palace—where I had been taken briefly during the latter part of the war—but how would they ever know? I comforted myself with this thought and turned my atten-tion to the others, who were all gathering to welcome Bran.

Oria, Julen, and I had designed a handsome new livery, and both women wore their new gowns. Little Calaub was proud of his new-sewn stablehand livery, which marked him out to his friends in the village for his exalted future as the Astiar Master of Horse. Village? *Town*, I thought, distracted, as the sound of pounding

orse hooves preceded Bran's arrival. Many of the artisans I'd hired
ad elected to remain, for everyone in the village had decided to
nprove their homes. We suddenly had lots of business for any who
anted it, and money—at last—to pay for it all.

The rattle up the new-paved road—our first project during
ummer—grew louder, and to our surprise, not one but four
oaches arrived, the first one a grand affair with our device boldly
ainted on its side. Outriders clattered in, their magnificent horses
icking up the powdery snow, and for a time all was chaos as the
:ablehands ran to see to the animals and lead them to our new
arn.

"Four coaches?" Julen said to me, frowning. "We've room for
1e one. Two, if they shift things around and squeeze up tightly."

"The last two will have to go to the old garrison barn," I said.
Leastwise it has a new roof."

Out of the first carriage stepped Bran, his hair loose and shining
nder a rakish plumed hat. He was dressed in a magnificent tunic
nd glossy high blackweave riding boots, with a lined cloak slung
ver one shoulder. He grinned at me—then he turned and, with a
esture of practiced grace that made me blink, handed out a lady.

A lady? I gawked in dismay at the impressive hat and muffling
loak that spanned a broad skirt, and looked down at myself, in an
ld skirt Oria had discarded, a worn tunic that I hadn't bothered
› change after my sword lesson that morning, and my bare feet.
'hen I noticed that Julen and Oria had vanished. I stood there all
lone.

In fine style Bran escorted the mysterious lady to the new slate
:eps leading to the big double doors where I stood, but then he
:ropped her arm and bounded up, grabbing me in a big hug and
vinging me around. "Sister!" He gave me a resounding kiss and
:t me down. "Place looks wonderful!"

"You *could* have let me know you were bringing a guest," I
·hispered.

"And spoil a good surprise?" he asked, indicating the lady, who was still standing on the first step. "We have plenty of room, and as you'd told me in your letter the place isn't such a rattrap anymore, I thought why not make the trip fun and bring 'em?"

" 'Them?' " I repeated faintly, but by then I already had my answer, for the outriders had resolved into a lot of liveried servants who were busy unloading coaches and helping stablehands. Through the midst of them strolled a tall, elegant man in a heellength black cloak. I looked at the familiar gray eyes, the long yellow hair—it was the Marquis of Shevraeth.

TWO

"Yes," Bran said carelessly, indicating his two
guests. "Nimiar—and Danric there, whom you already know." He
frowned. "Life, sister, why are there trees in here? Aren't there
enough of 'em outside?"

I gritted my teeth on a really nasty retort, my face burning
with embarrassment.

The lady spoke for the first time. "But Branaric, you liked them
well enough at my home, and I think it a very pretty new fashion
indeed." She turned to me, and I got a swift impression of wide-
set brown eyes, a dimpled smile, and a profusion of brown curly
hair beneath the elaborate hat. "I am Nimiar Argaliar," she said,
holding out a daintily gloved hand.

Trying desperately to force my face into a semblance of friendly
welcome, I stuck my own hand out, rather stiffly. She grasped it in
a warm grip for a moment as I said, "Welcome. I hope…you'll
enjoy it here."

"Do you have a welcome for me?" Shevraeth said with a faint
smile as he came leisurely up the steps and inside.

"Certainly," I said in a voice so determinedly polite it sounded
false even to my own ears. "Come into the parlor—*all* of you—
and I'll see to refreshment. It must have been a long trip."

"Slow," Bran said, looking around. "Roads are still bad down-mountain, but not up here anymore. You have been busy, haven't you, Mel? All I remember in this hallway is the mildew and the broken stone floor. And the parlor! What was the cost of this mosaic ceiling? Not that it matters, but it's as fine as anything in Athanarel."

I'd been proud of the parlor, over which I had spent a great deal of time. The ceiling had inlaid tiles in the same summer-sky blue that comprised the main color of the rugs and cushions and the tapestry on the wall opposite the newly glassed windows. Now I sneaked a look at the Marquis, dreading an expression of amusement or disdain. But his attention seemed to be reserved for the lady as he led her to the scattering of cushions before the fireplace, where she knelt down with a graceful sweeping of her skirts. Bran went over and opened the fire vents.

"If I'd known of your arrival, it would have been warm in here."

Bran looked over his shoulder in surprise. "Well, where d'you spend your days? Not still in the kitchens?"

"In the kitchens and the library and wherever else I'm needed," I said; and though I tried to sound cheery, it came out sounding resentful. "I'll be back after I see about food and drink."

Feeling very much like I was making a cowardly retreat, I ran down the long halls to the kitchen, cursing my bad luck as I went. There I found Julen, Oria, the new cook, and his assistant all standing in a knot talking at once. As soon as I appeared, the conversation stopped.

Julen and Oria turned to face me—Oria on the verge of laughter.

"The lady can have the new rose room, and the lord the corner suite next to your brother. But they've got an army of servants with them, Countess," Julen said heavily. Whenever she called me Countess, it was a sure sign she was deeply disturbed over something. "Where'll we house *them*? There's no space in our wing, not till we finish the walls."

"And who's to wait on whom?" Oria asked as she carefully brought my mother's good silver trays out from the wall-shelves behind the new-woven coverings. "Glad we've kept these polished," she added.

"I'd say find out how many of those fancy palace servants are kitchen trained, and draft 'em. And then see if some of the people from that new inn will come up, for extra wages. *Bran* can unpocket the extra pay," I said darkly, "if he's going to make a habit of disappearing for half a year and reappearing with armies of retainers. As for housing, well, the garrison does have a new roof, so they can all sleep there. We've got those new Fire Sticks to warm 'em up with."

"What about meals for your guests?" Oria said, her eyes wide.

I'd told Oria last summer that she could become steward of the house. While I'd been ordering books on trade, and world history, and governments, she had been doing research on how the great houses were currently run; and it was she who had hired Demnan, the new cook. We'd eaten well over the winter, thanks to his genius.

I looked at Oria. "This is it. No longer just us, no longer practice, it's time to dig out all your plans for running a fine house for a noble family. Bran and his two Court guests will need something now after their long journey, and I have no idea what's proper to offer Court people."

"Well, I do," Oria said, whirling around, hands on hips, her face flushed with pleasure. "We'll make you proud, I promise."

I sighed. "Then...I guess I'd better go back."

As I ran to the parlor, pausing only to ditch my blanket in an empty room, I steeled myself to be polite and pleasant no matter how much my exasperating brother inadvertently provoked me—but when I pushed aside the tapestry at the door, they weren't there.

And why should they be? This was Branaric's home, too.

A low murmur of voices, and a light, musical, feminine laugh drew me to the library. *At least this room is nothing to be ashamed of,* I thought, trying to steady my racing heart. I walked in, reassuring myself with the sight of the new furnishings and, on the wall, my framed map of the world, the unknown scribe's exquisitely exact use of color to represent mountains, plains, forests, lakes, and cities making it a work of art.

And on the shelves, the beginnings of a library any family might be proud of. Just last winter the room had been bare, the shelves empty. Ten years it had been so, ever since the night my father found out my mother had been killed; and in a terrible rage, he'd stalked in and burned every book there, from ancient to new. I now had nearly fifty books, all handsomely bound.

My head was high as I crossed the room to the groupings of recliner cushions, each with its lamp, that I'd had arranged about the fireplace. Of course this room was warm, for it had a Fire Stick, since I was so often in it.

Bran and his two guests looked up as I approached, and I realized that they had somehow gotten rid of their hats, cloaks, and gloves. *To one of their servants?* I should have seen to it, I realized, but I dismissed the thought. Too late—and it wasn't as if I'd known they were coming.

Lady Nimiar smiled, and Bran gave me his reckless grin. "Here y'are at last, Mel," he said. "We have something warm to drink on the way?"

"Soon. Also had to arrange housing for all those people you brought."

"Some of 'em are mine. Ours," he corrected hastily.

"Good, because we plan to put them all to work. The servants' wing is all still open to the sky. We're having it expanded. Had you ever *seen* the tiny rooms, and half of them with no fire vents? Anyway, the first snows came so early and so fierce we had to abandon the construction."

"They can go to the garrison," Bran said. "We saw it on the way in. Looks nice and snug. Where'd you get all these new books?"

"Bookseller in the capital. I'm trying to duplicate what Papa

228

destroyed, though nothing will restore the family histories that no one had ever copied."

"Most of 'em were dull as three snoring bears, burn me if they weren't!" he said, making a warding motion with one hand.

I wished I'd had the chance to decide for myself, but there was no purpose in arguing over what couldn't be fixed, so I just shook my head.

Right then Julen came in, her face solemn and closed as she bore the fine silver tray loaded with spiced hot wine and what I recognized as the apple tart we would have had after dinner, now all cut into dainty pieces and served with dollops of whipped cream on the gold-and-blue-edged porcelain plates that were our last delivery before the roads were closed. She set those down and went out.

Bran looked at me. "We serving ourselves?"

"Until we get some people from the inn," I said.

Bran sighed, getting up. "You were right, Nee. I ought to have written ahead. Thought the surprise would be more fun!" He moved to the table and poured out four glasses of wine.

Lady Nimiar also rose. She was short—just a little taller than —and had a wonderful figure that was round in all the right places. I tried not to think how I compared, with my skinny frame, and instead looked at her gown, which was a fawn color, over a rich dark brown underdress. Tiny green leaves had been embroidered along the neck, the laced-up bodice, and the hems of sleeves and skirt. I felt shabbier than ever—and studiously ignored the other guest—as I watched her pick up two wineglasses, turn, and come toward me without her train twisting round her feet or tripping her. She handed one glass to me, and Bran carried one to Shevraeth.

I tried to think of some sort of politeness to speak out, but then Bran held up his glass and said, "To my sister! Everything you've done is better than I thought possible. Though," he lowered his glass and blinked at me, "why are you dressed like that? The servants look better! Why haven't you bought new duds?"

229

"What's the use?" I said, feeling my face burn again. "There's still so much work to be done, and how can I do it in a fancy gown? And who's to be impressed? The servants?"

Lady Nimiar raised her glass. "To the end of winter."

Everyone drank, and Bran tried again. "To Mel, and what she's done for my house!"

"Our house," I said under my breath.

"Our house," he repeated in a sugary tone that I'd never heard before, but he didn't look at me. His eyes were on the lady, who smiled.

I must have been gaping, because Shevraeth lifted his glass. "My dear Branaric," he drawled in his most courtly manner, "never tell me you failed to inform your sister of your approaching change in status."

Bran's silly grin altered to the same kind of gape I'd probably been displaying a moment before. "What? Sure I did! Wrote a long letter, all about it—" He smacked his head.

"A letter which is still sitting on your desk?" Shevraeth murmured.

"Life! It must be! Curse it, went right out of my head."

I said, trying to keep my voice polite, "What is this news?"

Bran reached to take the lady's hand—probably for protection, I thought narrowly—as he said, "Nimiar and I are going to be married midsummer eve, and she's adopting into our family. You've got to come back to Athanarel to be there, Mel."

"I'll talk to you *later*." I tried my very hardest to smile at the lady. "Welcome to the family. Such as it is. Lady Nimiar."

"Please," she said, coming forward to take both my hands. "Call me Nee." Her eyes were merry, and there was no shadow of malice in her smile, but I remembered the horrible laughter that day in Athanarel's throne room, when I was brought as a prisoner before the terrible King Galdran. And I remembered how unreadable these Court-trained people were supposed to be—expressing only what they chose to—and I looked back at her somewhat

230

elplessly. "We'll soon enough be sisters, and though some families ke to observe the formalities of titles, I never did. Or I wouldn't ave picked someone like Branaric to marry," she added in a low oice, with a little laugh and a look that invited me to share her umor.

I tried to get my clumsy tongue to stir and finally managed to y, "Would you like a tour through the house, then?"

Instantly moving to Lady Nimiar's side, Bran said, "I can show ou, for in truth, I'd like a squint at all the changes myself."

She smiled up at him. "Why don't you gentlemen drink your ine and warm up? I'd rather Meliara show me about."

"But I—"

Shevraeth took Bran's shoulder and thrust him onto a cushion. it."

Bran laughed. "Oh, aye, let the females get to know one an-her."

Nimiar merely smiled.

So I led her all through the finished parts of the castle, tumbling ver my words as I tried to explain what I'd done and why. When et her get a word in, she made pleasant comments and asked easy uestions. By the time we were nearly done, though I didn't know er any better, I had relaxed a little, for I could see that she was erting herself to set me at ease. I reflected a little grimly on how aintaining an unexceptional flow of conversation was an art— e that neither Bran nor I had.

We ended up downstairs in the summer parlor, whose great assed doors would in a few months look out on a fine garden but w gave onto a slushy pathway lined by barren trees and rose-ashes. Still sitting where it had for nearly three decades was my other's harp.

As soon as Nimiar saw the instrument, she gave a gasp and essed her fingertips to her mouth. " 'Tis a Mandarel," she urmured reverently, her face flushed with excitement. "Do you ay it?"

I shook my head. "Was my mother's. I used to dance to the music she made. Do you play?"

"Not as well as this instrument deserves. And I haven't practiced for ages. That's a drawback of a life at Court. One gets bound up in the endless social rounds and forgets other things. May I try it sometime?"

"It's yours," I said. "This is going to be your home, too, and for my part, I think musical instruments ought to be played and not sit silent."

She caught my hand and kissed it, and I flushed with embarrassment.

And just then the two men came in, both wearing their cloaks again, and Bran carrying Nimiar's over his arm. "There you are. Found Mama's harp?"

"Yes, and Meliara says I may play it whenever I like."

Bran grinned at me. "A good notion, that. Only let's have it moved upstairs where it's warm, shall we?"

Nimiar turned at once to see how I liked this idea, and I spread my hands. "If you wish," I said.

Bran nodded. "Now, Mel, go get something warm on, and we'll take a turn in the garden and see what's toward outside."

"You don't need me for that," I said. "I think I'll go make sure things are working smoothly." And before anyone could say anything, I batted aside the door tapestry and fled.

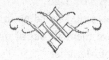

THREE

As soon as I reached my room I took out the Marquise's letter and reread it, even though by then I knew it word for word. It seemed impossible that Branaric's arrival on the same day—with Shevraeth—was a coincidence.

I sighed. Now I could not ask my brother outright about this letter. He was as tactless as he was honest. I could easily imagine him blurting it out over dinner. *He* might find it diverting, though I didn't think Shevraeth would, for the same reason I couldn't ask him his opinion of Arthal Merindar: because the last time we had discussed the possible replacement for Galdran Merindar, I had told him flatly I'd rather see my brother crowned than another lying courtier.

Remembering that conversation—in Shevraeth's father's palace, with his father listening—I winced. It wasn't just Bran who lacked tact.

Oria is probably right, I thought glumly, *there are too many misunderstandings between the Marquis and me.* The problem with gathering my courage and broaching the subject was the very fact of the kingship. If I hadn't been able to resolve those misunderstandings before Galdran's death, when Shevraeth was just the Marquis, it seemed impossible to do it now when he was about to take the crown. My motives might be mistaken and he'd think me one of those fawning courtiers at the royal palace. Ugh!

So I asked Oria to tell them I was sick. I holed up in my room with a book and did my best to shove them all out of my mind— as well as the mysterious Marquise of Merindar.

At sundown the next day there came a cough outside my room. Before I could speak, the tapestry swung aside as if swatted by an impatient hand, and there was Bran. "Hah!" he exclaimed, fists on his hips. "I knew it! Reading, and not sick at all. Burn it, Mel, they're our guests."

"They are your guests, and you can entertain them," I retorted.

"You don't like Nee?" He looked upset.

I sighed. "She seems as nice as any Court lady could possibly be, but how can she think I'm anything but an idiot? As for that Shevraeth, you brought him. He's yours to entertain. I don't need him laughing at me for my old clothes and lack of courtly finesse."

"He isn't going to laugh at you, Mel," Bran said, running his fingers through his hair. "Life! We didn't come all the way up here to talk to ourselves. Nee's going to play the harp before supper. She spent all afternoon retuning the thing. If you don't come, after all I said about how you like music, she'll get hurt—think you don't want her here. As for your clothes, you must have *something* nice."

I remembered my two remade dresses. "All right," I said grumpily. "I'll change and be right down."

He kissed the top of my head and left.

I opened my wardrobe, eyeing the two gowns. Most of my mother's things had been ruined when the weather got into her rooms. But we'd saved these, and Hrani the weaver had reworked them to fit me. One was a plain gown Mama had used for gardening, its fabric sturdy enough to have lasted. The other had taken some patient restitching, but I really loved it. The color was a soft gray blue, with tiny iridescent mois gems sewn over the tight sleeves and edging the square neck. It gathered at a high waist, opening onto a deep-blue skirt with gold birds embroidered on it. I had a vague memory of her having worn it, and I liked the idea of having something of hers for myself.

Besides, I thought it looked nice on me. She'd been a little taller, but otherwise our builds were much alike. I put the gown on, combed out my hair and rebraided it, and wrapped it up in its accustomed coronet.

Then I went down to the upper parlor that they seemed to have adopted. I could hear random notes from the harp, a shivery pleasant sound that plucked at old and beloved memories, just as wearing the gown did.

I slipped through the door tapestry, and three faces turned toward me.

And my dear brother snorted. "Mel! Where are your wits gone begging? Why d'you have to wear an old gown thirty years out-of-date when you can have anything you want?"

I turned right around and started to leave, but Nimiar rose and sped to my side, her small hand grasping my gem-encircled wrist. "This is a lovely dress, and if it's old, what's the odds? A lady has the right to be comfortable in her own home."

Bran rubbed his chin. "Don't tell me you ever looked like that?"

"Oh, Branaric. Take Lord Vidanric up to dinner. I'll play afterward. The harp isn't ready yet."

"But—"

"Please," she said.

Shevraeth's lips were twitching. He jerked his chin toward the doorway and my brother followed, protesting all the way.

My eyes stung. I stood like a stone statue as Nimiar sighed then said, "Your brother is a dear, and I do love him for the way he never fears to tell the truth. But he really doesn't understand some things, does he?"

"No," I squeaked. My voice seemed to come from someone else.

Nimiar ran her fingers along the harp strings and cocked her

235

head, listening to the sounds they produced. "No one," she said, "—well, no ordinary person—sits down to a harp and plays perfectly. It takes time and training."

I nodded stupidly.

She dropped her hands. "When Branaric came to Athanarel, he knew nothing of etiquette or Court custom. Arrived wearing cast-off war gear belonging to Lord Vidanric, his arm in a dirty sling, his nose red from a juicy cold. There are those at Court who would have chewed him like jackals with a bone, except he freely admitted to being a rustic. Thought it a very good joke. Then he'd been brought by the Marquis, who is a leader of fashion, and Savona took to him instantly. The Duke of Savona is another leader. And…" She hesitated. "And certain women who also lead fashion liked him. Added was the fact that you Astiars have become something of heroes, and it became a fad to teach him. His blunt speech was a refreshing change, and he doesn't care at all what people think of him. But you do, don't you?" She peered into my face. "You care—terribly."

I bit my lip.

She touched my wrist. "Let us make a pact. If you will come to Athanarel and dance at my wedding, I will undertake to teach you everything you need to know about Court life. And I'll help you select a wardrobe—and no one need ever know."

I swallowed, then took a deep, unsteady breath.

"What is it?" She looked unhappy. "Do you mistrust me?"

I shook my head so hard my coronet came loose, and a loop settled over one eye. "*They* would know," I whispered, waving a hand.

"They? Your servants? Oh. You mean Branaric and Lord Vidanric?"

I nodded. "They'll surely want to know my reasons. Since I didn't come to Court before." I thought of that letter hidden in my room and wondered if its arrival and Shevraeth's on the same day had some sinister political meaning.

She smiled. "Don't worry about Bran. All he wants, you must see, is to show you off at Athanarel. He knew you were refurbishing his castle, and I rather think he assumed you were—somehow—learning everything he was learning and obtaining a fashionable wardrobe as well. And every time he talks of you it's always to say how much more clever you are than he is. I really think he expected to bring us here and find you waiting as gowned and jeweled as my cousin Tamara."

I winced. "That sounds, in truth, like Branaric."

"And as for Vidanric, well, you're safe there. I've never met anyone as closemouthed, when he wants to be. He won't ask your reasons. What?"

"I said, 'Hah.'"

"What is it, do you mislike him?" Again she was studying me, her fingers playing with the pretty fan hanging at her waist.

"Yes. No. Not mislike, but more...mistrust. Not what he'll do, but what he might say," I babbled. "Oh, never mind. It's all foolishness. Suffice it to say I feel better when we're at opposite ends of the country, but I'll settle for opposite ends of the castle."

Her eyes widened. If she hadn't been a lady, I would have said she was on the verge of whistling. "Well, here's a knot. But—there's nothing for it." She closed the fan with a snap, then ran her hands over the harp.

"Why should it matter?" I asked, after a long moment. "If I don't want to be around Shevraeth, I mean."

She plucked a string and bent down to twist the key, then plucked it again, her head cocked, though I have a feeling she wasn't listening. Finally she said, "Of course you probably know he's likely to be the new king. His parents are in Athanarel now, his father making his first appearance in many years, and he came armed with a Letter of Regard from Queen Yustnesveas Landis of Sartor. It seems that in her eyes the Renselaeus family has the best claim to the kingdom of Remalna."

Half a year ago I would have been puzzled by this, but my

subsequent reading gave me an inkling of what protracted and ticklish diplomacy must have gone on beneath the surface of events to have produced such a result. "Well. So the Merindars no longer have a legal claim. If they mean to pursue one." I added hastily, "*Meant* to pursue one."

She gave a little nod. "Precisely. As it transpires, the Prince and Princess of Renselaeus do not want to rule. They're merely there to oversee what their son has accomplished and, I think, to establish a sense of order and authority. It is very hard to gainsay either of them, especially the Prince," she added with a smile.

When I nodded, she looked surprised. "You have met him, then?"

"Yes. Briefly."

"Would that be when you made the alliance? You know how bad Bran is at telling stories. A random sentence or two, then he scratches his head and claims he can't remember any more. And the Renselaeuses don't talk about the war at all."

This news surprised and amazed me. A portion of the tightness inside me eased, just a little.

"To resume—and we'd better hurry, or they'll be down here clamoring for our company before their supper goes cold—Lord Vidanric has been working very hard ever since the end of the war. Too hard, some say. He came to Athanarel sick and has been ill off and on since then, for he seldom sleeps. He's either in the saddle, or else his lamps are burning half the night in his wing of the Residence. He's here on his mother's orders, to rest. He and your brother have become fast friends, I think because Branaric, in his own way, is so very undemanding. He wants no favors or powers. He just likes to enjoy his days. This seems to be what Vidanric needs just now."

"Do you think he'll make a good king?" I asked.

Again she seemed surprised. "Yes," she said. "But then I've known him all my life."

As if that explains everything, I thought. Then I realized that to

er it did. He was a good prospect for a king because he was her
friend, and because they were both courtiers, raised the same way.

And then I wondered just who—if anyone—at Court was willing to speak not for themselves, but for the people, to find out who
really would be the best ruler?

A discreet tap outside the door brought our attention round.
Calden, the server from the inn, parted the tapestry and said,
"Count Branaric sent me to find out if you're coming?"

"In just a moment, thanks," I said.

"Will you agree to my pact, then?" Nimiar asked.

I opened my mouth to ask why they couldn't just marry here,
but I knew that was the coward's way out. I did not wish to get
involved in any more wars, but that didn't mean I ought not do
what I could to ensure that the next reign would be what Papa had
wished for when he commenced planning his revolt.

And the best way to find out, I realized as I looked into Nimiar's
face, would not be by asking questions of third parties, but by going
to the capital and finding out on my own.

So I squashed down my reluctance and said, "If you can teach
me not to make a fool of myself at that Court, I'll gladly come to
see you marry Bran."

"You will like Court life, I promise," she said, smiling sweetly
as we went out of the parlor.

I took care to walk behind her so she could not see my face.

For the next several weeks Nee and I spent nearly all our days
together as she tried to remake me into a Court lady. Most of the
time it was fun, a little like what I imagined playacting to be, as we
stood side by side facing a mirror and practiced walking and sitting
and curtsying. Nee seemed to enjoy teaching me. The more we
talked, the less opaque I found her. Beneath the automatic smiling
mask of Court, she was a quiet, restful person who liked comfort
and pleasant conversation.

239

In between lessons she talked about her friends at Court: what they liked, or said, or how they entertained. Pleasant, easy talk, meant to show all her friends in the best light; she did not, I realized, like politics or gossip. She never once mentioned the Marquise of Merindar.

In my turn I told her my history, bits at a time, but only if she asked. And ask she did. She listened soberly, wincing from time to time; one cold, blustery day I recounted how I had ended up in Baron Debegri's dungeon, and my narrow escape therefrom.

At the end of that story she shuddered and asked, "How could you have lived through that and still be sane?"

"Am I sane?" I joked. "There are some who might argue." Her reaction secretly cheered me, exactly like a ten-year-old who has managed to horrify her friends. *It isn't much of a claim to fame, but it's all I have*, I thought later as I stared down at the third fan I'd broken, and when—again—I'd forgotten which curtsy to make to which person under which circumstances.

The one thing I couldn't talk about was that terrible day when Shevraeth brought me to face Galdran before the entire Court. I did not want to know if Nimiar had been there, and had looked at me, and had laughed.

We saw Bran and Shevraeth only at dinner, and that seldom enough, for they were often away. When the weather was particularly bad, they might be gone for several days. On the evenings we were alone, Nee and I would curl up in her room or mine, eating from silver trays and talking.

Branaric and the Marquis managed to be around on most days when the weather permitted gatherings in the old garrison courtyard for swordfighting practice. Even though I was not very good at it, I enjoyed sword work. At least I enjoyed it when not rendered acutely conscious of all my failings, when the bouts were attended by someone tall, strong, naturally gifted with grace, and trained since childhood—such as the Marquis of Shevraeth. So after a couple of particularly bad practices (in which I tried so hard not to get laughed at that I made more mistakes than ever), I stopped going whenever I saw him there.

When Nee and I did join Bran and the Marquis for dinner, for the most part I sat in silence and watched Nee covertly, trying to copy her manners. No one—not even Bran—remarked on it if I sat through an entire meal without speaking.

Thus I was not able to engender any discussions about the Marquise of Merindar, so the letter—and the question of kingship—stayed dormant, except at night in my troubled dreams.

Nee had brought only one seamstress, whom she dispatched with outriders the day after our conversation in the parlor. Armed with one of my drafts on our bankers at Arclor House, this woman was entrusted to hire three more seamstresses and to bring back cloth suitable for gowns and accoutrements.

I don't know what instructions Nimiar gave her seamstress in private. I had expected a modest trunk of nice fabric, enough for a gown or two in the current fashions. What returned, though, just over a week later, was a hired wagon bearing enough stuff to outfit the entire village, plus three determined young journey-seamstresses who came highly recommended and who were ready to make their fortunes.

"Good," Nee said, when we had finished interviewing them. She walked about inspecting the fabulous silks, velvets, linens, and glorious array of embroidery twists, nodding happily. "Just what I wanted. Melise is a treasure."

"Isn't this too much?" I asked, astounded.

She grinned. "Not when you count up what you'll need to make the right impression. Remember, you are acquiring overnight what ought to have been put together over years. Morning gowns, after-noon gowns, riding tunics and trousers, party dresses, and perhaps one ball gown, though that kind of thing you can order when we get to town, for those take an unconscionable amount of time to make if you don't have a team doing it."

"A team? Doing nothing but sewing? What a horrible life!" I exclaimed.

"Those who choose it would say the same about yours, I think," Nee said with a chuckle. "Meaning your life as a revolutionary. There are many, not just women, though it's mostly females, who like very much to sit in a warm house and sew and gossip all day. In the good houses the tailors have music, or have books read to them, and the products are the better for their minds being engaged in something interesting. This is their art, just as surely as yon scribe regards her map and her fellows regard their books." She pointed toward the library. "And how those at Court view the way they conduct their public lives."

"So much to learn," I said with a groan. "How will I manage?"

She just laughed; and the next day a new arrival brought my most formidable interview yet: with my new maid.

"Her name is Mora," Nee told me, "and she's a connection of my own Ilvet. An aunt, I think. Ilvet promises she is deft and discreet. She was working for one of the northern families—low pay and too much work—but she stayed until her mistress married and adopted into a household even more huskscraping. Mora and the others suddenly found themselves each doing the work of three, while living in chambers that hadn't been altered for four hundred years—right down to the mold on the stones. If you like her, she will then hire your staff, whom you will never really see."

I shook my head. "Strange, to consider having a staff I won't see." But as I went to the interview, my thought was: *You mean, if she likes me.*

Mora was tall and thin, with gray-streaked dark hair. *Her face is more inscrutable even than Shevraeth's*, I thought with dismay. She bowed, then waited, her hands folded, for me to speak.

I took a deep breath. "I gather you're used to sophisticated

Court people, and I'd better tell you right out that I'm not
sophisticated and haven't been to Court. Well, except once, but that
was against my will. It's true that I'm going to Court, but I don't
know that I'll stay past the wedding; and then—most likely—it's
back here for the rest of my life. I go barefoot all summer, and
until now I've never owned more than one hat. And my friends
have all been village people."

She said nothing, but there was the faintest crinkling of humor
about her eyes.

"On the other hand," I said, "I'm used to cleaning up after
myself. I also won't interfere with your hiring whomever you need,
and you'll be paid whatever you think fair, at least while we *can*
pay. The fortune came to us on someone's whim, so I suppose it
could disappear the same way."

Mora bowed. "You honor me," she said, "with your honesty,
my lady."

"Does that mean you'll stay?" I asked, after an uncomfortable
pause.

She smiled then, just a little. "I believe, my lady," she said, "it
is for you to decide if you want me."

I clapped my hands, relieved that this formidable woman had
not left in disgust. "Great. Then start today," I said, and grinned.
"There's plenty to do if I'm to get properly civilized."

243

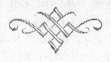

FOUR

MY FIRST GOWN WAS READY SHORTLY THEREAFTER.

It was a dinner gown; I was learning the distinctions between the types of clothing. Morning gowns were the simplest, designed to be practical for working at home. Afternoon gowns were for going visiting, for receiving visitors, and for walking. Dinner gowns were elaborate in the upper half, meant to make one look good while sitting, and narrow in the skirt, so one's skirts wouldn't drape beyond one's cushion. The distinction between party gowns and dinner gowns was blurring, Nee told me, because so frequently now there were dances directly after dinner; quite different again were the ball gowns, which were designed to look good moving. And then there was the formal Court gown, meant for state occasions, and few people had more than one, or possibly two, of these—they were meant to be seen again, and in these, the fashions had changed the least.

"Everyone will retire those they wore for Galdran's affairs, though, either giving them away, or consigning them to attics for their descendants to marvel at, or having them taken apart and remade into new gowns, for the materials are hideously expensive. At the coronation of the new ruler everything will be all new."

"So all these other fashions will change again?" I asked.

"They change all the time." She watched, smiling, as I put on ny first dinner gown and started lacing up the front. "Remind me to take you to the Heraldry Archive. There's been someone to draw pictures of what the rulers wear for, oh, centuries. It's astonishing to look through those pictures and see what our ancestors wore. I quite like the silken tunics and loose trousers of four hundred years ago, when we had Theraez of the West as our queen. Several generations before that, our climate must have been very warm, for all the hats were sun hats, and short hair was the fashion. No one wore gloves. Quite the opposite of the awful things they wore a hundred years ago—all gaudy, with odd angles, and those huge shoulders on the men, meant to cover up the fact that the king was as vain as he was fat. After him the clothes were more attractive in design, but everything was stiff with jewels and metallic embroidery. It was probably blinding in the sunlight! But that's in living memory, and my grandmother talks of how old all the Court leaders then were, and how very, very formal."

"And now?" I said, taking down my hair and unbraiding it.

"Now we're mostly young, for despite all the talk about Galdran liking young active folk, the truth was, we were there as hostages so our parents would not gainsay him." She smiled. "So though we are young, we prize delicacy of speech, and no one ever gets drunk in public. That kind of behavior, once a luxury, could get one killed under Galdran's rule. So could free speech, which is why fans became so popular. Speaking of fans, now that you know how to open one, and hold it, I'll teach you how to speak with it."

"Speak? With a fan?" I asked.

She grinned. "There are times when words say too much—or too little. For example, watch this." She tapped my wrist lightly with her closed fan. Her wrist was arched, her hand angled downward. "What does that seem to suggest?"

"That I stay where I am," I guessed, mildly intrigued.

She nodded. "But watch this." She tapped my wrist again, still holding the fan closed, but this time her hand was angled differently so that I saw the underside of her wrist.

"It's like a beckon," I said.

"Exactly. The first keeps a suitor at his distance, the second invites him to close the distance, all without speaking a word."

"That's flirting," I said in disgust. "I don't have any need for that. If any Court toady tries that on me, I'll be happy to use my words to send him to the rightabout. That's not why—" *I'm going to Court*, I started to say, but then I closed my mouth.

If she noticed the lapse, she gave no sign. "But it's not just for flirting," she said. "There are so many modes, all of which can change the meaning of one's words. I should add that we often used the fan language to make fun of Galdran or to give ourselves the lie when we had to flatter him. He had a habit—more and more in the last three or four years—of using threats to get flattery. I think he suspected that the end was near."

I whistled. "So the fan language is a kind of flag code? Like the navies use?"

"I guess you could think of it that way," she said. "I liked it because it gave us a bit of freedom, for Galdran never used a fan. Considered it female foolery, even when Savona and the other young men used it right before his face. Stars! Your hair *is* long!" She stood back and admired the waving auburn river of hair that hung just past my knees.

"I promised not to cut it until Mama was avenged, and now I find I can't," I said, and when I saw her odd expression, asked forebodingly, "Don't tell me I'll get laughed at..."

"Oh no," she said, brimming with sudden mirth. "It's becoming a fashion, very long hair—coming from the south, of course, where Queen Yustnesveas Landis has very long hair. She's young, you know, and so she leads fashion as well as rules. Anyway, everyone is trying to grow theirs; and...someone will be jealous."

"Someone?" I repeated, mentally reviewing her descriptions of various Court figures. She did not always name them, I had noticed, particularly when she made her—rare—criticisms. "Is this the same someone you've almost named once before?"

She smiled wryly. "I think I've already said too much. Won't

246

u leave yours down for dinner tonight? It looks quite lovely."

"Not to kneel on at the table," I said, swiftly rebraiding it. ince there's no one to impress. Now, back to the fans. Let's have me of that code."

"All right," she said. "This mode is called Within the Circle." e twirled her open fan gently in an arc. "It means that the speaker gards the listeners as friends. But if you wave it back—like this— en it alters to the Walled Circle Mode, which indicates trusted ends. It binds the listeners not to speak of what they've heard…"

r dinner that night we found Bran and Shevraeth waiting in the rlor next to the dining room. Nee had probably prepared them, ealized. This was new for me, but it was according to the rules etiquette; and if I looked at it as rehearsal—more of the ayacting—I found it easy to walk in beside her, minding my steps that my skirt flowed gracefully and my floor-length sleeves aped properly without twisting or tripping me up.

Nee walked straight to my brother, who performed a bow, and inning widely, offered his arm.

This left me with the Marquis, who looked tall and imposing dark blue embroidered with pale gold, which—I realized as I nced just once at him—was the exact same shade as his hair. He d nothing, just bowed, but there was mild question in his gray es as he held out his arm.

I grimaced, thinking: *You'll have to learn this some time. May's ll get it over quickly.* Putting my fingertips so lightly on his sleeve carcely felt the fabric, I fell into step beside him as we followed e other two into the dining room. Though this was my home, I ln't plop down cross-legged onto my cushion, but knelt in the proved style.

After I'd fortified myself with a gulp of wine, Bran said, "Life, el, you look fine. Getting some more of those duds?"

I nodded.

"What have you done with your day?" Nee asked, her fan spread in the attitude I recognized from our fan lesson as Harmonic Discourse.

"We had a bout with the group at the garrison, had a squint at some horses brought from up-mountain. Danric answered mail, and I went over to town with Calder to look at the plans for paving the streets."

This was Tlanth business. I said, "Did you talk to the elders? They want part of their taxes to go to that."

Bran nodded. "It's a fair plan," he said; and I sat back, relieved.

Nee put her chin in her hand. " 'Answered mail,' Vidanric? Is he referring to that formidable bag your equerries brought in this morning?"

"We're finishing the last of the dispersal and reassignment of Galdran's army," Shevraeth said.

"Dispersal?" I repeated, thinking immediately of my plans for evaluating his forming government. Surely it would raise no suspicions to ask about it, since he had introduced the subject. "You've dismantled that gigantic army?"

"A huge standing army with little to do is both—"

" '—a financial burden and a threat,' " I said. "I recognize the quote—and I agree," I added hastily, seeing consternation on Bran's face. "I just…wondered what was happening to them," I finished rather lamely.

To my surprise, Shevraeth said, "I shall be happy to discuss it with you. My decision did not meet with universal approval—there were advocates for extremes at either end—and some of my nearest associates grow tired of the whole affair." Here he saluted Bran with his wineglass, and Bran grinned unrepentantly.

"It's boring," my brother retorted. "And I can't even begin to keep it all in my head. Tlanth's affairs I see as my duty. Dealing with the affairs of the kingdom I regard as a narrow escape."

In disbelief I addressed the Marquis. "Don't you have advisers?"

"Quantities of them," he responded, "most of whom—nearly all, I very much regret to say—are precisely the people one wishes to listen to least: former Galdran toadies who are angling for new privileges, or to keep the ones they have; troublemakers; and then there are mere busybodies. I listen to them all, more to find out the trends of gossip in reaction to what I've done than to seek guidance for future decisions."

"Who are the troublemakers? People who want to rule?"

"Some of them," he agreed. "Among whom are a few with legitimate claims. Then there are those who are backing these claimants, with their own ends in view. Your own names have been put forth."

Bran grinned. "Grumareth kept after me the whole time I was in Athanarel."

"Well, maybe he thinks you'd rule well," I said.

Bran laughed. "He thinks I'd be easy to lead by the nose, yet too stupid to see him doing it."

I looked down at my plate, remembering again the terrible dinner with the Prince of Renselaeus when I had aired my views on how my brother would make a much better king than Shevraeth. Was that argument about to resurface?

But the Marquis said, "Poor Grumareth chose unwisely when he allied with Galdran. His was one of the duchies drained most by the 'volunteer taxes' and the forced levies for the army. I think he dreams of recouping what he lost. His people have to be clamoring for justice."

"He's a foolish man," Nee said, "but his great-niece isn't a fool."

Shevraeth nodded to her. "You're right. And I'm hoping that the duke will remain at Court to busy himself with plots and plans that won't work, so that Lady Elenet can stay in Grumareth and straighten things out."

Nee's eyes were sober as she glanced across the table, but her voice was exactly as pleasant and polite as ever. "So you will not strip the family of lands and title, despite his foolishness in the past?"

"The Duke of Grumareth was always a fool and will always be a fool," Shevraeth said, so lightly it was hard to believe he wasn't joking. His tone altered as he added, "I see no need to ruin the family over his mistakes. There is sufficient intelligence and good-will among them to see that their lands are restored to peace and thereby set on the way to recovering their former prosperity."

Nee smiled. "Trust Elenet for that." That was all she said, but I had a very strong feeling from both their tones of voice that there was an unspoken issue between them. Then I realized that she had been playing with her fan as they talked; I glanced at it, but if she'd used it to make more plain whatever it was that I sensed, it was too late now. She sat back, laying her fan in her lap as she reached for her wine.

"If everyone who compromised with Galdran out of fear, or greed, or even indifference, were to be penalized," Shevraeth went on, "Athanarel would soon be empty and a lot of people sent home with little to do but use their wealth and power toward recovering their lost prestige."

"More war," I said, and thinking again of my secret cause, I ventured a question. "Do you agree with Mistress Ynizang's writings about the troubles overseas and how they could have been avoided?"

Shevraeth nodded, turning to me. "That's an excellent book—one of the first my parents put into my hands when it became apparent I was serious about entering their plans."

"What's this? Who?" Bran asked, looking from one of us to the other.

Shevraeth said, "She is a historian of great repute in the Queen of Sartor's Court, and I believe what she says about letting social custom and the human habit of inertia bridge an old regime to a new, when there is no active evil remaining."

"Sounds dull as a hibernating snake. Saving your grace." Bran saluted the Marquis with his glass, then said, "Tell my sister about the army."

Shevraeth saluted my brother with his own glass and a slightly mocking smile. "To resume: Dispersal and reassignment. I have relied heavily upon certain officers whom I have come to trust—"

"Which is why you were up here against us last winter, eh?" Bran asked, one brow cocked up. "Scouting out the good ones?"

Old anger stirred deep inside me as I remembered the common talk from a year ago, about Shevraeth's very public wager with the Duke of Savona about how soon he could thoroughly squelch the rustic Tlanths—meaning Branaric and me. Fighting down my emotions, I realized that yet again I had been misled by surface events—and again I had misjudged Shevraeth's true motives.

"Precisely," the Marquis said. "Those who wish to stay are relatively easy; they await reassignment. Those who are unhappy, or incompetent, or for whatever reason are deemed ready for a civilian life are being cut loose with a year's pay. We are encouraging them to get training or to invest in some way so that they have a future, but a good part of that cash will inevitably find its way into the ready hands of pleasure houses. Still, each new civilian leaves with the warning that any bands of ex-soldiers roaming the countryside as brigands are going to find their futures summarily ended."

"So that's where the surplus money went," I said. "What about Galdran's bullies who *loved* their work?"

"The hardest part of our job is to determine who has the necessary qualifications for keeping order, and who merely has a taste for intimidating the populace. Those who fall between the two will be sent for a lengthy stint on border patrol up north, well away from events in the capital."

His readiness to answer my questions caused my mind to glitter with new ideas, like a fountain in the sunlight. I was suddenly eager to try my own theories of government, formed during my half year of reading. I launched a barrage of questions related to the merits of an all volunteer army paid from crown revenues, versus each noble being responsible for a certain number of trained and equipped soldiers should the need arise. To each question Shevraeth readily responded, until we had a conversation—not quite a debate—going about the strengths and weaknesses of each method of keeping the country safe.

Very soon I began to see where my lapses of knowledge were, for he knew the books I quoted from. Further, he knew the sources' strengths and weaknesses, whereas I had taken them as authorities. Still, I was enjoying myself, until I remembered what he'd said about listening to busybodies. Immediately full of self-doubt at the thought, I wondered if I sounded like one of those busybodies. Or worse, had I betrayed my secret quest?

Abruptly I stopped talking and turned my attention to my dinner, which lay cold and untouched on my plate. Stealing a quick glance up, I realized that I'd also kept Shevraeth talking so that his dinner was equally cold. I picked up my fork, fighting against another surge of those old feelings of helpless anger.

Into the sudden silence Branaric laughed, then said, "You've left me behind. What have you been reading, Mel? Life! You should go south to Sartor and help take the field against the Norsunder. Unless you're planning another revolution here!"

"Were you thinking of taking the field against me?" the Marquis addressed me in his usual drawl.

Aghast, I choked on a bite of food. Then I saw the gleam of humor in his eyes, and realized he'd been joking. "But I'm not," I squawked. "Not at all! I just like, well, reading and thinking about these things."

"And testing *your* knowledge, Danric," Bran added.

"Whether you are testing mine or your own, you really will get your best information firsthand," Shevraeth said to me. "Come to Athanarel. Study the records. Ask questions."

Was he really inviting me straight out to do what I'd resolved o secretly? I had no idea what to make of his words. "Promised Nimiar I'd come," I mumbled, and that ended the subject.

ater, Nee sat with me in my room. We were drinking hot chocolate and talking about music, something I usually enjoy. But the inner conversation was on my mind, and finally I said, "May I ask you a personal question?"

She looked up in query and made the graceful little gesture that had learned was an invitation.

"Isn't Shevraeth a friend of yours?"

"Yes," she said cautiously.

"Then why the fan, and the careful words when you asked about your friend Elenet?"

Nee set her cup down, her brow slightly furrowed. "We are iends to a degree... Though we all grew up at Court, I was never ne of his intimates, nor even one of his flirts. Those all tended to e the leaders of fashion. So I don't really know how close he was any of them, except perhaps for Savona. It took everyone by urprise to find out that he was so different from the person we'd rown up with." She shrugged. "He was always an object of gossip, ut I realized recently that though we heard much about what he d, we never heard what he thought."

"You mean he didn't tell anyone," I said.

"Exactly. Anyway, Elenet *is* an old friend, of both of us, which complicated by her family's machinations. Her safety is important me. Yet in referring to it, I don't want to seem one of the busy-odies or favor-seekers."

"I don't think you could," I said.

She laughed. "Anyone can do anything, with determination d an inner conviction of being right. Whether they really are ght..." She shrugged.

"Well, if he wants to be king, he'll just plain have to get used questions and toadies and all the rest of it," I said. Remembering the conversation at dinner and wondering if I'd made an idiot of myself, I added crossly, "I don't have any sympathy at all. In fact, I wish he hadn't come up here. If he needed rest from the fatigue of taking over a kingdom, why couldn't he go to that fabulous palace in Renselaeus? Or to Shevraeth, which I'll just bet has an equally fabulous palace?"

Nee sighed. "Is that a rhetorical or a real question?"

"Real. And I don't want to ask Bran because he's so likely to hop out with my question when we're all together and fry me with embarrassment," I finished bitterly.

She gave a sympathetic grin. "Well, I suspect it's to present a united front, politically speaking. You haven't been to Court, so you don't quite comprehend how much you and your brother have become heroes—symbols—to the kingdom. Especially you, which is why there were some murmurs and speculations when you never came to the capital."

I shook my head. "Symbol for failure, maybe. *We* didn't win— Shevraeth did."

She gave me an odd look midway between surprise and curiosity. "But to return to your question, Vidanric's tendency to keep his own counsel ought to be reassuring as far as people hopping out with embarrassing words are concerned. If I were you—and I know it's so much easier to give advice than to follow it—I'd sit down with him, when no one else is at hand, and talk it out."

Just the thought of seeking him out for a private talk made me shudder. "I'd rather walk down the mountain in shoes full of snails."

It was Nee's turn to shudder. "Life! I'd rather do almost anything than *that*—"

A "Ho!" outside the door interrupted her.

Bran carelessly flung the tapestry aside and sauntered in. "There y'are, Nee. Come out on the balcony with me? It's actually nice out, and we've got the moon up." He extended his hand.

Nee looked over at me as she slid her hand into his. "Want to come?"

I looked at those clasped hands, then away. "No, thanks," I said irily. "I think I'll practice my fan, then read myself to sleep. Good night."

They went out, Bran's hand sliding round her waist. The tapstry dropped into place on Nee's soft laugh.

I got up and moved to my window, staring out at the stars.

It seemed an utter mystery to me how Bran and Nimiar enjoyed looking at each other. Touching each other. Even the practical Oria, I realized—the friend who told me once that things were more interesting than people—had freely admitted to liking flirting.

How does that happen? I shook my head, thinking that it would never happen to me. Did I want it to?

Suddenly I was restless and the castle was too confining.

Within the space of a few breaths I had gotten rid of my civilized clothing and soft shoes and had pulled my worn, patched tunic, trousers, and tough old mocs from the trunk in the corner.

I slipped out of my room and down the stair without anyone seeing me, and before the moon had traveled the space of a hand across the sky, I was riding along the silver-lit trails with the wind in my hair and the distant harps of the Hill Folk singing forlornly in the mountaintops.

FIVE

THE BUDS WERE JUST STARTING TO SHOW GREEN ON the trees when Bran said suddenly at dinner one day, "We ought to start to Remalna-city, Mel. Danric has work to do, and Nee hasn't seen her people for all these weeks. And as for me—" He winced. "I'm glad when we have a clear enough day where the construction can go on, but life! The noise and mess make me feel like a cat in a dog kennel."

"Set the date," I said, which I think surprised them all.

But I had already realized that there was little to keep me in Tlanth. Our county was on its way to recovery. By this time the next year we would even have paved roads between the villages and down to the lowlands—everywhere but beyond that invisible line that everyone in Tlanth knew was the border of the Hill Folk's territory.

Nee and Bran began talking about what delights awaited us in the capital. My last order of books had come in three weeks before, and I hadn't ordered more, for Nee and Bran both assured me that the library at Athanarel was fabulous—fantastic—*full*. To all their other words I smiled and nodded, inwardly thinking about the Marquise of Merindar's letter and my own reason for going to Court.

Shevraeth didn't say anything, or if he did, I didn't hear it, for I avoided him whenever possible.

The day before our departure was mild and clear with only an occasional white cloud drifting softly overhead. Bran swooped down on us just after breakfast and carried Nee off for a day alone.

So during the afternoon I retreated to the library and curled up in the window seat with a book on my lap.

But for once the beautifully drawn words refused to make sense, and I gazed instead out the window at the rose garden, which would be blooming well after I was gone. "My last afternoon of peace," I muttered with my forehead against the glass, then I snorted. It sounded fine and poetic—but I knew that as long as I thought that way, the peace had already ended.

And what was I afraid of?

I now knew enough of the rules of etiquette to get by, and I was now the proud possessor of what I once would have thought the wardrobe of a queen. And I wouldn't be alone, for my brother and my sister-to-be would accompany me.

As for the Marquise of Merindar's letter, perhaps its arrival and Shevraeth's on the very same day were coincidences after all. No one had said anything to me about it. And if I were reasonably careful at Court, I could satisfy my quest....

Except, what then?

I was still brooding over this question when I heard a polite tap outside the tapestry, and a moment later, there was the equally quiet impact of a boot heel on the new tile floor, then another.

A weird feeling prickled down my neck, and I twisted around to face the Marquis of Shevraeth, who stood just inside the room. He raised his hands and said, "I am unarmed."

I realized I was glaring. "I hate people creeping up behind me," I muttered.

He glanced at the twenty paces or so of floor between us, then up at the shelves, the map, the new books. Was he comparing this library with the famed Athanarel one—or the equally (no doubt!) impressive one at his home in Renselaeus? I folded my arms and waited for either satire or condescension.

When he spoke, the subject took me by surprise. "You said once that your father burned the Astiar library. Did you ever find out why?"

"It was the night we found out that my mother had been killed," I said reluctantly. The old grief oppressed me, and I fought to keep my thoughts clear. "By the order of Galdran Merindar."

"Do you know why he ordered her murder?" he asked over his shoulder, as he went on perusing the books.

I shook my head. "No. There's no way to find out that I can think of. Even if we discovered those who carried out the deed, they might not know the real reasons." I added sourly, "Well do I remember how Galdran issued lies to cover his misdeeds: Last year, when he commenced the attack against us, he dared to say that it was *we* who were breaking the Covenant!" I couldn't help adding somewhat accusingly, "Did you believe that? Not later, but when the war first started."

"No." I couldn't see his face. Only his back, and the long pale hair, and his lightly clasped hands were in view as he surveyed my shelves.

This was the first time the two of us had conversed alone, for I had been careful to avoid such meetings during his visit. Not wanting to prolong it, I still felt compelled to amplify.

I said, "My mother was the last of the royal Calahanras family. Galdran must have thought her a threat, even though she retired from Court life when she adopted into the Astiar family."

Shevraeth was walking along the shelves now, his hands still behind his back. "Yet Galdran had taken no action against your mother previously."

"No. But she'd never left Tlanth before, not since her marriage. She was on her way to Remalna-city. We only know that it was his own household guards, disguised as brigands, that did the job, be-

ause they didn't quite kill the stablegirl who was riding on the
uggage coach and she recognized the horses as Merindar horses."

I tightened my grip on my elbows. "You don't believe it?"

Again he glanced back at me. "Do you know your mother's
errand in the capital?" His voice was calm, quiet, always with that
faint drawl as if he chose his words with care.

Suddenly my voice sounded too loud, and much too combative,
to my ears. Of course that made my face go crimson with heat.
"Visiting."

This effectively ended the subject, and I waited for him to leave.

He turned around then, studying me reflectively. The length
of the room still lay between us. "I had hoped," he said, "that you
would honor me with a few moments' further discourse."

"About what?" I demanded.

"I came here at your brother's invitation." He spoke in a conversational tone, as though I'd been pleasant and encouraging. "My
reasons for accepting were partly because I wanted an interlude of
relative tranquillity, and partly for diplomatic reasons."

"Yes, Nimiar told me about your wanting to present a solid
front with the infamous Astiars. I understand, and I said I'd go
along."

"Please permit me to express my profound gratitude." He
bowed gracefully.

I eyed him askance, looking for any hint of mockery. All I
sensed was humor as he added, "I feel obliged to point out
that...an obvious constraint...every time we are in one another's
company will not go unnoticed."

"I promise you I've no intention of trying again for a crown."

"Thank you. What concerns me are the individuals who seem
to wish to taste the ambrosia of power—"

"—without the bitter herb of responsibility. I read that one,
too," I said, grinning despite myself.

He smiled faintly in response, and said, "These individuals
might seek you out—"

My humor vanished. I realized then that he knew about the

259

letter. He *had* to. Coincidence his arrival might be, but this conversation on our last day in Tlanth was not. It could only mean that he'd had someone up in our mountains spying on me, for how else could he know?

My temper flared brightly, like a summer fire. "So you think I'm stupid enough to lend myself to the schemes of troublemakers just for the sake of making trouble, is that what you think?" I demanded.

"I don't believe you'd swallow their blandishments, but you'll still be approached if you seem even passively my enemy. There are those who will exert themselves to inspire you to a more active role."

I struggled to get control of my emotions. "I know," I said stiffly. "I don't want to be involved in any more wars. All I want is the good of Remalna. Bran and I promised Papa when he died." *Even if my brother has forgotten*, I almost added, but I knew it wasn't true. In Bran's view, he had kept his promise. Galdran was gone, and Tlanth was enjoying peace and prosperity. Bran had never pretended he wanted to get involved in the affairs of kings beyond that.

As if his thoughts had paralleled mine, Shevraeth said, "And do you agree that your brother—estimable as he is—would not have made a successful replacement for Galdran Merindar?"

The parallel was unsettling. I said with less concealed hostility, "What's your point?"

"No...point," he said, his tone making the word curiously ambiguous. "Only a question."

He paused, and I realized he was waiting for my answer to his. "Yes," I said. "Bran would make a terrible king. So what's your next question?"

"Can you tell me," he said slowly, "why you seem still to harbor your original resentment against me?"

Several images—spies, lying courtiers—flowed into my mind, to be instantly dismissed. I had no proof of any of it. So I looked out the window as I struggled for an answer. After the silence grew protracted, I glanced back to see if he was still there. He hadn't moved. His attitude was not impatient, and his gaze was on my hands, which were tightly laced in my lap. His expression was again reflective.

"I don't know," I said finally. "I don't know."

There was a pause, then he said, "I appreciate your honesty." He gave me a polite bow, a brief smile, and left.

That night I retreated for the last time to the mountain peaks behind the castle and roamed along moonlit paths in the cool end-of-winter air. In the distance I heard the harpwinds, but this time I saw no one. The harps thrummed their weird threnodies, and from peak to peak reed pipes sounded, clear as winged creatures riding on the air, until the night was filled with the songs of approaching spring, and life, and freedom.

The music quieted my restlessness and buoyed me up with joy. I climbed the white stone peak at Elios and looked down at the castle, silhouetted silvery against the darker peaks in the distance. The air was clear, and I could see on the highest tower a tiny human figure, hatless, his long dark cloak belling and waving, and star-touched pale hair tangling in the wind.

In silence I watched the still figure as music filled the valley between us and drifted into eternity on the night air.

The moon was high overhead when, one by one, the pipes played a last melody, and at last the music stopped, leaving only the sound of the wind in the trees.

It was time to return, for we would depart early in order to get off the mountain before nightfall. When at last I reached the courtyard and looked up at the tower, no one was there.

"Here's a hamper of good things," Julen said the next day, handing a covered basket into the coach where Nee and I were just settling.

Everyone in the village had turned out to see us off. We made

261

a brave-looking cavalcade, with the baggage coaches and the out-riders in their livery, and Branaric and the Marquis on the backs of fresh, mettlesome mounts, who danced and sidled and tossed their heads, their new-shod hooves striking sparks from the stones of the courtyard.

"Thank you," I said, pulling on my new-made traveling gloves. "Be well! 'Ria, keep us posted on Tlanth's business."

"I'll write often," Oria promised, bowed to Nee, and backed away.

"Let's go, then," Bran called, raising his hand. He flashed a grin at us then dropped his hand, and his impatient horse dashed forward.

Our carriage rolled more slowly through the gates; workers paused in their renovations and waved their caps at us. The trees closed in overhead, and we were on the road. I looked back until I had lost sight of the castle, then straightened round, to find Nee watching me, her face wistful within the flattering curve of her carriage hat.

"Regrets about leaving your home?" she asked.

"No," I said—making my first Court white lie.

Her relief was unmistakable as she sat back against the satin pillows, and I was glad I'd lied. "I hope we make it to Carad-on-Whitewater by nightfall," she said. "I really think you'll like the inn there."

"Why?" I asked.

She smiled. "You'll see."

I made a face. "You can't tell me? I think I've already had a lifetime's worth of surprises."

She laughed. "Dancing."

I rubbed my hands together. "Great. Strangers to practice on."

Still smiling, she shook her head. "I confess I find your attitude difficult to comprehend. When I learned, it was a relief to practice with my cousins before I tried dancing with people I didn't know."

"Not me," I said. "Like I told you, if I have to tread on

262

meone's toes, better some poor fellow I'll never see again—and ho'll never see me—than someone who'll be afraid whenever he es me coming. And as for practicing with Bran..."

She tried unsuccessfully to smother a laugh. "Well, he was just outspoken about his own mistakes when he was learning," she id. "Frequently had a roomful of people in stitches. Not so bad thing, in those early days," she added reflectively.

I shook my head. "I find it impossible to believe that anyone uld regret Galdran's defeat. Besides his family." And, seeing a rfect opportunity to introduce the subject of the Marquise of erindar, I said, "Even then, didn't they all hate one another?"

"They are...a complicated family," she said with care. "But of urse they must regret the loss of the perquisites from being re- ted to royalty. All that is gone now. They have only the family ldings."

"And we have his private fortune," I said, wondering if this lated to the letter in some way.

She glanced out the window, then said, "Do not feel you have speak of it, but it distressed me to realize that it is I who has en talking the most over the last days. Now I would very much e to listen."

"To what?" I asked in surprise. "I told you my history, and I n't *know* anything else."

"You know what the Hill Folk are like," she said with undis- ised awe.

I laughed. "Nobody really knows what they're like. Except emselves," I said. "But it's true I've seen them. We all have, we o live high enough in the mountains. We do as children, anyway. till do because I like to go up to them. Most of the others have t interest."

"What are they like?"

I closed my eyes, drawing forth the green-lit images. "Unlike ," I said slowly. "Hard to describe. Human in shape, of course, t taller, and though they don't move at all like us, I think them very graceful. They can also be very *still*. You could walk right by them and not notice their presence, unless they move."

"Strange," she said. "I think that would frighten me."

I shook my head. "They don't frighten me—but I think I could see how they might be frightening. I don't know. Anyway, they are all brown and green and they don't really wear clothes, but you wouldn't think them naked any more than a tree is naked. They do have a kind of mossy lace they wear...and flowers and bud garlands—lots of those—and when they are done, they replant the buds and blossoms, which grow and thrive."

"Are they mortal?"

"Oh, yes, though so long-lived they don't seem it—like trees. But they can be killed. I guess there's some grim stuff in our history, though I haven't found it. One thing, though, that's immediate is their sensitivity to herbs, particularly those brought here from other worlds. Like kinthus."

"Oh yes! I remember Bran talking about kinthus-rooting. The berries surely can't hurt them, can they? I mean, we use them for painkillers!"

"We never use kinthus in the mountains," I said. "Listerblossom is good enough. As for the Hill Folk, I don't know if the berries hurt them. The danger is if there's a fire."

"I know burned kinthus is supposed to cause a dream state," Nee said.

"Maybe in us. The Hill Folk also drop into sleep, only they don't wake up. Anyway, every generation or so there's a great fire somewhere, and so we make certain there's no kinthus that can burn and carry its smoke up-mountain."

"A fair enough bargain," she said. "Tell me about their faces."

"Their faces are hard to remember," I said, "like the exact pattern of bark on a tree. But their eyes are, well, like looking into the eyes of the animals we live among, the ones who make milk. Have you ever noticed that the eyes of the ones we eat—fowl and fish—don't look at yours; they don't seem to see us? But a milk animal will see you, just as you see it, though you can't meet minds. The Hill Folk's eyes are like that, brown and aware. I cannot tell you what I see there, except if I look one in the face, I always want to have a clean heart."

"Very strange," she said, hugging her elbows close. "Yet I think you are lucky."

"Sometimes," I said, thinking of the night before, after my conversation with Shevraeth, when I'd had an angry heart. I was glad I hadn't seen any Hill Folk face-to-face.

But I didn't tell Nee that.

We conversed a little more, on different matters, then I asked her to practice fan language with me again. We made a game of it, and so the time passed agreeably as we progressed steadily down the mountain, sometimes slowly over icy places or snowdrifts. As we got closer to the lowlands the air turned warmer; spring, still a distant promise in the mountains, seemed imminent. The roads were less icy than muddy, but our progress was just as slow.

We stopped only to change horses. Nee and I didn't even get out of the carriage but ate the food that Julen had packed.

It was quite dark, and a sleety rain was just starting to fall when our cavalcade rolled impressively into the courtyard of the Riverside Inn at Carad-on-Whitewater.

What seemed to be the entire staff of the place turned out, all bowing and scurrying, to make our debarkation as easy as possible. As I watched this—from beneath the rain canopy that two eager young inn-helpers held over our heads—I couldn't help remembering last spring's sojourn at various innyards, as either a prisoner or a fugitive, and it was hard not to laugh at the comparison.

We had a splendid dinner in a private room overlooking the river. From below came the merry sounds of music, about as different from the haunting rhythms of the Hill Folk's music as can be, yet I loved it too.

When we had finished, Nee said, "Come! Let's go dance."

"Not me," Bran said. He lolled back on his cushions and

grabbed for his mulled wine. "In the saddle all day. I'll finish this, then I'm for bed."

"I'll go with you," I said to Nee, rising to my feet.

Nee turned to Shevraeth, who sat with both hands round his goblet. "Lord Vidanric? Will you come with us?"

I looked out the window, determined to say nothing. But I was still angry, convinced as I was that he had been spying on me.

"Keep me company," Bran said. "Don't want to drink by myself."

The Marquis said to Nee, "Another time."

I kept my face turned away to hide the relief I was sure was plain to see, and Nee and I went downstairs to the common room, which smelled of spicy drinks and braised meats and fruit tarts.

In one corner four musicians played, and the center of the room was clear save for a group of dancers, the tables and cushions having been pushed back to make space. Nee and I went to join, for we had come in on a circle dance. These were not the formal Court dances with their intricate steps, where each gesture has to be just so, right down to who asks for a partner and how the response is made. These were what Nee called town dances, which were based on the old country dances—line dances for couples, and circles either for men or for women—that people had stamped and twirled and clapped to for generations.

Never lacking for partners, we danced until we were hot and tired, and then went up to the spacious bedrooms. I left my windows wide open and fell asleep listening to the sound of the river.

"I'll go in the rattler with you," Bran said the next morning, to Nee. Grinning at her, he added, "Probably will rain, and I hate riding horseback in the wet. And we never get enough time together as it is."

I looked out at the heavy clouds and the soft mist, thought of that close coach, and said, "I'll ride, then. I don't mind rain—" I looked up, realized who else was riding, and fought a hot tide of embarrassment. "You can go in the coach in my place," I said to Shevraeth, striving to sound polite.

He gave his head a shake. "Never ride in coaches. If you want to know the truth, they make me sick. How about a wager?"

"A wager?" I repeated.

"Yes," he said, and gave me a slow smile, bright with challenge. "Who reaches Jeriab's Broken Shield in Lumm first."

"Stake?" I asked cautiously.

He was still smiling, an odd sort of smile, hard to define. "A kiss."

My first reaction was outrage, but then I remembered that I was on my way to Court, and that had to be the kind of thing they did at Court. *And if I win I don't have to collect.* I hesitated only a moment longer, lured by the thought of open sky, and speed, and *winning.*

"Done," I said.

SIX

I WENT STRAIGHT BACK TO MY ROOM, SURPRISING Mora and one of her staff in the act of packing up my trunk. Apologizing, I hastily unlaced the traveling gown and reached for my riding gear.

Mora gave me a slight smile as she curtsied. "That's my job, my lady," she said. "You needn't apologize."

I grinned at her as I pulled on the tunic. "Maybe it's not very courtly, but I feel bad when I make someone do a job twice."

Mora only smiled as she made a sign to the other servant, who reached for the traveling gown and began folding it up. I thrust my feet into my riding boots, smashed my fancy new riding hat onto my head, and dashed out again.

The Marquis was waiting in the courtyard, standing between two fresh mares. I was relieved that he did not have that fleet-footed gray I remembered from the year before. On his offering me my pick, I grabbed the reins of the nearest mount and swung up into the saddle. The animal danced and sidled as I watched Bran and Nimiar come out of the inn hand in hand. They climbed into the coach, solicitously seen to by the innkeeper himself.

The Marquis looked across at me. "Let's go."

And he was off, with me right on his heels.

At first all I was aware of was the cold rain on my chin and the exhilaration of speed. The road was paved, enabling the horses to dash along at the gallop, sending mud and water splashing.

Before long I was soaked to the skin everywhere except my head, which was hot under my riding hat, and when we bolted down the road toward the Akaeriki, I had to laugh aloud at how strange life is! Last year at this very time I was running rain-sodden for my life in the opposite direction, chased by the very same man now racing neck and neck beside me.

The thought caused me to look at him, though there was little to see beyond flying light hair under the broad-brimmed black hat and that long black cloak. He glanced over, saw me laughing, and I looked away again, urging my mount to greater efforts.

At the same pace still, we reached the first staging point. Together we clattered into the innyard and swung down from the saddle. At once two plain-dressed young men came out of the inn, bowed, and handed Shevraeth a blackweave bag. It was obvious from their bearing that they were trained warriors, probably from Renselaeus. For a moment the Marquis stood conversing with them, a tall mud-splashed and anonymously dressed figure. Did anyone else know who he was? Or who I was? Or that we'd been enemies last year?

Again laughter welled up inside me. When I saw stablehands bring forth two fresh mounts, I sprang forward, taking the reins of one, and mounted up. Then I waited until Shevraeth turned my way, stuck my tongue out at him, and rode out at the gallop, laughing all the way.

I had the road to myself for quite a while.

Though I'd been to Lumm only that once, I couldn't miss the way, for the road to Lumm ran alongside the river—that much I remembered. Since it was the only road, I did not gallop long but pulled the horse back into a slower gait in order to keep it fresh. If I saw pursuit behind me, then would be the time to race again, to keep my lead.

So I reasoned. The road climbed gradually, until the area looked familiar again. Now I rode along the top of a palisade on the other side of the river; I kept scanning ahead for that rickety sheep bridge.

As I topped the highest point, I turned to look out over the valley, with the river winding lazily through it, and almost missed the fast-moving dot half obscured by the fine, silvery curtain of rain.

I reined in my horse, shaded my eyes, and squinted at the dot, which resolved into a horseback rider racking cross-country at incredible speed. Of course it could be anyone, but...

Turning my eyes back to the road, I saw Lumm in the distance, with a couple of loops of river between me and it.

Hesitating only a moment, I plunged down the hillside. The horse stumbled once in the deep mud, sending me flying face first. But I climbed back into the saddle, and we started racing westward across the fields.

I reached Lumm under a relentless downpour. My horse splashed slowly up the main street until I saw swinging in the wind a sign with a cracked shield. The wood was ancient, and I couldn't make out the device as my tired horse walked under it. I wondered who Jeriab was, then forgot him when a stablehand ran out to take my horse's bridle.

"Are you Countess of Tlanth?" she asked as I dismounted.

I nodded, and she bustled over to a friend, handed off the horse, then beckoned me inside. "I'm to show you to the south parlor, my lady."

Muddy to the eyebrows, I squelched after her up a broad stair into a warm, good-smelling hallway. Genial noise smote me from all directions, and people came and went. But my guide threaded her way through, then indicated a stairway with a fine mosaic rail, and pointed. "Top, right, all across the back is where your party will be," she said. "Parlor's through the double door." She curtsied and disappeared into the crowd.

I trod up the stairs, making wet footprints on the patterned arpet at each step. The landing opened onto a spacious hallway.

I turned to the double doors, which were of foreign plainwood, nd paused to admire the carving round the latch, and the painted attern of leaves and blossoms worked into it. Then I opened one, nd there in the middle of a lovely parlor was Shevraeth. He knelt t a writing table with his back to a fire, his pen scratching rapidly cross a paper.

He glanced up inquiringly. His hair seemed damp, but it wasn't nuddy, and his clothing looked miraculously dry.

I gritted my teeth, crossed my arms, and advanced on him, my old-numbed lips poonched out below what I knew was a ferocious lare.

Obviously on the verge of laughter, he raised his quill to top me. "As the winner," he murmured, "I choose the time and lace."

"You cheated," I said, glad enough to have the embarrassment ostponed.

"If you had waited, I would have shown you that shortcut," he etorted humorously.

"It was a trick," I snarled. "And as for your wager, I might as ell get it over now."

He sat back, eyeing me. "Wet as you are—and you have to be old—it'd feel like kissing a fish. We will address this another time. it down and have some cider. It's hot, just brought in. May I equest your opinion of that?" He picked up a folded paper and ossed it in my direction. He added, with a faint smile, "Next time ou'll have to remember to bring extra gear."

"How come you're not all soggy?" I asked as I set aside my odden hat and waterlogged riding gloves.

He indicated the black cloak, which was slung over a candle conce on the wall, and the hat and gloves resting on a side table. Water-resistant spells. Expensive, but eminently worthwhile."

"That's what we need in Remalna," I said, kneeling on the ushions opposite him and pouring out spicy-smelling cider into a porcelain cup painted with that same leaf-and-blossom theme. "A wizard."

Shevraeth laid his pen down. "I don't know," he said. "A magician is not like a tree that bears fruit for all who want it and demands nothing in return. A wizard is human and will have his or her own goals."

"And a way of getting them that we couldn't very well stand against," I said. "All right. No wizard. But I shall get me one of those cloaks." I drank some of the cider, which was delicious, and while its warmth worked its way down my innards, I turned to the letter he'd handed me.

The exquisite handwriting was immediately familiar—a letter from the Marquise of Merindar. Under my sodden clothing my heart thumped in alarm. Addressed to their Highnesses the Prince and Princess of Renselaeus, the letter went on at length, thanking them for their generous hospitality during her period of grief, and then, in the most polite language, stating that its writer must reluctantly return to her home and family, and take up the threads of her life once again. And it was signed, in a very elaborate script, Arthal Merindar.

I looked up, to find Shevraeth's gaze on me. "What do you think?"

"What am I supposed to think?" I asked slowly, wondering if his question was some kind of a trap. "The Marquise is going back to Merindar, and blather blather blather about her nice year at Athanarel."

"Wants to go back," he said, still mildly. "Do you see a message there?"

"It's not addressed to me," I muttered, hunching up in defense.

"Ostensibly it's addressed to my parents," he said. "Look closely."

I bent over the letter again. At first my conflicting emotions made the letters swim before my eyes, but I forced myself to look

272

again—and to remember my own letter, now hidden in one of my trunks. Then I made a discovery.

"The signature is different from the rest of the writing, which means she must have used a scribe—" I thought rapidly. "Ah. She *didn't* write this herself. Is that a kind of oblique insult?"

"Well, one may assume she intended this to be read by other eyes."

Like my letter, I realized. And that meant...

"And since the signature is so different, she wanted it obvious. Yes, I see that," I said, my words slow, my mind winging from thought to thought. Did this mean that Shevraeth *hadn't* spied on me after all—that the Marquise had sent that letter knowing he'd find out?

My gaze was still on the fine scribal hand, but my thoughts ranged back through winter. Of course Bran would have told all his Court friends that he was going home at last, and probably with whom.

I gulped in a deep breath and once again tried to concentrate. "But unless there's a kind of threat in that last bit about taking up the threads of her life, I don't see any real problem here."

He picked up the quill again and ran the feathered part through his fingers. "One of the reasons my parents are both in Remalna-city is to establish someone of superior rank there until the question of rulership is settled."

"You think Arthal Merindar wants to be queen, then?" I asked, and again thought of my letter and why she might have written it.

Unbidden, Shevraeth's words from the day before our departure sounded in my head: "...but you'll still be approached if you seem even passively my enemy." Cold shock made me shiver inside when I realized that the Marquise of Merindar might have attributed my refusal to come to Court to unspoken problems between Shevraeth and myself—which would mean her letter was meant either to capitalize on my purported enmity or to make him distrust me.

273

So did he?

"What is she like?" I asked.

"Like her brother, except much better controlled. She's the only one of the family who is still a danger, but she very definitely is a danger."

"She might be saying the same of you," I said, resolutely trying to be fair. As before, I had no proof, and last year I had gotten myself into trouble for making quick judgments based merely on emotions, not facts. "Not that I think all that much of the Merindars I've met so far, but they do have a claim on the throne. And their marquisate, like Renselaeus, takes its name from the family even if it isn't nearly as old."

It was impossible to read his expression. "You think, then, that I ought to cede to her the crown?"

"Will she be a good ruler?" I countered, and suddenly the shock was gone. My old feelings crowded back into my head and heart. "*I* don't know. Why are you asking me? Why does my answer make any difference at all, unless showing me this letter and asking me these questions is your own way of making a threat?" I got up and paced the length of the room, fighting the urge to grab something and smash it.

"No," he said, dropping his gaze to the papers on the desk. "I merely thought you'd find it interesting." He leaned forward, dipped the point of his pen into the ink, and went on writing.

The argument, so suddenly sprung up, was over. As I stood there watching that pen move steadily across the paper, I felt all the pent-up anger drain out of me as suddenly as it had come, leaving me feeling tired, and cold, and very, very confused.

Shevraeth and I did not speak again; he kept working through his mail, and I, still tired and cold, curled up on a cushion and slipped into uncomfortable sleep.

Waking to the sound of Bran's cheery voice and a bustle and

ustling of people, I got up, feeling horribly stiff. Though I'd tried
to stay with exercise through sword practice, I hadn't ridden that
hard all winter, and every muscle protested. It did my spirits no
good at all to see Shevraeth moving about with perfect ease. Resolving that I'd stay in the coach the rest of the way, crowded or
not, I greeted Bran and Nee, and was soon reunited with dry
clothing.

The four of us ate dinner together, and Shevraeth was exactly
as polite as always, making no reference to our earlier conversation.
This unnerved me, and I began to look forward to our arrival at
Athanarel, when he would surely disappear into Court life and we'd
seldom see one another.

As for the wager, I decided to forget about what had obviously
been some kind of aristocratic joke.

SEVEN

So once again on an early spring day, I was ensconced in a coach rolling down the middle of the Street of the Sun. Again people lined the street, but this time they waved and cheered. And as before, outriders joined us, but this time they wore our colors as well as the Renselaeuses'.

This had all been arranged beforehand, I found out through Nimiar. People expected power to be expressed through visible symbols, such as columns of armed outriders, and fancy carriages drawn by three matched pairs of fast horses, and so forth. Apparently Shevraeth loathed traveling about with such huge entourages—at least as much as Galdran used to love traveling with them—so he arranged for the trappings to be assumed at the last moment.

All this she told me as we rattled along the last distance through Remalna-city toward the golden-roofed palace called Athanarel.

When we reached the great gates, there were people hanging off them. I turned to look, and a small girl yelled, "Astiar!" as she flung a posy of crimson rosebuds and golden daisies through the open window of our carriage.

"They didn't shout last time," I said, burying my face in the posy. "Just stared."

"Last time?" Nee asked.

"When I had the supreme felicity of being introduced to Galdran by the esteemed Marquis," I said, striving for a light tone. "You don't remember?"

"Oh. I remember." Nimiar frowned, looking outside. "Though I was not there. I did not have duty that day. For which I was grateful."

"Duty?"

She gave me a pained smile. "Standing all afternoon in full Court dress was a pleasure for very few. It was a duty, and one strictly observed not out of loyalty or love but out of fear, for most of us."

"You were hostage to your families," I said.

"Essentially," she said, still looking out the window. Her profile was troubled.

"The Renselaeuses are keeping the Marquise of Merindar as a hostage, aren't they?"

Nee looked a little perplexed. "I'm certain she sees it in that light," she said quietly, and then she indicated the cheering people outside the coach. "You spoke of two kinds of crowds, the happy ones such as these, and the silent ones that you saw last year. Yet here is a third kind of crowd, the angry ones that are ready to fall on persons they hate and rend them if only someone brave enough—or foolhardy enough—steps forward to lead. I suspect that the Marquise of Merindar was kept here in part for her own protection from just that kind of crowd."

"Would she make a good queen?"

Nee bit her lip. "I don't know," she said. "I don't trust my ability to assess anyone that way. But I can tell you this: There were times she frightened me more than Galdran did, for his cruelties came out of rage, but hers came out of cold deliberation."

"Cold deliberation," I repeated, thinking of the letter—and of the way Shevraeth had let me know he knew about it. "So far, she and Shevraeth seem two buds on the same branch."

277

Nee said nothing. The atmosphere had changed, but before I could figure out how, and what it meant, we rolled to a stop before a fine marble terrace.

The carriage doors opened, and I looked out at servants in those fabulous liveries—still the crowned sun of Remalna, but now the green was deeper, and the brown had lightened back to gold.

I disembarked, gazing around. The terrace was part of a building, but in the other directions all I saw was greenery. "We're in a forest, or a garden. Where are the other buildings?"

She smiled again. "You can't see them from here. It's an artful design. Though the Family houses and the lesser guesthouses don't have quite this much privacy."

I looked up at the palace. Its walls were a warm peachy gold stone, with fine carving along the roof and beside each of its ranks of windows. Adjacent, glimpsed through budding trees, was another wing.

"That is the Royal Residence Wing." She pointed. "We're in the primary Guest Wing. On the other side of us, also adjacent, is the State Wing."

I whistled. "Do we have to eat in some vast cavern of a chamber with a lot of ambassadors and the like?"

"There are several dining rooms of varying size and formality, but I've been told we won't be using any of them except occasionally."

We were treading up the broad, shallow steps toward another pair of carved double doors. Someone opened them, and we passed through into a spacious entryway with a fabulous mosiac on the floor: a night sky with all the planets and stars, but with the sun at the center. Light shafted down from stained-glass windows above, overlaying the mosaic with glowing color. It was odd but interesting, and the golds and blues were beautiful.

Downstairs were the more public rooms; we were taken up a flight of beautifully tiled stairs to a long hall of suites. The servants had come up by some more direct way, for they were there before

s, busily making the beautifully appointed rooms into a semblance
f home.

I glanced around the rooms allotted to me. There was a little
arlor, a bedroom, and a dressing room with a narrow, tiled stair-
ay that led to the baths, below the first level. A cunningly hidden,
ven more narrow stairway led up to where the servants were
oused. All three windows overlooked a stream-fed pool sur-
ounded by trees. The rooms were done in soft greens; the tables
ere antique wood of a beautiful golden shade, the cushions and
urtains and hangings all pale blue satin stitched with tiny green
y and white blossoms.

I wandered through to Nee's suite, which was next to mine.
er rooms were done in quiet shades of rose, and they overlooked
flower garden.

She had been talking to her maids; when she was done and
ey had withdrawn, she sighed and sat down in a chair.

"What now?" I said.

She opened her hands. "What indeed? Protocol provides no
uswers. Instead it becomes a ticklish question itself, because there
no sovereign. Under Galdran, the days were strictly divided:
old, we spent with family; green, we spent at Court; blue was for
cial affairs—but he even made clear who was to give them, and
ho was to go."

"Aren't the Prince and Princess setting some kind of schedule?"

"Apparently State work gets done mostly during gold, and twice
week or so they hold court for petitioners at the customary green-
ne, and all who wish to attend can. But it's not required. The rest
us...do what we will." She lifted her hands. "I expect we'll
ceive an invitation for dinner from their Highnesses, at second-
ue, which will serve as an informal welcome."

I took a deep breath. "All right. Until then we're free? Let's
lk around," I said. "I'm not tired or hungry, but I still feel stiff
om—from sitting inside that coach for so long." I did not want
refer to my ride or the postponed wager.

If she noticed my hesitation and quick recovery, she gave no sign. She glanced out at the fair sky and nodded. "A good idea."

So we changed into afternoon dresses and walking hats and gloves, and went out. I told Mora that I'd like to have tea when we returned, thinking about how strange it was to be sending orders to a kitchen I'd probably never see. Before this past winter, the kitchen at home in Tlanth had been the center of my life.

Now I was buffered by Mora, and she by runners whose sole purpose seemed to be to wait about, in little anterooms at either end of the wing, to answer the summonses of our own personal servants, to fetch and carry. As Nee and I walked down the broad terrace steps onto a brick path, I reflected that anyone who really wanted to know what was going on at the palace would do better to question the runners than the aristocrats. Except, would they talk to me?

The day was fine, the cool air pleasant with scents of new blooms growing in the extensive gardens. We saw other people walking about, mostly in twos and threes. It was a great chance to practice my etiquette: nods for those unknown, and varying depths of curtsys for those Nee knew—the depth decided by rank and by the degree of acquaintance. Clues to status were in the way she spoke, and the order in which she presented me to people, or them to me if my rank was the higher. It was interesting to see people behave exactly the way she had told me they would—though I realized that, as yet, I couldn't read the tricks of gesture or smile, or the minute adjustments of posture that were additional messages.

For now, everyone seemed pleasant, and I even detected frank curiosity in the smiling faces, which braced me up: It seemed that they were not all accomplished dissemblers.

This was a good discovery to make just before the last encounter.

We strolled over a little footbridge that spanned a stream, then followed the path around a moonflower bed into a clearing beside a tree-sheltered pool.

The tableau we came upon was like a very fine picture. A beautiful lady sat on a bench, her blue skirts artfully spread at her feet, and ribbons and gems in her curling black hair. Watched by three young lords, she was feeding bits of something to the fish in the shallow pool. I gained only hazy impressions of two of the men— one red-haired, one fair—because my eyes were drawn immediately to the tallest, a man of powerful build, long waving dark hair, and a rakish smile. Dressed in deep blue with crimson and gold embroidery, he leaned negligently against the bench. The lady looked up at him with a toss of her head and smiled.

I heard a slight intake of breath from Nee, but when I looked over at her, I saw only the polite smile of her Court mask.

At first the people did not see us—or didn't notice us, I think would be a better way of saying it. For the lady had glanced up and then away, just as she dipped her hand into the beribboned little basket on her lap and, with a quick twist of her wrist, flung a piece of bread out over the light-dappled water of the pool. With a musical *plash*, a golden fish leaped into the air and snapped at the bread, diving neatly back into the water.

"Two to me," the lady cried with a gentle laugh, raising her eyes to the tall man, who smiled down at her, one hand gesturing palm up.

We were close enough now that I could see the lady's eyes, which were the same pure blue of her gown. Just then the tall man glanced over at us, and he straightened up, his dark eyes enigmatic, though he still smiled. He did not turn away, but waited for us to approach.

The lady looked up again, and I think I saw a faint impatience narrow those beautiful eyes; but then she gave us a breathtaking smile as she rose to her feet and laid aside her basket.

"Nimiar? Welcome back, dear cousin," she said in a melodious voice.

"We are returned indeed, Tamara," Nee said. "Your grace, may I present to you Lady Meliara Astiar?" And to me, "The Duke of Savona."

The dark eyes were direct, and interested, and very much

amused. The famous Duke responded to my curtsy with an elaborate bow, then he took my hand and kissed it. I scarcely heard the names of the other people; I was too busy trying not to stare at Savona or blush at his lingering kiss.

"My dear Countess," Lady Tamara exclaimed. "Why were we not told we would have the felicity of meeting you?"

I didn't know how to answer that, so I just shook my head.

"Though, in truth, perhaps it is better this way," Lady Tamara went on. "I should have been afraid to meet so formidable a personage. You must realize we have been hearing a great deal about your valiant efforts against our former king."

"Well," I said, "if the stories were complimentary, they weren't true."

The fellows laughed. Lady Tamara's smile did not change at all. "Surely you are overly modest, dear Countess."

Savona propped an elegantly booted foot on an edge of the bench and leaned an arm across his knee as he smiled at me. "What is your version of the story, Lady Meliara?"

Instinct made me wary; there were undercurrents here that needed thinking out. "If I start on that we'll be here all night, and I don't want to miss my dinner," I said, striving for a light tone. Again the lords all laughed.

Nee slid her hand in my arm. "Shall we continue on to find your brother?" she addressed me. "He is probably looking for us."

"Let's," I said.

They bowed, Lady Tamara the deepest of all, and she said, "I trust you'll tell us all about it someday, dear Countess."

We bowed and started to move on. One fellow, a young redhaired lord, seemed inclined to follow; but Lady Tamara placed her fingertips on his arm and said, "Now, do not desert me, Geral! Not until I have a chance to win back my losses…"

Nee and I walked on in silence for a time, then she said in a guarded voice, "What think you of my cousin?"

"So that is the famous Lady Tamara Chamadis! Well, she really s as pretty as I'd heard," I said. "But…I don't know. Somehow she embodies everything I'd thought a courtier would be."

"Fair enough." Nee nodded. "Then I guess it's safe for me to say—at risk of appearing a detestable gossip—watch out."

I touched the top of my hand where I could still feel the Duke of Savona's kiss. "All right. But I don't understand why."

"She is ambitious," Nee said slowly. "Even when we were young she never had the time for any of lower status. I believe that if Galdran Merindar had shown any interest in sharing his power, she would have married him."

"She wants to rule the kingdom?" I asked, glancing behind us. The secluded little pool was bounded by trees and hidden from view.

"She wants to reign over Court," Nee stated. "Her interest in the multitudes of ordinary citizens extends only to the image of them bowing down to her."

I whistled. "That's a pretty comprehensive judgment."

"Perhaps I have spoken ill," she said contritely. "You must understand that I don't like my cousin, having endured indifference or snubs since we were small, an heir's condescension for a third child of a secondary branch of the family who would never inherit or amount to much."

"She seemed friendly enough just now."

"The first time she ever addressed me as cousin in public," Nee said. "My status appears to have changed since I went away to Tlanth, affianced to a count, with the possible new king riding escort." Her voice took on an acidic sort of humor.

"And what about the Duke of Savona?" I asked, his image vivid in my mind's eye.

"In what sense?" She paused, turning to study my face. "He is another whose state of mind is impossible to guess."

I was still trying to disentangle all my observations from that brief meeting. "Is he, well, *twoing* with Lady Tamara?"

She smiled at the term. "They both are experts at dalliance,

283

but until last year I had thought they had more interest in each other than in anyone else," she said carefully. "Though even that is difficult to say for certain. Interest and ambition sometimes overlap and sometimes not."

As we wound our way along the path back toward Athanarel in the deepening gloom, I saw warm golden light inside the palace windows. With a glorious flicker, glowglobes appeared along the pathway, suspended in the air like great rainbow-sheened bubbles, their light soft and benevolent.

"I'm not certain what you mean by that last bit," I said at last. "As for the first, you said 'until last year.' Does that mean that Lady Tamara has someone else in view?"

"But of course," Nee said blandly. "The Marquis of Shevraeth."

I laughed all the way up the steps into the Residence.

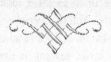

EIGHT

"I THINK YOU SHOULD WEAR YOUR HAIR DOWN," Nee said, looking me over.

"For a dinner? I might kneel on it," I protested.

She smiled. "We'll dine empire style, for Prince Alaerec will be here."

I remembered from my visit to the Renselaeus palace that Shevraeth's father had been wounded in the Pirate Wars many years before. He could walk, but only with difficulty; and he sat in chairs.

"So wear your hair bound with these." She picked up an enameled box and opened it. There lay several snowstone hair ties, with thin silken ribbons hanging down. The ribbons were all white or silver.

I looked at my reflection. My gown was so dark a violet it was almost black, and had tiny faceted snowstones embroidered in lily patterns across the front. Nothing would ever make me look tall or voluptuous—even after a year of excellent food, I was exactly as small and scrawny as ever—but the gown flattered what little figure I had, so I didn't look ten years old. "All right." I simpered at my reflection. "Think I'll start a new fashion?"

"I know you will." She laughed. "I want to watch it happen."

"They might not like me," I said, sitting down on a hassock while Mora's gentle fingers stroked and fingered my hair.

"Mmmm." Nee watched with the air of an artist looking at a painting. "Do not give that a thought. You're *interesting*—something new. I think..." She paused, gestured, and Mora adjusted the thin snowstone band higher on my brow, making it drape at a graceful angle toward the back of my head.

"Think what?" I played nervously with the new fan hanging at my waist.

"What's that?" Nee looked up, her eyes inscrutable for a moment, then she smiled reassuringly. "I think it will be fine."

And it started fine.

Branaric joined us out in the hallway, and the three of us crossed into the State Wing, to an exquisitely decorated parlor where the Prince and Princess of Renselaeus sat in great carved bluewood chairs on either side of a splendid fire. Instead of the customary tiled tiers round the perimeter of the room, the floor had been leveled to the walls, where there were more of the chairs. Several guests sat in these, and I mentally reviewed the etiquette for chairs: knees and feet together, hands in lap.

The Prince wore black and white. The Princess, who was no bigger than I, was a vision in silver and pale blue with quantities of white lace. She had green eyes and silver-streaked brown hair, and an airy manner. Seated at the Princess's right hand was a large, elaborately dressed woman with gray-streaked red hair. Her eyes, so like Galdran's they prompted in me a prickle of alarm, were bland in expression as they met my gaze briefly, then looked away. The Marquise of Merindar? My heart thumped.

"Ah, my dear," Princess Elestra said to me in her fluting voice—that very same voice I remembered so well from my escape from Athanarel the year before. "How delighted we are to have you join us here. Delighted! I understand there will be a ball in your honor tomorrow, hosted by my nephew Russav." She nodded toward the other side of the room, where the newly arrived Duke of Savona stood in the center of a small group. "He seldom bestirs himself this way, so you must take it as a compliment to you!"

"Thank you," I murmured, my heart now drumming.

I was glad to move aside and let Branaric take my place. I didn't hear what he said, but he made them both laugh; then he too moved aside, and the Prince and Princess presented us to the red-haired woman, who was indeed the Marquise of Merindar. She nodded politely but did not speak, nor did she betray the slightest sign of interest in us.

We were then introduced to the ambassadors from Denlieff, les Adran, and Sartor. This last one, of course, drew my interest, though I did my best to observe her covertly. A tall woman of middle age, the ambassador was polite, gracious, and utterly opaque.

"Family party, you say?" Branaric's voice caught at my attention. He rubbed his hands. "Well, you're related one way or another to half the Court, Danric, so if we've enough people to hand, how 'bout some music?"

"If you like," said Shevraeth. He'd appeared quietly, without causing any stir. "It can be arranged." The Marquis was dressed in sober colors, his hair braided and gemmed for a formal occasion; though as tall as the flamboyantly dressed Duke of Savona, he was slender next to his cousin.

He remained very much in the background, talking quietly with this or that person. The focus of the reception was on the Prince and Princess, and on Bran and me, and, in a strange way, on the ambassador from Denlieff. I sensed that something important was going on below the surface of the polite chitchat, but I couldn't discern what—and then suddenly it was time to go in to dinner.

With a graceful bow, the Prince held out his arm to me, moving with slow deliberation. If it hurt him to walk, he showed no sign, and his back was straight and his manner attentive. The Princess went in with Branaric, Shevraeth with the Marquise, Savona with the Sartoran ambassador, and Nimiar with the northern ambassador. The others trailed in order of rank.

I managed all right with the chairs and the high table. After we were served, I stole a few glances at Shevraeth and the Marquise of Merindar. They conversed in what appeared to be amity. It was equally true of all the others. Perfectly controlled, from their fingertips to their serene brows, none of them betrayed any emotion but polite attentiveness. Only my brother stood out, his face changing as he talked, his laugh real when he dropped his fork, his shrug careless. It seemed to me that the others found him a relief, for the smiles he caused were quicker, the glances brighter—not that *he* noticed.

Conversation during the meal was light and flowed along like water, sometimes punctuated by the quick, graceful butterfly movements of fans. Music, a comical play recently offered by a famous group of players, future entertainments, the difficulties of the winter—all were passed under review. I sat mute, sipping at the exquisite bluewine, which savored of sunshine and fresh nuts, and listening attentively to the melodic voices.

When the meal was over, the Princess invited everyone to yet another room, promising music after hot chocolate.

Dazzled by the glint of jewels and the gleam of silk in the firelight, I moved slowly until I found myself face-to-face with Princess Elestra.

"Has my son shown you the library yet, my child?" she asked, her gently waving fan flicking up for just a moment at the angle of Confidential Invitation.

"No," I said, instantly ill at ease. "Ah—we just arrived today, you see, and there hasn't been time to see much of anything."

"Come. We will slip out a moment. No one will notice." With a smile, she indicated the corner where Savona was telling some story, illustrating a sword trick with his forefinger amid laughter and applause. My brother was laughing loudest of all.

With the smoothest gesture, nod, and bow, she threaded through the crowd. Then we were suddenly in a quiet hall, its richness gleaming in the light of a double row of glowglobes placed in fabulously carved sconces.

"I am told that you like to read," the Princess said as we turned into an even more formal hall. Liveried servants stood at either side of the entry, and when they saw my companion, they bowed, ready for orders. With a little wave, she indicated the tall double doors between two spectacular tapestries dark with age. The servants sprang to open these doors.

As we passed inside, I glanced back at the nearest footman and caught a glimpse of curiosity before his face smoothed into imperiousness.

"A problem, dear child?"

I turned and saw awareness in the Princess's eyes.

So I said carefully, "I don't want to sound critical, Your Highness, but I was thinking how horrible it must be to stand about all day just waiting to open a door, even one as pretty as those."

"But they don't," she responded with a soft laugh. "They trade places regularly. Some stand out there, some are hidden from view waiting for summonses. It is very good training in patience and discretion, for they all want to advance into something better."

She touched a glowglobe, and one by one, in rapid succession, an array of globes flickered, lighting a long room lined with packed bookshelves.

"The books are all arranged by year," she said, nodding at the nearest shelves. "These on this wall concern Remalna. All those here are from other parts of the world. Some real treasures are numbered among that collection. And under the windows are plays and songs."

"Plays, Your Highness?" I repeated in surprise. "Do people write plays down? How can they, when the players change the play each time they do it?"

She nodded, moving along the shelves as though looking for something in particular. "In our part of the world, this is so, and it is common to some of the rest of the world as well. But there are places where plays are written first—usually based on true historical occurrence—and performed as written. It is an old art. At the Sartoran Court there is a current fashion for plays written at least four hundred years ago, with all their quaint language and custom and costume."

I thought this over and realized once again how much in the world I was ignorant of. "I thought plays were about dream people, that the events had never happened—that the purpose of plays is to make people laugh."

"There's a fine scholar in the south who has traveled about the world studying plays, and he maintains that, whether or not they are based on real experiences, they are the harbingers of social change," Princess Elestra replied. "Ah! Here we are."

She pulled down a book, its cover fine red silk, with the title in gilt: *The Queen from the Plains*.

"I know that book!" I said.

"It is very popular," she responded, then pulled down four books from nearby, each a different size and thickness. To my surprise, each had the same title. "We were speaking of plays, the implication being that history is static. But even it can change. Look."

I glanced through the histories, all of which were written in a scribe's exquisite hand. Two of them were purported to be taken from the queen's own private record, but a quick perusal of the first few lines showed a vast difference between them. Two of the books were written by Court-appointed historians—the heralds—like the one I'd read. One of them seemed familiar. The other had a lot fewer words and more decoration in the margins. When I flipped through it, I noticed there were conversations I didn't remember seeing in the one I had read.

"So some of these are lies?" I looked up, confused.

"A few are distorted deliberately, but one has to realize that aside from those, which our best booksellers weed out, there is truth and truth," the Princess said. "What one person sees is not always what another sees. To go back to our histories of the Marloven queen, we can find a fifth one, written a century later, wherein her story is scarcely recognizable—but that one was written as a lampoon of another queen."

"So...the scribes will change things?" I said.

She nodded. "Sometimes."

"Why?"

She closed the books and returned them to the shelves. "Occasionally for political reasons, other times because the scribes think they have a special insight on the truth. Or they think the subject was dull, so they enliven his or her words. Court historians are sometimes good, and sometimes foolish...and sometimes ambitious. The later histories are often the most trustworthy. Though they are not immediate, the writers can refer to memoirs of two or three contemporaries and compare versions."

"Going back to the memoirs, Your Highness, how does one know one is getting the words of the person whose name is in front?"

She pulled down three more books and flipped to the backs, each showing a seal and names and dates. Below these was written: *Fellowship of the Tower.*

"What is this, Your Highness, a sigil for a guild?"

"It is more than a guild. Men and women who join give up all affiliation with their own land. There are five or six establishments throughout the world. Members of the fellowship are not just scribes, but are sworn to stay with the written truth. If you find a copy of Queen Theraez's memoirs with the Fellowship of the Tower's sigil in back, you can trust that every word—every cross out—scrupulously reproduces the papers kept in the Heraldry Archive, written in the queen's own hand. Their purpose is to spread knowledge, not to comment or to alter or improve."

She closed the books and replaced them, then turned to face me. "This library was a haven for many of us during the late king's reign. He liked appearing suddenly hither and yon, but he never did come in here." She gave me a faint smile. "Are you chilled, my dear? Shall we rejoin the others? You can warm up again by dancing."

"Thank you for showing me the library, Your Highness," I said.

"I hope you will find time for exploring in here during your stay at Athanarel," she replied, leading the way to the doors.

She was kind and unthreatening; and because we were alone, I took a chance. "Did you know I was using your carriage to escape that night?" I blurted. My words sounded sudden, and awkward, and my face burned.

She sighed, looking down at her hand on the door's latch, but she did not open the door. "It was an ill-managed thing, not a memory one wishes to return to. Those were dangerous days, and we had to act quickly." Then she opened the door, and there were the footmen, and when she spoke again, it was about the new musicians that were to play.

We'd reached the reception room before I realized that her answer had admitted to a conspiracy without implicating anyone but herself—and that it had also been a kind of apology. But it was equally clear that she didn't want to return to the subject, and I remembered what Nee had told me during our first real conversation: *They don't talk of the war at all.*

Why? I thought, as we joined the rest of the company. The Renselaeuses won; surely such talk could no longer harm them. And it was impossible to believe that they wanted to protect those who had lost...those such as myself.

I shook my head as I made my way to Bran and Nee. *Impossible.*

The reception room was larger now. Folding doors had been thrown back, opening two rooms into one. The second room had the customary tiers along its perimeter, with gorgeously embroidered cushions and low tables for those who did not want to dance. Above, in a cozy gallery, musicians played horns and drums and strings, and in the center of the room, toes pointed and arched wrists held high, eight couples moved through the complicated steps of the taltanne.

The music was stirring and so well played I had to keep my feet from tapping. Among the Hill Folk it was also impossible to stay motionless when they played their music, yet it was very different from this. Up on the mountains the music was as wild as wind and weather, as old as the ancient trees; and the dances retold stories even older than the trees. This music was more controlled, with its artfully modulated melodies, themes, and subthemes; controlled too were the careful steps of the dance. Controlled, yet still beautiful. *And dangerous*, I thought, as I watched glances exchanged over shoulders and across the precise geometric figures of the dance.

Then the Duke of Savona appeared before me. He bowed, smiled, and held out his arm—and there was no time for thought.

It was my very first dance in Court, and I would have liked to try it with someone I knew. But at Court one didn't dance with one's brother. With the Hill Folk, dance was a celebration of life, sometimes of death, and of the changing of the seasons. Here dances were a form of courtship—one that was all the more subtle, Nee had said once, because the one you danced with might not be the one you were courting.

Savona did not speak until the very end, and then it was not the usual sort of compliment that Nee had led me to expect. Instead, he clasped my hand in his, leaned close so that I could smell his clean scent, and murmured, "Your favorite color, Meliara. What is it?"

No titles, just that soft, intimate tone. I felt slightly dizzy and almost said *Blue*, but I had just enough presence of mind to stop myself. Blue being the primary Renselaeus color, this might be misleading. "Lavender," I said. My voice sounded to my ears like a bat squeak.

The music ended then, and he bowed over my hand and kissed it. Then he smiled into my eyes. "Will you wear it tomorrow?" he asked.

"Certainly. Your grace," I managed.

"Call me Russav." Another bow, and he turned away.

"Here's Geral Keradec." Bran stepped up, took my arm, and turned me to face a tall red-haired young man. "Wants to dance with you, sister."

Desperately I tried to clear my thoughts and respond correctly.

293

Geral—he also insisted on abandoning titles right away—was funny, shy, and mild voiced. Encouraging him to talk, I discovered that he liked music and poetry, and that he was the heir to an old barony.

And so it went for the remainder of the evening. I was never still, never had time to stop or sit down—or to think. Increasingly I felt as if I had stepped down from a quiet pathway expecting to encounter firm stones, but had instead tumbled into a fast-moving river.

Twice I looked across the room to find Savona standing against the wall, his powerful arms crossed, watching me. When my eyes met his, he grinned. After the second time, I just had to know what the Marquis of Shevraeth made of all this, and I darted a fast glance at him under my partner's velvet-sleeved arm as we twirled.

Shevraeth was in the dance at the other end of the room, conversing quietly with his partner. He seemed completely oblivious to everyone else.

And the Marquise of Merindar was not there at all.

NINE

"Savona didn't dance with anyone else," Nee said.

We were curled up in my sitting room. Outside the window, the garden was a silhouette in the faint blue light of dawn.

"We only danced that once. But then he asked me that question about my favorite color," I said. "Ought I to wear it tonight?"

She pursed her lips. "I'll wager my best necklace all the decorations in that ballroom tonight will be lavender, even if he has to empty the entire city today to find them. Did he say anything else?"

"He asked me to call him Russav."

Her eyes widened. "I don't think *anyone* calls him that—except for Vidanric, and sometimes Tamara. I think I told you that he inherited when his parents died under mysterious circumstances, when he was very small. We all grew up calling him Savona."

"Well, I can't think of him as anything but Savona." Again that sense of rushing down a rock-strewn river engulfed me. "What does it all mean?"

"It means you are going to be very, very popular," Nee predicted.

"Is that it?" I said, frowning.

"You mean, what does it signify in personal terms?" she asked, her brows rising. "That question, my dear, you are the one to answer, not I."

"But I can't answer it," I wailed. "I feel like I'm in a whirlwind, and the wrong move will dash me on the rocks."

"You'll learn how to maneuver as you steer your own course," she said. "Everyone began with no experience."

I shook my head. "I think that Savona was born with experience."

She set her cup down. "He was always popular with the wilder children, the ones who liked dares and risks. He and Vidanric both. Only, Vidanric was so small and lightboned he had to work hard at it, while everything came easy to Savona, who was always bigger and faster and more coordinated than anyone else. I think it was the same when they discovered flirting—" She hesitated, then shrugged and closed her lips.

And since the subject had come to include Shevraeth, I didn't want to pursue it. Ever since our conversation on our arrival at Athanarel, Nee had stopped talking about him. I told myself I didn't want to hear any more anyway.

Now she drifted toward the door, her dressing gown trailing behind her. "We'd better get to sleep. We have a very long evening before us."

I nodded, wishing her a good rest. As I crawled into bed, I felt a happy sense of anticipation. Not just because I had a wonderful ball to look forward to—my very first. More important to me was that the day after that was my Name Day and the anniversary of the beginning of the long, terrible time I spent as a prisoner and a fugitive.

My Flower Day had also been last year, but because of the war there had been no music, no dancing, no celebration.

I remembered Bran's words just before I made the fateful spy trip, "Next year I promise you'll have a Name Day celebration to be remembered forever—and it'll be in the capital."

"With us as winners, right?" I'd said. Well, here we were in the capital after all, though we hadn't won the crown. I didn't want a party—not at Court, attended by strangers—but I looked forward to celebrating with Bran.

I didn't have a lavender ball gown, so Mora and her handmaids changed the ribbons on my white-and-silver one. I felt splendid when I looked at myself in the mirror as Mora brushed out my hair and arranged it to fall just right against the back of the silver gown.

Last was the headdress, which Mora's deft fingers pinned securely into place. It was mainly white roses with long white ribbons and one lavender one tied in a bow. I had another new fan, which hung from my waist on a braided silken cord of white.

My spirits were high as I joined Nee and Bran. But instead of walking down the stairs to go into the ballroom with the rest of the guests, Nee and Bran led the way across the hall, to the gallery that overlooked the ballroom, and stopped at the landing at the top of the grand stairway.

And there we found Shevraeth waiting for us, looking formidable and remote in his usual dark colors. Remembering with dismaying intensity that the last time we had talked with one another I had managed—again—to instigate a quarrel, I felt embarrassment chase away my anticipation.

Shevraeth greeted us in his customary calm manner. When he turned at last to Bran, I muttered out of the side of my mouth to Nee, "You mean we have to go down these stairs—with him—and everyone looking at us?"

"We're the guests of honor," she whispered back, obviously trying not to laugh. She looked fabulous in her dark brown velvet gown, embroidered all over with tiny gold leaves dotted with little rubies. "We're supposed to be looked at! We'll open the ball. You remember? I know I told you."

Bran flicked my shoulder. "Brace up, Mel. You'll like it. I promise."

My attempt at a bland face obviously wasn't convincing. I studied the toes of my dancing slippers, wishing with all my strength that I was back in Tlanth, riding the mountain trails with no humans in sight.

"Savona's waiting," Nee whispered to me.

Some invisible servant must have given a signal, for the music started: an entire orchestra filling the vaulted room with the strains of an ancient promenade. Had I been downstairs among the glittering throng, I would have loved it, but I now had Shevraeth standing right beside me, holding out his arm. I just *knew* I would manage to do something embarrassing.

I took a deep breath, straightened my shoulders, and tried my best to smooth my face into a polite smile as I put my hand on his sleeve.

Just before we started down, he murmured, "Think of this as a battle."

"A battle?" I repeated, so surprised I actually looked up at his face. He didn't look angry, or disgusted, or sarcastic. But there was suppressed laughter in the way his gray eyes were narrowed.

He replied so softly I could just barely hear it. "You've a sword in your hand, and vast numbers of ravening minions of some dreaded evil sorcerer await below. The moment you step among them, you'll leap into battle, mowing them down in droves..."

The absolute unlikelihood of it made me grin, on the verge of laughter. And I realized that while he'd spoken we had come safely down the stairs and were halfway along the huge room to the Duke of Savona, who waited alone. On either side people bowed and curtsied, as graceful as flowers in the wind.

I'd almost made it, and my smile was real—until I lost the image and remembered where I was, and who I was with, and I muttered defensively, "I don't really like battles, you know."

"Of course I know," he returned, still in that soft voice. "But you're used to them." And then we were before Savona, who was resplendent in black and crimson and gold; and as the Duke bowed, fanfare after fanfare washed over me like waves of brilliant light.

Because Shevraeth was also a guest of honor, and had the highest rank, it was his choice for the first dance, and he held out his hand to me. Savona went to Nee, and Bran went to Nee's cousin Tamara.

We danced. I moved through the complicated steps with sureness, my whole body in harmony with the singing strings, my eyes dazzled by the swirl of color all around me. Above our dancing figures, and around us, flowers and ribbons and hangings of every shade of violet and lavender made the room seem almost impossibly elegant.

When the dance ended, Shevraeth bowed and handed me to Savona, and once again I danced, relieved that I had somehow managed to get through the first one without any awkwardness at all. *It's the music,* I thought happily as I spun and stepped; *music is truly like magic.*

At the end of that dance I was surrounded by potential partners, and so it went for the rest of the night. I scarcely remembered any of the introductions, but it didn't seem to matter. A succession of smiling, handsome partners and a continual flow of compliments formed a background to the music, which filled me with the light air that makes clouds and rendered it impossible not to dance.

It wasn't until the night was nearly over that I discovered I was thirsty. It was my first quiet moment. Standing near one of the potted shrubs that isolated the food and drink, I sipped at the punch and started picking out individual voices from the chatter around me, and individual dancers from the mass.

I overheard a conversation from the other side of the shrub. "...see Tamara? That's the third time she's gotten him."

Curious, I looked at the dancers and easily found Lady Tamara—dancing with Shevraeth. They made a very handsome couple, her pale blue gown and dark hair, his colors the opposite.

Her eyes gleamed through her famous lashes as she smiled up into his face; she then spoke, though the words were inaudible. He, of course, was exactly as unreadable as always.

"Tsk tsk." A new voice joined in, drawling with sardonic amusement, "I suppose it's inevitable. She's always gotten what she's wanted; and beware whoever gets in her way."

"Everything?" the first voice said with a tinkly sort of laugh. "Compassing marriage to either of the cousins?"

"Come now, she's dropped the lesser prospect. Why settle for a duke when there's a king in reach?"

"Perhaps she's been dropped" was the answer. "Or else the glare while Savona danced with the little Tlanth countess was a sham to provide entertainment for our speculation."

Laughing, the speakers moved away. I stood where I was, watching Lady Tamara happily whirling about the room in Shevraeth's grasp, and I realized that he hadn't been near me since the beginning of the evening. Uncomfortable emotions began eroding my enjoyment. I tried to banish them, and also what I'd heard. *It's nothing to do with me*, I told myself firmly, hoping there wasn't some like conversation taking place elsewhere in the room—only with me as its subject. *I didn't do anything wrong.*

Still, it was hard during the remaining dances to recapture the earlier joy, and at the end I was glad to follow Bran and Nee back upstairs to our rooms, Nee yawning all the way. My feet were tired, but I buoyed myself with the reminder that my Name Day came with dawn. *What has Branaric planned?*

He gave me no hints as he bade me a good night outside my rooms.

The windows were bright with sunlight when I woke, and though I could have slept longer, the prospect of my Name Day got me up and dressed.

My first thought was to go to Nee's rooms. She would be a part of anything Bran planned.

300

I bustled down the hall. As I stretched out my hand to knock outside her tapestry, I heard Bran's genial voice booming from inside: "Enstaeus and Trishe went to kidnap him. We're to meet them at the stable."

And Nee said, "Then we'd better go before Meliara wakens. It'll be easier than trying to explain that she wouldn't enjoy this ride—"

My hand froze. Shock, dismay, and question all kept me from moving, even though I knew I ought to retreat—fast—to my room. Even in the rudest house among the most ignorant people, children grow up knowing that tapestry manners require you to make a noise as soon as you reach someone's room. You don't stand and listen.

Holding my hands straight at my sides so my skirts wouldn't rustle, I backed up one step, two—then Nee's tapestry lifted, and there were the three of us, face-to-face.

Bran snorted a laugh—of course. "Life, sister, you gave me a start!"

Nee's entire face went crimson, though the fault was mine for being there without warning. "Good morning," she said, looking unhappy.

I did my best to assume a sublimely indifferent Court mask. "I just stopped to tell you I was going to the library." And I walked away quickly.

Not enjoy a ride? I thought, and then I remembered that this was Court, and people didn't always say what they thought. Apparently even Nee. *They want to spend some time alone, of course,* I realized, and guilt overwhelmed me. I had monopolized Nee ever since the night in our palace when she offered to show me Court ways.

Well, I was at Court now, and I had made it through a grand ball without causing any disasters or making a complete fool of myself. *So now it is only fair to leave her some time alone with my brother,* I told myself firmly. After all, wasn't that a part of courtship, wanting to be alone with your intended, however much you liked the rest of his family?

I hurried down the silent halls toward the library as if I could outrun my emotions, forming a resolve to start making my own way, leaving Nee to get on with her life.

As I neared the State Wing, my heart thumped, and despite the Princess's kind invitation, I hoped I wouldn't encounter any of the Renselaeuses. But no one was about except silent footmen and occasional equerries passing to and fro. When I reached the library, the waiting footmen opened the doors for me, and I passed into the huge room and found myself alone.

I strolled slowly along the shelves, looking at titles without really comprehending them, wondering where I ought to begin. Remembering my conversation with Princess Elestra, I realized what I really wanted to see were the originals, the papers written by kings and queens in their own hands. Were they all in the Heraldry Archives, or were some of them here?

My gaze fell on a plain door-tapestry at the other end of the room. *A service access?* I turned and saw a narrow, discreet outline of a door tucked in the corner between two bookshelves; that was the service door, then. Might I find some kind of archive beyond that tapestry?

I crossed the room, heard no noise beyond, so I lifted the tapestry.

The room was small, filled with light. It was a corner room, with two entrances, floor-to-ceiling windows in two walls, and bookshelves everywhere else. In the slanting rays of the morning sun I saw a writing table angled between the windows—and kneeling at the table, dressed in riding clothes, was the Marquis of Shevraeth.

He put down his pen and looked up inquiringly.

Feeling that to run back out would be cowardly, I said, "Your mother invited me to use the library. I thought this might be an archive."

"It is," he said. "Memoirs from kings and queens addressed specifically to heirs. Most are about laws. A few are diaries of Court life. Look around." He picked up the pen again and waved it toward he shelves. "Over there you'll find the book of laws by Turic the Third, he of the twelve thousand proclamations. Next to it is his daughter's, rescinding most of them." He pushed a pile of papers in my direction. "Or if you'd like to peruse something more recent, here are Galdran's expenditure lists and so forth. They give a fairly comprehensive overview of his policies."

I stepped into the room and bent down to lift up two or three of the papers. Some were proposals for increases in taxes for certain nobles; the fourth was a list of people "to be watched."

I looked at him in surprise. "You found these just lying around?"

"Yes," he said, sitting back on his cushion. The morning light highlighted the smudges of tiredness under his eyes. "He did not expect to be defeated. Your brother and I rode back here in haste, as soon as we could, in order to prevent looting; but such was Galdran's hold on the place that, even though the news had preceded us by two days, I found his rooms completely undisturbed. I don't think anyone believed he was really dead—they expected one of his ugly little ploys to catch out 'traitors.' "

I whistled, turning over another paper. "Wish I could have been there," I said.

"You could have been."

This brought me back to reality with a jolt. Of course I could have been there—but I had left without warning, without saying good-bye even to my own brother, in my haste to retreat to home and sanity. And memory.

I glanced at him just in time to see him wince slightly and shake his head. Was that regret? For his words—or for my actions that day?

"What you said last night," I demanded, "about battles and me being used to them. What did you mean by that?"

"It was merely an attempt to make you laugh."

"I did laugh," I admitted, then frowned. "But did you *really* intend some kind of courtly double meaning? Hinting that I'm used to battles in the sense that I lost every one I was in? Or merely that I get into quarrels?"

"Neither." His tone was flat. "Forgive my maladroitness."

"Well, I *don't* get into quarrels," I said, suddenly desperate to explain, to accuse. "Except with—"

There came a tap outside the opposite doorway then.

I shut my mouth; and for a moment, there we were, in silence, me wishing I could run but feeling I ought not to. There was—something—I had to do, or say, though I had no idea what.

So I watched him rise, move the few steps to the other tapestry, and lift it. I did not see whoever was outside—I realized he was shielding me from sight. I could not hear the voice beyond, but I heard his: "Please inform Lady Trishe I will be along shortly. Thank you." He dropped the tapestry back into place and stood with his back to it, looking at me across the width of the room. "It seems," he said, "that seeking your opinion will not cease to embroil us in argument, whatever the cause. I apologize. I also realize trying to convince you of my good intentions is a fruitless effort, but my own conscience demanded that I make the attempt."

I couldn't think of any reply to make to that, so I whirled around and retreated into the library, my insides boiling with a nasty mixture of embarrassment and anger. Why did I always have to bring up that war—and pick a fight? What kind of answer was I looking for?

All I do is repeat the humiliations of last year. As if I haven't had enough of those, I thought grimly. And the worst thing was, I wouldn't dare to go near that room again, despite his offer at the beginning of the encounter—an encounter which was thoroughly my own fault.

Well, I'd have to console myself with the big room. Stopping along the row of biographies, I selected the histories of three well-hated tyrants, figuring they'd be good company for me, and I retreated to my rooms.

———

It was a while before my mind was quiet enough for reading. The conversation with Shevraeth I was determined not to think about. What was the use? It was over, and it was clear it wasn't going to be repeated.

Recalling the name he'd mentioned, Lady Trishe—one of the names Bran had spoken earlier that morning—I realized it was Shevraeth they were planning to go riding with. *She wouldn't enjoy this ride* was what Nee had said, meaning that I wouldn't enjoy it because Shevraeth would be along. What it probably also meant, I realized glumly, was that *they* wouldn't enjoy having *me* along if I glared at Shevraeth and started squabbling.

I grabbed up a book and flung myself down on my nest of pillows. At frequent intervals I set the book aside and listened, expecting to hear the noise of their return. But the sun marched across the sky without their reappearance, and just after sunset Nee knocked to ask if I was ready to go to a concert officially scheduled for the ambassadors.

I changed hastily, expecting my brother to appear. But what happened was that we went to the concert. Bran—indifferent to music—had gone off elsewhere with other friends. The choir was wonderful, and the songs from over the sea were beautiful, though I heard them through a damp veil of self-pity.

I finally had to admit to myself that my brother had forgotten all about my Name Day, and Nee had no idea. Before the revolt, my brother and I had been close. Obviously, more had changed since Galdran's defeat than I'd realized.

The main person in his life now is Nee—as it should be, I told myself as she and I walked across the flagged courtyard to the Residence Wing. But my mood stayed sober as I contemplated how life would change when we all returned to Tlanth. *I'm not oath-sworn as a countess, not until we gather before the new monarch when he or she is crowned; and Bran is the legal heir. And a county can't have two countesses...*

When we reached our hall, Nee offered to share hot chocolate with me. Shaking my head, I pleaded tiredness—true enough—and retreated to my rooms.

And discovered something lying on the little table in the parlor where letters and invitations were supposed to be put.

Moving slowly across the room, I looked down at an exquisite porcelain sphere. It was dark blue, with silver stars all over it, and so cunningly painted that when I looked closer it gave the illusion of depth—as if I stared deeply into the sky.

Lifting it with reverent care, I opened it and saw, sitting on a white silk nest, a lovely sapphire ring. Trying it on my fingers, I found to my delight it fit my longest one.

Why couldn't Bran give me this in person? There were times when I found my brother incomprehensible, but I knew he thought the same of me.

Puzzled, but content, I fell asleep with my ringed hand cradled against my cheek.

TEN

WHEN I HEARD BRANARIC CALL A MORNING GREET-
ing outside Nee's parlor, I rushed out and batted aside her tapestry.
They both looked at me in surprise as I hugged Bran. "Thank you.
It's really lovely!"

"Huh?" Bran looked half pleased, but half confused. Nee
looked completely confused.

"The gift egg! This ring!" I stuck out my hand. "The finest
Name Day gift I ever had!" I laughed.

Bran blinked, then grimaced. "Burn me, Mel—I forgot. I mean,
it ain't from me, the date went right out of my head. Life! I talked
to Nee about planning a boat party—didn't I?" He turned suddenly
to Nee, who looked stricken. He sighed. "But I guess I think we're
still back three or four months." He held out his arms and hugged
me. "I'm sorry."

I said with an unsteady laugh, "Well, I'll admit to being disappointed yesterday, until I found this—but if you didn't put it in
my room, who did?"

Nee also gave me a hug. I sensed how bad she felt. "We'll make
up for it," she whispered, and then, louder, "Was there a letter
with it?"

"No. But who else would know?"

"It might not be a Name Day gift at all, though it's awfully expensive for an admirer to start with," Nee said slowly.

"Savona, you think?" I felt my cheeks go red.

"Could be, except my understanding is, he usually writes love letters to go with gifts."

"Love letters," I said, grimacing. "I don't want those."

Nee and Branaric both grinned.

"Well, I don't," I protested. "Anyway, what ought I to do?"

Nee's maid brought coffee, which filled the room with its aromatic promise. When the woman was gone, Nee said, "You can put it away, which of course will end the question. Or you can wear it in public, to signify your approval, and see if anyone claims it, or even looks conscious."

That's what I did. A sudden spring shower prevented our going out immediately, but late in the afternoon the sky cleared and the air was balmy enough for one to carry one's walking gloves instead of wear them. I chose a dark gown to show off the ring, had my hair brushed out, and walked out with Nee, Branaric having disappeared earlier.

There were even more blooms in the garden than on my previous walk, scarcely two days before. Everyone seemed to be out and about—talking, laughing, watching the fish and ducks and swans. It was while we were walking along the big pool, admiring the swans and their hatchlings, that we found ourselves annexed by two energetic ladies, Lady Trishe and Lady Renna. The latter was tall, thin, and mild in manner, though Nee had told me she was a formidable rider—not surprisingly, as she was heir to the Khialem family, who were known for horse breeding. She had recently married, and her husband, second son to a baron whose family's lands bordered hers, was another horse-mad type.

Lady Trishe was the one who caught the eye. Also tall, with bright golden hair now worn in loose curls around her shoulders, she looked like the personification of spring in her light green gown. Nee had said she was a popular hostess.

They greeted us with expressions of delight, and Trishe said, "Have they finished their ride, then?"

Nee stiffened ever so slightly beside me. "That I do not know. Branaric went on ahead. It was too wet for my taste."

"You also did not want to go with them, Lady Meliara?" Trishe turned to me. "There has been much said in praise of your riding."

"About your everything," a new voice spoke with cool amusement from behind, and we turned to see Lady Tamara leading a small party of ladies and gentlemen. Tamara also wore her hair down, a cascade of glossy curls to her waist, with tiny gems braided into it. "Good day, Countess," she said, waving her fan slowly. I'd noticed that she always carried a fan, even at informal gatherings when the others didn't. "Is there any end to your accomplishments, then? Yesterday the air rang with acclaim for your grace on the ballroom floor. Shall you lead the way on horseback as well?" And she curtsied, a formal reverence, coming up with her fan spread half before her face in the mode denoting Modesty Deferring to Brilliance.

I was being mocked. Nothing in her manner gave it away, yet I knew that that particular fan gesture was not for social occasions but reserved for literary or artistic exchanges.

I bowed back, exactly the same bow, and because they all seemed to expect me to speak, I said, "I haven't had a chance to go riding as yet."

"I am surprised," Tamara exclaimed, her smile gentle, her hands making artful swirls with the fan. "But, I confess, not as surprised as I was that you did not join us at Petitioners' Court today."

Nee said quickly, "Court is not obligatory. You know that, Cousin."

"Obligatory, no indeed. Cousin." Now Tamara's fan gestured gracefully in query mode, but at a plangent angle. I couldn't get the meaning of it, and the other ladies were silent. "Surely the forming government would benefit from her advice?"

Was she referring to my having led a revolt, however unsuccessful, or was she digging at me for having lost a crown? I suspected the latter, not from any sign she gave but from the others' reactions, and I stood in silence, trying to find something to say that wouldn't start trouble. It was a relief when the sounds of laughter and voices heralded new arrivals.

We all turned, and my brother appeared with four other gentlemen. Branaric called jovially, "Found you, Mel, Nee." And he bowed to the other ladies, who in turn greeted the arrivals: Geral, Savona, Lord Deric of Orbanith, and Shevraeth.

"What's toward?" the Duke asked.

Tamara's gaze was still on me. I saw her open her mouth, and before she could say anything that might sting me with embarrassment, I stuck out my hand and said, "Look at my ring!"

Surprise, and a few titters of laughter, met my sudden and uncourtier-like gesture.

Trishe took my hand, turned it over so the ring caught the light. She made admiring noises, then looked up and said, "Where? Who?"

"Yesterday." I sneaked a look at Savona. He was grinning.

"Which finger?" Tamara asked, glancing down.

"The one it fits best," I said quickly, which raised a laugh. I cast a desperate look at Nee, who was biting her lip. I hadn't even thought to ask about meaning in ring fingers, though I ought to have, I realized belatedly. Rings would be a symbol just like flowers and fan language.

"I've seen it before," Trishe said, frowning in perplexity. "I know I have. It's very old, and they don't cut stones like this anymore."

"Who is it from?" Savona asked.

I looked up at him, trying to divine whether secret knowledge lay behind his expression of interest.

"Of course she cannot tell," Tamara said, her tone mock chiding—a masterpiece of innuendo, I realized. "But...perhaps a hint, Countess?"

"I can't, because it's a secret to me, too." I looked around. Nothing but interest in all the faces, from Savona's friendly skepticism to Shevraeth's polite indifference. Shevraeth looked more bored than ever. "The best kind, because I get the ring and don't have to do anything about it!"

Everyone laughed.

"Now that," Savona said, taking my arm, "is a direct challenge, is it not? Geral? Danric? I take you to witness." We started strolling along the pathway. "But first, to rid myself of this mysterious rival. Have you kissed anyone since yesterday? Winked? Sent a posy-of-promise?" He went on with so many ridiculous questions I couldn't stop laughing.

The others had fallen in behind. Conversations crossed the group, preventing it from breaking into smaller groups. Before too long Tamara brought us all together again. She was now the center of attention as she summoned Savona to her side to admire a new bracelet.

This was fine with me. I did not like being the center, and I felt jangled and uneasy. Had I betrayed myself in any important way? Had I been properly polite to Shevraeth? The few times he spoke I was careful to listen and to smile just like the others.

When I found myself on the edge of the group, I slipped away and hastened back to the Residence. In my room, I found Mora sewing. She looked at me in surprise, and hastily got to her feet to curtsy.

"Never mind that," I said. "Tell me, who brings letters and things?"

"The runners, my lady," she said.

"Can you find out who sent a runner?" When she hesitated, I said, "Look, I just want to find out who gave me these gifts. I know under the old king, people could be bribed. Is that true now? Please, speak plain. I won't tell anyone what you tell me, and I won't make trouble."

Mora pursed her lips. "There are times when the runners can be bribed, my lady," she said carefully. "But not all of them. Were it to get out, they could lose their position."

"So everyone belowstairs doesn't know everything?"

"No, my lady. Many people use personal runners to deliver things to the palace runners; and the loyal ones don't talk."

"Ah hah!" I exclaimed. "Then, tell me this: Can something be returned along the same route, even though I don't know to whom it's going?"

She thought a bit, then nodded. "I think that can be arranged."

"Good. Then let me pen a message, and please see that it gets sent right away." I dived down onto the cushions beside the desk, rummaged about, and came up with pen and writing paper. On the paper I wrote: *The gifts are beautiful, and I thank you, but what do they mean?*

I signed my name, sealed the letter, and handed it to Mora.

She left at once, and I was severely tempted to try to follow her, except I'd promised not to make trouble. And if I were caught at it, I suspected that the servants involved might get into trouble. I decided to look at this whole matter as a kind of challenge. I'd find some clever way of solving the mystery without involving anyone innocent.

So I pulled on a cloak and went out to take another walk. The sky was already clouding up again, and a strong, chilly wind kicked up my skirts. The weather reminded me of home, and I found it bracing. I set out in a new direction, away from the aristo gardens and the outlying great houses.

The buildings were still in the same style, but plainer. Presently I found myself midway between the royal stables and the military compound. My steps slowed. I remembered that the prison building was not very far from the stables, and I had no desire to see it again.

I turned around—and nearly bumped into a small group of soldiers in Renselaeus colors. They all stopped, bowed silently, and would have stepped out of my way, but I recognized one of them from my ride to Renselaeus just before the end of the war, and I cried, "Captain Nessaren!"

"My lady." Nessaren smiled, her flat cheeks tinged slightly with color.

"Is your riding assigned here now?"

"As you see, my lady."

The others bowed and withdrew silently, leaving us alone.

"Are you not supposed to talk to the civs?" Raindrops stung my face.

Her eyes crinkled. "They usually don't talk to us."

"Is this a good duty, or is it boring now that nothing is going on?"

Her eyes flickered to my face then down to the ground, and her lips just parted. After a moment she said, "We're well enough, my lady."

Which wasn't quite what I had asked. Resolving to think that over later, I said, "You know what I miss? The practice sessions we had when we were riding cross-country last year. I did some practice at home... but there doesn't seem to be opportunity anymore."

"We have open practice each day at dawn, in the garrison court when the weather's fine, the gym when it isn't. You're welcome to join us. There's no hierarchy, except that of expertise, by order of the Marquis himself."

"The Marquis?" I repeated faintly, realizing how close I'd come to making an even worse fool of myself than my spectacular attempts so far.

"There every day," she said. "Others as well—Lady Renna. Duke of Savona there most days, same as Baron Khialem. You wouldn't be alone."

I won't be there at all. But out loud I just thanked her.

She bowed. Her companions were still waiting at a discreet distance, despite the spatter of rain, so I said, "I won't keep you any longer."

313

As she rejoined her group, I started back toward the Residence. The wind had turned chill, and the rain started falling faster, but I scarcely noticed. *Was* there still some kind of danger? Instinct attributed Nessaren's deliberate vagueness to a military reason.

If the threat was from the borders, it seemed unlikely that I'd find Renselaeus warriors roaming around the royal palace Athanarel. So, was there a threat at home?

Like a rival for the kingship? My thoughts went immediately to the Marquise of Merindar—and to the conservation with Shevraeth at the inn. The Marquise had made no attempt to communicate with me, and I had not even seen her subsequent to that dinner the night of my arrival. In the days since, I'd managed to lose sight of my purpose in coming.

When I'd surprised Shevraeth in the archive, it had seemed he was actually willing to discuss royal business—at least that portion that pertained to cleaning up after Galdran—for why else would he offer me a look at the old king's papers? But I'd managed to turn the discussion into a quarrel, and so lost the chance.

I groaned aloud. What was *wrong* with me? As I hurried up the steps to our wing, I promised myself that next time Shevraeth tried to talk to me, I'd listen, and even if he insulted me, my family, and my land, I'd keep my tongue between my teeth.

"My own conscience demands that I make the attempt." Would there even be another try?

I sighed as I opened my door, then Nessaren and Shevraeth and the rain went out of my mind when I saw that my letter table was not empty.

Two items awaited me. The first was a letter—and when I saw the device on the heavy seal, my heart sped: the Marquise of Merindar.

I ripped it open, to find only an invitation to a gathering three weeks hence. No hint of any personal message.

Laying it aside, I turned my gaze to the other object.

Sitting in the middle of the table was a fine little vase cut from luminous starstone, and in it, bordered by the most delicate ferns, was a single rose, just barely blooming.

One white rose. I knew what that meant, thanks to Nee: *Purity of Intent.*

ELEVEN

My glimpses of Shevraeth were rare over the next three weeks, and all of those were either at State events or else at big parties held by mutual Court friends. I did not see the Marquise of Merindar or her two children at all—Nee said they rarely attended Court functions and entertained only in their family's house on the outskirts of Athanarel's garden, though the State rooms in the Residence could be hired by anyone. The Marquise's invitation sat on my table, looking rather like a royal summons.

Very different were the invitations that I received from the Court young people, for as Nee had predicted, I *had* become popular. At least on the surface, everyone was friendly, even Lady Tamara Chamadis, though her tone, and her fan, hinted that she didn't find me amusing because she thought I was a wit.

Others were more forthright in offering their friendship. Not just the ladies, either. To my vast surprise, I seemed to have collected several flirts. The Duke of Savona sought me out at every event we both attended, insisting on the first dance at balls—and lots more through the evening. He was an excellent dancer, and I thoroughly enjoyed him as a partner. His outrageous compliments just made me laugh.

My second most devoted admirer was Lord Deric Toarvendar,

Count of Orbanith. He was not content to meet me at balls but showered invitations on me—to picnics, riding parties, and other events that had to do with sport.

Among intimates, I'd discovered, young courtiers didn't write invitations, they spoke them, usually at the end of some other affair. Some people were overt—which meant they wanted others to overhear and thus to know they'd been excluded—but most were more subtle about it.

Not that Deric was particularly subtle. He made it obvious that he thought I was fun and funny, as good a loser as I was a winner. In the weeks after I received that rose, we had competed at all kinds of courtly games, from cards to horse racing. He was entertaining, and—unlike Certain Others—easy to understand, and also easy to resist when his flirting, wine- and moonlight-inspired, intensified to wandering hands and lips.

The night before the Merindar party, I had made myself easy to understand by planting a hand right in the middle of his chest and pushing him away. "No," I said.

He found that funny, too, and promptly offered to drive me to the Merindar party himself.

I accepted. By then I'd pretty much decided that he was the one who had sent me the ring and the rose, for despite his enthusiastic dedication to sport and his one energetic attempt at stealing a kiss, he was surprisingly shy about discussing anything as intimate as feelings.

This was fine with me. I felt no desire to tax him about it; if I did and it proved I was right, it might change a relationship I liked just where it was.

The night of the Merindar party, the weather was cold and rainy, so Deric drove his handsome pony-trap to the Residence to pick me up. It was not that long a distance to the Merindar house.

The Family houses were built around the perimeter of the

palace at Athanarel's extensive gardens, a tiny city within the city of Remalna. None of these were castles, and thus could never have been defended. They were palaces, designed for pleasure and entertaining—and for secret egress.

The finest two were at opposite ends, the one belonging to the Merindar family, and the other to the Chamadis family.

The Merindar palace most nearly resembled a fortress, for all its pleasing design; there were few windows on the ground level, and those on the upper levels seemed curiously blind. And all around the house stood guards, ostensibly to protect the Merindar family from grudge-holding citizens. I had discovered that this was in fact not new; Galdran Merindar had kept guards stationed around the house during his reign. As king, he had not had to give a reason.

"The food will be excellent, the music even better, but watch out for the Flower and the Thorn," Deric said to me at the end of the journey, just before we disembarked from the pony-trap. "Of the two, the Flower is the more dangerous," he added.

"Flower—is that the Marquise's son or daughter?"

"Lord Flauvic," Deric said with a twist to his lips and an ironic gleam in his black eyes. "You'll understand the moment you get a squint at him and hear his pretty voice. It was your brother gave him the nickname last year, after Flauvic returned from his sojourn at the king's court in Sles Adran. He spent almost ten years there as a page."

"A page," I repeated, impressed.

"Ten successful years," he added.

I considered this, making a mental note to stay away from Lord Flauvic—who had also been recently named his mother's heir, bypassing his older sister, Lady Fialma, the one called the Thorn. I'd learned about pages in my reading, for they had not been in use in Remalna for at least a century, and a good thing, too. Unlike runners, who were from obscure birth and kept—as servants—outside the main rooms until summoned, pages were from good homes and waited on their superiors within the State rooms. That meant that hey were privy to everything that went on—a very, very dangerous rivilege. According to my reading, pages who made political mistakes were seldom executed. Instead they were sent home before their term of indenture was over, which was a public disgrace and, s such, a lifelong exile from the provinces of power. Those who nished their time successfully tended to return home well trained nd formidably adept at political maneuvering. A page trained at the drani Court would be formidable indeed.

The only other thing I had known about Flauvic was that the Marquise had sent him out of the kingdom when he was small in rder to keep him alive, the year after his father and two of his ncles had met mysterious deaths. I hadn't met him yet—apparntly he never attended any State events or social events outside of is own home, preferring to remain there deep in his studies. An ristocratic scholar.

Studying what? I wondered, as we were bowed inside the house y blank-faced Merindar servants.

The grandeur around us was a silent testimony to wealth and ower. The air was scented with a complex mixture of exotic flowrs and the faintest trace of tanglewood incense, denoting peace nd kindred spirits.

"Easy over the fence," Deric said softly beside me.

We were already at the parlor. I suppressed a grin at the riding rm, then stepped forward to curtsy to the Marquise.

"My dear Countess," Lady Arthal said, smiling as she pressed y hand. "Welcome. Permit me to introduce my children, Fialma nd Flauvic. The rest of the company you know."

Lady Fialma was tall, brown-haired, with cold eyes and the evated chin of one who considers herself to be far above whomver she happens to be looking at—or down on. She was magnifintly gowned, with so many glittering jewels it almost hurt the es to look at her. She would have been handsome but for a very ng nose—which was the more obvious because of that imperious lt to her head—and thinly compressed lips.

"Welcome," she said, in so faint and listless a voice that it was

319

almost hard to hear her. "Delighted to…" She shrugged slightly, and her languidly waving fan fluttered with a dismissive extra flick.

Lord Flauvic, on the other side of their mother, was startlingly beautiful. His coloring was fair, his long waving hair golden with ruddy highlights. His eyes were so light a brown as to seem gold, a match for his hair. "…meet you, Countess," he said, finishing his sister's sentence. Politeness? Humor? Insult? Impossible to guess. His voice was the pure tenor of a trained singer, his gaze as blank as glass as he took my hand and bowed over it. Of medium height and very slender, he was dressed in deep blue, almost black, with a rare scattering of diamonds in his hair, in one ear, and on his clothing.

I realized I was staring and looked away quickly, following Deric into the next room. He fell into conversation with Branaric, Shevraeth, and Lady Renna Khialem, the subject (of course) horses. Deric's manner reminded me of someone relieved to find allies. Next to Bran sat Nee, completely silent, her hands folded in her lap.

Under cover of the chatter about horse racing, I looked around, feeling a little like a commander assessing a potential battlefield. Our hosts, despite their gracious outward manner, had made no effort to bind the guests into a circle. Instead, people were clumped in little groups, either around the magnificent buffet, or around the fireplace. As I scanned them, I realized who was there—and who was not there.

Present: counts, countesses, a duke, a duchess, heirs to these titles, and the only two people in the marquisate: Shevraeth and our hostess.

Absent: anyone with the title of baron or lower, except those —like Nee—who had higher connections.

Absent also were the Prince and Princess of Renselaeus.

"My dear Countess," a fluting voice said at my right ear, and Lady Tamara's soft hand slid along my arm, guiding me toward the lowest tier near the fireplace. Several people moved away, and we sank down onto the cushions there. Tamara gestured to one of the hovering foot-servants, and two glasses of wine were instantly brought. "Did I not predict that you would show us the way at the races as well?"

"I won only once," I said, fighting against embarrassment.

Deric was grinning. "Beat me," he said. "Nearly beat Renna."

"I had the best horse," I countered.

For a moment the conversation turned from me to the races the week before. It had been a sudden thing, arranged on the first really nice day we'd had, and though the course was purported to be rough, I had found it much easier than riding mountain trails.

As Deric described the last obstacles of the race in which I had beaten him, I saw the shy red-haired Lord Geral listening with a kind of ardent expression in his eyes. He was another who often sought me out for dances but rarely spoke otherwise. Might my rose and ring have come from him?

Tamara's voice recalled my attention "...the way with swords as well, dear Countess?"

I glanced at her, sipping at my wine as I mentally reached for the subject.

"It transpires," Tamara said with a glinting smile, "that our sharpest wits are also experts at the duel. Almost am I willing to rise at dawn, just to observe you at the cut and the thrust."

I opened my mouth to disclaim any great prowess with the sword, then realized that I'd walk right into her little verbal trap if I did so. Now, maybe I'm not any kind of a sharp wit, but I wasn't going to hand myself over for trimming so easily. So I just smiled and sipped at my wine.

Fialma's faint, die-away voice was just audible on Tamara's other side. "Tamara, my love, that is not dueling, but mere sword-play."

Tamara's blue eyes rounded with perplexity. "True, true, I had forgotten." She smiled suddenly, her fan waving slowly in query mode. "An academic question: Is it a real duel when one is favored by the opponent?"

Fialma said, "Is it a real contest, say, in a race when the better rider does not ride?" She turned her thin smile to Shevraeth. "Your grace?"

The Marquis bowed slightly, his hands at an oblique angle. "If a stake is won," he said, "it is a race. If the point draws blood, it is a duel."

A murmur of appreciative laughter met this, and Fialma sighed ever so slightly. "You honor us," she murmured, sweeping her fan gracefully in the half circle of Intimate Confidence, "with your liberality...." She seated herself at the other side of the fireplace and began a low-voiced conversation with Lady Dara, the heir to a northern duchy.

Just beyond Fialma's waving fan, Lord Flauvic's metal-gold gaze lifted from my face to Shevraeth's to Tamara's, then back to me. What had I missed? Nee's cheeks were glowing, but that could have been her proximity to the fire.

Branaric spoke then, saluting Shevraeth with his wineglass. "Duel or dabble, I'd hie me to those practices, except I just can't stomach rough work at dawn. Now, make them at noon, and I'm your man!"

More laughter greeted this, and Bran turned to Flauvic. "How about you? Join me in agitating for a decent time?"

Lord Flauvic also had a fan, but he had not opened it. Holding it horizontally between his fingers in the mode of the neutral observer, he said, "Not at any time, Tlanth. You will forgive me if I am forced to admit that I am much too lazy?"

Again laughter, but more subdued. Heads turned. As the smiling Marquise approached, she said, "You are all lazy, children." She gestured at the artfully arranged plates of food. "Come! Do you wish to insult my tastes?"

Several people converged on the table, where waiting servants piled indicated dainties on little plates. The Marquise moved smoothly through the milling guests, smiling and bestowing soft words here and there. To my surprise, she made her way to me, held out her hand, and said, "Come, my dear. Let's see what we can find to appeal to you."

I rose, trying to hide my astonishment. Deric's face was blank, and Bran looked puzzled. Behind him, Shevraeth watched, his expression impossible to interpret. As I followed the Marquise, I glanced at her son, and was further surprised to see his gaze on me. His fingers manipulated his fan; for just an instant he held it in the duelist's "guard" position, then his wrist bent as he spread the fan open with languid deliberation.

A warning? *Of course it is—but why?*

With a regal gesture the Marquise indicated a door—a handsome carved one—and a lackey sprang to open it. A moment later we passed inside a lamp-lit conservatory and were closed off in the sudden, slightly unsettling silence vouchsafed by well-fitted wooden doors. "I find young Deric of Orbanith a refreshing boy," she said. "He's been my daughter's friend through their mutual interest in horses since they were both quite small."

I cudgeled my mind for something diplomatic to say and came up with, "I hope Lady Fialma will join us for the next race, your race."

"Perhaps, perhaps." The Marquise stretched out a hand to nip away a dead leaf from one of her plants. She seemed completely absorbed in her task; I wondered how to delicately turn the discussion to the purpose of her letter when she said, "A little over a year ago there appeared at Court a remarkable document signed by you and your esteemed brother."

Surprised, I recalled our open letter to Galdran outlining how his bad ruling was destroying the kingdom. The letter, meant to gain us allies in the Court, had been the last project we had worked on with our father. "We didn't think anyone actually saw it," I said, unnerved by the abrupt change of subject. "We did send copies, but I thought they had been suppressed."

One of her brows lifted. "No one but the king saw it—officially. However, it enjoyed a brief but intense covert popularity, I do assure you."

"But there was no response," I said.

"As there was no protection offered potential fellow rebels,"

323

she retorted, still in that mild voice, "you ought not be surprised. Your sojourn here was brief. Perhaps you were never really aware of the difficulties facing those who disagreed with my late brother."

"Well, I remember what he was going to do to *me*," I said.

"And do you remember what happened instead?"

I turned to stare at her. "I thought—"

"Thought what, child? Speak freely. There is no one to overhear you."

Except, of course, the Marquise. But was she really a danger? The Renselaeuses now gripped the hilt-end of the sword of power, or she would have been home long since.

"The Princess Elestra hinted that they helped me escape," I said.

"Hinted," she repeated. "And thus permitted you to convince yourself?"

"You mean they didn't?"

She lifted one shoulder slightly. "Contradiction of the conqueror, whose memory is usually adaptable, is pointless, unless..." She paused, once more absorbed in clearing yellowed leaves from a delicate plant.

"Unless what, your grace?" Belatedly I remembered the niceties.

She did not seem to notice. "Unless one intends to honor one's own vows," she murmured. "I have not seen you or your respected brother at Court. Have you set aside those fine ideals as expressed in your letter?"

"We haven't, your grace," I said cautiously.

"Yet I have not seen you at Petitioners' Court. That is, I need hardly point out, where the real ruling takes place."

But Shevraeth is there. Remembering the promise I had made that last day at Tlanth, I was reluctant to mention my problems with him. I said with care, "I haven't been asked to attend—and I do not see how my presence or absence would make much difference."

"You would learn," she murmured, "how our kingdom is being governed. And then you would be able to form an idea as to whether or not your vows are in fact being kept."

She was *right*. This was my purpose in coming.

Ought I to tell her? Instinct pulled me both ways, but memory of the mistakes I had made in acting on hasty judgment kept me silent.

She bent and plucked a newly bloomed starliss, tucked it into my hair, then stepped back to admire the effect. "There are many among us who would be glad enough to see you and your brother honor those vows," she said, and took my arm, and led me back to the reception room.

At once I was surrounded by Nee and Deric and Renna—my own particular friends—as if they had formed a plan to protect me. Against what? Nothing happened after that, except that we ate and drank and listened to a quartet of singers from the north performing ballads whose words we could not understand, but whose melancholy melodies seemed to shiver in the air.

The Marquise of Merindar did not speak to me again until it was time to leave, and she was gracious as she begged me to come visit her whenever I had the inclination. There was no reference to our conversation in the conservatory.

When at last Deric and I settled into his carriage, he dropped back with a sigh of relief. "Well, that's over. Good food and good company, but none of it worth sitting mum while Fialma glared daggers at me."

Remembering the Marquise's opening statement, I realized suddenly what I'd missed before—some of what I'd missed, anyway—and tried unsuccessfully to smother a laugh. It seemed that Deric was deemed an appropriate match for the daughter of a Merindar.

Deric grinned at me, the light from glowglobes flickering in his black eyes. "Cowardice, I know. But burn it, that female scares me."

I remembered the gossip about Lady Fialma and her recent return from Eidervaen, where she was supposed to have contracted an appropriately brilliant marriage alliance but had failed. Which was why the Marquise had passed her over for the heirship of Merindar.

But that wasn't all; as Deric drove away and I mounted the steps of the Residence, I realized that he could, in fact, be subtle when he wanted. And that there were consequences to bluntness that one could not always predict. He had asked me to accompany him as a hint to the Merindars that he was courting me, and therefore wouldn't court Fialma.

Interesting, though, that he asked to take me to that party right *after* I had rejected his attempts to kiss me.

I'll never understand flirting, I thought, fighting the impulse to laugh. *Never.*

In my rooms, I sat at the window, looking out at the soft rain and thinking about that conversation with the Marquise. Was she, or was she not, inviting me to join her in opposing Shevraeth's rule?

Ought I to attend Petitioners' Court, then, and begin evaluating the Renselaeus policies? Where was the real truth between the two families?

I remembered the hint that the Marquise had dropped. According to her, Princess Elestra had not, in fact, had anything to do with my escape. If she hadn't, who, then? The Marquise? Except why didn't I find out before? Who could I ask?

Deric? No. He showed no interest whatever in Crown affairs. He lived for sport. Renna as well. Trishe and the others?

I bit my lip, wondering if my opening such a discussion would be a betrayal of the promise to Shevraeth. I didn't know any of these people well enough to enjoin them to secrecy, and the thought of Shevraeth finding out about my purpose in coming made me shudder inside.

Of the escape, at least, I could find out some of the truth. I'd rite to Azmus, our trusted spy during the war, who had helped e that night. Now he was happily retired to a nice village in 'lanth. I moved to my writing table, plumped down onto the pillows without heeding my expensive gown, and reached for a pen. he letter was soon written and set aside for dispatch home.

Then I sat back on the pillows. As I thought about the larger uestion, a new idea occurred to me: Why not ask the Secret dmirer who'd sent the ring and the rose?

He certainly knew how to keep a secret. If he was only playing game, surely a serious question would show him up. I'd phrase it refully....

I remembered the starliss in my hair and pulled it out to look own into the silver-touched white crown-shaped petals. I thought out its symbolism. In Sartor it was known as Queensblossom; at I'd learned from my mother long ago. Nowadays it symbolized nbition.

My scalp prickled with a danger sense. Once again I dipped my ill. I wrote:

Dear Unknown,
You probably won't want to answer a letter, but I need some
advice on Court etiquette, without my asking being noised around,
and who could be more closemouthed than you? Let's say I was at a
party, and a high-ranking lady approached me...

TWELVE

As soon as I finished the letter I asked Mora to have it sent, just so I wouldn't stay awake changing my mind back and forth during the night.

When I woke the next morning, that letter was the first thing on my mind. Had I made a mistake in writing it? I'd been careful to make it seem like a mental exercise, a hypothetical question of etiquette, describing the conversation in general terms and the speakers only as a high-ranking lady and a young lady new to Court. Unless the unknown admirer had been at the party, there would be no way to connect me to the Marquise. And if he had been at the party—as Deric, Savona, and Geral, all of whom flirted with me most, had been—wouldn't his not having given away his identity make him obliged to keep my letter secret as well?

So I reasoned. When Mora came in with my hot chocolate, she also brought me a gift: a book. I took it eagerly.

The book was a memoir from almost three hundred years before, written by the Duchess Nirth Masharlias, who married the heir to a principality. Though she never ruled, three of her children married into royalty. I had known of her, but not much beyond that.

There was no letter, but slipped in the pages was a single petal of starliss. The text it marked was written in old-fashioned language, but even so, I liked the voice of the writer at once:

...and though the Count spoke strictly in Accordance with Etiquette, his words were an Affront, for he knew my thoughts on Courtship of Married Persons...

I skipped down a ways, then started to laugh when I read:

...and mock-solemn, matching his Manner to the most precise Degree, I challenged him to a Duel. He was forced to go along with the Jest, lest the Court laugh at him instead of with him, but he liked it Not...

...and at the first bells of Gold we were there on the Green, and lo, the Entire Court was out with us to see the Duel. Instead of Horses, I had brought big, shaggy Dogs from the southern Islands, playful and clumsy under their Gilt Saddles, and for Lances, we had great paper Devices which were already Limp and Dripping from the Rain....

Twice he tried to speak Privily to me, but knowing he would apologize and thus end the Ridiculous Spectacle, I heeded him Not, and so we progressed through the Duel, attended with all proper Appurtenances, from Seconds to Trumpeteers, with the Court laughing themselves Hoarse and No One minding the increasing Downpour. In making us both Ridiculous I believe I put paid to all such Advances in future...

The next page went on about other matters. I laid the book down, staring at the starliss as I thought this over. The incident on this page was a response—the flower made that clear enough—but what did it mean?

And why the mystery? Since my correspondent had taken the trouble to answer, why not write a plain letter?

Again I took up my pen, and I wrote carefully:

Dear Mysterious Benefactor:

I read the pages you marked, and though I was greatly diverted, the connection between this story and my own dilemma leaves me more confused than before. Would you advise my young lady to act the fool to the high-ranking lady—or are you hinting that the young one already has? Or is it merely a suggestion that she follow the duchess's example and ward off the high-ranking lady's hints with a joke duel?

If you've figured out that this is a real situation and not a mere mental exercise, then you should also know that I promised someone important that I would not let myself get involved in political brangles; and I wish most straightly to keep this promise. Truth to tell, if you have insights that I have not—and it's obvious that you do—in this dilemma I'd rather have plain discourse than gifts.

The last line I lingered over the longest. I almost crossed it out, but instead folded the letter, sealed it, and when Mora came in, I gave it to her to deliver right away. Then I dressed and went out to walk.

In the past, when something bothered me, I'd retreat up into the mountains to think it through. Now I strolled through Athanarel's beautiful garden, determined to review the entire sequence of events as clearly as memory permitted.

During the course of this I remembered one vital hint, which I then wondered how I could be so stupid as to forget: Lord Flauvic's little gesture with the fan. *On guard.*

That, I decided, I could pursue.

Running and walking, I cut through the gardens. The air was cold and brisk, washed clean from rain. The sky was an intense, smiling blue.

Growing up in the mountains as I had, I'd discovered that maintaining a true sense of direction was instinctive. As I homed in on Merindar House, taking the straightest way rather than the ordered paths, I found ancient bearded trees and tangled grottos. Just before I reached the house, I had to clamber over a mossy wall that had begun to crumble over the centuries.

Pausing to run my fingers over its small, weather-worn stones, I wondered if the wall had been set during the time my mother's family had ruled. Had one of my ancestors looked on then, and what had been her hopes and fears? What kind of life had she seen at Athanarel?

Vaulting over into the tall grass on the other side, I turned my attention to the problem at hand. For there was a problem, I realized as I emerged from the protective shelter of silvery-leaved argan trees and looked across the carefully planted gardens at the house. Its blind windows and slowly strolling guards served as a reminder of the hidden eyes that would observe my walking up and demanding to talk to the heir.

I stepped back beyond the curtain of breeze-stirred leaves and made my way over a log that crossed a little stream, then crossed the rough ground on a circuit round the house as I considered the matter.

I had no conscious plan in mind, but it turned out I did not need one; when I reached the other side of the house, I glimpsed through a wall of vines a splendid terrace, and seated at a table on it was Lord Flauvic. Exquisitely dressed in pale shades of peach and gray, he was all alone, absorbed in reading and writing.

I stooped, picked up some small gravel, and tossed it in his direction.

He went very still. Just for a moment. Then his head turned deliberately. When he saw me he smiled slightly. Moving with swift grace, he swung to his feet and crossed the terrace. "Serenades," he said, "are customarily performed under moonlight, or have fashions here changed?"

"I don't know," I said. "No one's serenaded me, and as for my serenading anyone else, even if I wanted to, which I don't, my singing voice sounds like a sick crow."

"Then to what do I owe the honor of this delightful—but admittedly unorthodox—visit?"

"That." I demonstrated his gesture with my hands. "You did that when your mother took me away last night. I want to know what you meant by it."

His fine brows lifted just slightly, and with leisurely grace he stepped over the low terrace wall and joined me among the ferns. "You do favor the blunt, don't you?"

It was phrased as a question, but his lack of surprise hinted fairly broadly that he'd heard gossip to this effect. My chin came up; I said, "I favor truth over style."

He retorted in the mildest voice, "Having endured the blunt style favored by my late Uncle Galdran, which had little to do with truth as anyone else saw it, I beg you to forgive me when I admit that I am more dismayed than impressed."

"All right," I said. "So there can be truth with style, as well as the opposite. It's just that I haven't been raised to think that I'd find much truth in Court, though there's plenty of style to spare there."

"Will I seem unnecessarily contentious if I admit that my own life experience has engendered in me a preference for style, which at least has the virtue of being diverting?" It seemed impossible that Flauvic was exactly my age. "Not so diverting is the regrettable conviction that truth doesn't exist." His golden eyes were wide and curiously blank.

"Doesn't exist? Of course it does," I exclaimed.

"Is your truth the same as mine? I wonder." He was smiling just slightly, and his gaze was still as limpid as the stream rilling at our feet, but I sensed a challenge.

I said gloomily, "All right, then, you've neatly sidestepped my question—if you even intended to answer it."

He laughed, so softly I just barely heard it, and bowed, his hands moving in a quick airy gesture. I gasped when I saw the bouquet of flowers in his hands. As I reached, they poofed into glowing cinders of every color, which then swirled around and re-formed into butterflies. Then he clapped his hands, and they vanished.

"Magic!" I exclaimed. "You know magic?"

"This is merely illusion," he said. "It's a kind of fad in Sles Adran. Or was. No one is permitted to study true magic unless invited by the Council of Mages, which is agreed on by the royal treaty."

"I'd love to learn it," I exclaimed. "Real magic or not."

We were walking, randomly I thought; in the distance I heard the sweet chiming bells announcing second-gold.

Flauvic shrugged slightly. "I could show you a few tricks, but I've forgotten most of them. You'd have to ask a play magician to show you—that's how we learned."

"Play magician?" I repeated.

"Ah," he said. "Plays here in Remalna are still performed on a bare stage, without illusion to dress it."

"Well, some players now have painted screens and costumes, as in two plays here during recent days. I take it you haven't seen them?"

"I rarely leave the house," he said apologetically.

We reached a path just as the beat of horse hooves sounded from not far ahead. I stepped back; Flauvic looked up as two riders trotted into view.

My first reaction was blank dismay when I saw Savona and Shevraeth riding side by side. The three lords greeted one another with practiced politeness; and when the newcomers turned to me, I curtsied silently.

By the time I had realized that the very fineness of their manners was a kind of message, somehow it was agreed—amid a barrage of mutual compliments—that Flauvic's escort could be dispensed with and the two would accompany me back to the Residence. Savona swung down from his mount and took the reins in hand, falling in step on my left side. Shevraeth, too, joined me on foot, at my right. They were both informally dressed—just returning from the swordfighting practice, I realized. Meanwhile Flauvic had disappeared, as if he'd dissolved into the ground.

All my impressions and speculations resolved into one question: Why did they think I had to be accompanied? "Please don't think you have to change your direction for my sake," I said. "I'm just out wandering about, and my steps took me past Merindar House."

"And lose an opportunity to engage in converse without your usual crowd of swains?" Savona said, bowing.

"Crowd? Swains?" I repeated, then laughed. "Has the rain affected your vision? Or am I the blind one? I don't see any swains. Just as well, too."

A choke of laughter on my right made me realize—belatedly—that my comment could be taken as an insult. "I don't mean you two!" I added hastily and glanced up at Savona (I couldn't bring myself to look at Shevraeth). His dark eyes narrowed in mirth.

"About your lack of swains," Savona murmured. "Deric would be desolated to hear your heartless glee."

I grinned. "I suspect he'd be desolated if I thought him half serious."

"Implying," Savona said with mendacious shock, "that I am not serious? My dear Meliara! I assure you I fell in love with you last year—the very moment I heard that you had pinched a chicken pie right from under Nenthar Debegri's twitchy nose, then rode off on his favorite mount, getting clean away from three ridings of his handpicked warriors."

Taken by surprise, I laughed out loud.

Savona gave me a look of mock consternation. "Now don't—*please* don't—destroy my faith in heroism by telling me it's not true."

"Oh, it's true enough, but heroic?" I scoffed. "What's so heroic about that? I was hungry! Only got one bite of the pie," I added with real regret. I was surprised again when both lords started laughing.

"And then you compounded your attractions by keeping my

azy cousin on the hop for days." He indicated Shevraeth with an iry wave of the hand.

Those memories effectively banished my mirth. For it wasn't just Galdran's bullying cousin Baron Debegri who had chased me halfway across the kingdom after my escape from Athanarel. Shevraeth had been there as well. I felt my shoulders tighten against the old embarrassment, but I tried not to show it, responding as lightly as I could. "On the contrary, it was he who kept me on the hop for days. Very long days," I said. And because the subject had been broached and I was already embarrassed, I risked a quick look at the Marquis and asked, "When you said to search the houses. In the lake town. Did you know I was inside one?"

He hesitated, looking across at Savona, who merely grinned at us both. Then Shevraeth said somewhat drily, "I...had a sense of it."

"And outside Thoresk. When you and Debegri rode by. You looked right at me. Did you know that was me?"

"Will it make you very angry if I admit that I did? But the timing seemed inopportune for us to, ah, reacquaint ourselves." All this was said with his customary drawl. But I had a feeling he was bracing for attack.

I sighed. "I'm not angry. I know now that you weren't trying to get me killed, but to keep me from getting killed by Debegri and Galdran's people. Except—well, never mind. The whole thing stupid."

"Come then," Savona said immediately. "Forgive me for straying into memories you'd rather leave behind, and let us instead discuss tonight's prospective delights."

He continued with a stream of small talk about the latest entertainments—all easy, unexceptionable conversation. Slowly I relaxed, though I never dared look at Shevraeth again.

So it was another unpleasant surprise when I glanced down an adjoining pathway to find the tight-lipped face of Lady Tamara framed in a truly spectacular walking hat.

Tight-lipped for the barest moment. In the space of a blink she

335

was smiling prettily, greeting me with lavish compliments as she fell in step on my right. Shevraeth moved to the outside of the path to make room, his gray still following obediently behind.

The conversation went on, but this time it was Tamara who was the focus. When we reached the bridge just before the rose garden where several paths intersected, she turned suddenly to me. "You did promise me, my dear Countess, a little of your time. I think I will hold you to that promise, perhaps tomorrow evening?"

"I—well—" Answers and images cartwheeled wildly through my mind. "I think—that is, if I haven't forgotten—"

She spoke across me to Savona. "You'll have the evening free?"

He bowed; though I hadn't heard or seen anything untoward in that brief exchange, I saw her eyes narrow just the slightest degree. Then she looked up over her shoulder at Shevraeth. "And you, Vidanric?"

"Regrettably, my mother has a previous claim on me," he said.

Tamara flicked a curtsy, then turned back to me. "I'll invite a few more of your many friends. Do not distress me with a refusal."

There was no polite way to get around that, or if there was, it was beyond my skills. "Of course," I said. "Be delighted."

She curtsied gravely, then began talking with enviable ease about the latest play.

Silent, I walked along until we came to an intersection. Then I whirled to face them all. "I fear I have to leave you all now. Good day!" I swept a general curtsy then fled.

When I returned from that night's dinner party at Nee's family's house, I found two letters on my table. One was immediately recognizable as Oria's weekly report on Tlanth's affairs, which I left for later; Tlanth had been flourishing peacefully. All my problems were here.

The second letter was sealed plainly, with no crest. I flung myself onto my pillows, broke the seal impatiently, and read:

My Dear Countess:

You say you would prefer discourse to gifts. I am yours to command. I will confess my hesitancy was due largely to my own confusion. It seems, from my vantage anyway, that you are surrounded by people in whom you could confide and from whom you could obtain excellent advice. Your turning to a faceless stranger for both could be ascribed to a taste for the idiosyncratic if not to mere caprice.

I winced and dropped the paper to the table. "Well, I asked for the truth," I muttered, and picked it up again.

But I am willing to serve as foil, if foil you require. Judging from what you reported of your conversation with your lady of high rank, the insights you requested are these: First, with regard to her hint that someone else in power lied about rendering assistance at a crucial moment the year previous, you will not see either contender for power with any clarity until you ascertain which of them is telling the truth.

Second, she wishes to attach you to her cause. From my limited understanding of said lady, I suspect she would not so bestir herself unless she believed you to be in, at least potentially, a position of influence.

There was no signature, no closing.

I read it through three times, then folded it carefully and fitted it inside one of my books.

Pulling a fresh sheet of paper before me, I wrote:

Dear Unknown:

The only foil—actually, fool—here is me, which isn't any pleasure to write. But I don't want to talk about my past mistakes, I just want to learn to avoid making the same or like ones in future. Your

*advice about the event of last year (an escape) I thought of already
and have begun my investigation. As for this putative position of
power, it's just that. I expect you're being confused by my proximity
to power—my brother being friend to the possible king and my living
here in the Residence. But believe me, no one could possibly be more
ignorant or less influential than I.*

With a sense of relief I folded that letter up, sealed it, and gave
it to Mora to send along the usual route. Then I went gratefully to
sleep.

I dressed carefully for Tamara's party, choosing a gown that became
me well—the effect of knowing one looks one's best is enormously
bracing—but which was subdued enough that even the most critical
observer could not fault me for attempting to draw the eye from
my beautiful hostess.

Neither Bran nor Nee was invited, which dismayed me. I remembered Tamara having promised to invite my friends, and I
knew I would have refused had I known Bran and Nee would be
overlooked. But Nee insisted it would be a terrible slight not to go,
so alone I went.

And nothing could have been more gracious than my welcome.
With her own hands Tamara pressed a glass of iced punch on me.
The liquid was astringent with citrus and blended fruit flavors. "Do
you like it, Countess?" she said, her brows raised in an anxious line.
"It is a special order. I tried so hard to find something new to please
you."

"It's wonderful," I said, swallowing a second sip. My throat
burned a little, but another sip of the cool drink soothed that.
"Lovely!"

"Please drink up—I'll get you another," she said, smiling as she
led me to the honored place by the fire.

And she waited on me herself, never permitting me to rise.

at there and sipped at my punch cup, which never seemed to be empty, and tried to follow the swift give and take of the conversational circle. The talk reminded me of a spring river, moving rapidly with great splashes of wit over quite a range of territory. Like a river, it wound and doubled back and split and re-formed; as the evening progressed I had more and more difficulty navigating it. I was increasingly distracted by the glowing candles, and by the brilliance with which the colorful fabrics and jewels and embroidery reflected back the golden light. Faces, too, caught my eye, though at times I couldn't follow what the speakers said. With a kind of fixed attention I watched the swift ebb and flow of emotion in eyes, and cheeks, and around mouths, and in the gesturing of hands with or without fans.

Then suddenly Tamara was before me. "But we have strayed far enough from our purpose. Come, friends. I bid you to be silent. The Countess did promise to entertain us by describing her adventures in the late war."

I did? I thought, trying to recall what she'd said—and what I'd promised. My thoughts were tangled, mixing present with memory, and finally I shook my head and looked around. Every face was turned expectantly toward me.

My vision seemed to be swimming gently. "Uh," I said.

"Mouth dry?" Tamara's voice was right behind me. "Something to wet it." She pressed a chilled goblet into my hands.

I raised it and saw Savona directly across from me, a slight frown between his brows. He glanced from me to Tamara, then I blocked him from my view as I took a deep sip of iced—bristic.

A cold burn numbed my mouth and throat, and my hand started to drop. Fingers nipped the goblet from mine before I could spill it. I realized I had been about to spill it and looked aside, wondering how I'd gotten so clumsy. My hand seemed a long way from my body.

Even farther away was Tamara's voice. "Did you really fight a duel to the death with our late king?"

"It was more of a duel to the—" I felt the room lurch as I stood up.

That was a mistake.

"A duel," I repeated slowly, "to—" I wetted my lips again. "To—burn it! I actually had a witty saying. Fer onsh...once. What's wrong with my mouth? A duel to the dust!" I giggled inanely, then noticed that no one else was laughing. I blinked, trying to see, to explain. "He knocked me outa the saddle...y'see...an' I fell in the—in the—"

Words were no longer possible, but I hardly noticed. The room had begun to revolve with gathering speed. I lost my footing and started to pitch forward, but before I could land on my face, strong hands caught my shoulders and righted me.

I blinked up into a pair of very dark eyes. "You're not well," said Savona. "I will escort you back to the Residence."

I hiccuped, then made a profound discovery. "I'm drunk," I said and, as if to prove it, was sick all over Lady Tamara's exquisite carpet.

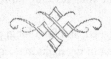

THIRTEEN

I WOKE UP FEELING TERRIBLE, IN BODY AND IN SPIRIT.

I recalled Nee's exhortations about drinking, and control, and how it was a sure way to social ruin. Our grandparents had apparently considered it fashionable to drink until one was insensate, but during Galdran's threat, that had changed. Was I socially finished?

A light scent like fresh-cut summer grass reached me; I turned my head, wincing against the pounding inside my skull, and saw a teacup sitting on a plate beside my bed. Steam curled up from it. For a time I watched the steam with a strange, detached sort of pleasure. My eyes seemed to ache a little less; the scent made me feel incrementally better.

"Can you drink this, my lady?" a soft voice murmured.

I turned my head. "Mora," I croaked. "I think I got drunk."

"Yes, my lady."

I sighed, closing my eyes.

"Please, my lady. Do drink my elixir. It's a special one."

Groaning and wincing, I sat up, took the cup, and sipped the liquid in it. The taste was bitter and made me shiver, but within the space of two breaths I felt a wondrous coolness spread all through me. When I gulped down the rest, the coolness banished most of the headache.

I looked up at Mora gratefully. She gave me a short nod of satisfaction, then said, "I have laid out your dressing gown." And noiselessly she left.

So I was alone with my regret. I sighed, and for a long, pleasant moment envisioned myself sneaking out in my nightdress, grabbing a horse from the stables, and riding hard straight for home. Tlanth was safe. Tlanth was friendly and honest and respectful. *Mother was right*, I thought aggrievedly. Court was nothing but betrayal in fine clothing.

I certainly hadn't meant to get drunk. And Tamara had certainly made it easy for me, keeping my cup filled; but of course she hadn't forced me to drink it. *Whether she meant it to happen or not, there is little purpose in blaming her*, I thought morosely. That was the coward's way out.

And so was sneaking back to Tlanth, leaving Nee and Bran to face the inevitable gossip.

No, I'd have to brave it out; and if people really did snub me, well, a snub wasn't permanent like a sword through one's innards. I'd live. I'd just spend my time in the library until the wedding, and *then* ride home.

This plan seemed eminently reasonable, but it left me feeling profoundly depressed. I rose at last, reaching for my dressing gown so I could go downstairs to the bath. My spirits were so glum I almost overlooked the two letters waiting on my writing table.

When I did see them, my heart gave one of those painful thumps, and I wondered if these were letters of rejection. The top one had my name written out in a bold, slanting hand, with flourishing letter-ends and underlining. I pulled it open.

My Dear Meliara:
You cannot deny me the pleasure of your company on a picnic this afternoon. I will arrange everything. All you need to do is appear and grace the day with your beautiful smile. To meet you will be some of our mutual friends...

Named were several people, all of whom I knew, and it ended with a promise of undying admiration. It was signed *Russav*.

Could it be an elaborate joke, with me as the butt, as a kind of revenge for my social lapse? I reread the note several times, dismissing automatically the caressing tone—I knew it for more of his flirtatious style. Finally I realized that I did not see Tamara's name among the guests, though just about all of the others had been at the party the night before.

A cold sensation washed through me. I had the feeling that if anyone was being made a butt, it was not Meliara Astiar, social lapse notwithstanding.

I turned to the next letter and was glad to see the plain script of my Unknown:

> Meliara—
>
> In keeping faith with your stated desire to have the truth of my observations, permit me to observe that you have a remarkable ability to win partisans. If you choose to dismiss this gift and believe yourself powerless, then of course you are powerless; but the potential is still there—you are merely pushing it away with both hands.
>
> Ignorance, if you will honor me with permission to take issue with your words, is a matter of definition—or possibly of degree. To be aware of one's lack of knowledge is to be merely untutored, a state that you seem to be aggressively attempting to change. A true ignorant is unaware of this lack.
>
> To bring our discourse from the general to the specific, I offer my congratulation to you on your triumph in the *Affair Tamara*. She intended to do you ill. You apparently didn't see it, or appeared not to see it. It was the most effective—perhaps the only effective—means of scouting her plans for your undoing. Now her reputation is in your hands.
>
> This is not evidence of lack of influence.

And it ended there.

Two utterly unexpected communications. The only facts that seemed certain were that the Unknown had been at that party and like Savona (maybe it was he?) had sat up very late penning this letter. Or both letters.

I needed very much to think these things out.

Nee tapped outside my door and asked if I'd like to go down to the baths with her.

"How do you feel?" she asked, looking concerned, as we walked down the stairs.

I felt my face burn. "I suppose it's all over Remalna by now."

She gave me a wry smile. "I think I received six notes this morning, most of which, I hasten to add, affirm their partisanship for you."

Partisan. The term used by the Unknown.

"For me?" I said. "But I got drunk. Worse, I got sick all over Tamara's carpet. Not exactly courtly finesse." I ducked my head under the warm water.

When I came up, Nee said, "But she was the one who served an especially potent punch, one they all knew you probably hadn't tasted before, as it's a Court delicacy..." She hesitated, and I hazarded a guess at what she was leaving out.

"You mean, people might want to see Tamara in trouble?"

She nodded soberly.

"And apparently I can do something about that?"

"All you have to do is give her the cut," Nee said quietly. "When you appear in public, you don't notice her, and she'll very shortly come down with a mysterious ailment that requires her to withdraw to the family estate until the next scandal supplants this one."

"Why would she do it?" I asked. "I am very sure I never did anything to earn her enmity."

Nee shrugged. "I can't say I understand her, cousins though we be. She's always been secretive and ambitious, and I expect she sees you as competition. After all, you appeared suddenly, and it seems effortless how you have managed to attract the attention of the most eligible of the men—"

I snorted. "Even I know that a fad can end as suddenly as it began. Savona could get bored with me tomorrow, and all the rest would follow him to the next fad, just as if they had ribbons tied round their necks and somebody yanked."

Nee smiled as she wrung out her hair. "Well, it's true, but I think you underestimate the value of Savona's friendship."

"But it isn't a friendship," I retorted without thinking—and I realized I was right. "It's just a flirtation. We've never talked about anything that really matters to either of us. I don't know him any better now than I did the first day we met." As I said the words I felt an unsettling sensation inside, as if I were on the verge of an important insight. Pausing, I waited; but further thoughts did not come.

Nee obviously thought that sufficed. "If more people recognized the difference between friendship and mere attraction, and how love must partake of both to prosper, I expect there'd be more happy people."

"And a lot fewer poems and plays," I said, laughing as I splashed about in the scented water.

Nee laughed as well.

We talked more about what had happened, and Nee maintained that Savona's picking me up and walking out was the signal that had finished Tamara.

This made me wonder, as I dressed alone in my room, if there had been an unspoken struggle going on all along between the two of them. If so, he'd won. If she'd been the more influential person, his walking out with me would not have mattered; her followers would have stayed and dissected my manners, morals, and background with delicacy and finesse and oh-so-sad waves of their fans.

And another thing Nee maintained was that it was my forthright admission that I was drunk that had captivated Savona. Such honesty was considered risky, if not outright madness. This inspired some furious thinking while I dressed, which produced two resolutions.

Before I could lose my courage, I stopped while my hair was half done, and dashed off a note to my Unknown:

I'll tell you what conclusion I've reached after a morning's thought, and it's this: that people are not diamonds and ought not to be imitating them.

I've been working hard at assuming Court polish, but the more I learn about what really goes on behind the pretty voices and waving fans and graceful bows, the more I comprehend that what is really said matters little, so long as the manner in which it is said pleases. I understand it, but I don't like it. Were I truly influential, then I would halt this foolishness that decrees that in Court one cannot be sick; that to admit you are sick is really to admit to political or social or romantic defeat; that to admit to any emotions usually means one really feels the opposite. It is a terrible kind of falsehood that people can only claim feelings as a kind of social weapon.

Apparently some people thought it took amazing courage to admit that I was drunk, when it was mere unthinking truth. This is sad. But I'm not about to pride myself on telling the truth. Reacting without thinking—even if I spoke what I thought was true—has gotten me into some nasty situations during the recent year. This requires more thought. In the meantime, what think you?

I signed it and got it sent before I could change my mind, then hastily finished dressing. *At least*, I thought as I slipped out the door, *I won't have to see his face when he reads it, if he thinks it excessively foolish.*

Wrapping my cloak closely about me, I ran down the Residence steps, immediately left the flagged pathway, and faded into the garden.

One thing I still remembered from my war days was how to move in shrubbery. With my skirts bunched in either hand so the hems wouldn't get muddy, I zigzagged across the grounds so that

346

no one would see me. I emerged from behind a scree of ferns and
tapped at the door at the wing of the Chamadis House where I
knew that Tamara had her rooms.

The door was opened by a maid whose eyes widened slightly,
but her voice was blank as she said, "Your ladyship?" She held
the door close, as if to guard against my entry; I expect she would
have denied me had not Tamara herself appeared in the background.

"Who is it, Kerael?" The drawl was completely gone, and
her voice was sharp with repressed emotion—I almost didn't recognize it.

In silence the maid opened the door wider, and Tamara
saw me. Her blue eyes were cold and angry, but her countenance betrayed the marks of exhaustion and strain. She curtsied,
a gesture replete with the bitterest irony; it was the bow to a
sovereign.

I felt my neck burn. "Please. Just a bit of your time."

She gestured obliquely, and the maid stepped aside; I walked
in. A moment or two later we stood facing one another alone in a
lovely anteroom in shades of celestial blue and gold.

She took up a stance directly behind a chair, her back straight,
her hands laid atop the chair back, one over the other, the image
of perfect control. She was even beautifully gowned, which made
me wonder if she had been expecting someone else to call.

She stared at me coldly, her eyes unblinking; and as the silence
grew protracted, I realized she would not speak first.

"Why did you get me drunk?" I asked. "I'm no rival of yours."

She made a quick, sharp gesture of negation. A diamond on
her finger sparkled like spilled tears, and I realized her fingers were
trembling.

"It's true," I said, watching her bury her hands in the folds of
her skirts. "What little you know of me ought to make one thing
plain: I don't lie. That is, I don't do it very well. I don't fault you
for ambition. That would be mighty two-faced when my brother

347

and I plotted half our lives to take the crown from Galdran. Our reasons might be different, but who's to fault that? Not me. I gave that over last year. As for Savona—"

"Don't," she said.

"Why?" I demanded. "Can't you see he's just flirting with me? I don't know much of romance—well, nothing, if you only count experience—but I have noticed certain things, and one is that in a *real* courtship, the two people endeavor to get to know one another." Again I had that sensation of something important hovering just out of my awareness, but when I paused, frowning—trying to perceive it—my thoughts just scattered.

"I think," she said, "you are being a trifle too disingenuous."

I sighed. "Humor me by pretending I am sincere. You know Savona. Can't you see him making me popular just to...well, prove a point?" I faltered at the words *pay you back for going after Shevraeth and a crown?*

Not that the meaning escaped her, for I saw its impact in the sudden color ridging her lovely cheeks. Her lips were pressed in a thin line. "I could...almost...believe you had I not had your name dinned in my ear through a succession of seasons. Your gallantry in facing Galdran before the Court. The Astiar bravery in taking on Galdran's army with nothing but a rabble of half-trained villagers on behalf of the rest of the kingdom. Your running almost the length of the kingdom with a broken foot and successfully evading Debegri's and Vidanric's warriors. The duel-to-the-death with Galdran."

I had to laugh, which I saw at once was a mistake. But I couldn't stop, not until I saw the common omission in all of this: my disastrous encounters with Shevraeth. Had he spoken about my defeats, surely this angry young lady would have nosed it all out—and it was apparent she'd have no compunction about flinging it in my teeth.

No. For some incomprehensible reason, he hadn't talked about any of it.

This realization sobered me, and I gulped in a deep, shaky breath.

Tamara's grimness had given way to an odd expression, part anger, part puzzlement. "You will tell me that your heroism is all lies?" she asked.

"No," I said. "But it's—well, different. Look, if you really want to hear my story, we can sit down and I'll tell you everything, from how I ran about barefoot and illiterate in the mountains joyfully planning our easy takeover, right down to how Galdran knocked me clean out of my saddle after I warded a single blow and nearly lost my arm in doing it. I think he attacked me because I was the weakest—it's the only reason that makes sense to me. As for the rest—" I shrugged. "Some of it was wrong decisions made for the right reasons, and a little of it was right decisions made for the wrong reasons; but most of what I did was wrong decisions for the wrong reasons. That's the plain truth."

She was still for a long, nasty space, and then some of the rigidity went out of her frame. "And so you are here to, what, grant mercy?"

I closed my eyes and groaned. "Tamara. *No one* knows I'm here, and if you don't like my idea, then no one *will* know I was here unless *you* blab. I won't. I just wondered, if I invite you to come with me to Savona's picnic this afternoon, think you things might just go back to how they were?"

She flushed right up to her hairline, a rose-red blush that made her suddenly look like a young girl. "As his supplicant? I bow to your expertise in wielding the hiltless knife." And she swept a jerky curtsy, her hands shaking.

"Life! I didn't mean that," I said hastily. "Yes, I think I can see it's a bad idea. All right, how's this: You and I go out for a walk. Right now. You don't even have to talk to me. But wouldn't that shut up all the gossipmongers—leastwise pull the teeth of their gossip—if we seem to be on terms of amity, as if last night was just a very good joke?"

Again her posture eased, from anger to wariness. "And in return?"

"Nothing. I don't need anything! Or what I need no one can give me, which is wisdom." I thought of my mistakes and winced. Then said, "Just let things go back to the way they were, except you don't have to think of me as an enemy. I'm not in love with Savona any more than he is with me, and I don't see myself changing my mind. If I did, I don't believe he'd like it," I added, considering the elusive Duke. "No, I don't think I could fall in love with him, handsome though he is, because I don't accept any of that huff he gives me about my great beauty and all that. I'd have to trust a man's words before I could love him. I think."

She took a deep, slightly shaky breath. "Very well."

And so we went.

It wasn't a very comfortable walk. She hardly exchanged five words with me; and every single person who saw us stared then hastily recovered behind the remorselessly polite mask of the true courtier. It would have been funny if I had been an observer and not a participant, an idea that gave me a disconcerting insight into gossip. As I walked beside the silent Tamara, I realized that despite how entertaining certain stories were, at the bottom of every item of gossip there was someone getting hurt.

When we were done with a complete circuit of the gardens and had reached her house again, I said, "Well, that's that. See you at the ball tonight, right?"

She half put out a hand, then said, "Your brother's wedding is nearing."

"Yes?"

"Did you know it is customary for the nearest relation to give a party for the family that is adopting into yours?"

I whistled. "No, I didn't. And I could see how Nee would feel strange telling me. Well, I'm very grateful to you."

She curtsied. Again it was the deep one, petitioner to sovereign, but this time it was low and protracted and wordlessly sincere.

FOURTEEN

ON THE SURFACE, SAVONA'S PICNIC WAS A DELIGHT. All his particular friends—except Shevraeth—were there, and not one of them so much as mentioned Tamara. Neither did I.

When a lowering line of clouds on the horizon caused us to pack up our things and begin the return journey, I wondered how many notes would be dispatched before the morrow.

Savona escorted me back to the Residence. For most of our journey the talk was in our usual pattern—he made outrageous compliments, which I turned into jokes. Once he said, "May I count on you to grace the Khazhred ball tomorrow?"

"If the sight of me in my silver gown, dancing as often as I can, is your definition of grace, well, nothing easier," I replied, wondering what he would do if I suddenly flirted back in earnest.

He smiled, kissed my hand, and left. As I trod up the steps alone, I realized that he had never really *talked* with me about any serious subject, in spite of his obvious admiration.

I thought back over the picnic. No serious subject had been discussed there, either, but I remembered some of the light, quick flirtatious comments he exchanged with some of the other ladies, and how much he appeared to appreciate their flirting right back. Would he appreciate it if I did? *Except I can't*, I thought, walking down the hall to my room. Clever comments with double meanings; a fan pressed against someone's wrist in different ways to hint at different things; all these things I'd observed and understood the meanings of, but I couldn't see myself actually performing them even if I could think of them quickly enough.

What troubled me most was trying to figure out Savona's real intent. He certainly wasn't courting me, I realized as I pushed aside my tapestry. What other purpose would there be in such a long, one-sided flirtation?

My heart gave a bound of anticipation when I saw a letter waiting and I recognized the style of the Unknown.

> *You ask what I think, and I will tell you that I admire without reservation your ability to solve your problems in a manner unforeseen by any, including those who would consider themselves far more clever than you.*

That was all.

I read it through several times, trying to divine whether it was a compliment or something else entirely. *He's waiting to see what I do about Tamara*, I thought at last.

"And in return?" That was what Tamara had said.

This is the essence of politics, I realized. One creates an interest, or, better, an obligation, that causes others to act according to one's wishes. I grabbed up a paper, dipped my pen, and wrote swiftly:

> *Today I have come to two realizations. Now, I well realize that every courtier in Athanarel probably saw all this by their tenth year. Nonetheless, I think I finally see the home-thrust of politics. Everyone who has an interest in such things seems to be waiting for me to make some sort of capital with respect to the situation with Tamara, and won't they be surprised when I do nothing at all!*
>
> *Truth to say, I hold no grudge against Tamara. I'd have to be a mighty hypocrite to fault her for wishing to become a queen, when*

*I tried to do the same a year back—though I really think her heart
lies elsewhere—and if I am right, I got in her way yet again.*

*Which brings me to my second insight: that Savona's flirtation
with me is just that, and not a courtship. The way I define courtship
is that one befriends the other, tries to become a companion and not
just a lover. I can't see why he so exerted himself to seek me out, but
I can't complain, for I am morally certain that his interest is a good
part of what has made me popular. (Though all this could end tomorrow.)*

"Meliara?" Nee's voice came through my tapestry. "The concert begins at the next time change."

I signed the letter hastily, sealed it, and left it lying there as I
hurried to change my gown. *No need to summon Mora*, I thought;
she was used to this particular exchange by now.

Not many were at that night's concert, and none of Court's leading
lights. By accident I overheard someone talking and discovered that
most of them had been invited to Merindar House to see some
players from Erev-li-Erval.

When I heard this, I felt strange. So, I hadn't been invited. I
suspected that this was a message from the Marquise, to whom I
had given no answer. Either that or she had simply decided I was
not worth her attention after all.

Well, what *had* I done to investigate the rival rulers and how
they might rule? Shevraeth's policies I might learn something of if
I could nerve myself to attend Petitioners' Court sessions. But how
to investigate the Marquise of Merindar as a potential ruler?

Before my eyes rose an image of the beautiful and utterly unreadable Flauvic. I felt an intense urge to find him, ask him, even
though I had learned firsthand that he was very capable of turning
off with oblique replies whatever he did not wish to answer directly.

The problem was, he never left Merindar House, and I had no

excuse to visit there that wouldn't cause all kinds of speculation.

As the singers spun away the evening with lovely melodies, my mind kept returning to the problem, until at last I got what seemed to me to be an unexceptionable idea.

When I returned from the concert I wrote, in my very best hand, a letter to Flauvic requesting the favor of his advice on a matter of fashion. I sent it that night, and to my surprise, an answer awaited me when I woke in the morning. In fact, two answers awaited: one, the plain paper I had grown used to seeing from my Unknown, and the second, a beautifully folded and sealed sheet of imported linen paper.

This second one I opened first, to find only a line, but Flauvic's handwriting was exquisite: He was entirely at my disposal, and I was welcome to consult him at any time.

The prospect was daunting and fascinating at the same time. Resolving to get that done directly after breakfast, I turned eagerly to the letter from the Unknown:

> *I can agree with your assessment of the ideal courtship, but I believe you err when you assume that everyone at Court has known the difference from age ten—or indeed, any age. There are those who will never perceive the difference, and then there are some who are aware to some degree of the difference but choose not to heed it. I need hardly add that the motivation here is usually lust for money or power, more than for the individual's personal charms.*
>
> *But I digress. To return to your subject, do you truly believe, then, that those who court must find themselves of one mind in all things? Must they study deeply and approve each other's views on important subjects before they can risk contemplating marriage?*

Well, I had to sit down and answer that.

I scrawled out two pages of thoughts, each following rapidly on the heels of its predecessor, until I discovered that the morning was already advancing. I hurried through a bath, put on a nice gown, and grabbed up a piece of fruit to eat on the way to Merindar House.

Again I made certain that no one knew where I was going. When I emerged from the narrow pathway I'd chosen, just in view of the house, the wind had kicked up and rare, cold drops of rain lashed against my face, promising a downpour very soon.

The servant who tended the door welcomed me by name, his face utterly devoid of expression, offered to take my hat and gloves, which I refused, then requested that I follow him.

This time I visited a different part of the house; the room was all windows on one side, but the air was cool, not cold, with a faint trace of some subtle scent I couldn't quite name. Directly outside the windows was a flowery hillock, down from which poured a small waterfall that splashed into a pool that reached almost to the long row of windows.

Flauvic was standing by the middle window, one slim hand resting on a golden latch. I realized that one window panel was, in fact, a door, and that a person could step through onto the rocks that just bordered the pool. Flauvic was looking down, the silvery light reflecting off rain clouds overhead, and water below throwing glints in his long golden hair.

He had to know I was there.

I said, "You do like being near to water, don't you?"

He looked up quickly. "Forgive me for not coming to the door," he said directly—for him. "I must reluctantly admit that I have been somewhat preoccupied with the necessity of regaining my tranquillity."

I was surprised that he would admit to any such thing. "Not caused by me, I hope?" I walked across the fine tiled floor.

He lifted a hand in a gesture of airy dismissal. "Family argument," he said. Smiling a little, he added, "Forbearance is not, alas, a hallmark of the Merindar habit of mind."

Again I was surprised, for he seemed about as forbearing as anyone I'd ever met—but I was chary of appearing to be a mere flatterer, and so I said only, "I'm sorry for it, then. Ought I to go? If the family's peace has been cut up, I suppose a visitor won't be welcome."

Flauvic turned away from the window and crossed the rest of the floor to join me. "If you mean you'd rather not walk into my honored parent's temper—or more to the point, my sister's—fear not. They departed early this morning to our family's estates. I am quite alone here." He smiled slightly. "Would you like to lay aside your hat and gloves?"

"Not necessary," I said, stunned by this unexpected turn of events. Had the Marquise given up her claim to the crown, or was there some other—secret—reason for her sudden withdrawal? If they had argued, I was sure it had not been about missing social events.

I looked up—for he was half a head taller than I—into his gold-colored eyes, and though their expression was merely contemplative, and his manner mild, I felt my neck go hot. Turning away from that direct, steady gaze, I just couldn't find the words to ask him about his mother's political plans. So I said, "I came to ask a favor of you."

"Speak, then," he said, his voice just a shade deeper than usual.

I looked over my shoulder, and realized that he was laughing. Not loud, but internally. All the signs were there; the shadows at the corners of his mouth, the sudden brightness of his gaze. He was laughing at me—at my reaction.

I sighed. "It concerns the party I must give for my brother's coming marriage," I said shortly, and stole another quick look.

His amusement was gone—superficially, anyway.

"You must forgive my obtuseness," he murmured. "But you could have requested your assistance by letter."

"I did. Oh." I realized what he meant, and then remembered belatedly one of Nee's more delicate hints about pursuit—and pursuers. "*Oh!*" So he *hadn't* guessed why I'd really come—instead he thought I'd come courting him? And, well, here we were alone.

My first reaction was alarm. I did find him attractive—I realized it just as I was standing there—but in the way I'd admire a beautifully cut diamond, or a sunset above sheer cliffs. Another person, finding herself in my place, could probably embark happily

356

into dalliance and thus speed along her true purpose, but the prospect simply terrified me.

He touched my arm, lightly, sliding his fingers up to my shoulder, and then under my hair to the back of my neck. His touch made me shiver. I closed my eyes—and gasped when lips met my own.

Heat flooded down my body, replacing the cold shock of his touch. I leaned into that kiss as his hands caressed me. So this was dalliance; this was why the others paired off and disappeared, why the lifted brows, the secretive smiles. It was powerful, mind-numbing pleasure.

But it was not joy.

I knew what would come next, right there in that room, in his house, for no one would stop us. But the last shreds of my consciousness arrowed ahead, and I knew I would not want to find myself lying next to Flauvic when the pleasure had gone, as go it must; I'd seen couples for whom the absence of pleasure made one another a burden to be borne.

Two things caught and steadied my will against the sensory flood: I did not know him.

And: he did not know me.

So what he had been initiating had to be no more than a game. A game, or—

I wrenched my lips away, breathing fast. My fingers trembled as I straightened my gown.

Flauvic was also breathing fast, but he—of course—had more control than I, and he just smiled, but made no move of pursuit. "Change your mind, little Countess?"

I couldn't speak yet. I shook my head—nodded—then rolled my eyes and shrugged.

This time he laughed out loud, a soft, pleasant sound, before he touched me again, just enough to guide us back to his window. "It is not merely the sight of water that I find salubrious," he said. "Its function as a metaphor for study is as...as adaptable—"

"You were going to say fluid," I cut in, almost giddy with relief at the deft change of subject.

357

Once again I saw that quirk to his eyes that indicated internal laughter. "I wasn't," he insisted. "I would never be so maladroit."

Forgive my maladroitness— For an instant I was back in that corner room in the State Wing, with Shevraeth standing opposite me.

I dismissed the memory as Flauvic went on. "As adaptable, to resume our discourse, as its inherent properties. The clarity, the swift change and movement, the ability to fill the boundaries it encounters, all these accommodating characteristics blind those who take its utility and artistry for granted and overlook its inexorable power."

As if to underline his words—it really was uncanny—the threatening downpour chose that moment to strike, and for a long moment we stood side by side as rain thundered on the glass, running down in rivulets that blurred the scene beyond.

Then he turned his back to it. "How may I be of service?"

"My brother's party. I want it to be special," I said. "I should have been planning it long before. I just found out that it's a custom, and to cover my ignorance I would like to make it *seem* I've been planning it a long time, so I need some kind of new idea. I want to know what the latest fashion for parties in Sartor's—or Sles Adran's—court is, and I thought the best thing I could do would be to come to you."

"So you do not, in fact, regard me as an arbiter of taste?" He placed a hand over his heart, mock-solemn. "You wound me." His tone said, *You wound me again.*

Once again I blushed, and hated it. "You *know* you're an arbiter of taste, Flauvic," I said with some asperity. "If you think I'm here just to get you to parrot out Nente's latest fad, then you're, well, I know you don't believe it. And I didn't think you prodded for compliments."

He laughed out loud a second time, a musical sound that suddenly rendered him very much more like the age we shared. It also made him, just for that moment, devastatingly attractive. If he ouched me again, I was not so certain I could say no—but through the dazzle of attraction, instinct prompted me to move. Away. If I did not get out of there I would plunge myself into trouble that it would take a lifetime to get out of.

"There's never any one fad," he said. "Or if there is, it changes from day to day. A current taste is for assuming the mask of the past."

"Like?" I looked out at the rain streaming down the window-panes.

"Like choosing a time from history, say six hundred years ago, and everyone who comes must assume the guise of an ancestor from that time."

"Well, my mother was a Calahanras, but it seems to me—and I know I'm not exactly subtle—that it would not be in the best of taste to assume the guise of royalty for this party."

"But you have your father's family as well. For example, Family Astiar and Family Chamadis have intermarried, ah, twice that I know of. One of those was a love match, almost three hundred years ago. Your brother and prospective sister would be charming in the guises of Thirav Astiar and Haratha Chamadis. It would also be a compliment to Nimiar, for it was her ancestor Haratha who considerably boosted the family's prestige by her part in the Treaty of the Seven Rivers."

"Oh!" Relief chased away the intense awareness of his proximity. "I knew you'd think of something! But is there a part for me? I have to be prominent, being hostess."

"You don't know your own family's history?" He raised his brows.

"We barbarians are ignorant, yes," I retorted, "mostly because my father burned most of our books after my mother died."

"He did?" Flauvic's blank gaze seemed curiously intent. "Now, why was that—do you know?"

"I don't have any idea. Probably will never find out. Anyway, there was no history of any kind for me to read until I began last year by ordering new ones, and very few of those mention the Astiar family."

He bowed, gesturing apology. "Forgive me," he said. "I had not known. As for your part, that's a shade more difficult, for Thirav had no sisters. However, there were two female cousins, either of whom you might assume the guise of. Ardis was the more prominent of the two."

"Ardis. I suppose there are no portraits—"

"—but you could safely order a gown based on court fashions of the time," he finished. "The point here is, if people are to get their costumes ordered in time, you must be speedy with your invitations."

"Costumes are easily ordered," I said, smiling sourly. "What you mean is, to give everyone time to dive into their family histories if they aren't as well read as you are."

"Precisely," he said with a gentle smile. "It is a shame that so few have the time or inclination for scholarship these days. There is much entertainment to be afforded in perusing the mistakes of our forebears."

He said it exactly like he said everything else, but once again that sense of warning trickled through me. "For what purposes?" I asked, daring my real subject.

"More curiosity," he murmured, still smiling. "I never involve myself in political brangles."

So that was that.

"Thanks for the advice," I said briskly. "I'd better get to my own studies."

"You do not wish to stay for some refreshment?" he asked.

I shook my head, pointing at the window, which was now clear. The downpour, as downpours will, had slackened just as suddenly as it had come, and there was a brief glimpse of blue through the tumbling clouds. "I think I'd better go now, before it comes back."

He bowed, silent and gracious, and I was very soon gone.

I decided that that would be my last visit to the heir to the Merindars, at least uninvited and when he was alone. I'd learned something, all right, about the power of attraction, and Nee was right, it *was* potent.

But I'd also learned that the self might want one thing, but that didn't mean it was right. Isn't that why we have minds? I thought as I tramped my fastest away from Merindar House.

Meanwhile one thing I did know: I didn't want any more lessons.

And there was still his suggestion for my party to be researched.

What time was it? Just then the bells for first-green pealed. Green—time for Petitioners' Court, Nee had said. Meant that the Renselaeuses ought to be safely ensconced in the throne room.

Despite the fact that I was somewhat damp from the rain that had begun again in earnest just before I reached the Residence, I fled down the halls to the State Wing, slowing to a sedate walk just before I reached the areas where the door servants could be found.

My heart thumped hard when I reached that last hallway, but the big library was empty. Relieved and grateful, I dashed inside and started scouring the shelves. I knew I would not find anything directly relating to the Astiars—they weren't particularly famous for anything. I'd have to find memoirs or histories that might mention them. The best source for researching the Chamadis family, of course, would be a history of the Battle of the Seven Rivers, or else a history about relations between Remalna and Denlieff or Lamanca. Chamadis lands being on the border, there was sure to be mention of them—and maybe the marriage with the Astiars.

Unfortunately, there was only one book that dealt with that battle, and it was written by the ambassador at the time, who featured himself so prominently that the negotiations for the Treaty were presented only through a long and self-praising catalogue of the entertainments he gave. There was just one brief mention of Lady Harantha.

Remembering what the Princess had told me about histories, I had to grin as I replaced the dusty book for what would probably be another hundred years. So now where?

Of course I knew where.

I turned toward the corner, staring at the tapestries to the little alcove where the memoirs for the heirs were stored. Bunching my skirts in either hand so they wouldn't rustle, I moves stealthily to the tapestry and stood listening. No voices, certainly, and no sounds beyond the drumming of the rain against the near window.

So I lifted the tapestry—and looked across the room into a pair of familiar gray eyes. Dressed splendidly in black and gold, as if for Court, Shevraeth knelt at the desk, writing.

For the third time that day, my face went hot. Resolutely reminding myself of my promise not to initiate any quarrels, I said, "Harantha Chamadis. Thirav Astiar. The Treaty of Seven Rivers. Is there a record?"

Shevraeth didn't say a word. He lifted his pen, pointed at a particular shelf, then bent his head and went right back to his task.

For a moment I watched his pen traversing swiftly over the paper in close lines. Then my gaze traveled to the smooth yellow hair, neatly tied back, and from there to the lines of his profile. For the very first time I saw him simply as a person and not as an adversary, but I did not give myself the space to gauge my reactions. The curl of danger, of being caught at my observations and once again humiliated, caused me to drag my gaze away, and I trod to the shelf to which I'd been directed.

A few swift glances through the books, and I found the memoirs of the queen of that time. A quick glance through showed the names I wanted repeated on a number of pages. Gripping the book in one hand and brushing back a strand of my wet hair with the other, I said, "Do you need my reason—"

He cut in, lightly enough: "Just put it back when you're done."

He kept his gaze on his writing, and his pen scarcely paused. Scrawl, dip, scrawl, dip.

Two or three more words—then the pen stopped, and he glanced up again. "Was there something else?" he asked. Still polite, but very remote.

I realized I'd been staring for a protracted time, my reactions frozen as if behind a layer of ice. I said in a rush, "The party, for Bran and Nee. Do you—should I send you—"

He smiled just a little. "It would cause a deal of talk if you were to avoid inviting any of my family."

"Oh." I gulped. "Yes. Indeed."

He dipped his pen, bent his head, and went back to his task. I slipped out the door and fled.

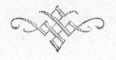

FIFTEEN

FLAUVIC'S REMARK ABOUT SCHOLARSHIP, I DECIDED before the day ended, was a kind of double-edged sword. When I discovered my ancestor Ardis was not so much prominent as notorious, my first reaction was a snort of laughter, followed by interest—and some indignation.

The queen's memoir, which was replete with gossip, detailed Ardis's numerous and colorful dalliances. Her ten-year career of flirtation came to a close not long after she became engaged to a Renselaeus prince. This engagement ended after a duel with the third Merindar son—no one knew the real reasons why—and though both men lived through the duel, neither talked of it afterward. Or to her. She wound up marrying into a minor house in the southwest and passed the rest of her days in obscurity.

She was beautiful, wealthy, and popular, yet it appeared, through the pages of this memoir anyway, that the main business of her life had been to issue forth in the newest and most shocking gown in order to shine down the other women of the Court, and to win away lovers from her rivals. There was no hint that she performed any kind of service whatever.

In short, she was a fool.

This made me drop the book and perform a fast and furious

eview of my conversations with Flauvic. Did he think I was a fool? Did he think that I would find Ardis in the records and admire her?

Or was this some kind of oblique challenge? Was he hinting that I ought to do more than my ancestor—such as get involved in fight for the crown?

The answer seemed pretty obvious. I decided not to communicate with Flauvic about my foolish ancestor. Instead, I'd use his idea but find my own time period and historical personages. A much more elegant answer.

This time I planned my foray. When I saw Shevraeth dancing at the Khazhred family ball that night, I excused myself after a short time as quietly as I could, retreated to the Residence, changed out of my gown, lit a candle, and sped through the library to the alcove.

It was empty. I knelt at the desk, which was bare except for pen and ink, and leafed through book after book, names and events filling my mind and overlaying the present until I felt as if I existed in two times at once—as in a dream.

And I realized that if Flauvic had intended some kind of obscure statement through his choice of the time and the ancestors, I could do the same.

For instance, Branaric and I were also descendants of royalty through the Calahanras family. The Calahanras rulers had been some of the best kings and queens this kingdom had ever known; it would be a nice gesture to Flauvic, I thought wryly, if I were to assume the guise of one of my Calahanras ancestors. I could select one who was not famous—thus who wouldn't draw attention to me and away from my brother and his betrothed.

Furthermore, I realized I ought to know something of the ancestors of the other guests, if I could, in case there was some ancient scandal or disgrace that I might accidentally dredge up. So I read until my vision flickered with the candle flames. Before I left, I held my candle up, scanning that barren desk. Why would Shevraeth work there when he had what was rumored to be a fabulous suite of rooms in the Royal Wing—including at least one study?

Because he could be alone, of course.

Except for a certain snotty countess bounding in and starting quarrels.

Sighing to myself, I retreated to my rooms to think out my strategy. I didn't notice the waiting letter until I sank down on my pillows. I grabbed it, saw the familiar handwriting, and tore into the envelope eagerly.

It was a long response to my letter, talking freely about all manner of things. Several times I laughed out loud. Other times I felt the impulse to go hunting books again, for he made easy reference to historical events and people he assumed I was familiar with. It was a relief that, though he knew I was ignorant, he did not think I was stupid. Despite my tiredness, I sat up most of the night happily penning my reply.

And so passed the next several days.

I prowled around the various Court functions to mark where Shevraeth was, and if I spotted him I'd invariably sneak back to the State Wing and slip into the memoirs room to read some more—when I wasn't writing letters.

My response to the Unknown had caused a lengthy answer in kind, and for a time we exchanged letters—sometimes thrice a day. It was such a relief to be able to express myself freely and without cost. He seemed to appreciate my jokes, for his style gradually metamorphosed from the carefully neutral mentor to a very witty kind of dialogue that verged from time to time on the acerbic—just the kind of humor that appealed most to me. We exchanged views about different aspects of history, and I deeply enjoyed his trenchant observations on the follies of our ancestors.

He never pronounced judgment on current events and people, despite some of my hints; and I forbore asking directly, lest I inadvertently say something about someone in his family—or worse, him. For I still had no clue to his identity. Savona continued to flirt with me at every event we met at. Deric claimed my company for every sporting event. And shy Geral always gravitated to my side at balls; when we talked—which was a lot—it was about music. Though others among the lords were friendly and pleasant, these three were the most attentive.

None of them hinted at letters—nor did I. If in person the Unknown couldn't bring himself to talk on the important subjects that increasingly took up time and space in his letters, well, I could sympathize. There was a person—soon to be king—whom I couldn't bring myself to face.

Anyway, the only mention of current events that I made in my letters was about my own experience. Late one night, when I'd drunk a little too much spiced wine, I poured out my pent-up feelings about my ignorant past, and to my intense relief he returned to me neither scorn nor pity. That did not stop me from going around for a day wary of smiles or fans hiding faces, for I'd realized that though the letters could be pleasant and encouraging, I could very well be providing someone with prime material for gossip. Never before had I felt the disadvantage of not knowing who he was, whereas he knew me by name and sight.

But no one treated me any differently than usual; there were no glances of awareness, no bright, superior smiles of those who know a secret. So it appeared he was as benevolent as his letters seemed, yet perfectly content to remain unknown.

And I was content to leave it that way.

At the end of those three days my life changed again when I received a surprise visitor: Azmus, our former spy.

Bran and Nee had already departed for some early morning event. Unspoken between us was the understanding that they would go off to enjoy purely social affairs for Shevraeth's personal friends, and I would stay behind. They didn't mention them ahead of time, they just went.

So I was alone that morning when Mora came in and said, "The vendor you summoned is here to show you some new wares."

"Vendor?" I asked, surprised.

"I think—you wished to see him," Mora said quietly, and so I thanked her, my surprise changing to intense curiosity.

A moment later there was Azmus's round face and snub nose. He was dressed as a goldsmith, and he even carried a bulging satchel.

"Azmus!" I exclaimed in delight. "I didn't think you'd come— I hope you didn't think I'd summoned you." I finished on an apologetic note. "If anyone has earned retirement, it is you."

Azmus grinned. "Neither Khesot nor I like retirement," he said, his voice so quiet it was just above a whisper. "Makes us feel too old. I believe Oria informed you that he's now the head of your border riders—"

"Yes."

"—and as for me, I was glumly sitting at home planning out a garden when your most welcome letter came."

"You can speak to be heard," I said, and grinned. "I think Mora knew who you were—and even if she's listening, I believe she's got our interests to heart. As to why I wrote; oh, Azmus, I truly need help. The Marquise of Merindar wrote me last winter, hinting that I ought to join her, and the one time I spoke with her she twitted me for not keeping the vows of our letter last year. But I do want to keep those vows, and those we made to Papa as well! *Ought* I to help her gain the throne? Would she be better than Shevraeth? Or will he make a good king? I can't find out on my own—either the courtiers don't care, or they take sides, and the one person I could ask..." I thought of my unknown admirer, and sighed. "Well, I can't ask him, either, lest my asking be misconstrued."

He bowed his head slightly, his brows knit. "May I speak freely, my lady?" he said at last.

"Please," I said, and hastened to point to the pillows. "Sit down, Azmus. Speak plainly with me. I desperately need that."

He pursed his lips. "First. Have you gone to Petitioners' Court,

368

or talked to the Renselaeuses? When his grace the Marquis of Shevraeth was up at Tlanth during winter, he rode around the county with Lord Branaric and answered questions very freely, no matter who asked."

"No. I...keep running afoul of him."

"Running afoul on political questions?" he asked.

"It never gets that far." I felt my face burn. "Purely personal questions—usually with me misconstruing his motivations. I can't ask him."

Once again he pursed his lips, but this time his countenance seemed more serious. "We can begin with your question to me, then. The Princess of Renselaeus did indeed aid us in our escape that day, though it was indirect aid. I retraced the steps not long after, for my own peace of mind. The Marquise had no involvement whatever with the escape. If she spoke to her brother on your behalf, there's no way of knowing. From what I know of her, I doubt it. But it is entirely possible," he amended scrupulously.

"Ah-hah," I said. "So *she* lied to me. Go on."

"It wasn't a lie so much as indirection," Azmus said. "She did make certain that copies of your letter to Galdran were given into important hands." He grinned. "Her servant was most discreet, yet most insistent that the copies be distributed through the Marquise. I didn't mind, so long as they got read."

"Yet from what you hint about her character, there ought to be a reason beyond altruisim, am I right?"

"You are." He nodded. "More than one person in Court was overheard surmising that it was her way of undermining her brother's position even more thoroughly than he was doing on his own."

"Shev—it's been hinted that she wants the throne."

He nodded again. "Of course I have never overheard her say anything to prove it, nor have I intercepted any correspondence to prove it. But I can well believe it."

"She has recently gone home," I said. "Do you think she gave up?"

He shook his head. "She has never retreated in her life. Every movement was an advance, even when it seemed she retreated. If she went back to her estates, then she has some kind of plan."

I thought furiously. "Her initial request to go home was denied—this was just before we came. Shevraeth showed me her letter. And the other day, I visited Lord Flauvic, and he said that he'd had some kind of argument with his mother and sister, just before they left for Merindar."

Azmus's eyes lowered to his plump hands. "You have established a relationship with Lord Flauvic?"

I grimaced. "Well, let's say I had the opportunity. But I suspect that even if I had continued talking to him, I'd be no more knowledgeable than I am now. He's very good at deflecting questions and giving misleading answers."

Azmus nodded slowly. "We can assume, then, that he wishes this news of the family fight to get about."

"I'm not telling anyone," I said. "Not even about my visit to him."

Azmus's face went bland.

"But you knew," I said, not even making it a question.

"Those who wanted to know, knew," he said.

"So there *is* someone spying on me?" I cried.

"Not on you. On the Merindar House. I arrived two days ago and resumed some of my old contacts and found this out. I also found out that the Merindars have their own spy network, and not just here at Athanarel."

"Spies! Did one intercept my letter to you?" I asked in alarm.

"I did not think a proper answer to your questions ought to be put on paper—though your letter did arrive at my home with its seal intact. I do know how to unseal and seal a letter again, and I know how to tell the difference when it's been done," he assured me. "It appears that the Renselaeus family never did release my name after they identified me, and so most folk believe me to be a retired goldsmith. The letter arrived unmolested."

"Well that's good to know." I sighed in relief. "I hadn't even

hought about tampering. Maybe it's best that I stay ignorant and
oolish," I added bitterly. "You know how successful Bran and I
vere with our revolt, and messing with politics is just as likely to
eave me mud-covered now."

"If you so choose," Azmus said, "I will return to Tlanth."

"I don't know." I played restlessly with my fan. "I want to do
he right thing, yet I can't outthink Flauvic—I proved that recently,
ver a relatively simple question of social usage—and your re-
uinder about the letters makes me realize I could stupidly do some-
ning disastrous without meaning to."

"If you want information," he said in his low tones, "I am
illing to take up my old connections and provide it. You need
rite to no one or speak to no one. It's common enough for people
o summon their own artisans for special projects." He patted his
atchel. "You are wealthy enough to enable me to sustain the
over."

"You mean I should order some jewelry made?"

He nodded. "If you please, my lady."

"Of course—that's easy enough. But to backtrack a bit, what
ou said about spies on both sides worries me. What if the
.enselaeuses find out you're here? Will they assume I'm plotting?"

"I have taken great care to avoid their coverts," he said. "The
wo who met me face-to-face last year are not in Athanarel. And
one of the family has actually seen me."

Once again I sighed with relief. Then an even more unwelcome
nought occurred. "If my movements are known, then other things
ave been noticed," I said slowly. "Are there any I ought to know
oout?"

He gave his nod. "It is known, among those who observe, that
ou do not attend any private social functions that are also attended
y the Marquis of Shevraeth."

So much for my promise, I thought dismally. Yet Shevraeth
adn't said anything. "So…this might be why Flauvic granted me
aat interview?"

"Possibly," he said.

"I take it servants talk."

"Some," he agreed. "Others don't."

"I suppose the Merindar ones don't."

He smiled. "They are very carefully selected and trained, exceedingly well paid—and if they displease, they have a habit of disappearing."

"You mean they're found dead, and no one does anything?"

He shook his head, his mouth now grim. "No. They disappear."

I shuddered.

"So whatever I find out must be by observation and indirection."

"Well, if you can evaluate both sides without endangering yourself," I said, deciding suddenly, "then go ahead. The more I think about it, the less I like being ignorant. If something happens that might require us to act, you can help me choose the correct thing to do and the way to do it."

He bowed. "Nothing would please me more, my lady," he promised.

"Good," I said, rising to fetch my letter from the Marquise. "Here's her letter. Read it—and as far as I care, destroy it." I handed it to him, relieved to have it gone. "So, what's in your bag? I will want something special," I said, and grinned. "For someone special."

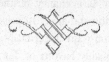

SIXTEEN

THE UNKNOWN WAS NOT LIKELY TO WEAR THE JEW-
elry I sent. I knew that. Yet it gave me pleasure to plan the design
and select just the right gem.

It was a ring I wanted, a fitting return for my own ring, which
I wore frequently. Around it Azmus etched laurel leaves in an abstract, pleasing pattern. Leaves, spring, circles—all symbols that
complemented the friendship. The gemstone was the best ekirth
that Azmus could find, carefully faceted so it glittered like a nightstar, so deep a blue as to seem black, except when the light hit it
just so and it would send out brilliant shards of color: gold, blue,
crimson, emerald.

Ekirthi traditionally symbolized mystery, but I didn't think an
old meaning so bad a thing. I sent it the night following Azmus's
second visit. After wasting much paper and time in fruitless endeavor to write a graceful note to accompany it, I decided to simply
send it in a tiny cedar box that my mother had apparently brought
from Colend and that I'd had all my life.

There was no response the next morning, when I rose early,
which disappointed me just a little, but I shrugged off the reaction
and dressed swiftly. For I'd found out that Trishe was having a
riding party before breakfast, and I intended to encounter it by
accident.

Encountering a party by accident is a chancy business. You can't just appear at the party's destination and affect surprise to find everyone gathered there, not unless you want to seriously discommode either the host or yourself. Probably Savona or Tamara—or Flauvic—were expert at managing such a thing gracefully, but I knew I wasn't.

So what I had to do was take a ride on my own, find their path, and see to it that we fell in together. That was the easy part.

The hard part was reacting with delight and no hint of embarrassment when I did find them, for of course most of them exclaimed in various kinds of surprise when they saw me, especially Nee and Bran. A quick glance showed me that Shevraeth was indeed with them, riding next to a young lady I had never seen before.

I reined in my borrowed mount and reached forward to stroke her braided mane, pretending not to notice Nee's confusion. On the periphery of the group I saw the golden-haired hostess, Lady Trishe. She smiled, but her eyes showed worry. I turned to my brother. For once, I hoped, his disastrous habit of loudly saying whatever he thought would be a boon.

"Bran! You're up already. What a surprise to find you out here!" And of course for Bran it was a surprise. His usual habit on days when he had no engagements was to sleep in, or if he did rise betimes, he'd go with some of his cronies to the gymnasium and take up the swords for a bout or two.

Bran looked at me now, saying in his clear voice, "Not as surprising as finding you here, Mel. We take a morning ride once a week, unless it rains. Trishe puts on a breakfast spread in some nice grassy spot—"

And here I was able to cut in and say in an equally jovial and penetrating voice, " 'Tis true I haven't seen much of anyone these mornings, but I've been locked up studying for a special project. But I'm nearly done, and so I find myself free."

Then Trishe had her opportunity to come forward and request that I join them, which I professed myself honored to do, and the

374

vkward moment passed. I urged my mount in on the other side
f Trishe's and, in the friendliest voice I could assume, told her
ow they would all know about my secret project very soon.

I didn't actually look at little red-haired Lady Arasa Elbanek or
r skinny, long-nosed brother, but I could sense them both listen-
g avidly. This meant, I thought happily as I dropped back to ride
ext to Nee, that my confidential conversation with Trishe would
e all over Athanarel before the bells for green-change rang.

So I congratulated myself on a fine, subtle social save—until
e reached Trishe's picnic site. In the chaos of dismounting and
ndering the horses to the waiting servants, I happened to catch
evraeth's gaze. Those gray eyes, always so accursedly observant,
ere now narrowed with humor, but his mouth was mock-solemn
he said, "I have the honor to introduce to you Lady Elenet
heraev of Grumareth."

I curtsied, wondering where I'd heard that name before. Elenet
as a tall, slim young lady with a heart-shaped face and wide-set
ay-blue eyes. Her hair was fine and somewhat thin, of a tint mid-
ay between blond and brown, but it had been dressed by a master
nd; and her gown, though of sober hues that suited her subdued
loring, was as finely made as any of Fialma's. She gave me a quiet
nile, but there was no time for conversation because Trishe beck-
ned and everyone had to follow along a narrow path up a short
ll, where we found blankets and baskets spread out invitingly on
e grass overlooking one of the ponds.

A quick side-glance showed Trishe addressing a hurried ques-
n to one of her servants, which was answered with a nod. So they
d enough cups and plates—probably carried against breakage.
ood. Then I wouldn't have to pretend I'd already eaten.

Next transpired the sort of flutter of well-bred activity atten-
nt upon being seated and served with cups of gently steaming
t chocolate and light, flaky little pan-breads covered with fresh
eenhouse berries. During the course of this I got a chance to scan
e company and assess positions and attitudes. Not that I could

believe everything I saw, I knew. Most of them were probably dissembling as much as I and probably more successfully. But, bent as I was on eradicating negative gossip, I made myself wander from group to group, chocolate cup in hand.

First to my hostess, who sat with Lady Renna, her husband, and some of the other horse-mad people. We talked a little about horses, and the coming races, and who was likely to bet on—or against—whom. Then I passed on to Arasa, sitting with Geral and the Turlee heir. On the outskirts of this conversation hovered Arasa's sour, clapper-tongued brother Lord Olervec, tolerated only because his sister was so popular.

Arasa, whose blue silk gown flattered her attractive, plump figure, seemed perfectly happy to share her two swains with me. She greeted me with a smile and complimented me sunnily on my gown. "Were you hinting about a special party?" she asked, hugging herself. "Oooh, I do hope so!"

"I was," said I, watching Geral and Alcanad Hazhlee watch her. I dropped some hints about costumes and mysteries, and she giggled and shivered. I realized that I was very probably talking to the present-day equivalent of my forebear Ardis. It was hard not to laugh at the idea.

As I bowed to them and moved away, I wondered if she were in fact as empty-headed as she seemed. Everyone liked her, but with the sort of tolerant attitude one expresses when one admits to a taste for spun sugar. Her name was coupled almost constantly with this or that gentleman by those who liked that kind of gossip. Such as, for instance, her brother.

Next was the foursome I had been bracing myself to face all along: Tamara, Savona, the newly met Lady Elenet, and the Marquis of Shevraeth. Very conscious of Olervec's pale eyes following me, I forced myself to greet the Marquis first: "Good morning," I said, as if we'd been talking just the day before. "How much I wish to thank you for putting me in the way of finding the proper books for my project."

Again that laughter was evident in his glance as he sketched a bow. "If you have any further questions," he said, "it would be my pleasure to accommodate you."

"I'd be honored." I curtsied, my hands making the fan gesture of Unalloyed Gratitude. The shadow of humor in the corners of his mouth deepened.

Then I turned to the others. Savona grinned at me, one hand moving slightly in the fencer's salute of a good hit. I fought the urge to blush as Tamara murmured, "You'll be in the race to-morrow?"

"Of course," I said, lifting my hands. "I have to prove whether my wins last time were luck, skill—or the kindness of well-wishers."

Tamara smiled a little. "And once you've proved which it is?"

"Why then I either celebrate, commiserate—or fulminate!"

They all laughed at that, even the quiet Elenet, though her laughter was so soft I scarcely heard it.

I turned to Shevraeth and said, "Will you be there?"

"I hope to be," he said.

"Riding your gray?"

"Is that a challenge?" he replied with a hint of a smile.

I opened my mouth, then a stray memory brought back our private wager before we reached Athanarel and nothing could prevent the heat that burned up my neck into my face; so I quickly bent over, making a business of ordering one of the flounces on my gown. After I had straightened up I'd have an excuse for a red face, or at least enough of one to pass the notice of the three who (presumably) knew nothing of that unpaid wager.

"I think," I said, retying a ribbon and patting it into place, then unbending with what I hoped was an expression of nonchalance, "I'd better find out if my luck is due to skill or kindness before I make any pledges."

"Very well," he said. "A friendly race will suffice."

When the conversation came to a natural close, I retreated to Nee's side and finished the rest of the picnic with her and Bran.

The morning was chill and the sky steadily darkened. Trishe gave a signal to the servants as soon as the last plate was picked up; it was not a morning to linger.

Scattered drops of rain rustled the leaves overhead as we pulled our gloves on and resettled our hats. Within moments the sweetly chiming harness bells announced that the mounts waited below, and very soon the company was in motion again. I rode back with Nee and Bran, and despite the increasing cold and the strengthening rain I had that inner glow of satisfaction that comes with having attempted the right thing—and actually managing to carry it off.

When we returned to the Residence I decided I had better make the most of my virtuous mood. I sat down at my desk, drew forth the papers I had ordered, which resembled age-yellowed paper from the past, and in my very best writing, began my invitations. I would not insult my brother and Nee by foisting the job off on a scribe.

The historical period I had selected for my party was five hundred years before. The king, young and popular and handsome, had married a lady from the house of Noarth, forebears of the Chamadis family. Those two sterling historical personages would do for Bran and Nee. The king, Jhussav, had had a sister, whose guise I could adopt without causing any kind of political repercussions. She had departed on a world tour not long after she reached my age, and had settled somewhere else. It was a quiet time in our history—no wars or great changes—and there were no exceptionally villainous members of any of the families whose names were prominent now, nor were there any great fools. We could enjoy the masquerade, dress like our ancestors, eat food that was fashionable then, and everyone could find out the idiosyncrasies of their forebears, without embarrassment, and come to the party to do some playacting.

I was thus congratulating myself on having successfully routed Flauvic when a chilling thought made me drop my pen and groan.

Flauvic! What could have possessed me to forget to look up

378

the Merindars? I had checked on everyone else except the forebears of the one who had given me the idea.

No use scolding myself, I thought as I hurried out into the hallway. As I'd done my reading, pausing to run through names of friends, acquaintances, and neutral parties, the Merindars had somehow stood outside of this group. They did not spring naturally to mind, either, when I considered my guest lists. But of course I had to invite Flauvic, and his mother and sister if they returned.

Had I read their names as I did my research? I couldn't remember, which made me fear that something distasteful had been done to them or by them, either of which would be disastrous to call attention to now.

My friendly guise of the morning notwithstanding, I had no wish to blunder into the memoir room if Shevraeth was working there. *This time I will be more stealthy*, I vowed....

The thought vanished when I happened to glance out one of the many arched windows lining the long hallway and saw two figures in one of the private courtyards.

The glass was old and wavery, but something about the tall figure made me stumble to a halt and reach to unlatch the window. As I did, my mind went back to another time when I stood inside a building with distorted glass and stared out at the Marquis of Shevraeth. And somehow he had sensed I was there.

I opened the window just a crack, telling myself that they could see me if they chanced to look up, so it wasn't really spying. He was walking side by side with Lady Elenet, his head bent, his hands clasped behind him. His manner was completely absorbed. I could not hear her voice, but I could see urgency in her long hands as she gestured, and intensity in the angle of her head. Then she glanced up at him and smiled, just briefly, but the expression in her face made me back away without closing the window. I had seen that look before, in the way Nee and Bran smiled at one another, and in the faces of Lady Renna and her new husband. It was love.

Almost overwhelming was the sense that I had breached their

privacy, and instinctively I started back to my room until I realized I was in retreat. Why? No one had seen me. And now I knew I would not accidentally encounter Shevraeth in the alcove where he kept the royal memoirs.

Still, it was with shaking hands and pattering heartbeat that I raced back to the archive room and searched through the appropriate years looking for mentions of the Merindars. In one old, crumbling book there was a dull listing of everyone who attended formal Court functions, and the Merindars showed up there. The next book revealed the fact that the most prominent of them five hundred years ago was an elderly man. This was certainly innocuous enough.

I closed the book, carefully replaced it, and left.

The rain had turned the sky to slanting sheets of gray by afternoon, a steady, pelting shower that kept the humans from promenading the paths. Even the spring birds were quiet and invisible.

As Bran had gone off in pursuit of some kind of pleasure, Nee joined me in my room. I'd bade Mora to bring us hot chocolate, which had arrived creamy and perfect as always. Nee poured it out, then settled at my desk to read her letters. For a time I stood at the window, toying with my cup and breathing the gentle, aromatic steam rising up. For some reason the scent of chocolate threw me back to my first taste of it—at the Renselaeus palace. I looked out at the rain and thought about my past.

My thoughts lengthened into reverie, which was broken only by the sound of Nee's voice. "Something amiss?"

I turned my back to the shower-drenched garden. Nee laid down her pen and looked at me from over her cup, held in both hands. Her manner indicated it was not the abstract question of one who would hardly spare the time to listen to the answer. She was in a mood for converse.

So I shrugged, and forced a smile. "Thinking about the rain," I said.

"Rain?" Her brows arched in inquiry.

"Here I stand, regretting our missed opportunity to walk. A year ago I would have happily run up in the hills, whether it rained or not. And I was thinking that I could go out, in spite of the weather, but I wouldn't enjoy it like I used to."

She gestured in amicable agreement. "There's no fault in misliking the feel of a water-soaked gown."

"That's part of it," I said, seizing on the image. "Last year I wore the same clothes year round. My only hat was a castoff that Julen found me somewhere. I loved the feel of rain against my face, and never minded being soaked. I never noticed it! Now I own carriage hats, and walking hats, and riding hats, and ball headdresses—and none of them except the riding hats can get wet, and even those get ruined in a good soak. My old hat never had any shape to begin with, or any color, so it was never ruined." I turned to face the window again. "Sometimes I feel like I didn't lose just my hat, I lost my *self* that horrible night when I walked into Bran's trap."

Nee was silent.

I ran my thumb around the gilt rim of the cup a couple of times, then I made myself face her. "You think I'm being foolish?"

She put her palms together in Peaceful Discourse mode. "Yes I do," she said, but her tone was not unkind. "One doesn't lose a self, like a pair of gloves or a pin. We learn and change, or we harden into stone."

"Maybe I've changed too fast. Or haven't changed enough," I muttered.

"Have you compromised yourself in any important way?" she asked.

I opened my mouth to say *Of course, when we were forced to give up our plans to defeat Galdran*, but I knew it would be an untruth as soon as it left my lips. "I think," I said slowly, "I lost my purpose that day. Life was so easy when all I lived for was the revolt, the accomplishment of which was to bring about all these wondrous miracles. Nothing turned out to be the way we so confidently expected it to. Nothing."

381

"So…" She paused to sip. "…if you hadn't walked into that trap, what would be different?"

"Besides the handsomeness of my foot?" I forced a grin as I kicked my slippered toes out from under my hem. No one could see my scarred foot, not with all the layers of fine clothing I now wore, but the scars were there.

She smiled, but waited for me to answer her question.

I said, "I suppose the outcome in the larger sense would have been the same. In the personal sense, though, I suspect I would have been spared a lot of humiliation."

"The humiliation of finding out that your political goals were skewed by misinformation?"

"By ignorance. But that wasn't nearly as humiliating as—" *my encounters with a specific individual.* But I just shook my head, and didn't say it.

"So you blame Vidanric," she said neutrally.

"Yes…no…I don't know," I said, trying not to sound cross. "I don't." I looked down, saw my hand fidgeting with the curtain and dropped it to my side. "Tell me about Elenet. Why haven't I met her before? Or is she another who abjured Court?"

"On the contrary," Nee said, and she seemed as relieved as I was to have the subject changed. "She grew up with the rest of us. In fact, she was my greatest friend until she went back to Grumareth. As young girls we were both very minor members of our families, largely ignored by the others. She's solitary in habit. Serious. Though her humor comes out in her art."

"Art?"

"Yes. She's very, very gifted at painting. The fan she made for me is so beautiful and so precious I use it maybe once a year. She makes them only when she wishes to. Screens as well. They can change a room."

"I remember you talking about her once."

"She went home two years ago, when she was unexpectedly made the heir to Grumareth." Nee's mouth tightened. "It was another of Galdran's workings, though no one could point to any proof. Until two years ago the Duke of Grumareth had been a very bright man working hard to counter Galdran's worse excesses. Then there was some kind of power struggle and the Duke had one of the accidents that has decimated so many of our families. Galdran got rid of most of the rest of the smart ones in that family, either by accidents or by sending them out of the kingdom. Elenet's mother then moved back to her family in Denlieff, leaving Elenet here. Galdran settled on the present duke, Elenet's great-uncle, to take the title and quiet, obedient Elenet to be heir. The new duke stayed here to pay lip service to Galdran, and Elenet was sent back to run the province."

The memory of my first formal dinner back in Tlanth, when Shevraeth and Nee fenced verbally over the question of reversion of titles, came clear. Nee had defended her friend. "She's done a good job?"

"A superlative job," Nee said fervently. "No one expected it of her, except me. Just because she seldom speaks doesn't mean she doesn't notice, or think. She's saved her people untold grief, deflecting Galdran when she could, and her great-uncle the rest of the time."

"Do you know what brings her here now?"

"I don't," Nee said. "I've scarcely had an opportunity to exchange two words with her. I trust I'll have the chance tonight. I expect, though, that she's here partly because Grumareth has finally gone home ill."

I'd scarcely noticed the absence of the obnoxious duke. Full of patently false flattery and obsequiousness mixed with superciliousness, he was thoroughly repellent—and stupid. Luckily he favored the older generation as gambling cronies, only paying lip service to those young people he thought would somehow advantage him. He'd apparently decided we Astiars were not worth his exalted efforts; though he'd courted my brother all the year before, he'd largely ignored us both since my arrival.

"Ill? But no one admits to being sick—it always means something else."

"Probably gambling debts," Nee said, shrugging. "That's what it usually is, with *him*. Elenet will have informed him they haven't the wherewithal for his latest squanderings, and he'll have gone home to save face until they can raise what's needed."

"You mean they are that close to ruin?"

Nee grinned. "Oh, not as bad as they were, thanks to Elenet. It's just that his foolishness is now the very last priority, over land improvement. It's she who governs the finances, not he. He's so afraid of anyone finding out, he perforce permits it. I shall make certain the two of you have a chance to talk. I think you will really like her."

"Thank you," I said, sweeping a curtsy. "I'm flattered."

SEVENTEEN

THE NEXT DAY'S RACE WAS CANCELED ON ACCOUNT of rain. My invitations had been delivered, however, causing a spate of notes to cross and recross the elegant pathways, borne by patient runners under drooping rain canopies.

Bran and Nee were delighted—and I think Nee was just a little relieved as well. With every appearance of enthusiasm, they both summoned their clothier staffs to start planning their costumes.

I also received a note from Azmus saying that he needed to talk to me, so I asked Mora to help me arrange my schedule for the following day so that I could see him alone when everyone else was to be busy. Mora gave no sign that I knew she knew all my affairs—she just said she'd help, and did.

I also received a note from the Unknown, the first in two days. I pounced on it eagerly, for receiving his letters had come to be the most important part of my day.

Instead of the long letter I had come to anticipate, it was short.

I thank you for the fine ring. It was thoughtfully chosen and I appreciate the generous gesture, for I have to admit I would rather impute generosity than mere caprice behind the giving of a gift that cannot be worn.

> *Or is this a sign that you wish, after all, to alter the circum-*
> *scriptions governing our correspondence?*
>
> *I thought—to make myself clear—that you preferred your ad-*
> *mirer to remain secret. I am not convinced you really wish to relin-*
> *quish this game and risk the involvement inherent in a contact*
> *face-to-face.*

I dropped the note on my desk, feeling as if I'd reached for a blos-
som and had been stung by an unseen nettle.

My first reaction was to sling back an angry retort that if gifts
were to inspire such an ungallant response, then he could just return
it. Except it was I who had inveighed, and at great length, against
mere gallantry. In a sense he'd done me the honor of telling the
truth—

And it was then that I had the shiversome insight that is probably obvious by now to any of my progeny reading this record: that
our correspondence had metamorphosed into a kind of courtship.

A *courtship.*

As I thought back, I realized that it was our discussion of this
very subject that had changed the tenor of the letters from my
asking advice of an invisible mentor to a kind of long-distance
friendship. The other signs were all there—the gifts, the flowers.
Everything but physical proximity. And it wasn't the unknown gentleman who could not court me in person—it was I who couldn't
be courted in person, and he knew it.

So in the end I sent back only two lines:

> *You have given me much to think about.*
> *Will you wear the ring, then, if I ask you to?*

I received no answer that day, or even that night. And so I sat
through the beautiful concert of blended children's voices and tried
not to stare at Elenet's profile next to the Marquis of Shevraeth,
while feeling a profound sense of unhappiness, which I attributed
to the silence from my Unknown.

The next morning brought no note, but a single white rose.

Despite Nee's good intentions, there was no opportunity for any real converse with Elenet after that concert. Like Nee, Elenet had unexpectedly risen in rank and thus in social worth. If she'd been confined to the wall cushions before, she was in the center of social events now.

But the next morning Nee summoned me early, saying she had arranged a special treat. I dressed quickly and went to her rooms to find Elenet there, kneeling gracefully at the table. "We three shall have breakfast," Nee said triumphantly. "Everyone else can wait."

I sank down at my place, not cross-legged but formal kneeling, just as Elenet did. When the greetings were over, Nee said, "It's good to have you back, Elenet. Will you be able to stay for a while?"

"It's possible." Elenet had a low, soft, mild-toned voice. "I shall now for certain very soon."

Nee glanced at me, and I said hastily, "If you are able to stay, I hope you will honor us with your presence at the masquerade ball I am hosting to celebrate Nee's adoption."

"Thank you." Elenet gave me a lovely smile. "If I am able, I would be honored to attend."

"Then stay for the wedding," Nee said, waving a bit of bread in the air. "It's only scarce days beyond—midsummer eve. In fact, Vidanric will just make up his mind on a day—and I don't know why he's lagging—you'll have to be here for the coronation, anyway. Easier to stay than to travel back and forth."

Elenet lifted her hands, laughing softly. "Easy, easy, Nee. I have responsibilities at home that constrain me to make no promises. I shall see what I can contrive, though."

"Good." Nee poured out more chocolate for us all. "So, what think you of Court after your two years' hiatus? How do we all look?"

"Older," Elenet answered. "Some—many—have aged for the

387

better. Tastes have changed, for which I am grateful. Galdran never would have invited those singers we had last night, for example."

"Not unless someone convinced him that they were all the rage at the Sartoran Court and only provincials would not have them to tour."

"It must be expensive to house so many," Elenet observed.

"Princess Elestra brought them." Nee picked up her fan, snapped it open, and gestured in Acknowledgment of Superior Aesthetics mode, which caused Elenet to smile. "Apparently they have those children up in Renselaeus every year, and I understand one or two of their own youth have been deemed good enough to join the choir and travel the world. It's a long association." She leaned back on her pillows. "It's been like that of late, Elenet. You really must stay and enjoy it while the Princess is still arranging royal entertainments. Remember those long, hideous nights of watching Galdran win at cards?"

"I never watched him," Elenet admitted. "I watched the others, always. It took consummate skill to lose to him."

"I take it people had to lose," I said.

They both looked at me quickly, as if they'd forgotten I was there. *So others can lose themselves in memories of the past*, I thought. And obviously not good memories, either.

"Yes," Nee said. "If you didn't, he got his revenge. Mostly, though, if you wanted to live—if you wanted your family to be safe—then you pretended to be much stupider than he was."

Elenet made a quick gesture of warding. "Banish those old fears. Let us talk of pleasant things. Have you been keeping up with your own music?"

"I blush to say no," Nee admitted, "but a beautiful harp awaits me when we remove to Tlanth, and then I know I will have the time to practice every day. Maybe even make my own songs again."

I looked at her in surprise—I hadn't known that she wrote music.

"Your songs are beautiful," Elenet said.

"But sad," Nee said, wrinkling her nose. "I promised myself no more sad songs, and so I stopped. Now I think I can make happy ones. You?" Nee asked.

"Every day," Elenet said. "Acquit me of heroic efforts, though! It has been my solace to sit at my harp each morning, just before first-gold."

"If I painted like you do, I'd have solace enough," Nee said, sighing.

Elenet's smile was slight, and her eyelids lowered as she stared down at her hands. "It seems that my...sad songs...took a different form."

"No more sad songs for you, either," Nee said, touching her friend's wrist. "You've earned happiness. I command you to have it!"

All three of us laughed, and the remaining conversation was about inconsequentials, such as gowns and materials, and then music again, before Nee realized it was late and we all had things to do. We parted with mutual compliments and expressions of esteem.

Azmus leaned forward and said, "I have only one fact to give you: The Duke of Grumareth met with the Marquise and her daughter on their way to Merindar."

"On their way?" I repeated. "Merindar is north, and Grumareth west."

Azmus's round, pleasant face hardened into a kind of sardonic amusement. "For a half day's journeying, their path could lie together."

"Which could be innocuous," I said. "Anything else?"

"Only that the rain forced them to stop at an inn for a full time-change. Admittedly the rain was heavy that day, but it was also intermittent; yet only after second-green did both parties deem it possible to ride on."

"I take it you got this from inn servants, or Grumareth's?"

"One of the duke's people." Azmus nodded. "They are loyal enough to their land, but some loathe the Merindars with deadly passion."

"Ah-hah!" I exclaimed. "So, what now?"

Azmus's gaze was serious. "It is time for the truth, my lady, if you will honor me with the privilege of speaking frankly."

"Do," I said, hiding the wail of dismay that shivered through my head. Everyone seemed to want to tell me the truth, when I wasn't sure I wanted to hear it. *Except Flauvic, who says there is no truth.*

"I can pursue this," he said, "but it will take a great deal of work, and it will also be costly."

"How so?" I asked uneasily. "Bribery?"

He shook his head. "Not at all. The person who gives information for bribes is usually worthless; someone else could be paying a higher price either for the information you want—or for you to get the wrong information. I told you before that the Merindars' servants are mum. What I must do is reassemble many of my old contacts and gather the information we need by finding patterns. This is exhaustive and complicated if it is to be done well—and without causing comment."

"Patterns?"

He nodded, smiling. "The very first lesson I learned when I first began spying for my lord your father was that information that cannot be gathered on where someone is can usually be inferred by where the individual isn't. This is particularly true for runners." He looked at me expectantly.

I drew a deep breath. "So. What you're saying is that you—and whomever else you need—must visit all the likely inns along likely paths and find out if Merindar runners have been there, and when, and how long?"

"That's close enough," he said. "Bear in mind that the best of them take different routes quite often, but humans are creatures of habit, and they are also creatures of comfort. At some point they will go where they know there are clean beds or a particularly good table set, or where they can do their own listening. And of course, there are their horses."

"But wealthy people like the Merindars and the Renselaeuses have horses stabled all over the kingdom," I protested. "I noticed that last year."

"Yes, but good stablehands know those horses, and thus know when they're taken out, and for how long, and where they went. For one stablehand to talk about the fine roan Windrunner and how he did in the bad weather last week is merely horse talk and seldom raises comment. But Windrunner's movements put together with Jerrec of Ilvan-town's movements make a pattern."

"I see. So you want to know if I'll pay for it?"

He shook his head. "I want to know, my lady, what you will do with the information."

My first thought was that the Marquise would probably make my servant disappear who spoke thus with her. But I had given Azmus the right. He loved a challenge, this I knew, but he also loved the kingdom. When I first took charge of Tlanth's accounting books, I had discovered that Azmus had been paid only sporadically over the years. He had used his ostensible trade as goldsmith in order to pursue his clandestine vocation on our behalf. My father, and then my brother and I, had helped little, beyond sending him back to Remalna-city with a basket of fresh food and one of our good mounts after he'd made one of his reports.

So he was not in any sense a mere lackey to go silently and carry out my whims. He was a co-conspirator, and he wanted to discuss the goal.

So what was my goal?

Images fled through my mind, chased by phantom emotions: my descending on Shevraeth to inform him of whatever it was the Marquise was planning; my sending him an anonymous letter with the same information. Fine, triumphant gestures, but to what end? And why?

I shook my head, as if that would dispel the images. If I was going to dip my hand into public affairs, then I had to dismiss personal considerations.

"To help the new king," I said. "To make certain that no Merindar sits again on that throne, because none of them are worthy."

Azmus smiled, clapped his hands to his knees and bowed with slow deliberation. "I shall communicate with you as soon as I know something, my lady," he said, and slipped out.

EIGHTEEN

THE DAYS IMMEDIATELY FOLLOWING PASSED VERY swiftly.

Now that summer had begun, the spring rains, which had held off for weeks, inundated us steadily. I noticed worried conversations once in a while, among people whose lands lay along the coast, and runners dashed and splashed back and forth to report on crops and roads and floods.

Meanwhile, the peculiar life of Athanarel continued. We did not have a king, yet the government was somehow carried forward, and foreign diplomats attended the constant round of social events, and they all seemed content with things as they were. Not so the more serious of the courtiers, but as yet the questions everyone most wanted to ask—"When will we have a king? Why does he wait?"—were as yet discussed only in quiet corners of informal parties and never by those most closely concerned.

The weather curtailed outside activities. For now the races and picnics were set aside for inside diversions: readings, music, dancing, parties, chocolate, and talk. I think four new dances were introduced during that time, but what I really enjoyed was the resumption of sword work. Parties to pursue the martial arts were organized, and fencing tourneys replaced racing for those who liked competition.

I competed only for fun, and no one bet on me, not even Savona, because, despite my enthusiasm, I wasn't very good. Neither was Bran, though he shared my enthusiasm. The others who favored the blade had been well trained from childhood, and our lack showed. But this did not stop either of us from trying.

One of the topics of conversation was my party, which was perhaps the more anticipated because people kept inside perforce had more time to spend on their costumes. My own involvement with the preparations had escalated accordingly, about which I'll have something to say anon.

From Flauvic, of course, nothing was seen, nor did he entertain—but after enough days had passed that I had quite given up on him, I received a witty note, gracefully written by his own hand, stating that he would attend my party.

And so, on the surface, all was serene enough. Tamara remained cool but friendly, and Nee told me over chocolate one morning when Elenet was not there that Tamara never mentioned me but in praise.

Trishe held her weekly breakfast parties in her rooms at Khialem House; Derec and Geral continued to flirt with me; Savona continued his extravagant compliments; I was often in company with Shevraeth now, and we both smiled and conversed, but always, it seemed, with other people.

And on most mornings, Elenet joined Nee and me for breakfast. Sometimes Bran was there, and sometimes not. I cannot say that I came to know Elenet any better as the days wore on. She was reserved and never made any reference to anything personal. Still, when she was there, we had some of our best discussions of reading, music—always music—art, and history.

One morning when we three were alone, Nee leaned forward and said, "Elen, you've been closeted with Vidanric a lot, I've noticed. Has he said aught about a coronation? I confess it makes me nervous to have it not decided—as if they are waiting for something terrible to happen."

Elenet's expression did not change, but high on her thin cheeks appeared a faint flush. "I trust we will hear something soon," she murmured. And she turned the conversation to something general.

Were they in love? I knew that she was. Elenet would make a splendid queen, I told myself, and they both certainly deserved happiness. I found myself watching them closely whenever we were all at an event, which occurred more and more often. There were no touches, no special smiles, none of the overt signs that other courting couples gave—but she was often by his side. I'd inevitably turn away, thinking to myself that it was none of my business. It wasn't as if I didn't have admirers, both the social kind and one real one—though I didn't know his name. Still, the subject made me restless, which I attributed to my knowledge of how badly I had behaved to Shevraeth. I knew I owed him an apology, or an explanation, two things I could not bring myself to offer lest—someone—misconstrue my motives. And think me angling for a crown.

So I hugged to myself the knowledge of my Unknown. No matter how my emotions veered during those social occasions, it was comforting to realize that I would return to my room and find a letter from the person whose opinions and thoughts I had come to value most.

I *preferred* courtship by paper, I told myself. No one feels a fool, no one gets hurt. And yet—and yet—though I loved getting those letters, as the days went by I realized I was becoming slightly impatient of certain restraints that I felt were imposed on us.

Like discussing current events and people. I kept running up against this constraint and finding it more irksome as each day passed. We continued to range over historical events, or the current entertainments such as the Ortali ribbon dancers or the piper-poets from faraway Toar—all subjects that I could have just as well discussed with an erudite lady.

The morning of Nee's question to Elenet about coronations, I found the usual letter waiting when I returned to my room. I decided to change everything. Having scanned somewhat impatiently down the well-written comparison of two books about the Land of the Chwair, I wrote:

> *I can find it in myself to agree with the main points, that kings ought not to be sorcerers, and that the two kinds of power are better left in the charge of different persons. But I must confess that trouble in Chwairsland and Colend seems a minor issue right now. The problems of wicked mage-kings are as distant as those two kingdoms, and what occupy my attention now are problems closer to home. Everyone seems to whisper about the strange delay concerning our own empty throne, but as yet no one seems willing to speak aloud. Have you any insights on why the Renselaeus family has not made any definite plans?*

That sent, I changed into my riding clothes, summoned a rain canopy, and set out for sword practice, wondering about the silence from Azmus.

The long room now used as a gymnasium had formerly been some kind of drill hall for Galdran's private army, and before that it had obviously served mostly military purposes, for flags, ancient and modern, hung high on the walls, celebrating past ridings and regiments that had been deemed worthy of fame. These were not as spectacular as the House banners that were displayed on angled poles in the Throne Room, testament to Remalna's unity, but they carried their own prestige; now that I was better read about our past I recognized some of them, and there was a kind of thrill in seeing the physical evidence of past glory.

At one end of the room was a group of young teens busy with swordplay, and at the other a swarm of children circled round on ancient carved horses mounted on cart wheels or played at stick-and-ball.

I wandered toward my friends and was soon hailed by Renna, who offered me a bout. Time passed swiftly and agreeably. I finished my last engagement with one of Nee's cousins and was just beginning to feel the result of sustained effort in my arm and back when a practice blade thwacked my shoulder. I spun around, and gaped.

Shevraeth stood there smiling. At his elbow my brother grinned, and next to him, Savona watched with appreciation apparent in his dark eyes.

"Come, Lady Meliara," the Marquis said. "Let's see how much you've learned since you took on Galdran."

"I *didn't* take on Galdran," I protested, feeling hot and cold at once.

"I don't know what you'd call it, then, Mel." Bran leaned on his sword, still grinning. "Looked like you went have-at-'im to me."

"I was just trying to defend *you*," I said, and the others all laughed. "And a fat lot of good it did, too," I added when they stopped. "He knocked me right out of the saddle!"

"Hit you from behind," Shevraeth said. "Apparently he was afraid to confront so formidable a foe face-to-face."

They laughed again, but I knew it was not at me so much as at the hated King Galdran.

Before I could speak again, Shevraeth raised his point and said, "Come now. Blade up."

I sighed. "I've already been made into cheese by Derec, here, and Renna, and Lornav, but if you think I merit another defeat..."

Again they laughed, and Savona and my brother squared off as Shevraeth and I saluted. My bout with the Marquis was much like the others. Even more than usual I was hopelessly outclassed, but stuck grimly to my place, refusing to back up, and took hit after hit, though my parrying was steadily improving. Of course I lost, but at least it wasn't so easy a loss as I'd had when I first began to attend practice—and he didn't insult me with obvious handicaps, such as never allowing his point to hit me.

Bran and Savona finished a moment later, and Bran was just

suggesting we exchange partners when the bells for third-gold rang, causing a general outcry. Some would stay, but most, I realized, were retreating to their various domiciles to bathe and dress for open Court.

I turned away—and found Shevraeth beside me. "You've never sampled the delights of Petitioners' Court," he said.

I thought of the Throne Room again, this time with Galdran there on the goldenwood throne, and the long lines of witnesses. I repressed a shiver.

Some of my sudden tension must have exhibited itself in my countenance because he said, "It is no longer an opportunity for a single individual to practice summary justice such as you experienced on your single visit."

"I'm certain you don't just sit around happily and play cards," I muttered, looking down at the toes of my boots as we walked.

"Sometimes we do, when there are no petitioners. Or we listen to music. But when there is business, we listen to the petitioners, accept whatever they offer in the way of proof, and promise a decision at a later date. That's for the first two greens. The last is spent in discussing impressions of the evidence at hand; sometimes agreement is reached, and sometimes we decide that further investigation is required before a decision can be made."

This surprised me so much I looked up at him. There was no amusement, no mockery, no threat in the gray eyes. Just a slight question.

I said, "You listen to the opinions of whoever comes to Court?"

"Of course," he said. "It means they want to be a part of government, even if their part is to be merely ornamental."

I remembered that dinner when Nee first brought up Elenet's name, and how Shevraeth had lamented how most of those who wished to give him advice had the least amount worth hearing.

"Why should I be there?" I asked. "I remember what you said about worthless advisers."

"Do you think any opinion you would have to offer would be worthless?" he countered.

"It doesn't matter what *I* think of my opinion," I retorted, and then caught myself. "I mean to say, it is not me making the decisions."

"So what you seem to be implying is that I think your opinion worthless."

"Well, don't you?"

He sighed. "When have I said so?"

"At the inn in Lumm, last year. And before that. About our letter to Galdran, and my opinion of courtiers."

"It wasn't your opinion I pointed up, it was your ignorance," he said. "You seem to have made truly admirable efforts to overcome that handicap. Why not share what you've learned?"

I shrugged, then said, "Why don't you have Elenet there?"—and hated myself for about as stupid a bit of pettiness as I'd ever uttered.

But he took the words at face value. "An excellent suggestion, and one I acted on immediately after she arrived at Athanarel. She's contributed some very fine insights. She's another, by the way, who took her own education in hand. Three years ago about all she knew was how to paint fans."

I had talked myself into a corner, I realized—all through my own efforts. So I said, "All right, then. I'll go get Mora to dig out that Court dress I ordered and be there to blister you all with my brilliance."

He bowed, lifted his gray-gloved hand in a casual salute, and walked off toward the Royal Wing.

I retreated in quick order to get ready for the ordeal ahead.

As the bells for first-green echoed sweetly up the stone walls of the great hall built round the Throne Room, I passed through the arched entrance into the room itself. I felt very self-conscious in my never-worn pale rose satin gown and gloves. I glanced down at the gemstones winking in the light, and the cunning silver and maroon embroidery, then I raised my head carefully so as not to dislodge the formal headdress.

People seemed to be milling about in an orderly fashion, the rare sunlight from the high window sparking rich highlights from brightly colored velvets and satins and jewels.

Elenet and Savona appeared, arm in arm, she dressed in forest green and he in a very dark violet that was almost black. They came directly to me, smiling welcome, and with a pretty fan-flourish of Friends' Recognition, Elenet said, "You look lovely, Meliara. Do come stand with us; we have found a good place."

And it was a good place, from which we could see all three Renselaeuses plus the petitioners. We could hear them all without too much distortion from the echoes in the huge room, for there were only twenty or thirty of us at most; not the hundreds that Galdran had required to augment his greatness.

The throne was empty, and above it hung only the ancient flag of Remalna, tattered in places from age. Galdran's banners were, of course, gone. No one was on the dais. Just below it, side by side in fine chairs, sat the Prince and Princess.

At their feet Shevraeth knelt formally on white cushions before a long carved table. He now wore white and silver with blue gemstones on his tunic and in his braided hair. *He looks like a king,* I thought, though he was nowhere near the throne.

Each petitioner came forward, assisted by stewards in the gold-and-green of Remalna. They did not have to stand before the Renselaeuses, but were bade to take a cushion at that long table, which each did, first bowing and then kneeling in the formal manner.

It really was a civilized way of conducting the business, I realized as time wore on. The Prince and Princess remained silent, except when they had a question. Their son did all the speaking, not that he spoke much. Mostly he listened, then promised a decision on this or that day; as the number of petitioners increased, I realized he'd been doing it long enough to gauge about how long each piece of business was likely to take. Then he thanked them for coming forward, and they bowed and rose, and were escorted away to the side table, where refreshments awaited any who wanted them.

I noticed some of the courtiers with cups in their hands, or tiny plates of delicately made foods. The room was chill, and the rain had come back, drumming against the high windows. The Renselaeuses did not eat or drink, and I realized I was so fascinated with the process that I did not want to steal away to get food for myself.

The last petitioner left well before the second-green, which meant that there would be no Court the following day. I suspected they'd need to use the time to go over the petitions; one change was not going to do for all that I had heard that day.

Nor did it. When the great doors at the other end were closed, we repaired into a beautiful antechamber of pink marble, where more food and drink were spread, hot and fresh.

This time everyone partook liberally and seated themselves on narrow stools along a long, high table. When I realized that these were to accommodate the women, I wanted to laugh. Court gowns, having wide skirts and delicate, costly decoration, are not made to be sat in, but one could manage with a stool. I wondered when the stools had been made, and with whom in mind, as I harkened back to elder days of fashion when it was the men whose tight, constraining clothing made sitting difficult, while the ladies knelt at their ease in their flimsy gowns.

The Prince and Princess sat at either end of the table. Both had foreign diplomats at their right and left hands. Prince Alaerec caught my eye and smiled a welcome, then he said, "So who has thoughts about Guild Mistress Pelhiam's request?"

"Seems straightforward," Baron Orbanith said, sounding, as usual, slightly pompous. "Cloth makers want glowglobes for their street for night work, citing the sail makers and the scribes as having glowglobes on theirs. They'll contact the magicians, order them, pay for them."

Savona lowered his wineglass. "It is straightforward. The question is, is this the time to be raising prices? Because we all know that the Guild will duly raise prices in order to meet the extra expense."

"It is not the time to be raising prices." The Princess's fluting voice was pleasant but firm. "The people who will be most affected by the price rise will need another year or more to recover from the recent hardships."

Several more people spoke then, some of them merely repeating what had already been said, and one person, Lord Olervec Elbanek, declaring that if the poor simply worked harder they could afford to buy more.

Others spoke more sensibly, and then finally Elenet said, "Perhaps the request should be granted, contingent on the Guild using some of its own funds and not raising prices. If that's summarily refused, the subject could be brought forward again in a year's time."

Shevraeth nodded. "If they want light at night badly enough, they'll unpocket the funds. If not, then they can wait."

General agreement murmured round the table, and Shevraeth leaned over to speak to the quiet scribe who sat at his elbow. He then wrote swiftly on the petition and laid it aside.

The second petition caused longer debate, which led to calls for more investigation. It seemed that one of the fortresses on the northern border—I wondered if it was one to which the troublesome army officers had been sent—was charging increasing amounts of tax money to the people they protected. The petitioners, from a nearby town, begged for a royal decree placing a ceiling on the taxes. "They claim they have more new recruits than ever before, which accounts for all the supplies and equipment and horses they are ordering. But we're no longer at war. So if they really are ordering all this, against what?" one man had said.

The debate went on, listened to but not commented on by the three Renselaeuses. Then when all seemed to have had their say, the petition was set aside pending investigation.

The third petition caused more general talk, led by the Prince; and so time sped on, the bells for blue ringing before the pile was half done. There was general agreement to meet the next day at green in the Exchequer First Chamber and then all rose and departed.

I left, having not spoken during the entire proceeding. I realized I was glad that I had gone and that I was fascinated by what I'd seen. As I walked down the long halls, listening to the *swish-swish* of my skirts on the fine mosaic tiles, I wondered how they'd investigate, who they'd hire—and just how one went about building the unseen part of a government.

When I reached my rooms, I saw a letter lying on my table.

Hastily stripping off my gloves, I sank down onto my pillows, heedless of the costly fabric of my court gown crinkling and billowing about me, and broke the seal with my finger.

The Unknown had written:

You ask why there has been no formal announcement concerning a coronation. I think this question is better addressed to the person most concerned, but I do know this: Nothing will be announced until the sculptors have finished refashioning a goldenwood throne for a queen.

NINETEEN

WELL, I HAD NO ANSWER TO MAKE TO THAT; THINK-
ing about Elenet, or Shevraeth, or that carved throne, caused a cold
ache inside, as if I had lost something I had not hitherto valued.

So I didn't write back that day. Or the next. The following
morning I received a letter that did not refer to thrones, queens,
or coronations, to my intense relief. And so, for a handful of days
anyway, things went right back to normal.

Except, what is normal at any given time? We change just as
the seasons change, and each spring brings new growth. So nothing
is ever quite the same. I realize now that what I wanted was comfort,
but that, too, does not often come with growth and change.

I did not go back to Petitioners' Court the next day, or the
next; and the morning after that, when Nee had arranged a
breakfast for Elenet and me, I moved so reluctantly that I arrived
outside Nee's tapestry somewhat late. From inside came the
sound of Elenet's laughing, and then her voice, talking swiftly.
Either she was happy over something specific, or else she felt constrained while in my company. Either way, I did not know how to
react, so I backed away from the tapestry and retreated to my
rooms.

"Mora, I think the time has come for me to remain here to

oversee the last of the preparations for the party," I said as soon as I slipped inside. And there was no mistaking the relief in her face.

One could, of course, issue orders through servants for this or that group of performers to appear, promising a sizable purse. There were many of these groups earning their living in and around Remalna-city: players, dancers, singers, musicians whose livelihood depended on their knowing the latest trends and tastes.

My idea was to transport everyone five hundred years into the past as soon as they entered the portals. The building, of course, was appropriate; I hired a ballroom near the Residence that had not been renovated for generations, knowing that the marble therein was more than five hundred years old.

As for the rest, I did not want to issue orders through servants. I wanted to see the project through myself. What I discovered was that in discussing my vision with each artist I encountered, these artists altered from hirelings into individuals—and conversely for them, I altered from a faceless courtier with money into an individual with an interest and appreciation for their expertise.

This, in turn, led to offers of cousins, friends, relations—some so distant they were beyond our borders—who were experts at this or that art. Over the month in which I prepared for that ball, my own vision slowly transformed into a much greater reality, one conceived in willing collaboration with many minds.

I'd thought to have someone scout out enough five-hundred-year-old tapestries from houses around town to borrow for suitable wall hangings. When I mentioned this to one of the palace servants Mora introduced to me, I was brought an uncle who specialized in re-creating ancient arts.

"No, no," said this wizened little old man, his eyes bird-bright. 'Never tapestries for a ball, not then. Always a chimerical garden, so arranged that the air always smells sweet and fresh." His hands whirled around his head, reminding me of wings, then he darted

405

back and forth, showing me where this or that herb would hang, and describing streams of water that one heard but did not see, which would somehow help the air to move.

One day, near the end of my planning, I traveled into the city to hear the music of the time, and to help choose the songs. In a low-roofed inn room I sat on the cushions set for me, and the group picked up the old instruments they had assembled and began to play.

At first the sounds were strange to my ear, and I marveled at how music could change so greatly over the years. There were no strumming instruments, such as the harp or tiranthe, which formed the essential portion of any ensemble nowadays. Instead the instruments were drums and air and sweet metallic bells and cymbals, combining complicated rhythms with a light-edged, curiously physical kind of sound that made one's feet itch to be moving. The drums also, I realized as I listened on, caused an echo in memory of those heard on the mountains from the unseen folk there.

Recognizing that, I laughed. "I like it! That will be perfect."

"Of course we'll have our own instruments laid by," the group mistress told me. "So we can play any of the modern dances your guests ask for. But for the arrivals, the start of the event—"

"—we will make them feel they have stepped into the past," I said.

And so it went, even with the mimery. It turned out that the Court during that period had been fond of entertaining itself, and more frequently than not had performed for one another. Thus I bade my hired players to guise themselves as figures of the period, that some of my guests might be surprised to see themselves mirrored in art.

My greatest coup was when Mora brought to me her brother, who with a few quiet words and a low bow, offered to take charge of the food, from preparation to serving. I'd been at Court long enough by then to know that he was—justly—famous. "You're the hief steward for the Renselaeuses," I said. "Surely you haven't left hem?"

"I came to offer my services," he said, as blank-faced as his ister. "With the full permission of the Princess."

I accepted gratefully, knowing now that the food and drink vould be the very best and perfectly served.

The morning of the ball dawned.

When I reached the ballroom for my last inspection and saw he faces awaiting me, I realized I had fully as many people working or me as there would be guests. I could feel the excitement running igh among performers and servers alike, showing me this or that etail, all rehearsing their arts. As I moved about admiringly, it eemed to me that my event served as a symbolic representation of ne kingdom: These artists, like the aristocrats, came to be seen as vell as to see; and the servants, who worked to make all smooth, vere unseen but saw everything. Everyone would have a tale to ike home, a memory of performance, whether a countess or a carf dancer or a server of pastries.

But my preparations were nearly done. I went back to my ooms to get ready.

s the bells for second-blue echoed from wall to pillar to gloriously ainted ceiling, then died away, I stood alone at the midpoint of ne ballroom to welcome the guests of honor. Everyone was there, r nearly everyone. Only Flauvic was missing, which did not par- cularly bother me.

Nee and Bran came down the stairs, arm in arm, both dressed a the violet-and-white of the royal Calahanras family.

My own gown was mostly white and dove gray, with knots of olet ribbon as acknowledgment of my role as Bran's sister. But ere the reference to the royal family ended, for my colors in the ballroom were Remalna's green and gold—the green of the plant leaves, and all shades of gold, from ocher to palest yellow, picked out in the blooms. The focus, therefore, was quite properly on Nee and Bran, who grinned like children as they came to me.

I glanced up at the balcony, and a ruffle of drums brought the quiet tide of murmurings to a cease. Then an extravagant cascade of sound from all the instruments of the air, flutes to greathorns, announced the ancient promenade, and all took their places to perform the dance that their ancestors had toed-and-heeled through hundreds of years before.

Backs straight, heads high, fingertips meeting in an archway under which the honored two proceeded, followed by everyone else in order of rank.

So it began. By the end of the promenade I knew my ball was a triumph. I breathed the heady wine of success and understood why famous hosts of the past had secreted knowledge of their artists, sometimes hiring them exclusively so that no one could reproduce the particular magic that so much skill had wrought.

For a time the focus was equally on me as I made my way round the perimeter and accepted the compliments of the guests. But gradually they turned to one another, or to the entertainment, and I remained on the perimeter and thus faded into the background.

Or attempted to, anyway. For as I moved away from a group of young ladies bent on dancing, I suddenly found myself face-to-face with Flauvic. Could I possibly have overlooked him?

Not likely. He was magnificent in black, white, and gold, the candlelight making a blaze of his hair. His eyes were brilliant, their expression hard to read, but I sensed a kind of intensity in him when he bowed over my hand. "Beautifully done," he said with an elegant lift of his hand.

"It was your suggestion," I reminded him—knowing full well he didn't need to be reminded.

"You do great credit to my poor idea," he returned, bowing slightly.

And because he did not move away, I invited him to stroll with me.

He agreed, and as we walked around the perimeter, he commented appreciatively—and knowledgeably—on the fine details of my evocation of our shared past, until he was seen and claimed by friends.

As I watched him walk away, I contemplated just how skillfully he had contrived his entrance. He had managed, while saluting me as hostess, to avoid paying honor to Bran and Nee. One always arrives at a ball before the guests of honor, unless one wishes to insult them. Great dramas had been enacted in the past just this way, but he'd slipped in so quietly, no one—except me, it seemed—knew that he had not been there all along.

I watched him for a time, sipping at my wine. He moved deftly from group to group, managing to speak to just about every person. When I finished the wine, I set the glass down, deciding that Flauvic would always constitute an enigma.

Realizing I ought to be circulating as well, I turned—and found myself confronted by the Marquis of Shevraeth.

"My dear Countess," he said with a grand bow. "Please bolster my declining prestige by joining me in this dance."

Declining prestige? I thought, then out loud I said, "It's a tartelande. From back then."

"Which I studied up on all last week," he said, offering his arm.

I took it and flushed right up to my pearl-lined headdress. Though we had spoken often, of late, at various parties, this was the first time we had danced together since Savona's ball, my second night at Athanarel. As we joined the circle I sneaked a glance at Elenet. She was dancing with one of the ambassadors.

A snap of drums and a lilting tweet caused everyone to take position, hands high, right foot pointed. The musicians reeled out a merry tune to which we dipped and turned and stepped in patterns round one another and those behind and beside us.

In between measures I stole looks at my partner, bracing

for some annihilating comment about my red face, but he seemed preoccupied as we paced our way through the dance. The Rense-laeuses, completely separate from Remalna five hundred years before, had dressed differently, just as they had spoken a different language. In keeping, Shevraeth wore a long tunic that was more like a robe, colored a sky blue, with black and white embroidery down the front and along the wide sleeves. It was flattering to his tall, slender form. His hair was tied back with a diamond-and-nightstar clasp, and a bluefire gem glittered in his ear.

We turned and touched hands, and I realized he had broken his reverie and was looking at me somewhat quizzically. I had been caught staring.

I said with as careless a smile as I could muster, "I'll wager you're the most comfortable of the men here tonight."

"Those tight waistcoats do look uncomfortable, but I rather like the baldrics," he said, surveying my brother, whom the movement of the dance had placed just across from us.

At that moment Bran made a wrong turn in the dance, paused to laugh at himself, then hopped back into position and went on. Perhaps emboldened by his heedless example, or inspired by the unusual yet pleasing music, more of the people on the periphery who had obviously not had the time, or the money, or the notion of learning the dances that went along with the personas and the clothes, were moving out to join. At first tentative, with nervously gripped fans and tense shoulders here and there betraying how little accustomed to making public mistakes they were, the courtiers slowly relaxed.

After six or seven dances, when faces were flushed and fans plied in earnest, the first of my mime groups came out to enact an old folktale. The guests willingly became an audience, dropping onto waiting cushions.

And so the evening went. There was an atmosphere of expectation, of pleasure, of relaxed rules as the past joined the present, rendering both slightly unreal.

I did not dance again but once, and that with Savona, who insisted that I join Shevraeth and Elenet in a set. Despite his joking remarks from time to time, the Marquis seemed more absent than merry, and Elenet moved, as always, with impervious serenity and reserve. Afterward the four of us went our ways, for Shevraeth did not dance again with Elenet.

I know, because I watched.

The two tones of white-change had rung when the scarf dances began.

To the muted thunder of drums the dancers ran out, clad in hose and diaphanous tunics of light gray, each connected to the dancer behind him or her by ropes of intertwined gold and green. Glints of silver threads woven into the floating, swirling tunics flashed like starlight, as well-muscled limbs moved with deliberate, graceful rhythm in a difficult counterpoint to the drums.

Then, without warning, notes from a single flute floated as if down on a breeze, and with a quick snap of wrists the dancers twitched the ropes into soaring, billowing squares of gauze.

A gasp from the watchers greeted the sudden change, as the gauzy material rippled and arched and curled through the air, expertly manipulated by the dancers until it seemed the scarves were alive and another kind of dance altogether took place above the humans.

Then the dancers added finger cymbals, clinking and clashing in a syncopated beat that caused, I noted as I looked about me, responsive swayings and nods and taps of feet.

Why this gift, o pilgrim, my pilgrim,
Why this cup of water for me?

I give thee the ocean, stormy or tranquil,
Endless and boundless as my love for thee...

Now it was time for the love songs, and first was the ancient Four Questions, sung in antiphony by the women and the men, and then reversed. High voices and deep echoed down from the unseen gallery, as the dancers below handed out smaller versions of the scarves and drew the guests into the dance.

...why this firebrand for me?

Dancers, lovers, all turned and stepped and circled, connected only by the scarves which hid them, then revealed them, then bound them together as they stepped in, his corner held high by the shoulder, hers low at her waist.

...just so my love burneth for thee

The music, flawlessly performed, the elusive perfume on the scarves—all made the atmosphere feel charged with physical awareness. In the very center of all the dancers were Branaric and Nimiar, circling round one another, their faces flushed and glowing, eyes ardent.

I scarcely recognized my own brother, who moved now with the unconscious ease that makes its own kind of grace, and in a dainty but provocatively deliberate counterpoint danced Nee. It was she, and not Bran, who—when the gauze was overhead, making a kind of canopy that turned their profiles to silhouettes—leaned up to steal a kiss. Then they separated, she casting a look over her shoulder at him that was laughing and not laughing, and which caused him to spin suddenly and crush her in both arms, just for a moment, as around them the others swirled and dipped and the gauzes rose and fell with languorous grace.

As I watched, images flitted through my mind of little Ara, the girl I'd met last year who talked so cheerily of twoing. And of Oria, and of the summer dances on our hills; and I realized, at last, how emotion-parched I was and how ignorant of the mysteries of love.

I had seen ardency in men's eyes, but I had only felt it once. With Flauvic, false and therefore easy to dismiss. I suddenly wished

412

that I could feel it now. No, I *did* feel it. I did have the same feeling, only I had masked it as restlessness, or as the exhortation to action, or as anger. I thought how wonderful it would be to see that spark now, in the right pair of eyes.

Looking away from the dancers, I glanced around the room—straight into Flauvic's coin-glinting gaze. He continued to stare straight at me across the width of the ballroom, those large eyes half closed, and a pensive smile on his perfect lips.

After a moment he started toward me at a deliberate pace.

And my first reaction was to panic.

I suppressed the urge to retreat, bolstering myself with the observation that he would never be so obvious as to touch me in public.

As if he read my mind his smile widened, just slightly, and when he was near enough to speak he bowed, hand on heart, and said, "I make you my compliments, Meliara. A remarkable achievement."

I did not ask what he meant.

For a time we stood there, watching the others, as the dancers wound about the floor in intersecting circles that drew imperceptibly tighter.

"Do you think your dances will become a fad again?" he asked, still watching.

"Depends who asks for them to be played—if anyone does," I said with a shrug. "You always could," I added. "Guaranteed, the latest rage."

He laughed, one thin, well-made hand rising in the fencer's salute for a hit. Then he stepped close, still without touching me, but I could smell the clean, astringent scent he used in his hair. "I wish," he murmured, "that you had been granted the right tutor."

Tutor in what? I was not about to ask.

And then he was on his way, bowing here, smiling there, a careless flick of the hand to a third. Moments later he was gone.

Though few had seen him go, his leaving seemed to constitute a kind of subtle signal, for slowly, as white wore on, my guests slipped away, many of them in pairs. Elenet left with the Orbanith family, all but her laughing.

The Renselaeuses came all three to thank me formally for a splendid—memorable—evening, and then departed in a group.

After they left, I felt tiredness pressing on my shoulders and eyelids; and though I stood there, back straight and smile steady on my aching face, I longed for my bed.

The lake blue light of morning was just paling the eastern windows when the last guests departed and I stepped wearily up to my rooms.

They were lit, and steaming listerblossom tea awaited. A surge of gratitude rose in me as I wondered how many times Mora had summoned fresh tea that I might come back to this.

I sank down onto my cushions, wondering if I'd be able to get up again to undress and climb into my bed. My hand clattered the cup and saucer as I poured—and then froze when I heard a slight noise come from my bedroom.

I froze, not breathing.

The tapestry stirred, and then, looking two steps from death, Azmus came forward and sank down onto his knees a pace away from me.

"They're going to war," he wheezed. "The Merindars. They're going to march on Remalna-city as soon as the last of their hirelings arrive."

TWENTY

I HEARD AZMUS'S WORDS, BUT AS YET THEY MADE NO sense.

So I held out my cup of tea. He took it carefully into his trembling fingers and downed it almost at one gulp. Then he gasped and blinked, and his eyes were noticeably clearer, though nothing could banish the bruiselike smudges under them.

"Now," I prompted, pouring more tea for him. "Tell me again."

"The Merindars," he said. "Forgive me, my lady. I have not left the saddle for nearly two days. Six horses—" He paused to drink. "I dared not entrust a message to anyone. Six horses I ran near to death, but I am here. After days and days of incremental progress and extrapolation by inference, I had luck at last and chanced to position myself to overhear a conversation between the Duke of Grumareth's valet and a scout from Denlieff. The Marquise of Merindar, the Duke, and three of their supporters are all ranged at the border. Over the last several months, 'volunteers' have poured into two of the northern garrisons. Those volunteers are mercenaries—at least the Marquise thinks they are mercenaries. They are soldiers from Denlieff."

"And they're going to march on us here?"

He nodded. "Taking each town as they come. But that is not all."

"Wait. Do the Renselaeuses know? I can't believe they haven't been investigating any of this."

"I don't know how much they know," he said. "I did see some of their equerries, the ones I recognized, but of course I never spoke to them, as you desired my investigations to remain secret."

He paused to drink again. His voice was a little stronger now. "You must realize the Renselaeus equerries are constrained by the past. In the countryside, there are those who are slow to trust them because of the ambivalent role that Shevraeth was forced to play under Galdran. I might therefore have access to better information." He smiled faintly, despite cracked lips, then he slurped down more tea. "So, to conclude, they probably know about the pending attack. That kind of thing is hard to hide if you know what you are looking for. But there is a further threat that no one knows, I'm sure, because I happened upon it only by accident."

"Speak," I said, gripping my hands together.

"Wagons of supplies," he said, fighting back a huge yawn that suddenly assailed him. "Had to hide in one. Supposed to be paving stone for road-building, and there was some, but only a thin layer. Under it—I know the smell—cut and stacked kinthus."

"*Kinthus?*" I repeated. "They're harvesting kinthus as, what, pay for the mercenaries?"

He shook his head, smiling bleakly. "You have never traveled beyond our borders, my lady. You have no idea how precious our rare woods are, for they *are* rare. Nowhere on this world is there anything like our colorwoods, especially the golden. What I overheard is that the Merindars and their allies have granted permission for the hired forces to take a given amount of colorwoods from Orbanith, Dharcarad—and Tlanth—in trade for military aid."

"But—the kinthus. Are they going to plant it?" I tried to get my tired mind to comprehend what I was hearing.

He shook his head, his face blanching again. "No. They will burn it."

416

Shock rang through my head as though someone had struck it. "Burn," I repeated stupidly. "Burn kinthus? In the woods? Then they must want to *kill* the Hill Folk! Is that it?"

"Easiest way to get the wood unmolested," he said.

I glanced up, to find Mora standing, still as a statue, just inside the servants' door. "My riding gear," I said to her. "And send someone to have the fastest and freshest mount saddled and ready. Please." To Azmus I said, "You've got to go over to the Royal Wing and tell Shevraeth. Tell him everything. Either him or the Prince and Princess. Only they can get an army raised here to meet those mercenaries."

"What are you going to do?" Azmus murmured, rising slowly to his feet.

I was already tearing at my laces, beyond considering the proprieties. "To warn the Hill Folk, of course," I said. "There is no one who knows how to find them as quickly as I do."

I dressed with reckless speed, tearing costly cloth and flinging jewels to the floor of my room like so many seed husks. As I dressed, Mora and a palace runner—who had suddenly appeared—discussed the best route I ought to take. No pretense of secrecy. We all had to work for the good of Remalna—of the Hill Folk. We all agreed that Orbanith was where I ought to go, for that was where the mountains jutted east. They both felt that the dangers of riding the river road were not as pressing as the need for speed. Also I'd be able to hire fresh horses at inns known to both; they told me their names, repeating them so I would remember.

Then I threw together a saddlebag of money and clothing, and departed, to find the horse I'd ordered waiting on the steps of the Residence Wing, held by a worried-looking stablehand. I knew without speaking that somehow the word was spreading through the palace—at least among the servants.

The bells of first-gold began ringing just as my horse dashed past the last houses of Remalna-city. Soft rain cooled my face, and the bracing wind helped revive me. I bent my head low and urged my mount to stretch into a canter so fast it seemed we flew over the road.

As we splashed eastward, I scanned ahead. If I saw any more than two riders, or anyone the least suspicious looking, I'd ride alongside the road, much as it slowed me. Though I had asked for a short saddle-sword, it was almost mere decoration. I knew how little I could defend myself against trained soldiers.

Occasionally the rain lifted briefly, enough to enable me to see ahead when I topped the gentle rises that undulated along the road. And after a time I realized that though no suspicious riders were approaching, for I had passed nothing but farmers and artisans going into the city, I was matching the pace of a single rider some distance before me. Twice, three times, I spotted the lone figure, cresting a hill just as I did. No bright colors of livery, only an anonymous dark cloak.

A messenger from Flauvic? Who else could it be? For Azmus would have reached the Royal Wing to speak his story just as I set out. No one sent by the Renselaeuses could possibly be ahead of me.

Of course the rider could be on some perfectly honest business affair that had nothing to do with the terrible threat of warfare looming like thunderclouds over the land. This thought comforted me for a hill or two, until a brief ray of light slanting down from between some clouds bathed the rider in light, striking a cold gleam off a steel helm.

Merchants' runners did not wear helms. A messenger, then.

I rode on, squinting ahead despite a sudden downpour that severely limited visibility. It also slowed my horse. Despite the paved road, the deep puddles interfered with speed and made the ride more of an effort. When bells rang over the hills, indicating the change from gold to green, both my horse and I were weary.

The plan had been for me to halt at the Farjoon Anchor. My drooping horse could stop, I decided, though whether or not I did would depend on what the rider ahead did.

Presently I crested a hill. Spread below me in a little valley was the village I'd been told to look for. I scanned the road ahead and saw the mysterious rider splash up the narrow lane into the village, disappearing among the small cluster of houses.

My mount trotted slowly down the hill and into the village. The inn was a long, low building in the center, with an anchor painted on its swinging sign. I hunched into my wet cloak, though no one could possibly recognize me, and slid off my steaming mount as stablehands ran to the bridle. "Fresh horse," I said, surprised at how husky my voice came out—and when my feet hit the mud, the world seemed to spin for a moment.

Before I ate or drank I had to find out who that rider was.

I stepped into the common room, scanning the few people seated on cushions at the low, rough tables. They all had gray, brown, or blue cloaks hung behind them, or hats. No dark cloaks or helms. So I wandered farther inside and encountered a young woman about my age.

"Hot punch? Stew?" she offered, wiping her hands on her apron.

"My companion came in just ahead of me. Wearing a helm. Where—"

"Oh! The other runner? Wanted a private room. Third down, that hall," she said cheerily. "What'll I bring you?"

"I'll order in a moment." The savory aroma of stew had woken my insides fiercely, and I realized that I had not eaten a bite the entire day before.

As I trod down the hall, I made and discarded plausible excuses. When I reached the tapestry I decided against speaking at all. I'd just take a quick peek, and if the livery was Merindar, then I'd have to hire someone to ride back and warn the Renselaeuses.

I pulled my soggy cloak up around my eyes, stuck out my gloved finger, and poked gently at the edge of the tapestry.

Remember the surmise I recorded on my arrival at the Residence that day in early spring—that if anyone were to know everyone's business, it would be the servants?

419

I glanced inside in time to see a pale, familiar face jerk up.

And for a long, amazing moment, there we were, Meliara and Shevraeth, mud-spattered and wet, just like last year, looking at one another in silence. Then I snatched my hand back, now thoroughly embarrassed, and spun around intending retreat. But I moved too fast for my tired head and fell against the wall, as once again the world lurched around me.

I heard the faint metallic *ching* of chain mail, and suddenly he was there, his hand gripping my arm. Without speaking, he drew me inside the bare little parlor and pointed silently at a straw-stuffed cushion. My legs folded abruptly, and I plopped down.

"Azmus—" I croaked. "How could you—I sent him—"

"Drink." Shevraeth put a mug into my hands. "Then we can talk."

Obediently I took a sip, felt sweet coffee burn its way pleasantly down my throat and push back the fog threatening to enfold my brain. I took a longer draught, then sighed.

The Marquis looked back at me, his face tense and tired, his eyes dark with an intensity that sent a complexity of emotions chasing through me like darting starlings.

"How did you get ahead of me so fast?" I said. "I don't understand."

His eyes widened in surprise, as if he'd expected to hear anything but that. "How," he asked slowly, "did you know I was here? We told no one when I was leaving, or my route, outside of two servants."

"I *didn't* know you were here," I said. "I sent Azmus to you. With the news. About the Merindars. You mean you already *knew*?"

"Let us backtrack a little," he said, "if you will bear with my lamentable slowness. I take it, then, that you were not riding thus speedily to join me?" With his old sardonic tone he added, "Because if you were, your retreat just now is somewhat puzzling, you'll have to admit."

I said indignantly, "I peeked in because I thought you might

420

be one of the Merindars, and if so, I'd send a warning back to you. I mean, you if you were there. Does that make sense?" I frowned, shook my head, then gulped down the rest of the coffee.

He smiled just slightly, but the intensity had not left his eyes. The serving maid came in, carrying a bowl of food and some fresh bread. "Will you have some as well?" she said to me.

"Please," Shevraeth said before I could speak. "And more coffee." He waited until she went out, then said, "Now, begin again, please. What is it you're trying to tell me, and where are you going?"

"I'm going to Orbanith," I said, and forced myself to look away from the steam curling up from the stew at his elbow. My mouth watered. I swallowed and turned my attention to pulling off my sodden gloves. "I guess I am trying to tell you what you already seem to know—that the Merindars are going on the attack, with hired mercenaries from Denlieff. But—why do you want me to tell you when you *do* already know all this?" I looked up from wringing out my gloves.

"I am trying," he said with great care, "to ascertain what your place is in the events about to transpire, and to act accordingly. From whom did you get your information?"

The world seemed to lurch again, but this time it was not my vision. A terrible sense of certainty pulled at my heart and mind as I realized what he was striving so heroically not to say—nevertheless, what he meant.

He thought I was on the other side.

Seen from an objective perspective, it was entirely possible that *I* was the phantom messenger from the Merindars. After all, last year I'd made a try for the crown. Since then, on the surface I'd been an implacable enemy to Shevraeth—and even though that had changed, I had not given any sign of those changes. Meanwhile I seemed to have suddenly acquired information that no one else in Athanarel had. Except for him.

And, probably, Flauvic.

I saw it now, the real reason why Flauvic had made the public gestures of friendship with me. What an easy way to foster Shevraeth's distrust, to force him to divide his attentions! The most recent gesture having been just measures ago at my ball.

The maid came in with another bowl and bread, then, and set them at my elbow, but I scarcely heeded the food. Now I couldn't eat. I couldn't even explain, because anything I gabbled out would seem mere contrivance. The fact was, I had refused all along any kind of straightforward communication with the man now sitting across from me, and too many lives were at stake for him to risk being wrong.

The real tragedy was that there were too many lives at stake in both races. And so even though I could comprehend why I might end up as a prisoner, just like last year, I also knew that I would fight, as hard as I was capable, to remain free.

I looked at him, sick and miserable.

"Tell me where you got your information," he said.

"Azmus. Our old spy." My lips were numb, and I started to shiver. Hugging my arms against my stomach, I said, "My reasons were partly stupid and partly well-meaning, but I sent him to find out what the Marquise was after. She wrote me during winter—but you knew about that."

He nodded.

"And you even tried to warn me, though at the time I saw it as a threat, because—well, because." I felt too sick inside to go on about that. Drawing a shaky breath, I said, "And again. At her party, when she took me into the conservatory. She tried again to get me to join her. Said I hadn't kept my vows to Papa. So I summoned Azmus to help me find out what to do. The right thing. I know I can't prove it," I finished lamely.

He pulled absently at the fingers of one glove, then looked down at it, and straightened it again. Unnecessary movements from him were so rare, I wondered if he too was fighting for clear thought.

422

He lifted his gaze to me. "And now? You were riding to the border?"

"No," I said. "To Orbanith."

Again he showed surprise.

"It's the other thing that Azmus found out," I said quickly. "I sent him to tell you as soon as I learned—but there's no way for you to know that's true. I realize it. Still, I *did*. I have to go because I know how to reach the Hill Folk."

"The Hill Folk?"

"Yes," I said, leaning forward. "The kinthus. The Merindars have it stowed in wagons, and they're going to burn it up-slope. Carried on the winds, it can kill Hill Folk over a full day's ride, all at once. That's how they're paying Denlieff, with our woods, not with money at all. They're breaking our Covenant! I *have* to warn the Hill Folk!"

"Orbanith. Why there, why this road?"

"Mora and the servants told me this was the fastest way to Orbanith."

"Why did you not go south to Tlanth where you know the Hill Folk?"

I shook my head impatiently. "You don't *know* them. You can't know them. They don't have names, or if they do, they don't tell them to us. They seem to be aware of each other's concerns, for if you see one, then suddenly others will appear, all silent. And if they act, it's at once. Some of the old songs say that they walk in one another's dreams, which I think is a poetic way of saying they can speak mind to mind. I don't know. I *must* get to the mountains to warn them, and the mountains that source the Piaum River are the closest to Remalna-city."

"And no one else knows of this?" he asked gently.

I shook my head slowly, unable to remove my gaze from his face. "Azmus discovered it by accident. Rode two days to reach me. I did send him..."

There was no point in saying it again. Either he believed me, and—I swallowed painfully—I'd given him no particular reason to, or he didn't. Begging, pleading, arguing, ranting—none of them would make any difference, except to make a horrible situation worse.

I should have made amends from the beginning, and now it was too late.

He took a deep breath. I couldn't breathe, I just stared at him, waiting, feeling sweat trickle beneath my already soggy clothing.

Then he smiled a little. "Brace up. We're not about to embark on a duel to the death over the dishes." He paused, then said lightly, "Though most of our encounters until very recently have been unenviable exchanges, you have never lied to me. Eat. We'll leave before the next time-change, and part ways at the crossroads."

No "You've never lied *before*." No "*If* I can trust you.'" No warnings or hedgings. He took all the responsibility—and the risk—himself. I didn't know why, and to thank him for believing me would just embarrass us both. So I said nothing, but my eyes prickled. I looked down at my lap and busied myself with smoothing out my mud-gritty, wet gloves.

"Why don't you set aside that cloak and eat something?"

His voice was flat. I realized he probably felt even nastier about the situation than I did. I heard the scrape of a bowl on the table and the clink of a spoon. The ordinary sounds restored me somehow, and I untied my cloak and shrugged it off. At once a weight that seemed greater than my own left me. I made a surreptitious swipe at my eyes, straightened my shoulders, and did my best to assume nonchalance as I picked up my spoon.

After a short time, he said, "Don't you have any questions for me?"

I glanced up, my spoon poised midway between my bowl and my mouth. "Of course," I said. "But I thought—" I started to wave my hand, realizing too late it still held the spoon, and winced as stew spattered down the table. Somehow the ridiculousness of it released some of the tension. As I mopped at the mess with a corner

424

of my cloak, I said, "Well, it doesn't matter what I thought. So you knew about the plot all along?"

"Pretty much from the beginning, though the timing is new. I surmised they would make their move in the fall, but something seems to have precipitated action. My first warning was from Elenet, who had found out a great deal from the Duke's servants. That was her real reason for coming to Court, to tell me herself."

"What about Flauvic?"

"It would appear," he said carefully, "that he disassociated with this plan of his mother's."

"Was that the argument he alluded to?"

He did not ask when. "Perhaps. Though that might have been for effect. I can believe it only because it is uncharacteristic for him to lend himself to so stupid and clumsy a plan."

"Finesse," I drawled in a parody of a courtier's voice. "He'd want finesse, and to make everyone else look foolish."

Shevraeth smiled slightly. "Am I to understand you were not favorably impressed with Lord Flauvic?"

"As far as I'm concerned, he and Fialma are both thorns," I said, "though admittedly he is very pretty to look at. More so than his sour pickle of a sister. Anyway, I hope you aren't trusting him as far as you can lift a mountain, because I wouldn't."

"His house is being watched. He can't stir a step outside without half a riding being within earshot."

"And he probably knows it," I said, grinning. "Last question, why are you riding alone? Wouldn't things be more effective with your army?"

"I move fastest alone," he said. "And my own people are in place, and have been for some time."

I thought of Nessaren—and the fact that I hadn't seen her around Athanarel for weeks.

"When I want them," he said, reaching into the pouch at his belt, "I will summon them with this." And he held up something that glowed blue briefly: the summons-stone I had seen so long ago. "Each riding has one. At the appropriate moment, we will converge and, ah, convince the Marquise and her allies to accompany us back to Athanarel. It is the best way of avoiding bloodshed."

In the distance the time-change rang. "What about those Denlieff warriors?" I asked.

"If their leaders are unable to give them orders, they will have to take orders from me."

I thought about the implied threat, then shook my head. "I'm glad I have the easy job," I said. "Speaking of which..."

He smiled. "There's a room adjacent. I suggest you change your clothes and ride dry for a time." Before I could say anything, he rose, stepped to the tapestry, and summoned the maid.

Very soon I was in the little bedroom, struggling out of my soggy clothing. It felt good to get into dry things, though I knew I wouldn't be dry long. There was no hope for my cloak, except to wring it out and put it back on. But when I left the room, I found my cloak gone, and in its place a long, black, waterproof one that I recognized at once.

With very mixed feelings I pulled it on, gathering it up in my arms so it wouldn't drag on the ground behind me. Then I settled my hat on my head, and very soon I was on the road to the east.

TWENTY-ONE

I WAS VERY GRATEFUL FOR THAT CLOAK BEFORE MY
journey's end.

The weather steadily turned worse. I forbore hiring horses in
favor of sturdy mountain ponies, on whose broad backs I could doze
a little.

For I did not dare to stop. The driving rain and the deep mud
made a swift pace impossible. Halting only to change mounts and
stuff some hasty bites of food into my mouth, I kept going, even
in the dark, and hired a glowglobe to carry with me as I neared the
mountains.

The third morning I reached the foothills below Mount Toar.
My road rounded a high cliff from which I could see the road to
the northwest. On this road I descried a long line of wagons
trundling their way inexorably toward the mountains. They were
probably half a day's journey behind me—and I knew that they
wouldn't have to go as high.

This sight was enough to kindle my tired body into renewed
effort.

At the next inn, I mentioned the wagons to a friendly stablehand as I waited for my new mount. "Do you know anything about
them?"

The stablegirl gave me a quick grin. "Sure do," she said cheerily. "Orders came straight from the Duke of Grumareth himself, I'm told. Those wagons are full of paving stones for the castle upmountain. Halt 'em, get in the way, and you're dead. Too bad! We wouldn't mind pinching a few. Maybe next time they'll think of us. Ever seen such a wet summer? Roads are like soup."

I thanked her and left, my spirits dampening again. So much for rousing the locals to stop those wagons. Of course they might be willing to fight for the Covenant despite the orders given the Duke's forces—but what if these were not the right wagons? And even if they were, sending unarmed villagers against warriors would be a slaughter. All I could think was that I had to solve this myself.

I bought some bread and cheese, and was soon on my way, eating as I rode. Very soon the rain returned, splashing down at a slant. I pulled the edge of Shevraeth's cloak up onto my head and my hat over it, then arranged the rest as a kind of tent around me, peering through the thin opening to see the road ahead. Not that I had to look, except for the occasional low branch, for the pony seemed to know its way.

As we climbed, the air got colder. But when the woods closed around me at last, I forgot about the discomfort. I was breathing the scents of home again, the indefinable combination of loam and moss and wood and fern that I had loved all my life.

And I sensed presence.

The woods were quiet, except for the tapping of raindrops on leaves and, once or twice, the sudden crash and scamper of hidden animals breaking cover and retreating. No birds, no great beasts. Yet I felt watchers.

And so, tired as I was, I tipped back my head and began to sing.

At the best of times I don't have the kind of voice anyone would want to hear mangling their favorite songs. Now my throat was dry and scratchy, but I did what I could, singing wordlessly some of the old, strange patterns, not quite melodies, that I'd heard in my childhood. I sang my loudest, and at first echoes rang off stones and trees and down into hollows. After a time my voice dropped to a husky squeak, but as the light bent west and turned golden, I heard a rustle, and suddenly I was surrounded by Hill Folk, more of them than I had ever seen at once before.

They did not speak. Somewhere in the distance I heard the breathy, slightly sinister cry of a reed pipe.

I began to talk, not knowing if they understood words, such as "Marquise" and "mercenary," or if they somehow took the images from my thoughts. I told them about the Merindars, and Flauvic, and the Renselaeuses, ending with what Azmus had told me. I described the wagons on the road behind me. I finally exhorted them to go south and hide, and that we—Shevraeth and his people and I—would first get rid of the kinthus, then find a way to keep the Covenant.

When I ran out of words, for a long moment there was that eerie stillness, so soundless yet full of presence. Then they moved, their barky hides dappling with shadows, until they disappeared with a rustling sound like wind through the trees.

I was alone again, but I felt no sense of danger. My pony lifted her head and blinked at me. She hadn't reacted at all to being surrounded by Hill Folk.

"All right," I said to her. "First thing, water. And then we have some wagons to try to halt. Or I do. I suppose your part will be to reappear at the inn as mute testimony to the fallen heroine."

We stopped at a stream. I drank deeply of the sweet, cold water and splashed my face until it was numb. Then we started on the long ride down. From time to time quick flutings of reed pipes echoed from peak to peak, and from very far away, the rich chordal hum of the distant windharps answered. Somehow these sounds lifted my spirits.

I remained cheery, too, as if the universe had slipped into a kind of dream existence. I was by now far beyond mere tiredness, so that nothing seemed real. In fact, until I topped a rise and saw the twenty wagons stretched out in a formidable line directly below me, the worst reaction I had to rain, to stumbles, to my burning eyes, was a tendency to snicker.

The wagons sobered me.

I stayed where I was, squarely in the center of the muddy road, and waited for them to ascend my hill. I had plenty of time to count them, all twenty, as they rumbled slowly toward me, pulled by teams of draught horses. When I caught the quick gleam of metal on the hill beyond them—the glint of an errant ray of sun on helms and shields—my heart started a rapid tattoo inside my chest.

But I stayed where I was. Twenty wagons. If the unknown riders were reinforcements to the enemy, I couldn't be in worse trouble than I already was. *But if they weren't…*

"Halt," I said, when the first wagon driver was in earshot.

He'd already begun to pull up the horses, but I felt it sounded good to begin on an aggressive note.

"Out of the way," the man sitting next to the driver bawled. Despite their both being clad in the rough clothing of wagoneers, their bearing betrayed the fact that they were warriors.

That and the long swords lying between them on the bench.

"But your way lies back to the north," I pointed.

The second driver in line, a female, even bigger and tougher looking than the leader, had dismounted. She stood next to the first wagon, squinting up at me in a decidedly unfriendly manner. She and the leader exchanged looks, then she said, "We have a delivery to make in yon town."

"The road to the town lies that way," I said, pointing behind me. "You're heading straight for the mountains. There's nothing up here."

They both grinned. "That's a matter for us and not for you. Be about your business, citizen, or we'll have to send you on your way."

"And you won't like the way we do the sending," the woman added.

They both laughed nastily.

I crossed my arms. "You can drop the paving stones here if you wish, but you'll have to take the kinthus back to Denlieff."

Their smiles disappeared.

I glanced up—to see that the road behind the last wagon was empty. The mysterious helmed riders had disappeared. What did that mean?

No time to find out.

"Now, how did you know about that?" the man said, and this time there was no mistaking the threat in his voice. He laid his hand significantly on his sword hilt.

"It's my business, as you said." I tried my best to sound assured, waving my sodden arm airily in my best Court mode.

The woman bowed with exaggerated politeness. "And who might you be, Your Royal Highness?" she asked loudly.

The leader, and the third and fourth drivers who had just joined the merry group, guffawed.

"I am Meliara Astiar, Countess of Tlanth," I said.

Again the smiles diminished, but not all the way. The leader eyed me speculatively for a long breath. "Well, then, you seem to have had mighty good skill in the past, if half the stories be true, but even if they are, what good's your skill against forty of us?"

"How do you know I don't have eighty-one armed soldiers waiting behind that rise over there?" I waved my other hand vaguely mountainward.

They thought that was richly funny.

"Because if you did," the female said, "they'd be out here and we wouldn't be jawin'. Come on, Kess, we've wasted enough time here. Let's shift her majesty off our road and be on our way."

The man picked up his sword and vaulted down from his wagon. I yanked my short sword free and climbed down from my pony. When I reached the ground, the world swayed, and I staggered back against the animal, then righted myself with an effort.

The man and woman stood before me, both with long swords

431

gripped in big hands. They eyed me with an odd mixture of threat and puzzlement that made that weird, almost hysterical laughter bubble up inside my shaky innards. But I kept my lips shut and hefted my sword.

"Well?" the woman said to her leader.

They both looked at me again. I barely came up to the middle of the shortest one's chest, and my blade was about half the length and heft of theirs.

The man took a slow swing at me, which I easily parried. His brows went up slightly; he swung again, faster, and when I parried that he feinted toward my shoulder. Desperately, my heart now pounding in my ears, I blocked the next strike and the next, but just barely. His blade whirled faster, harder, and that block shook me right down to my heels. The man dropped his point and said, "*You're* the one that whupped Galdran Merindar?"

Unbidden, Shevraeth's voice spoke inside my head: "You have never lied to me..." I thought desperately, *Better late than never!* And for a brief moment I envisioned myself snarling *Yes, ha ha! And I minced fifty more like him, so you'd better run!* Except it wasn't going to stop them; I could see it in their eyes and in the way the woman gripped her sword.

"No," I said. "He knocked me off my horse. But I'd taken an oath, so I had to do my best." I drew in a shaky breath. "I know I can't fight forty of you, but I'm going to stand here and block you until you either go away or my arms fall off, because this, too, is an oath I took."

The woman muttered something in their home language. Her stance, her tone, made it almost clear it was "I don't like this."

And he said something in a hard voice, his eyes narrowed. It had to mean "We have no choice. Better her than us." And he took up a guard position again, his muscles tightening.

My sweaty hand gripped my sword, and I raised it, gritting my teeth—

And there came the beat of hooves on the ground. All three of us went still. Either this was reinforcements for them, in which case I was about to become a prisoner—or a ghost—or...

Blue and black and white tunicked riders thundered down through the trees toward the wagons. On the other side of the road, another group rounded the rise, and within the space of ten heartbeats, the wagons were surrounded by nine ridings of warriors, a full wing, all with lances pointed and swords at the ready.

One of them flashed a grin my way—Nessaren! Then my attention was claimed when the wing commander trotted up, stopped, and bowed low over his horse's withers. "Your orders, my lady?" He was utterly serious, but the impulse to dissolve into helpless laughter was shaking my already watery insides. "These gentle people may unload their stones, and pile them neatly for the locals to collect," I said. "And then the drivers and their companions are yours. I think local villagers might be hired to drive the cargo of the wagons to the sea. Brine-soaked kinthus won't hurt anyone and becomes mere wood. The wagons then might be offered to said villagers as partial payment."

The wing commander bowed again, turned, and issued orders. I noted from the salutes that Nessaren had risen in rank—she now appeared to have three ridings under her.

Within a very short time, the prisoners were marched off in one direction and the wagons trundled slowly in another, driven by warriors whose fellows had taken their horses' reins.

All except for one riding. Nessaren presented herself to me and said, "My lady, if it pleases you, I have specific orders."

"And they are?"

"You're to come with us to the nearest inn, where you are to sleep for at least two candles. And then—"

I didn't even hear the "and then." Suddenly, very suddenly, it was all I could do to climb back onto my pony. Nessaren saw this and, with a gesture, got her group to surround me. In tight formation we rode slowly back down the mountain....

And I dismounted...

And walked inside the inn...

I don't even remember falling onto the bed.

The next morning I awoke to find a tray of hot food and drink awaiting me, and, even better, my wet clothes from my saddlebag, now dry and fresh.

When I emerged from the room, I found the riding all waiting, their gear on and horses ready.

I turned to Nessaren. Until that moment I hadn't considered what it meant to have them with me. Was it possible I was a prisoner?

She bowed. "We're ready to ride, my lady, whenever you like."

"Ride?" I repeated.

She grinned—all of them grinned. "We thought you'd want to get caught up on events as quick as could be." Her eyes went curiously blank as she added, "If you wish, we can ride to the city. We're yours to command."

An honor guard, then.

I rubbed my hands together. "And be left out of the action?" They laughed, obviously well pleased with my decision. In very short order we were flying westward on fast horses, scarcely slowed by a light rain. The roads down-mountain were good, and so we made excellent progress. At the end of the day's ride, we halted on a hill, and Nessaren produced from her saddlebag a summons-stone. She looked down at it, turning slowly in a circle until it gleamed a bright blue, and then she pointed to the north. We rode in that direction until we reached an inn, and next morning she did the same thing.

That afternoon we rode into an armed camp. I glanced about at the orderly tents, the soldiers in battle tunics of green and gold mixing freely with those in the blue with the three white stars above the black coronet. As we rode into the camp, sending mud flying everywhere, people stopped what they were doing to watch. The closest ones bowed. I found this odd, for I hadn't even been bowed to by our own warriors during our putative revolt. Attempting a Court curtsy from the back of a horse while clad in grubby, wet clothes and someone else's cloak didn't seem right, so I just smiled, and was glad when we came to a halt before a large tent.

Stablehands ran to the bridles and led the horses to a picket as Nessaren and I walked into the tent. Inside was a kind of controlled pandemonium. Scribes and runners were everywhere that low tables and cushions weren't. Atop the tables lay maps and piles of papers, plus a number of bags of coinage. In a corner was stacked a small but deadly arsenal of very fine swords.

Seated in the midst of the chaos was Shevraeth, dressed in the green and gold of Remalna, with a commander's plumed and cor-oneted helm on the table beside him. He appeared to be listening to five people, all of whom were talking at once. One by one they received from him quick orders, and they vanished in different di-rections. Then he saw us, and his face relaxed slightly. Until that moment, I hadn't realized he was tense.

Meanwhile the rest of his people had taken note of our arrival, and all were silent as he rose and came around the table to stand before us. "*Twenty* wagons, Lady Meliara?" he said, one brow lifting.

I shrugged, fighting against acute embarrassment.

"We've a wager going." His neatly gloved hand indicated the others in the tent. "How many, do you think, would have been too many for you to take on single-handed?"

"My thinking was this," I said, trying to sound casual, though by then my face felt as red as a glowing Fire Stick. "Two of them would trounce me as easy as twenty wagons' worth. The idea was to talk them out of trying. Luckily Nessaren and the rest of the wing arrived when they did, or I suspect I soon would have been part of the road."

Shevraeth's mouth was perfectly controlled, but his eyes gleamed with repressed laughter as he said, "That won't do, my

435

lady. I am very much afraid if you're going to continue to attempt heroic measures you will have to make suitably heroic statements afterward—"

"If there is an afterward," I muttered, and someone in the avidly watching group choked on a laugh.

"—such as are written in the finest of our histories."

"Huh," I said. "I guess I'll just have to memorize a few proper heroic bombasts, rhymed in three places, for next time. And I'll also remember to take a scribe to get it all down right."

He laughed—they all did. They laughed much harder than the weak joke warranted, and I realized that events had not been so easy here.

I unclasped his cloak and handed it over. "I'm sorry about the hem," I said, feeling suddenly shy. "Got a bit muddy."

He slung the cloak over one arm and gestured to a waiting cushion. "Something hot to drink?"

A young cadet came forward with a tray and steaming coffee. I busied myself choosing a cup, sitting down, and striving to reestablish within myself a semblance of normalcy. While I sipped at my coffee, one by one the staff finished their chores and vanished through the tent flaps, until at last Shevraeth and I were alone.

He turned to face me. "Questions?"

"Of course! What happened?"

He sat down across from me. "Took 'em by surprise," he said. "That part was easy enough. The worst of it has been the aftermath."

"You captured the commanders, then. The Marquise and—"

"Her daughter, the two mercenary captains, the two sellout garrison commanders, the Denlieff wing commander, Barons Chaskar and Hurnaev, and Baroness Orgaliun, to be precise. Grumareth's nowhere to be found; my guess is that he got cold feet and scampered for home. If so, he'll find some of my people waiting for him."

"So the Marquise is a prisoner somewhere?" I asked, enjoying the idea.

He grimaced. "No. She took poison. A constitutional inability to suffer reverses, apparently. We didn't find out until too late. Fialma," he added drily, "tried to give her share to me."

"That must have been a charming scene."

"It took place at approximately the same time you were conversing with your forty wagoneers." He smiled a little. "Since then I have dispatched the real mercenaries homeward, unpaid, and sent some people to make certain they get over the border. What they do in Denlieff is their ruler's problem. Fialma is on her way back—under guard—to Sles Adran, where I expect she'll become a permanent royal Court pest. The Denlieff soldiers I'm keeping in garrison until the ambassador can squeeze an appropriate trade agreement from his soon-to-be apologetic king and queen. The two sellouts we executed, and I have trusted people combing through the rest to find out who was coerced and who not."

"Half will be lying, of course."

"More. It's a bad business, and complete justice is probably a dream. But the word will get out, and I hope it won't be so easy to raise such a number again."

I sighed. "Then the Merindar threat is over."

"I sincerely hope so."

"You do not sound convinced."

He said, "I confess I'll feel more convinced when the courier from Athanarel gets here."

"Courier?"

"Arranged with my parents. Once a day, even if the word was 'no change.' Only she's late."

"How late?" I asked, thinking of a couple of measures, or maybe a candle, or even two. "The rain was bad yesterday—"

"A day."

Warning prickled at the back of my neck. "Oh, but surely if there was a problem, someone would either send a runner or come in person."

"That's the most rational way to consider it," he agreed.

"And of course you sent someone to see if something happened to the expected courier? I mean something ordinary, like the horse threw a shoe, or the courier fell and sprained her leg?"

He nodded. "I'll wait until the end of blue, and make a decision then." He looked up. "In the meantime, do you have any more questions for me?" His voice was uninflected, but the drawl was gone.

I knew that the time for the political discussion was past, for now, and that here at last were the personal issues that had lain between us for so long. I took a deep breath. "No questions. But I have apologies to make. I think, well, I *know* that I owe you some explanations. For things I said. And did. Stupid things."

He lifted a hand. "Before you proceed any further..." He gave me a rueful half smile as he started pulling off his gloves, one finger at a time. When the left one was off he said, "This might be one of the more spectacular of *my* mistakes—" With a last tug, he pulled off the right, and I saw the glint of gold on his hand.

As he laid aside the gloves and turned back to face me, I saw the ring on his littlest finger, a gold ring carved round with laurel leaves in a particular pattern. And set in the middle was an ekirth that glittered like a nightstar.

"That's my ring," I said, numb with shock.

"You had it made," he replied. "But now it's mine."

I can't say that everything suddenly became clear to me, because it didn't. I realized only that he was the Unknown, and that I was both horrified and relieved. Suddenly there was too much to say, but nothing I *could* say.

As it turned out, I didn't have to try. I looked up to see him smiling, and I realized that, as usual, he'd been able to read my face easily.

By then my blood was drumming in my ears like distant thunder.

"It is time," he said, "to collect on my wager."

He moved slowly. First, his hands sliding round me and cool light-colored hair drifting against my cheek, and then softly, so

438

softly, the brush of lips against my brow, my eyes, and then my lips. Once, twice, thrice, but no closer. The sensations—like starfire—that glowed through me chased away from my head all thoughts save one, to close that last distance between us.

I locked my fingers round his neck and pulled his face again down to mine.

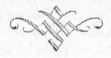

TWENTY-TWO

I DIDN'T WANT THAT KISS TO EVER STOP. HE DIDN'T
seem to, either.

But after a time, I realized the drumming sound I heard was
not my heart, it was hoofbeats, and they were getting louder.

We broke apart, and his breathing was as ragged as mine. We
heard through the tent the guard stop the courier, and the courier's
response, "But I have to report right away!"

A moment later the courier was in the tent, muddy to the chin,
and weaving as he tried to stand at attention. "You said to return
if I found Keira, or if I saw anything amiss," he gasped out.

"And?" Shevraeth prompted.

"Streets are empty," the courier said, knuckling his eyes. I
winced in sympathy. "Arrived...second-gold. Ought to have been
full. No one out. Not a dog or a cat. No sign of Keira, either.
Didn't try to speak to anyone. Turned around, rode back as fast as
I could."

"Good. You did the right thing. Go to the cook tent and get
something to eat. You're off duty."

The courier bowed and withdrew, staggering once.

Shevraeth looked grimly across the tent at me. "Ready for a
ride?"

It was well past sunset before we got away. All the details that couldn't be settled had to be delegated, which meant explanations and alternative orders. But at last we were on the road, riding flat out for the capital. The wind and our speed made conversation under a shout impossible, so for a long time we rode in silence.

It was just as well, leastwise for me. I really needed time to think, and—so I figured—if my life was destined to continue at such a headlong pace, I was going to have to learn to perform my cerebrations while dashing back and forth cross-country at the gallop.

Of course my initial thoughts went right back to that kiss, and for a short time I thought wistfully about how much I'd been missing. But I realized that, though it was splendid in a way nothing had been hitherto and I hoped there'd be plenty more—and soon—it didn't solve any of the puzzles whose pieces I'd only recently begun to comprehend. If anything, it made things suddenly more difficult.

I wished that I had Nee to talk to, or better, Oria. Except what would be the use? Neither of them had ever caused someone to initiate a courtship by letter.

I sighed, glad for the gentle rain, and for the darkness, as I made myself reconsider all of my encounters with Shevraeth—this time from, as much as I was able, his perspective.

This was not a pleasant exercise. By the time we stopped, sometime after white-change, to get fresh horses and food and drink, I was feeling contrite and thoroughly miserable.

We stepped into the very inn in which we'd had our initial conversation; we passed the little room I had stood outside of, and I shuddered. Now we had a bigger one, but I was too tired to notice much beyond comfortable cushions and warmth. As I sank down, I saw glowing rings around the candles and rubbed my eyes.

When I looked up at Shevraeth, it was in time to catch the end of one of those assessing glances. Then he smiled, a real smile of humor and tenderness.

"I knew it," he said. "I knew that by now you would have managed to see everything as your fault, and you'd be drooping under the weight."

"Why did you do it?" I answered, too tired to even try to keep my balance. Someone set down a tray of hot chocolate, and I hiccuped, snorted in a deep breath, and with an attempt at the steadying influence of laughter, added, "Near as I can see I've been about as pleasant to be around as an angry bee swarm."

"At times," he agreed. "But I take our wretched beginning as my own fault. I merely wanted to intimidate you—and through you, your brother—into withdrawing from the field. What a mess you made of my plans! Every single day I had to re-form them. I'd get everyone and everything set on a new course, and you'd manage to hare off and smash it to shards again, all with the best of motives, and actions as gallant as ever I've seen, from man or woman." He smiled, but I just groaned into my chocolate. "By the time I realized I was going to have to figure you into the plans, you were having none of me, or them. At the same time, you managed to win everyone you encountered—save the Merindars—to your side."

"I understand about the war. And I even understand why you had to come to Tlanth." I sighed. "But that doesn't explain the letters."

"I think I fell in love with you the day you stood before Galdran in the Throne Room, surrounded by what you thought were enemies, and glared at him without a trace of fear. I knew it when you sat across from me at your table in Tlanth and argued so passionately about the fairest way to disperse an army, with no other motive besides testing your theories. It also became clear to me on that visit that you showed one face to all the rest of the world, and another to me. But after you had been at Athanarel a week, Russav insisted that my cause was not hopeless."

"Savona? How did he know?"

The Marquis shook his head. "You'd have to address that question to him."

I rubbed my eyes again. "So his flirtation *was* false."

"I asked him to make you popular," Shevraeth admitted. "Though he will assure you that he found the task thoroughly enjoyable. I wanted your experience of Court to be as easy as possible. Your brother just shrugged off the initial barbs and affronts, but I knew they'd slay you. We did our best to protect you from them, though your handling of the situation with Tamara showed us that you were very capable of directing your own affairs."

"What about Elenet?" I asked, and winced, hating to sound like the kind of jealous person I admired least. But the image of that goldenwood throne had entered my mind and would not be banished.

He looked slightly surprised. "What about her?"

"People—some people—put your names together. And," I added firmly, "she'd make a good queen. Better than I."

He lifted his cup, and I saw my ring gleaming on his finger. He'd worn that since he left Bran and Nee's ball. He'd been wearing it, I thought, when we sat in this very inn and he went through that terrible inner debate on whether or not I was a traitor.

I dropped my head and stared into my cup.

"Elenet," he said, "is an old friend. We grew up together and regard one another as brother and sister, a comfortable arrangement since neither of us had siblings."

I thought of that glance she'd given him when I spied on them in the Royal Wing courtyard. She had betrayed feelings that were not sisterly. But he hadn't seen that look because his heart lay otherwise.

I pressed my lips together. She was worthy, but her love was not returned. Suddenly I understood why she had been so guarded around me. The honorable course for me would be to keep to myself what I had seen.

Shevraeth continued, "She spent her time with me as a mute

443

warning to the Merindars, who had to know that she came to report on Grumareth's activities, and I didn't want them trying any kind of retaliation. She realized that our social proximity would cause gossip. That was inevitable. But she heeded it not; she just wants to return to Grumareth and resume guiding her lands to prosperity again." He paused, then said, "As for her quality, it is undeniable. But I think the time has come for a different perspective, one that is innate in you. It is a problem, I have come to realize, with our Court upbringing. No one, including Elenet, has the gift you have of looking every person you encounter in the face and accepting the person behind the status. We all were raised to see servants and merchants as faceless as we pursued the high strategy. I'm half convinced this is part of the reason why the kingdom ended up in the grip of the likes of the Merindars."

I nodded, and for the first time comprehended what a relationship with him really meant for the rest of my life. "The goldenwood throne," I said. "In the letter. I thought you had it ordered for, well, someone else."

His smile was gone. "It doesn't yet exist. How could it? Though I intend for there to be one, for the duties of ruling have to begin as a partnership. Until the other night, I had no idea if I would win you or not."

"Win me," I repeated. "What a contest!"

He smiled, but continued. "I was beginning to know you through the letters, but in person you showed me that same resentful face. Life! That day you came into the alcove looking for histories, I was sitting there writing to you. What a coil!"

For the first time I laughed, though it was somewhat painful.

"But I took the risk of mentioning the throne as a somewhat desperate attempt to bridge the two. When you stopped writing and walked around for two days looking lost, it was the very first sign that I had any hope."

"Meanwhile you had all this to deal with." I waved northward, indicating the Marquise's plots.

"It was a distraction," he said with some of his old irony.

I thought about myself showing up on his trail, put there by servants who were—I realized now—doing their very best to throw us together, but with almost disastrous results. It was only his own faith that saved that situation, a faith I hadn't shared.

I looked at him, and again saw that assessing glance. "The throne won't be ordered until you give the word. You need time to decide if this is the life you want," he said. "Of all the women I know you've the least interest in rank for the sake of rank."

"The direct result of growing up a barefoot countess," I said, trying for lightness.

He smiled back, then took both my hands. "Which brings us to a piece of unpleasant news that I have not known how to broach."

"Unpleasant—oh, can't it wait?" I exclaimed.

"If you wish."

At once I scolded myself for cowardice. "And leave you with the burden? Tell me, if the telling eases it."

He made a faint grimace. "I don't know that anything can ease it, but it is something you wanted to know and could not find out."

I felt coldness turn my bones to water. "My mother?"

"Your mother," he said slowly, still holding my hands, "apparently was learning sorcery. For the best of motives—to help the kingdom, and to prevent war. She was selected by the Council of Mages to study magic. Her books came from Eidervaen. Apparently the Marquise found out when she was there to try to find Fialma a Sartoran marriage alliance. She sent a courier to apprise her brother."

"And he had her killed." Now I could not stop the tears from burning my eyes, and they ran unheeded down my cheeks. "And Papa knew about the magic. Which must be why he burned the books."

"And why he neglected your education, for he must have feared that you would inherit her potential for magic-learning. Anyway, I

445

found the Marquise's letter among Galdran's things last year. I just did not know how to tell you—how to find the right time, or place."

"And I could have found out last year, if I'd not run away." I took a deep, unsteady breath. "Well. Now I know. Shall we get on with our task?"

"Are you ready for another ride?"

"Of course."

He kissed my hands, first one, then the other. I felt that thrill run through me, chasing away for now the pain of grief, of regret.

"Then let's address the business before us. I hope and trust we'll have the remainder of our lives to talk all this over and compare misguided reactions, but for now…" He rose and pulled me to my feet. Still holding on to my hands, he continued, "…shall we agree to a fresh beginning?"

I squeezed his hands back. "Agreed."

"Then let me hear my name from you, just once, before we proceed further. My name, not any of the titles."

"Vidanric," I said, and he kissed me again, then laughed.

Soon we were racing side by side cross-country again, on the last leg of the journey to Remalna-city.

I now had fresh subjects to think about, of course, but it is always easier to contemplate how happy one is than past betrayal and murder—and I knew my mother would want my happiness above anything.

Who can ever know what turns the spark into flame? Vidanric's initial interest in me might well have been kindled by the fact that he saw my actions as courageous, but the subsequent discovery of passion, and the companionship of mind that would sustain it, seemed as full of mystery as it was of felicity. As for me, I really believe the spark had been there all along, but I had been too ignorant—and too afraid—to recognize it.

I was still thinking it all over as dawn gradually dissolved the shadows around us and the light strengthened from blue to the peach of a perfect morning. There was no wind, yet the grasses and shrubs in the distance rustled gently. Never near us, always in the distance either before or behind, as if a steady succession of breezes rippled just ahead of us, converging on the capital. Again I sensed presence, though there was nothing visible, so I convinced myself it was just my imagination.

We clattered into the streets of Remalna under a brilliant sky. The cobblestones were washed clean, the roofs of the houses steamed gently. A glorious day, which should have brought everyone out not just for market but to talk and walk and enjoy the clear air and sunshine.

But every window was shuttered, and we rode alone along the main streets. I sensed eyes on us from behind the barriers of curtain, shutter, and door, and my hand drifted near the saddle-sword that I still carried, poor as that might serve as a weapon against whatever awaited us.

And yet nothing halted our progress, not even when we reached the gates of Athanarel.

It was Vidanric who spotted the reason why. I blinked, suddenly aware of a weird singing in my ears, and shook my head, wishing I'd had more sleep. Vidanric edged his mount near mine. He lifted his chin and glanced up at the wall. My gaze followed his, and a pang of shock went through me when I saw the white statues of guards standing as stiff as stone in the place where living beings ought to be.

We rode through the gates and the singing in my ears intensified, a high, weird note. The edges of my vision scintillated with rainbow sparks and glitters, and I kept trying—unsuccessfully—to blink it away.

Athanarel was utterly still. It was like a winter's day, only there was no snow, just the bright glitter overlaying the quiet greenery and water, for even the fountains had stopped. Here and there more of the sinister white statues dotted the scene, people frozen mid-stride, or seated, or reaching to touch a door. A danger sense, more profound than any I had yet felt, gripped me. Beside me Vidanric rode with wary tension in his countenance, his gaze everywhere, watching, assessing.

We progressed into the great courtyard before the Royal Hall. The huge carved doors stood wide open, the liveried servants who tended them frozen and white.

We slowed our mounts and stopped at the terraced steps. Vidanric's face was grim as he dismounted. In silence we walked up the steps. I glanced at the door attendant, at her frozen white gaze focused beyond me, and shuddered.

Inside, the Throne Room was empty save for three or four white statues.

No, not empty.

As we walked further inside, the sun-dazzle diminished, and in the slanting rays of the west windows we saw the throne, its highlights firelined in gold and crimson.

Seated on it, dressed entirely in black, golden hair lit like a halo round his head, was Flauvic.

He smiled gently. "What took you so long, my dear cousin Vidanric?" he said.

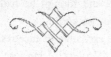

TWENTY-THREE

COUSIN? I THOUGHT.

Vidanric said, "Administrative details."

Flauvic made an ironic half bow from his seat on the throne. "For which I thank you. Tiresome details." The metallic golden eyes swept indifferently over me, then he frowned slightly and looked again. "Meliara. This is a surprise; I took you for a servant." His voice was meant to sting.

So I grinned. "You have an objection to honest work?"

As a zinger it wasn't much, but Flauvic gave me an appreciative smile. "This," he waved lazily at Vidanric, "I hadn't foreseen. And it's a shame. I'd intended to waken you for some diversion, when things were settled."

That silenced me.

"You included sorcery among your studies in Nente?" Vidanric asked.

Personal insults vanished as I realized what it was my inner senses had been fighting against: magic, lots of it, and not a good kind.

"I did," Flauvic said, stretching out his hands. "So much easier and neater than troubling oneself with tiresome allies and brainless lackeys."

I sighed, realizing how again he'd played his game by his own rules. He'd showed me that magic, and though he had called it illusion, I ought to have let someone else know.

"I take it you wish to forgo the exchange of niceties and proceed right to business," he went on. "Very well." He rose in a fluid, elegant movement and stepped down from the dais to the nearest white statue. "Athanarel serves as a convenient boundary. I have everyone in it under this stone-spell. I spent my time at Meliara's charming entertainment the other night ascertaining where everyone of remotest value to you would be the next day, and I have my people with each right now. You have a choice before you. Cooperate with me—obviating the need for tedious efforts that can be better employed elsewhere—or else, one by one, they will suffer the same fate as our erstwhile friend here."

He nodded at the statue, who, I realized then, was the Duke of Grumareth. The man had been frozen in the act of groveling or begging, if his stance was any indication. An unappealing sight, yet so very characteristic.

Flauvic suddenly produced a knife from his clothing and jabbed the point against the statue, which tipped and shattered into rubble on the marble floor.

"That will be a nasty mess when I do lift the spell," Flauvic went on, still smiling gently. "But then we won't have to see it, will we?" He stopped, and let the horrifying implications sink in.

The Prince and Princess. Savona. Tamara. Bran and Nee. Elenet. Good people and bad, silly and smart, they would all be helpless victims.

I'd left my sword in the saddle sheath, but I could still try. My heart crashed like a three-wheeled cart on a stone road. *I must try*, I thought, as I stepped forward.

"Meliara," Vidanric said quickly. He didn't look at me, but kept his narrowed gaze on Flauvic. "Don't. He knows how to use that knife."

Flauvic's smile widened. "Observant of you," he murmured,

saluting with the blade. "I worked so hard to foster the image of the scholarly recluse. When did you figure out that my mother's plans served as my diversion?"

"As I was walking in here," Vidanric replied just as politely. "Recent events having precluded the luxury of time for reflection."

Flauvic looked pleased; any lesser villain would have smirked. He turned to me and, with a mockingly courteous gesture, said, "I fault no one for ambition. If you wish, you may gracefully exit now and save yourself some regrettably painful experience. I like you. Your ignorance is refreshing, and your passions amusing. For a time we could keep each other company."

I opened my mouth, trying to find an insult cosmic enough to express my rejection, but I realized just in time that resistance would only encourage him. He would enjoy my being angry and helpless, and I knew then what he would not enjoy. "Unfortunately," I said, striving to mimic Vidanric's most annoying Court drawl, "I find you boring."

His face didn't change, but I swear I saw just a little color on those flawless cheeks. Then he dismissed me from his attention and faced Vidanric again. "Well? There is much to be done, and very soon your militia leaders will be here clamoring for orders. We'll need to begin as we mean to go on, which means *you* must be the one to convince them of the exchange of kings." He smiled—a cruel, cold, gloating smile.

Flauvic was thoroughly enjoying it all. He obviously liked playing with his victims—giving me a nasty little hint of what being his companion would be like.

My eyes burned with hot tears. Not for my own defeat, for that merely concerned myself. Not even for the unfairness. I wept in anger and grief for the terrible decision that Vidanric faced alone, with which I could not help. Either he consigned all the Court to death and tried to fight against a sorcerer, or he consigned the remainder of the kingdom to what would surely be a governance more dreadful than even Galdran's had been.

Vidanric stood silently next to me, his head bowed a little, his forehead creased with the intensity of his thought. There was nothing I could do, either for him or against his adversary. I had from all appearances been dismissed, though I knew if I moved I'd either get the knife or the spell. So I remained where I was, free at least to think.

And to listen.

That was how I became aware of the soughing of the wind. No, it was not wind, for it was too steady for that. But what else could it be? A faint sound as yet, like a low moan, not from any human voice. The moan of the wind, or of—

I sucked in a deep breath. Time. I sensed that a diversion was needed, and luckily there was Flauvic's penchant for play. So I snuffled back my tears and said in a quavering voice, "What'll happen to us?"

"Well, my dear Meliara, that depends," Flauvic said, with that hateful smile.

Was the sound louder?

"Maybe I'll change my mind," I mumbled, and I felt Vidanric's quick glance. But I didn't dare to look at him. "Will you save Branaric and Nimiar from being smashed if I—" I couldn't say it, even to pretend.

Flauvic's gold-lit eyes narrowed. "Why the sudden affect of cowardice?"

The sound was now like muted drums, though it could be the rushing of my own blood in my ears. But the scintillation had intensified, and I felt a tingle in my feet, the faintest vibration.

Flauvic looked up sharply, and the diversion, brief as it was, was lost. But it had been enough.

"For time," I said. "Look outside."

Flauvic shoved past us and ran in a few quick strides to the doors. Vidanric and I were a step behind. Meeting our eyes was the strangest sight I believe ever witnessed at Athanarel: Standing in a ring, reaching both ways as far as we could see, was what appeared at first glance to be trees. The scintillation in the air had increased so much that the air had taken on the qualities of light in water, wavering and gleaming. It was hard to see with any clarity, but even so it was obvious what had happened—what the mysterious breezes just before dawn had been.

By the hundreds, from all directions, the Hill Folk had come to Athanarel.

Flauvic's mouth tightened to a line of white as he stared at me. "This is *your* work!" And before I could answer, his hand moved swiftly, grasping my wrist. I tried to pull free—I heard Vidranric rip his blade out of its sheath—then Flauvic yanked me to him with a vicious twist so that my arm bent up behind me, and my other was pinioned between our bodies. A hot line of pain pricked me just under the ear: the knife.

With me squirming and struggling, Flauvic backed into the Throne Room again. "Tell them to vanish," he said to Vidanric. "Or she dies."

"Don't do it—" I yelled, but the arm around me tightened and my breath whooshed out.

Flauvic backed steadily, right to the edge of the dais. Vidanric paced forward, sword in hand.

The moaning sound increased and became more distinct. The rubbing of wood against hollow wood drums had slowly altered into a rhythmic tapping, the deliberate thunder of Hill Folk magic, a sound deep with menace.

For a moment no one moved, or spoke. The thunder intensified.

"Tell them *now*!" Flauvic yelled, his voice cracking.

And the pain in the side of my neck sent red shards across my vision; warmth trickled down my neck. I gasped for breath, then suddenly I was free, and I fell onto my hands and knees on the dais. The knife clattered on the marble next to me.

I heard the sound of boot heels on stone, once, twice, and arms scooped me up as the ground trembled.

I flung my head back against Vidanric's chest in time to see Flauvic raise his arms and cry a series of strange words. A greenish glow appeared between his hands, then shot out toward us—but it diminished before reaching us and evaporated like fog before the sun. The air between Flauvic and us now wavered, and through it we saw Flauvic twist, his arms still raised, his head thrown back and his golden hair streaming down.

Loud cracks and booms shook the building, and with a flourish of bright light, Flauvic's limbs grew and hardened, reaching and branching. Down through the marble of the dais, roots ramified from his feet. His legs and body twisted and grew, magnificent with red and gold highlights. And with a resounding smash, the branches above breached the high ceiling and sent mortar and stone and glass raining harmlessly down around us.

Abruptly the sound disappeared. Movement ceased. We remained where we were, looking up at a great goldenwood tree where once the throne had been.

Behind us we heard a cough, and we both turned, me dizzily, to see one of the liveried door attendants fall to her knees, sobbing for breath. A moment later she fell full length into what appeared to be sleep. Her companion slumped down and snored. On the floor near the great tree, the remains of the Duke of Grumareth had turned into clear stones.

Beyond the doors, the street and the gates were empty. The Hill Folk had vanished as mysteriously as they had come.

A shuddering sigh of relief, not my own, brought my attention home and heartward. I shut my eyes, smiling, and clung with all my strength to Vidanric as kisses rained on my hair, my eyes, and finally—lingeringly—on my lips.

The duel was over, and we had won.

AFTERWORD

IT HAS TAKEN ME VERY NEARLY A YEAR TO WRITE down this record. In fact, today is my Name Day. As my adventures began on that day two years ago, it seems appropriate to end the story of my life thus far on its anniversary.

Will there be more adventures to write down? I don't know. Vidanric thinks I am the kind of person who is destined to be in the midst of great events despite herself. Flauvic's mighty tree in the Throne Room is silent testimony to how great events can overtake even the provincial denizens of a small, unknown kingdom like Remalna. Word of the tree, and how it got there, certainly spread beyond our borders, because visitors from far beyond Sartor have traveled here just to see it.

Who is to say if any among these observers have been the ones who trained Flauvic in his magic? The Hill Folk do not easily take lives. Flauvic might well continue to grow there, silent witness to all that is good and bad in government, for centuries. I suspect that the Hill Folk somehow know how to commune with him, and it is my fancy, anyway, that someday, should he suffer a change of heart, they will release him.

Unless, of course, those Norsundrian sorcerers from whom he learned appear first, and we awaken one morning to find the tree gone.

But that's for the future—generations ahead, I trust.

What I need to finish up is the past.

By the time everyone in Athanarel, from the highest to the lowest status, had woken from the groggy slumber they'd fallen into when released from that spell, Vidanric and I had had a chance to comb through Merindar House. We found very little of interest. The Marquise had taken her papers with her, and Flauvic apparently kept all his plotting in his head. What we did find were his magic books, which we took away and locked safely in an archive.

After that, events progressed swiftly. On midsummer Branaric and Nimiar were married amid great celebration. They withdrew to Tlanth soon after, leaving me behind to lay down the stones, one by one, for a new life-path—one I wanted, one that gave me new things to learn every day. But from time to time, usually when the wind rose, I would stop and look eastward and think about roaming freely over my beloved mountains, hearing the distant windharps and reed pipes. I've promised myself that when I have children, they will spend more than one summer up there, running barefoot through the ancient mosses and dancing through soft summer nights to the never-ending music of the Hill Folk.

But here I am again, looking ahead.

Except there is little enough left to tell. At least, no events of great import, save one, which I will come to anon. The days passed swiftly in a series of little happinesses, each forging a bright link in the living chain with which Vidanric and I bound ourselves into a partnership. One can imagine how many nights were needed to talk through, until dawn, to lay to rest all the shadows of past misunderstanding. And of course the business of government had to be carried on, for no longer were our lives our own.

There were no more thrones in the Royal Hall, not with that awe-inspiring monument to what can happen when ambition goes astray. We sit on cushions, as do our petitioners—and the Court, which in turn caused an alteration in Court fashions. In fact, there is less constraint of formality—a loosening of masks, and a corresponding increase in laughter—which Vidanric insists has been like a fresh breeze blowing through the ancient buildings, and which he attributes directly to my influence.

Perhaps. I still wander sometimes from room to room in the Royal Wing here and think back on the days when I slept in the kitchen of our crumbling old castle at Erkan-Astiar, wearing my single suit of clothes, and I marvel at how far my life has come—and wonder where it might yet lead.

There is left to tell only that on New Year's Day was Vidanric's and my wedding, and the coronation. I don't need to describe those because the heralds and scribes wrote them up exhaustively, right down to the numbers and quality of jewels on each guest's clothing. The rituals are long, and old, and I felt like an effigy most of that day. I still can't remember most of it. The resulting celebrations— a much more pleasant business!—went on for a month, after which the Prince and Princess withdrew to Renselaeus, to take up once again the quiet threads of their own lives.

And so I come to the end of my tale. I look through my window at the early buds of spring and think of placing this little book on the shelf here with all the other memoirs of queens and kings past. Who is reading my words now? Are you a great-granddaughter many years ahead of me? Ought I to offer you advice? Somehow it doesn't seem appropriate to detail for you how to properly go about organizing a revolt—and likewise it seems kind of silly to exhort you to look, if you should suddenly start receiving mysterious letters of courtship, for possible inkstains on the fingers of the fellow you quarrel with the most.

So let me end with the wish that you find the same kind of happiness, and laughter, and love, that I have found, and that you have the wisdom to make them last.

THE TALE ISN'T *QUITE* OVER YET!

Here is a special addition for the Firebird
paperback, a never-before-published
short story by Sherwood Smith.

Turn the page for
VIDANRIC'S BIRTHDAY SURPRISE

VIDANRIC AND I STOOD SIDE BY SIDE IN THE THRONE room, staring up at Flauvic's great tree, all blond wood with gold and amber and even silver streaks winding up the smooth bark. Way, way beyond the roof his silver-green leaves had turned to gold, for the time was autumn, and the leaves would soon come drifting down.

Whatever you thought about Flauvic Merindar, you had to admit he made a really handsome tree.

"Let's go," I said.

Vidanric smiled down at me somewhat quizzically. "You really think he listens to us?"

"Oh, I'm sure of it. And while I don't have the least objection to his hearing lots of good government"—I pointed at the cushions before what was once the throne dais—"I don't care for him to hear anything else."

Vidanric laughed. We started out, and he glanced once over his shoulder, then said, "I must admit, the idea that he hears every judgment I make keeps me honest."

"As if you weren't already," I muttered. His lips twitched; he gave me one of those speculative looks from his long gray eyes, and he slid his hand under my swinging hair to hold me close. His touch still gave me that fizzing shiver inside, as strong as our very first kiss. I think it will always give me shivers. I look forward to a lifetime of shivers, I thought happily—though at the same time I was somewhat apprehensive, for once again, I'd embarked on what had seemed a splendid idea in the middle of the night earlier in the season, but since then, I'd begun to wonder.

But Vidanric had been away a great deal, particularly now that the summer rains had diminished. There was still much in the kingdom to be overseen with his own eyes, especially along the border.

We passed through one of the hallways and then up to our own suite, which was empty of servants. We were alone, behind real carved-wood doors instead of tapestries. No one could overhear us.

Vidanric stopped in the middle of our sitting room and put his hands on my shoulders. "Now," he said. "Let's have it. You've been giving me funny looks and grimaces all day, and I have to leave soon, but I won't until you tell me what's disturbing you. Unless, of course, you're just anxious to get rid of me for a week so you can whistle up the army and do some conquering."

At one time his jokes would have sent me into a lather of expostulations and angry denials, but I'd gotten accustomed to Vidanric and Savona's particular style of humor, so I said, "How did you guess? I've got my sword and my armor in the other room, all ready." My reward was the sudden lift to his eyelids, letting the light in, and his quick, soft laugh.

Then I sighed. "And I thought I was being so subtle! All right." I took a deep breath. "You know, next week is your birthday."

"I vaguely remember something of the sort," he murmured, eyes still curved with laughter.

I plunged grimly on. "I had this surprise. I've been wondering, though, if I ought to tell you first. Before you're in front of everyone." I felt my face burning. "Ugh! I'm doing this worse than I dreaded."

462

He leaned down to kiss me. "Bring on your surprise next week. I shall look forward to it."

I sighed again. "If you're certain."

He stepped back. He still had that quizzical smile. "You are not?"

I waved my hands, as if those could express my thoughts better than words. "Well, it seemed like a good idea, but the more I think about it—the more time will get taken up—oh, I don't know. It might be all a big mistake, that's what I'm afraid—"

His smile was still there, but only on his lips. "Can we postpone this discussion until next week?" he asked in his gentlest voice. "I have a courtyard full of riders waiting. It would be most remiss of me to have insisted on their promptitude at the bell-change and I linger."

I opened my mouth, then shook my head. "No. You're right. Go ahead. You've got to reach Grumareth by nightfall, or Elenet's supper will be all ruined. And you know she'll have a splendid one all planned, because she has such good ones when she's here."

"Very well," he said. "Do I take any message to her?"

"Only my very best greetings," I said automatically, for my mind was still several exchanges back.

But there was no time to catch up, for he kissed me, picked up his riding cloak, and then was gone. Next thing I knew I was waving through the upper windows as he mounted his long-tailed gray and, amid the ringing of iron-shod hooves on the fine mosaic tiles, his honor guard formed round him and they raced through the gates and vanished up the road.

I turned away, feeling desolate. It wasn't just the empty room, it was something . . . something. . . .

Yes. There was indeed something wrong. He could still hide his feelings when he wanted to, though I'd seen that polite mask very rarely indeed, and then mostly in Court.

Why would I see it now? When exactly did I first see it?

I tried thinking back. Was it when I mentioned Elenet's supper? No, before that. When, exactly? What had I said? Not when I first mentioned my surprise—it had to be afterward.

I was still brooding about it when my door opened and Nee came in, carrying my new niece.

I gave a foolish grin when I glimpsed that tiny head with its dusting of silken dark hair and reached out to touch her with just one finger lest I disturb her. "Trouble sleeping again?"

Nee nodded. "Bran took night duty, so here I am. This is our second tour of the palace. I'm glad it's plenty large."

Nee and Bran had come down to celebrate their baby's Name Day, since Vidanric and I could not leave Athanarel and go to Tlanth. I had convinced them to stay for Vidanric's birthday—and his surprise.

Nee said, her eyes considering, "Are you feeling all right?"

"Oh, Nee, I'm afraid my surprise is a mistake. I was thinking, maybe my magic lessons might have some kind of state significance. You know I'm not very good at thinking ahead about things like that. And what if he doesn't like it?"

She laughed—silently, so as not to waken the babe. "But you just did look ahead! Seriously, what possible bad effect could there be from your learning a little magic?"

I flopped down onto the pillows and propped my chin on my hands. "I don't know," I moaned. "But something did upset him. I'm sure of that much."

"Did he say so?"

"No, but he went blank on me. At first I thought it was just because he was going away, but there was something else. It was when I mentioned my surprise—and incidentally, he wasn't surprised. I mean, I didn't tell him it was magic, but he knows. I'd swear that much. Did I leave one of my practice books out by mistake? And why would he be so blank? Does magic practice somehow draw evil mages?" I groaned again. "When I first began learning, I thought it would be so wonderful—but now I wonder if I've just made a disastrous mistake, and he doesn't want to tell me

464

it's a disaster lest it hurt my feelings. That, I assure you, makes me feel worse."

Nee was still laughing, a quiet, shaking laugh that reminded me of a boiling kettle. The baby stirred in her arms, and she walked toward the floor. "I'd better put her down," she whispered. "But I think you're imagining things. Don't fret. Just practice, so your birthday concert will go perfectly. I am absolutely certain he will be charmed."

"He will be delighted," Savona said that night.

We were alone in the royal suite's private dining room. Tamara had gone off to Chamadis to oversee the harvest, he'd said, when inviting himself to supper. I could tell from the careless way he'd said it that they'd had one of their rather frequent quarrels—but they always took just as much pleasure in making up, Vidanric had told me, so I pretended not to notice anything amiss. I was not about to interfere in their lives; Savona had become like a brother, but a sort of oblique, hard-to-comprehend brother, and Tamara, while remaining steadfastly (and surprisingly) loyal, was still as prickly as holly leaves.

Since Savona and I were alone, I'd sounded him out on my fears. He knew Vidanric better than anyone did, and he just shook his head while I talked. "I don't believe it," he kept saying. "I can't believe he'd think anything but good of your decision to learn magic. He's said often enough that he wished he had the time to learn it, but he doesn't. I think he'll welcome your surprise with heartfelt relief."

"Thanks," I said, but inwardly I still had doubts. I thought: but you didn't see his face.

So I was only half comforted when I finally fell into bed that night. I lay with the drapes all pulled open so I could stare out the windows at the stars. Was Vidanric also looking out at them? Or was he busy with Elenet still?

I sighed. It was me she had come to, not him, about the still unresolved problems in Grumareth, left over from the bad old Galdran Merindar days. And it was me who had suggested that he go himself, rather than sending messengers—and that he should stay for a week, and visit every problem person himself.

The fact that she had come to me, and not to him, suggested to me that she was still trying to resolve her feelings; and I knew that having him there for a whole week would be difficult for her, which meant she truly needed the help.

I silently wished them both well, and slid into troubled dreams.

That was the last free time I had for the week. I still had to arrange the last details of the party, which was to be quite spectacular. The entertainment was to be music, and I was going to make illusions to go with it. So in between sitting alone on the cushions before Flauvic's great goldenwood tree and hearing petitioners who came to Court and presiding over the subsequent discussions and dealing with the constant stream of domestic details and visiting and being visited by foreign diplomats, I practiced my spells alone and with the musicians until I was muttering them almost in my sleep.

The week melted away with all the swiftness of a spring waterfall, and suddenly Vidanric was back, riding in through the gray mist on his birthday. I waited anxiously, but I was not alone, for kingship does not afford much of the luxury of privacy. Others had been on the watch for him, and footmen and errand runners from an astonishing number of people, mostly military, waited in the courtyard as he and his riders dismounted. I was not able to resolve any matters dealing with the army or with border disputes; my experience as a revolutionary countess had really only trained me well in comprehending the intricacies of trade.

Vidanric gave one glance my way. His tired eyes were dark with appraisal. I smiled, hoping that for once I managed to hide the anxiousness that made my heart thunder in my ears.

That glance was all we had, but I could tell instantly that my face had somehow betrayed me yet again, for his brow was tense before he turned away, and then all I saw was his long wind-tousled yellow hair lying against the black cloak as he and the train of messengers went inside.

And there was a continual stream of messengers dashing in and out of his interview room as the afternoon progressed; when the evening bells rang out, I gave up trying to get a moment with him and ran to dress. I proceeded alone to the salon to receive the guests and look over the last-moment details—muttering spells under my breath the entire time.

As it was, he nearly was late. Savona brought him in, thrusting him down by the shoulder onto the cushions at the table of honor. He bent to whisper to me, "I almost had to challenge him to a duel in order to get him to leave business. Make it good."

Well, I made it good. At least, it seemed good.

The food was delicious, the musicians played better than they ever had at rehearsals, and my illusion spells made the guests gasp and exclaim with delight. I realized that one's mood really did affect magic—that the more intense one's emotions, the stronger the magic. Stars streamed across the ceiling, great rainbow-clouds of color drifted through the air; scenes of beauty blanketed the room, selected from each of the seasons.

The guests loved it, I could see, but their reception registered only on the periphery of my mind, for my heart, my whole attention, was reserved for Vidanric.

He watched and nodded approval and clapped with them all, and when, at the last, courtiers and relatives alike exclaimed over my magical skills (not that illusion-making is very hard, but it looks difficult if you don't know anything about magic!), Vidanric nodded and smiled, but the smile was his polite smile, his court smile, and his eyes just looked—tired.

Was there going to be a scene? Did he dread pointing out to me some obscure law, or some complicated danger, that I had managed to overlook?

Nee appeared at my side. "Do you not feel well?" she whispered, peering with concern into my face.

I shook my head. My throat hurt too much for me to risk speech.

"Slip out the servants' door," she murmured. "No one will notice, now that Vidanric is back. And if they do, I'll say that the magic wore you out. No one will have trouble believing that," she added with a grin.

I pressed her hand. A step here, duck an arm there, open the door—and the voices and tinkle of crystal were gone, and quiet enveloped me.

I raced along little-used passages to our rooms.

It wasn't until I was alone that the weeping came, great snorting, gulping sobs. Hot tears bounced off the beads so beautifully embroidered on the bodice of my new gown. I heeded them not. Snuffling, I dug out my magic books, so carefully studied—so long awaited—and began to stack them in a sturdy wooden chest. As soon as I was done, I'd call a footman to carry them off and burn them—and thus save Vidanric the heartache of remonstrance.

But before I could close the lid, the door opened behind me and he was there.

"What are you doing?"

I jumped. Looked up guiltily, the last book in my hands. I saw him framed in the doorway, a look of pain on his face.

I threw the book into the box. "You don't have to s-say a thing," I wailed. Snort! Sniff! "I guess I didn't think—couldn't see there might be some problem—you know I'm not very good at that kind of thing. Never w-was—"

He crossed the room in two steps. "Mel." He breathed my name into my hair.

"I'm sorry," I gibbered. "I know I'm making it worse—can't help it. I'm afraid I get a little moody these days—"

He tightened one arm around me, then reached out with the other to touch the top book. "Do you need to keep these in this kind of wooden container?" he asked. "May I know the reason? Some obscure magical law?"

I gulped. "No—that is, I don't think so. But I thought they'd be easier to burn this way. See, I thought it would be easier on you if I just got rid of them right away—"

The lid slammed down, unheeded.

Vidanric took my shoulders in both hands and gently turned me so we were face-to-face.

"What?" he asked. "Mel. What were you doing?"

"Getting rid of my books. You don't need to say anything. I know I'm not exactly subtle—but I did see it in your face. You weren't pleased. I made some kind of mistake, but I'm trying to make it better—"

"Mel."

Sniff! Hiccup! "—I meant to do it before you came back, so you wouldn't have to—"

"Mel?"

"—s-s-s-ay anything we'd both hate, you saying, and me hearing, and us b-b-both f-f-f-eeling t-t-t-err-ib—"

"Meliara!"

I whooped in my breath, knuckled the blur from my eyes, and stared up into the most intense gaze I had ever seen in those gray eyes.

"Huh?" I squeaked.

He gave a sharp sigh, and let me go, and crossed the room to stand by the window. His hands ran along the sill, back and forth, with a quickness that betrayed—what? Fear? Nerves?

I stared. I'd never seen this mood before.

He turned to face me. "Perhaps we'd better begin again." A deep breath. "And I will start. I love the magic," he said. "I loved your surprise. I can't tell you how delighted I am that you commenced learning magic, for you know I have often wished I could learn it myself. But there is no time, and I do not believe I'd have the aptitude."

"Huh?" I exclaimed, but at least the tears had stopped. "But—I don't understand."

"You do have the aptitude," he went on. "You inherited it from your mother, but I did not want to ask you to take on this kind of study, because—" He turned away, then back. "Oh, for several reasons." He did not look at me now, but out the window at the slanting rain.

I came forward and touched his hand. "I don't understand. When I said it was to be a surprise, just before you left, you looked—well, I thought you knew, and you didn't like it, but didn't know how to tell me."

"I thought I knew something else," he said, to the window, and not to me. "And I was afraid that you were trying to tell me that it made you unhappy."

I stared at his profile, lamplit against the dark window, the runnels of rain on the glass sparkling as brightly as the diamond in his ear. My thoughts had scattered like that fast-running light, leaving behind an empty head.

Deep breath. Another. And when he didn't speak, out of all the impossible images came a small one, a conviction that hereto I had not had the time to even consider.

But I had to be sure.

"So there is no arcane political reason I ought not to study magic? Real magic, I mean, and not this illusion stuff, fun as it is for entertainment?"

He turned. Seemed to feel the need to speak as carefully as I did. "I know of no possible reason why you should not become a mage."

I gave a shuddering sigh of relief, one that seemed to start at my toenails. "Well then," I said, so relieved that I was now giddy.

Giddy and suddenly shy and awkward—which was an old mood for me.

To hide it I turned to the books and busied myself taking them out.

But he read me too well for that. Another step and he was

470

there right beside me, and I had to look up. "I thought your surprise would be of an entirely different nature," he said tentatively.

And my face burned. I know it was red—probably scarlet.

"Well," I said. "Um. There is. But that was going to be my private present to you. When we were alone. I mean, maybe it's all right in court circles, but I can't—I just can't stand up before all those people and blab out that we're going to have a little prince or princess come spring!"

He let out an exclamation of joy and grabbed me up—and then set me down again, so suddenly my head rocked.

"Is that a mistake?" he asked, looking anxiously into my face.

I laughed. "No! I'm not suddenly made of glass! Oh, Vidanric, I've been so happy, it was so hard to keep it to myself, but I had to be certain. The Healer said I had to wait, and I did, and then it seemed I could wait just a bit longer for your birthday—you mean you guessed?"

He grinned, a boyish grin. "I suspected when Nee and Bran arrived with your new niece, but instead of looking longingly at her like you used to look at babies, you kept taking her and holding her like you were, well, practicing."

"I was! Practicing spells and baby care. Oh! And—the other day—you thought I wasn't happy about this?" I tapped my still-flat middle.

He took my hands. "Let us make a vow. Never again will we attempt to read one another without instantly asking if we are right. No more sparing the other's supposed feelings. I don't think I can stand another week like this last, thinking you had regrets— were unhappy—"

"Never. Never," I said into his tunic breast. "And I almost burned my books, and it took months to get them—"

"They're safe," he said. "And you're not made of glass." He swept me up in his arms.

I laughed. "And I'm not made of glass."

He carried me into our room and kicked the door shut behind us.

471